LOVE SIGNALS

MELANIE SUMMERS

Books by Melanie Summers

SPICY ROMANCE

The Full Hearts Series

Break in Two (Full Hearts Book One)

Don't Let Go (A Full Hearts Novella) – Prequel to Breaking Love – E-book only

Breaking Love (Full Hearts Book Two)

Letting Go (A Full Hearts Novella) – Prequel to Breaking Clear

Breaking Clear (Full Hearts Book Three)

Breaking Hearts (Full Hearts Book Four)

ROMANTIC COMEDIES

The Crown Jewels Series

The Royal Treatment

The Royal Wedding

The Royal Delivery

Braniacs in Love

The Space Between Us ⟵

Love Signals (Coming Soon)

Paradise Bay Series

The Honeymooner

Whisked Away

The Suite Life

Resting Beach Face

The Accidentally in Love Series

Text Me on Tuesday
The Text God
Text Wars
Text in Show
Mistle Text
Text and Confused

A Gamble on Love Mom-Com Series

No Ordinary Hate
A Hate Like This
Hate, Rinse, Repeat

For my sweet, funny grandma who hated having her picture taken, loved feeding people, had the best wheezy laugh, and taught me that ice cream is just for fun.
Miss you lots and lots,
Love,
Melanie

Letter to the Reader

Dear Lovely Reader,

Welcome to Allie and Hudson's story! Prepare yourself for a journey that includes two complete opposites who would fit perfectly together, if only they could silence those pesky voices in their heads saying nasty things like "I'm not good enough," or "love is not for me."

Buckle up for a crazy ride because there are a lot of twists, turns, and drops that you'll encounter between now and *The End*, including but not limited to: a big, crazy Italian family, an adorable mini-dachshund, and an extremely determined woman hell-bent on revenge.

I've thrown some real-life stuff in here this time:

- Like Allie, I had a grandma who refused to let us call her Nonna for the same reasons as Allie's grandma,
- The Dennis Quaid story is absolutely true, except it happened to me a few weeks before this book came out,

- When the big incident happens, the symptoms listed are all medically correct. (You'll know it when you get to it.) 😊

I hope their story will make you laugh and leave you with a big grin on your face. Because that's why I write.

And on with the show…

Xoxo,

mel

Gnarly Waves, Green Drinks, and Hair Plugs...

Hudson Finch - Malibu, California

THE THING no one tells you about life in Hollywood is how rare it is to see a clear blue sky. It's almost always smoggy, occasionally there are clouds, but that pure blue that lets you see all the way from Malibu to the Channel Islands? Almost never happens. Which is why giving shit news on a day like today should be outlawed.

I glance out at the perfect swells of the Pacific, itching to grab my board and run out into the water while my agent, Paul, prepares to give me whatever bad news he's got coming for me. I can tell by the 'too bright' smile that has been plastered on his face since he strolled through my front door with a tray of green juices for him, my brother/manager, Gershwyn, and me. Paul is a total health nut, and I sometimes wonder if it's because he likes it, or because he's trying to normalize the whole L.A. body-obsessed lifestyle for his clients. Keeping us in shape makes his job a lot easier. But maybe that's me being cynical, which isn't my norm. Although, if any place on earth will bring out the cynic in you, it's Hollywood. Everybody's lying about everything all the time. And I'm no different.

"Say, Hudson, you might want to change out of that wetsuit. This conversation is going to take a minute," Paul tells me, settling himself on my tan leather sectional.

I glance out the wall of windows just in time to see a barrel wave roll toward shore, feeling like a broke kid standing outside a candy store. In about an hour, the barrels will be gone and I'll be left with ankle slappers not worth getting wet for. "Can this wait, Paul?" I ask, pointing to the ocean. "I know you drove all this way, but…"

"Wish it could, bud, but it's really important."

My gut tightens and I glance at Gershwyn, who looks as dumbfounded as I am. He has a sip of his juice. "Is this about the *Lightningman* reboot? Because we already knew they were looking at McAuliffe for that one."

"Yeah, you don't have to break it to me gently, Paul," I add. "I'm totally okay not donning a pair of tights to pretend I can shoot lightning bolts out of my dick."

Paul scrunches up his face. "I think it was out of his fingertips, but glad you're okay with it because you didn't get the part."

Nodding quickly, I say, "Yup, totally fine with it. In fact, I'm great. Don't mind taking a break from acting for the next few months. Maybe do a little surfing…" I give a head nod toward the ocean.

"It's not just the *Lightningman* thing. It's also the whole *Beach Cops III* flop and…" Paul says, rubbing his forehead. "Why don't you sit down?"

I suddenly feel like I swallowed a twenty-pound kettle bell. My wetsuit tugs as I drop onto my Eames Lounge Chair, the high neckline pressing against my throat. Oscar, my mini-dachshund, gets up from his bed and trots over, pawing at my leg. I reach down and scoop him up, then give him a scratch behind his long, brown ears. In exchange, he gives me a couple of licks on my chin with his tiny tongue. "Lay it on me, Paul. What's going on?"

"There comes a time in every actor's career when we need to have the talk."

I grin at Gersh, then back at Paul. "I already know about the birds and the bees."

He offers me a polite smile, then his face grows serious again. "You've had a great run as the wild, fun, daring young guy, and I mean, let's face it, the ladies love you. *Love* you…"

"You don't have to sugarcoat it," Gershwyn tells him. "Hudson's not one of your clients with a porcelain ego."

I offer my brother a nod. "Thanks, Gersh. I appreciate that."

"No problem, bro."

We both turn back to Paul who stares at me for a moment before he blurts out, "Your leading man days are over."

What the actual fuck?! "Okay, you could protect my ego a little. I'm not made of stone."

"Sorry, but it's better to rip off the Band-Aid," Paul answers.

"What are you talking about?" Gersh asks him. "He just wrapped a movie with Margot and it hasn't even come out yet."

"Yeah, well, the testing isn't going as hoped."

Uh-oh. Here it comes. "What do you mean?"

"The audience isn't seeing you as 'that guy' anymore. I don't want to get into specifics, but the studio is thinking of shelving it." Paul picks up his juice and sucks down a few gulps while I sit with my jaw somewhere around my knees. "In fact, they *are* shelving it."

Shelving it. The two worst words you can hear as an

actor. One shelved movie can make you a pariah in Hollywood. *Oh fuck, is this seriously happening?* My mind races to figure out how the hell this happened until I key in on Paul's comment about not wanting to get into specifics. "Be specific."

"Yeah, Paul, be specific. Otherwise, how will we know what to fix?" Gersh asks.

Shaking his head, Paul says, "This isn't something you can fix. It's just … part of aging."

"Aging?! He's only thirty-nine years old!"

I stare at the shag rug, trying to make sense of what's happening while Paul and Gershwyn go back and forth.

"Overwhelmingly, the audience thought you would've been better cast as … the villain."

Gersh gasps. "The villain? Hudson is not a villain! Villains are played by washed-up has-beens."

Paul pulls a face that says the phrase washed-up has-been suits me perfectly.

"Hudson? You okay, buddy?" Paul asks.

Plastering on a wide grin, I say, "I'm great. Well, not terrific. I'm a little sweaty. I should've taken your suggestion and gotten changed." I chuckle a little and look over at my brother. "This thing should be called a sweat suit, not a wet suit."

"A sweat suit is already a thing," Paul says.

"He knows that, Paul," Gershwyn snaps. "He was making a joke."

"Right, yeah." Paul nods. "Good one."

Standing up, I carry Oscar over to the window again and stare out. The waves are already dying—the perfect metaphor for my career. Taking a deep breath, I turn to face Paul, doing my best to look breezy. "So? What do we do? How do we pivot?"

"There is one option, but I don't think you'll like it."

"Hey, a few seconds ago, you told me my career was over. If you've got a Hail Mary pass in that playbook of yours, you better believe I'm going to take the ball and run."

"We go full McConaughey."

"Full McConaughey?" Gersh asks, wrinkling up his eyes in confusion. "Hudson doesn't need hair plugs. He's got great hair."

"For the record, Matthew didn't actually get hair plugs," Paul says. "He uses some sort of cream. Rubs it into his head for ten minutes a day."

"Really?" Gersh says. "Huh."

Are they really talking about hair loss treatments right now?

"Yeah, apparently it's some sort of miracle cream."

What the fuck is going on?

"You wouldn't think that would work."

Oscar wiggles a little in my arms and I put him down on his bed, where he curls up into a tight ball. A wave of nausea comes over me and I pull on my collar again. "Could we get back to the matter at hand? Because, honestly, I'm freaking out just the littlest bit."

"Right, sorry," Paul answers. "The full McConaughey. We prove you've got the acting chops to play serious roles. Meaty stuff. I'm talking *Oppenheimer*, *Killers of the Flower Moon*. Get you a real Oscar," he says, glancing down at my dog.

"Hey, Oscar is a real Oscar," I answer, feeling defensive on behalf of my tiny buddy.

"It's what you've always wanted, isn't it, Hud? It's why you named your dog after a trophy," Paul says.

Yes, yes it is. But I certainly can't admit that. Shaking my head, I say, "He's a wiener dog. His full name is Oscar Mayer."

Oscar opens his eyes, his ears perking up, but when no

one says the magic words 'walk time' or 'treats,' he closes his eyes again.

"I don't know. I'm not a drama guy. You said it yourself —I've been playing the wild, fun guy my entire career. I'm a lifeguard, a bodyguard, a ski champion."

"Yes, up until now, but it's time to expand your skills. Go deeper. Try something new. Show everyone in this town you've got what it takes to be up there with the big dogs," Paul says. "DeNiro, Pacino, Streep."

There is no way I've got what it takes to do that. I look over at Gersh, knowing I'll be able to read the truth all over his face. If there's one thing Gersh isn't, it's an actor.

He nods at me, looking one part proud and two parts scared. "You can do it. You're constantly underestimating yourself."

"I'd say I'm more of a realist."

"No," Gersh says. "What you are is your harshest critic."

He's not wrong about that. Well, I'm probably *third* harshest, right behind my father and this nasty little guy who reviews movies for the *Harvard Crimson*. He hates my guts. Planting my hand on my hip, I say, "Even if I did have what it takes to do a serious drama—and I doubt I do —who's even going to give me a shot?"

"I'm repping a new director—Peter Ma. Super talented. Up and coming. He's the next Scorsese. He's working on a new project with the woman who wrote *The After Wife*," Paul tells me.

"I loved that movie." Gershwyn shakes his head and puts a fist up to his chest. "The part when she saves Olive from drowning? And then you find out Liam's dying?"

Paul nods at him, looking suddenly verklempt. "It was too much for one family to go through." He glances at me and winces a little when he sees the glare on my face. "Anyway, this script? It's one hundred times better. It's a once-in-a-lifetime role, I'm telling you," Paul says, leaning down and flipping open his messenger bag. He pulls out a script and tosses it onto the coffee table. "Galaxy Studios has agreed to a package deal—Ma, Summers, and you."

"What's the catch?" Gersh asks.

Paul pauses just long enough for me to know we're getting to something else I won't like. "It's a pay cut."

"How much of a cut are we talking?"

"Like, indie film pay," Paul tells me.

Gersh and I both cringe. Before either of us can answer, he adds, "But doing indie films is cool these days. It says to the world that the art matters more than the money. You get to be the hero that brings a big name to the film. Plus, it's your chance to go to Sundance and Cannes. You'll finally be taken seriously."

My muscles feel all rubbery at the thought of having a film at the serious festivals. No way I belong there. "I've never wanted to be taken seriously. My whole thing is to keep it fun."

"There's only so long you can do that," Paul tells me. "And I'm afraid we've reached the end of what's been a great run."

My shoulders drop and I let out a long puff of air, trying to absorb what's happening. I'm being shuffled off stage and into oblivion, that's what. Folding my arms, I glance down at the script. "What's it about?"

He offers me his best salesman smile and spreads his arms out to the side as he announces, "A radio astronomer."

I stare at him for a second, then say, "I don't even know what that means."

"People who study space. In this case, the astronomer in question was a man on a quest to find intelligent life in the Universe." Pointing to the script, he says, "Here, take a look."

My gut tightens as it always does when I'm asked to read something in front of people. Gersh, the only person other than my parents who knows the truth, gets up and swipes the script off the table, saving me from the embarrassment. "So it's a space movie?" he asks, opening it up and flipping a few pages. "That's almost a superhero movie."

Paul shakes his head. "No, it's not actually set in space. It's historical fiction based on something called Radio Silence Day that took place in the 1920s. This guy, David Todd, convinced the US government to get the entire country to shut down all radio signals for five minutes an hour, every hour, so they could listen for signals from Mars. Quite a feat, if you think about it."

"So, it's a movie about something that failed," I say.

"No, it didn't fail. There just weren't any Martians up there to talk to," Paul says. "Todd was an extraordinary man. He also suffered from mental illness. It's a complicated role, but it's also about the strength of the human spirit and love and determination. Honestly, it's a masterpiece. You can't go wrong with a script like this."

"It sounds like something we should look at," Gershwyn says.

"Yes, you absolutely should," Paul answers. "And I need an answer by tomorrow morning."

Narrowing my eyes, I say, "Why so fast?"

He swallows hard. "It took a little … massaging to get them to give you the part."

"Massaging?" Gersh asks, his face turning slightly red. "Hudson is a *star*. A leading man. And you're telling us you needed to convince these guys to take him at an *indie rate*?"

Looking over at me, he says, "I think it's time for a new agent."

Putting up one hand, I say, "All right, Gersh. Let's not get crazy here. Paul's been my champion through everything. If he says this is our only move, then it's our only move."

"It really is," Paul tells me. He sighs, and I can tell he feels bad about what's happening. "Look, you are a talented actor, Hudson. You *really* are." He pauses, then adds, "This is your shot to prove it."

Nodding, I say, "Give me the night to read it, okay?"

"Take all the time you need," he says, standing up. "Well, until the morning, that is. It's a great script. It made me bawl like a baby. Well, it made Tanya cry. I haven't read the whole thing yet. But she loved it." He picks up his bag and starts toward the door. "And if you do take it—which you should—I can get you set up shadowing at a SETI research facility upstate. It'll be the perfect publicity for the film and a chance to start showing the world a new, serious side of Hudson Finch at the same time. The guy who prepares for his roles instead of just showing up. The guy that can carry a film all the way to the Academy Awards."

"And if I don't?"

He stares at me for a second. "They're looking for someone to play the dad in *Diary of a Wimpy Kid Six*."

————

Instagram Reel: Hollywood Dish with Ferris Biltmore

The video starts up, showing a young man sitting behind a large glass desk wearing a black turtleneck sweater and a bright pink beret. He grins into the camera. "Hello, bitches! It's me, Ferris. Yes, I'm back after my impromptu trip to Paris. France, not Texas, obviously, because eww!

"And I know some of my lambs were upset that I left without so much as a 'see you next Tuesday,' but fear not because I always come back. And hey, sometimes a man's got a hankering for baguettes that simply cannot be cured by the stuff they're trying to pass off here in L.A. No thank you! I need the original. Get over it already!"

The background changes to show a silhouette of a woman. "Guess which celeb, fresh out of her third marriage, is sporting a gigantic engagement ring? I'll give you a hint. Her last husband just won the World Series." He taps his lips, then adds, "I'll tell you later. But first, huge, horrible, awful, makes-me-want-to-curl-up-in-a-ball news coming out of LaLa Land. You know that movie I've been dying, and I mean, *dying*, to see? With Hudson Finch and the beautiful Miss Barbie herself?"

He pauses dramatically and shakes his head with his eyes closed, then whispers, "Shelved."

Nodding, he says, "Yes, bitches, you heard me right. My cousin's barber's best friend's podiatrist heard the news straight from the dog walker of one of the execs at Tuxedo Studios who shelved the film. And this bit of shit news brings us to a little segment I like to call, 'Suck My Left Nut,' where I will speak directly to the inhumans responsible for this debacle." A graphic reading "Suck My Left Nut" appears behind Ferris's head and he raises his voice to a high-pitched squeal. "You shelved Hudson?! You shelved *Hudson*?! *You* shelved Hudson Fucking Finch, the sweetest piece of man candy to ever —and I mean *ever*—light up the big screen? You should be ashamed of yourselves, you horrible, awful excuses for people. You … you robots with teeth! You complete wastes of oxygen! How dare you?! You wouldn't know talent if it bit you on the ass. I hope your dog gets infested with super-fleas, and the fleas have billions of baby super-fleas that you can never get rid of so you spend the rest of your life scratching incessantly until you finally go insane and have to live out your days in a mental hospital for shitty movie executives with fleas. You can suck my left nut. But not righty because righty is perfectly symmetrical. You can suck the one that looks like a meatball that fell off the counter before it was put in the oven. Suck. It."

He lowers his voice and takes a deep breath, then mouths, "Suck it."

Ferris closes his eyes and says, "Okay, now, I know you're all as upset as me, so now it's time for a new segment I like to call, 'Don't Worry Darling.'

He points above his left shoulder where the graphic appears. "This message is for Hudson Finch. Don't worry, darling. You're not going anywhere. I promise. Yes, for other lesser actors, one shelved movie would be a career-killer, but not for you. You're too perfect for that. Too perfect. You're ethereal. You're the living representation of an actual Greek god come to life, with your chestnut locks that fall perfectly, even if you just escaped a massive under-water explosion, and your chiseled everything, and that jawline that could serve as a ruler at NASA, and those green eyes that look like a forest bathed in sunlight. You're going to bounce back. You will. And you will bounce higher than any freaking ball has ever bounced because you, sir, are Hudson Fucking Finch—king of the big screen, lord of the ladies, master of the disaster movies. You, my darling, are just getting *started* in this biz. You're going to own this town someday soon. Own it! You will. I know you will. At least you better, or I'm going to be forced to binge watch *Beach Cops* and *Beach Cops II* then cry myself to sleep every night for the rest of my life."

A photo of Hudson in swim trunks appears behind Ferris as he sighs heavily. "You know what, bitches? I'm too upset to tell you who got engaged. My heart's just not in it. Maybe tomorrow. For now, I'm going to sign off and go treat myself to a bubble bath and a bottle of Nyquil because there is no way I'm going to be able to sleep after what happened to my Hudson. No way in hell."

2

Good Men Giving Bad News...

Allie Cammareri – Mountain View, California

THERE ARE two things I hate: spiders and liars. And not necessarily in that order. The first one is because of my cousin Emilio, who thought it would be hilarious to hide a sack of spider eggs in my sock drawer when I was eight. Yeah, what a little fucker, right? Not something you get over, to be honest. I'm thirty-five and I still break out in a cold sweat at the very mention of arachnids. Fun fact: I also gag whenever I see one—even just a photo. But enough about 'those things' because I'm feeling a little woozy just thinking about them.

Onto liars, which are far more dangerous (and despicable) than the eight-legged among us. Spiders don't mean to be creepy and awful, whereas liars know exactly what they're doing, *and* that it's wrong, but they do it anyway. And, yes, I know everybody hates it when people lie. I get that. I'm not special in that regard. But I hate being lied to with a deep, burning passion that burns inside me day and night. I don't have to go to therapy to discover the cause because it's pretty damn obvious.

Twice in my life, I've fallen head over heels for big, fat liars. My first love (or so I thought) was Ian Miller, a big dumb jock I went to high school with, who made me believe we were a couple so I would do all his homework. He was in danger of being kicked off the football team because of his crappy grades and I was too naive to realize I was just his tutor who he occasionally left hickeys on. Turns out, while I was writing Mrs. Allegra Miller in my notebook and dotting the 'I' with a heart, he had an actual girlfriend. She was the head cheerleader from another high school and he was with her the entire time he was pretending to be in love with me. In Ian's case, you could say, he was just a stupid kid, and leave it at that. I'm not that charitable, however. I'm still mildly pleased at the fact that he never made a college team, never went pro, and now works for animal control. He and the cheerleader had two kids right out of high school, then got divorced and she married a successful realtor. Poor, poor Ian. I feel so bad for him.

My second hugely disappointing teller of non-truths was Lando Allegro. We studied astrophysics together in grad school, and I thought I'd found love—the real and everlasting kind. It was so different than with Ian, because not only did we have a lot in common, we were best friends, and we had a slamming sex life. As an added bonus, Lando comes from a nice Italian family, so he had my parents' approval. Well, my mom's anyway. I'm not sure there's a man on this planet my dad would find acceptable for his little girl. I was one-hundred-percent sure we were going to get married (with me obviously keeping my last name to avoid becoming Allegra Allegro), have little smart babies together, and work side-by-side at

NASA every day. I was so in love, I missed *all* the red flags, and believe me, there were some big ones, like the times he'd go straight to the bathroom when he'd come over and wash his penis in the sink. Yep, not a good sign. Long story short, not only was he cheating on me, but he also stole all my research, took credit for it, and dumped my ass.

Unlike with Ian (who I only think about a couple of times a year), I'm still filled with a level of indignant rage toward Lando that I can't quite describe. It's partly due to the fact that we work in the same field. He's also a radio astronomer working for a rival SETI team, so I not only have to hear about the fabulous advancements he makes (all of which I'm sure he's stealing from co-workers), but I also have to see him at every conference. Just the sight of his weasely face causes me to seethe with anger. On my more petty days, I've googled 'glitter bomb companies,' and also may or may not have considered going down to the local dog park for 'samples' to ship to his house in Virginia. I haven't done it though, because I have a much better way to get back at him—I'm going to out-astronomer him. It's taken me ten long years to figure out how, but it's about to happen. At least, I hope.

In exactly two minutes, I'm going to find out if my shot at taking down Lando the Liar is still a possibility. I'm currently walking upstairs to my boss's third floor office, where he's going to give me the good news. Or the bad news. My stomach is in knots as I stare at his name placard: Keenan Edward, Director.

It's definitely going to be a yes. Keenan's an amazing boss. He trusts his staff, and more than that, he believes in us. I'm sure he has every faith I'll finish my project in time to present at the International SETI Forum. It takes place in two months in Zurich and is pretty much the SETI Olympics in that it only happens once every four years and only the best of the best get to speak. The rest of us peons have to sit there and listen. I've never been allowed to present, which is fine because I've never had anything cutting edge to share. Until now, that is. Well, almost. Not quite yet, but if I stay focused for another couple of days (okay, weeks), I'm going to have a presentation that will blow the roof off the auditorium.

But presenting at the conference isn't the only reason I've been replacing sleep with caffeine and sugar for months. There's another researcher working on the same thing—and it's none other than Lando Allegro. Actually, he's got a team of three people, whereas I'm working alone (which is my preferred way to work after getting screwed over by Lando, the Screwer-Over). We're in a sprint to the finish and, as in all races, to the victor will go all the spoils. In this case, it'll mean having your name in bold face in future astronomy textbooks the world over as the person responsible for advancing humanity's knowledge of extraterrestrial intelligence by hundreds of years all in one shot. I intend to have my name in bold, and more importantly, I want Lando the Liar to go down in history as the nothing he is. I'm going to beat him for once. And it's going to be glorious. Wonderful. Freeing. All my rage will instantly disappear. Poof. Gone. I'll finally be able to evict him from my brain, where he's been squatting for a pathetic twelve years.

I can just picture myself standing at the podium delivering my speech while he sits fuming in the audience, knowing I got the best of him. I can almost taste the justice of that moment now, and it is sweet. *Suck on that, Lando, you hack. I am the better scientist.* Mic drop.

Taking a deep breath, I knock at the door.

"Come in," Keenan calls.

When I do, he gestures for me to have a seat across

from his desk. His space heater is humming under his desk and piles of papers are stacked on every surface. His curly gray hair pokes out from behind a particularly tall stack, and he has to shift to the right so we can make eye contact. "Allegra, how's your project coming?"

"I am so close, Keenan. So close," I tell him.

"Really?" he asks with a bright smile. "So you're ready for the validation phase?"

Crap. Why couldn't he just let me leave it at 'so close?' "Not just yet, but once I get there—"

"It'll happen at lightning speed," he says, quoting me from the last several times we've spoken about my AI project I lovingly call Frank after Frank Drake, the father of SETI.

"I know I keep saying that, but seriously, it will go really, *really* fast, and Frank is getting so much better at detecting repeated signals."

Nodding, Keenan says, "What's he detected so far?"

"A lighthouse off the coast of Finland."

Keenan purses his lips and makes a little *hmph* sound. "That's definitely some real progress, Allie."

"Thanks. I know it's not what we were hoping for at this point, but trust me, now that Frank's done it once, the sky is the limit." (That's the astronomy equivalent of a dad joke, by the way.)

"Unfortunately, you're still quite far from getting results you can test and verify," Keenan says. "Whereas, aside from a few tweaks, Chad's project is basically done."

No, no, no, no, no. Not Chad. Anyone but Chad. Chad's the assistant director. Think Dwight Schrute from *The Office*, only without the charm or sense of style.

Before I can protest, Keenan continues. "I've spoken to the organizers of the forum, and, unfortunately, we can only have one speaker. With the influx of programs around the globe since the last summit, we'd be there for several weeks if everyone got a chance to present."

Crap. He's saying no, isn't he?

"I'm truly sorry, but I'm afraid I'm going to have to call it. I'm submitting Chad's name as our team's speaker."

Don't cry. Do not cry, whatever you do. I dig my nails into my palms and blink quickly while trying to smile. "Are you sure you can't give me a few more weeks?"

"I'm positive. I know you were really hoping to make your mark this year and I'm sorry it's not going to happen. Four years feels like a very long time when you're young, but believe me, it'll zip by," he says with a knowing smile.

Four years feels like a very long time because it *is* a very long time. "It's really not just about presenting at the forum. It's about sharing my research and changing the entire way SETI researchers do our work."

"And you'll still be able to share it. Just not at the forum."

"But if the Virginia team gets to present, everyone is going to use their system instead of mine, and I know for a fact, mine is going to outperform theirs." Sitting forward in my chair, I say, "Can you just give me one more month, Keenan? One more. I'll work literally around the clock. I'm so close. I know I can get there in time."

"I don't want you running yourself into the ground," he says. "Remember, good science is not done in a hurry."

"Yeah, but … in this case, it's just so vital to me that I get a shot at it at least," I tell him.

"Why's it so important to you?" he asks.

Because this is my one chance to beat a lying sack of crap. "Because I truly believe that if implemented on a global scale, Frank is going to advance our project exponentially. We've always thought contact could take another four hundred years, but what if it could actually be achieved in our lifetime?"

He stares at me just long enough for hope to build in my chest. Then he shakes his head. "In that case, rushing it is most definitely a mistake. Take your time. If your system truly is superior, once you publish your results, people will switch over, even if they've already adopted the Virginia team's system."

"But—"

"For your own sake, the answer is no."

———

Five minutes later, I'm back at my desk stewing about being given a hard no. My best friend, Gwen, floats into our office with Starbucks for both of us. "Good morning," she says, just shy of actually singing. Gwen is madly in love with Ty Sterling, the billionaire who backs our program. She smiles down at me as she sets my latte on my desk, reminding me very much of Snow White as she bats her eyelashes. If I didn't love her so much, I'd totally hate her.

"Thank you," I say, picking up my drink and having a sip of the warm, frothy liquid. "Is there booze in this? Because I could definitely use some alcohol right now."

"I take it your meeting with Keenan didn't go well?" she asks, flopping down onto her chair.

I shake my head, tears pricking the backs of my eyes.

Gwen scrunches up her face. "Please tell me he's not picking Chad."

"That's exactly what he's doing."

We both shudder and say, "Chad."

"I'm sorry, sweetie," she says. "That sucks fur balls."

"It really does, especially because I know Frank can do it. We just need a few more weeks." I look at my screen, squinting my eyes at Frank's latest attempt at tweezing out a needle from the haystack of signals I've given him. "Crap. I'm pretty sure he's just detected a Boeing 707 again."

"Just like a man. Can't find anything, even if it's in plain sight." She puts on a goofy man voice and says, "Honey, are we out of ketchup?" Returning her voice to normal, she says, "It's right there. Behind the olives."

"I should've named him after a woman."

There's a knock on the door, then Chad comes strolling in and plants himself on the corner of my desk. "I guess you've heard the big news by now."

"Yup," I answer.

He smirks down at me. "Look, it'll happen for you eventually. You're just not ready yet, Allie. But don't feel bad. Few people are. As assistant director, I have an edge. It just looks better for us to send one of the men at the top to represent our team."

The fact that he said 'men' is no accident. Chad's as sexist as a day on Venus is long, and since a single day on Venus is the equivalent of 243 Earth days, he's pretty fucking sexist. He looks over at Gwen. "Pretty cool that I get to present, hey?"

She just blinks slowly at him in response.

"What? Don't tell me you think *she* should go instead of me? I know you're friends and all, but seriously, even you must admit I'm the guy who's getting things done around here."

Picking up her coffee, Gwen has a long swig of it without breaking eye contact, and it occurs to me that Chad makes Frank look like a freaking genius at picking up signals.

"Oh, I get it. The ladies of STEM have to stick

together, right? Forget logic and reason, you're all about girl power." He does a fist pump to emphasize his point.

Gwen glares at him. "Allie is on the precipice of the biggest breakthrough in SETI history. If she can get it done in time, she should one-hundred-percent be presenting."

"Well, Keenan and I don't think she's ready," he says, turning to me. "So it would be a lot better if you can just learn to accept that."

There's no way in hell Keenan consulted Chad on the matter. And yet, like the giant douche waffle he is, Chad's pretending he had something to do with the decision.

Fixing him with a steely gaze, Gwen says, "If there's nothing else you came to say, we should all get back to work."

"You're not my boss, Gwendolyn," Chad tells her. "You're the person sleeping with him, which, quite frankly, is a whole different thing."

Ah, hell no. "Did you just say that?!" I snap. "Did you actually just say that to Gwen? Our hero?! The woman who single-handedly saved our program?"

He shrugs. "If you call what she did heroic."

"You certainly couldn't have done it," I tell him.

"Yeah, because Mr. Sterling isn't gay."

"He did *not* give us funding because she slept with him." Turning to Gwen, I say, "Although I'm sure you're very talented in that department." Glaring at Chad, I continue. "She convinced him with her beautiful mind. And for that, she's owed a debt of gratitude. If it weren't for her, you'd be ... living in your parents' basement, spending your days trolling people online."

"Don't *you* live in your parents' basement?" he asks.

"I live upstairs, thank you very much," I answer, my

voice shaking with anger. "And I only moved back in with them because my father had a stroke."

Chad snorts, then stands up. "Yeah, years ago, and if I'm not mistaken, he's fine now. Anyway, you ladies should get back to work. I'd hate to have to tell Keenan you're slacking."

He hurries out before Gwen can throw a stapler at him.

As soon as he's gone, I get up and shut the door. Turning to Gwen, I let out a growl. "Oh my God, Gwen, if that jackass gets to present instead of me, I'm going to lose it."

"Um, it sounds like it's a done deal."

"Yeah, he may believe that and Keenan may believe that, but they're both dead wrong," I tell her, sitting back down.

"But Keenan's putting Chad's name forward."

"Well as soon as I get Frank up and running, he won't have a choice but to change his mind. No way Keenan's going to let Chad give his stupid 'Space is Big' presentation." Putting on a face, I say, "Oh, is space big? We had no idea, numb nuts."

Gwen laughs, then her smile fades. "Listen, you might have to accept that there's a really good chance Keenan is going to let him present."

"What makes you think that?"

She looks at me like I'm insane. "Because he said he is."

"Oh, that." I wave off her words. "I'm about to make the biggest leap forward in SETI history. If I can do it before the conference starts, even if Keenan puts Chad's stupid name down, the conference organizers will make room for me. They'll have to because it'll be the only thing anyone will want to talk about."

She gives me a 'that could work' look. "All right, I see where you're going with this."

"Yeah, you do!" I give her a firm nod. "No way am I letting Lando win. Or Chad. Even if I have to stay awake for the next six weeks straight. Even if I have to start wearing adult diapers. Even if it kills me!" Tilting my head, I add, "Well, maybe not the diaper thing. But the point is, I'm not letting the opportunity to crush either of those assholes pass me by. And I'm not just doing it for me. I'm doing it for women in STEM everywhere because it's time for us to triumph over the sexist, cheating, lying asshats of the world."

"Amen, sister."

"Amen."

Now, if only I knew how to get this freaking thing to work...

3

Burgers, Fries, and Comfort Milkshakes

Hudson

WELL, today certainly hasn't turned out the way I expected. I thought I'd do some surfing, hit the gym, and spend the rest of the day hanging out with Gersh and Oscar. Instead, I not only found out my career as a leading man is effectively over (and let's face it, it is because there's no way I'm going to pull this off), but I rode exactly zero waves. By the time Paul left, the ocean had already calmed down and the clouds had rolled in. I got out of my sweat suit (I'd be chuckling about that still if I weren't so depressed) and took a quick shower while Gersh scanned the script and put it in Dyslexie font for me. Then the two of us read it through once, looked over the publicity package Paul included, and are now sitting staring at each other, both dumbfounded. The film is called *Radio Silent*, and Paul wasn't kidding about this David Peck Todd character being complicated. He was a brilliant astronomer, an inventor, a philandering husband, and a petty thief who wound up in a mental institution. Tackling a character like this would require ... well, someone who isn't me.

Gersh tosses the package onto the coffee table. "Well, there's only one thing we can do at a time like this."

"In-N-Out?"

Nodding gravely, he says, "It's burger time."

Oscar lifts his head and gives me a hopeful look. I stand and smile down at him. "Yup, you can come."

He springs out of his bed and over to the interior garage door, his entire body wagging. I throw on my ball cap and sunglasses, grab Oscar's leash, and we pile into my new electric Range Rover. Pulling out of the garage, we then wait for the dark wood and black iron gate to slowly slide open. I roll to a stop at the edge of the driveway, glad there's no paparazzi here today. After a few minutes on Pacific Coast Highway, we take a right and head north for a thirty-minute drive through the countryside to Westlake Village where a juicy cheeseburger, fries, and a chocolate shake are waiting. Well, hopefully they're not waiting yet. That would mean the hot stuff'll be cold and the milk-shake will be warm.

"It's been a good run," I say, glancing over at my brother, who has Oscar on his lap. Oscar is standing on his hind legs, with his front paws pressed against the glass as he watches the world go by.

"Come on, dude, you're just getting started."

Shaking my head, I say, "You read the script yourself. There is no way in hell anyone is going to buy me as a genius astrologer."

"Astronomer."

"See? I can't even remember the job title. There's no way people will think I went to school for eight years to learn how to do that."

"You're underestimating yourself again," Gersh tells me. "You're so much smarter than you think."

When I don't answer, he says, "You know what? You seem hangry. Let's talk about this after we eat."

"Sure." I let out a sigh, knowing he's right.

He connects his phone to my truck and plays *Starboy* by The Weeknd. I hit the gas and let my mind wander while the music plays. I'm lucky. I really am. And I know it. I have a life most people would kill to have, and so much of it is because of my big brother.

Gershwyn is two years older than me and whizzed through school without any trouble, while I struggled to even write a sentence as a little kid. The letters just kept moving around on me and getting jumbled up. I was diagnosed with dyslexia in the second grade. But there was no way my parents were going to accept that. My father, the principal of the Manhattan private school we attended, insisted on hiding it. He couldn't possibly admit to all the hoity-toity, Tribeca parents that his own son had a serious learning disability. Instead, he and my mom tutored me every night until well after bedtime. Sight word memorization, reading ahead in every subject so I could learn the material before I got to class the next day. The arguing, the fighting, the shame they passed on to me. It was a horrible secret and there was no way they were going to let it out, even if it nearly killed us all.

By the time I was in high school, I started to fight back. I just wouldn't come home until late every night so I could avoid those torturous study sessions. But I still found a way to hide it. I became the class clown. I made it seem like I wasn't working because I didn't *want* to, not because I couldn't. It was the start of my acting career, and believe me, those years gave me all the experience I needed to make it in Hollywood.

In junior year, my parents gave up on the idea that I'd ever amount to anything, but Gershwyn always knew I was going places. He'd tell me all the time that there are thousands of great jobs out there that require very little reading at all, and that I was going to find my place in the world and be a huge success someday. And he was right. I've gone farther and made more money than I ever thought possible. I've certainly done better than my parents expected. It's all thanks to him. The best brother anyone could have asked for. My best friend. Gersh has kept my secret all these years. No one in the biz knows that I can barely read because he helps me distract and redirect people, then he helps me prepare.

I never pick up a script in front of anyone. Instead, I pretend like I've got far more fun and exciting things to do than to read it right now, but I'll get to it. And as soon as we're alone, that's exactly what happens. He records himself reading it over and creates a copy in a font that's easier for me to read. I listen to the recording until I have the entire thing memorized and can follow along in my version of the script for table reads. It's a hell of a lot of work, but it lets me go on pretending I'm just as capable as everyone else in the room. And yeah, I know there are a lot of famous people who are open about being dyslexic, but for me, it's different. Too shameful to admit out loud. And I also know technically having dyslexia doesn't make me stupid. But honestly, what's the first insult people go to when they want to attack someone's intelligence? They say, "I bet he can't even read."

By the time we pull up in front of In-N-Out, my stomach is growling. It's only four in the afternoon, but I was so thrown by the conversation with Paul, I forgot to eat lunch. "Nice, it looks dead in there."

"That's cause we're 'old people' early," Gersh answers, opening his door.

I snort laugh, then scoop up Oscar and we go inside to order. I know I'm not supposed to bring him in, but I'll hold him the entire time, and we frequent this location enough that the staff lets us get away with it. (Okay, it's also possibly because of the whole fame thing, but I'd rather think it's because Oscar's so adorable and we're friendly.)

Ten minutes later, we're outside at a table noshing on our meals and sucking back milkshakes. I dip a hot fry into some ketchup and take a bite, letting all that wonderful grease soothe my nerves. "It's not the end of the world. We can easily live on our investments, especially if we sell the house." I pick up my burger and hold it up to my mouth. "We could move somewhere cheap, like Nebraska."

Gershwyn's head snaps back. "Nebraska? Are you nuts? There's no way we're moving there."

"Hey, I'm just spitballing here. Trying to figure out what our next move is because clearly it's not making this movie," I say, taking a big bite of my double-double.

"Look, I know Paul's got you rattled. Totally understandable. But you're quitting before you've even given it a shot." He has a sip of milkshake, then adds, "It's a role, just like any other role. You memorize the script, you go spend a few weeks with those alien-hunting people, and you transform yourself into one of them just like you turned yourself into a bodyguard, a lifeguard, and a famous movie star."

I give him a look, then say, "Come on, that last one wasn't exactly a stretch."

He shrugs. "Okay, yeah, but every other role you've had, you had to figure it out. There's no reason you can't figure this out too. You just have to put in the work."

Wiping my mouth, I say, "Did you notice anything in common among the roles you just listed?"

"Nope."

He does. He just doesn't want to admit it.

"I've played a bodyguard, a lifeguard, a surfer——"

"Surfing world champion."

"Irrelevant. The point is, I've never played a lawyer, a doctor, a scientist, or an archaeologist. And there's a reason for that."

"It's called typecasting."

"It's called reality," I answer. "The reality is, I'm not one of *those* people. Those people were my bullies."

"Sure, back in grade school, but they're singing a different tune now, aren't they?"

"Which is why I can't do this movie," I tell him. "I'll be a joke, Gersh. A total joke. I won't even last a day at that research place before some nerd sniffs out what's really going on with me. And contrary to popular belief, nerds aren't always these nice, gentle wallflowers waiting to be noticed. Some of them are really freaking mean."

Gershwyn stares at me for a second. "You're not that kid anymore, Hudson. You hold the power now. And those nerds are going to suck up to you and adore you just like every other person on this planet does. Because you're famous and talented and you know how to make people love you. I promise, it's going to be different than it was in school. It's going to be easy, in fact."

"Easy? What makes you think that?" I ask, my words coming out harsher than I intend.

"Because you're going to have a whole team of geniuses at your disposal for six weeks. Think of how much you'll learn. By the time you leave, you'll practically *be* a radio astronomer."

"Oh dude, don't fall for our own hype. At the end of

the day, we're all just playing pretend on those sets." A cute woman in a tank top and yoga pants walks by, flashing me a grin while eye-fucking me. I give her a little upward head nod and smile back. Huh, she certainly doesn't think I'm washed up. "You know, maybe Paul's wrong. Maybe I *do* have a few more years of being a leading man in me. Maybe I just tell Paul I'm taking a pass on this one and wait for something more in my wheelhouse to come in."

I can tell by the expression in my brother's eyes that he agrees with Paul's assessment of the state of the union. He offers me an unconvincing smile. "That's one way you could go, for sure."

"But you don't think it's a good idea."

"I think you'd only be putting off the inevitable. At some point, even if it's not right now, you're going to end up facing this exact same dilemma. This is an opportunity to get ahead of what's coming your way," he says. "It's a great role, and it really could open a whole new set of doors for you. Redefine your career."

"What if I don't want to redefine things? What if I'm happy doing what I've been doing?" I ask, having another bite of my burger. I chew for a second, then swallow before saying, "I mean, look at Brad Pitt. The guy has a good twenty years on me and he's still getting leading roles. And Tom Cruise? Hit after hit, and he's over sixty."

I feel someone tapping on my shoulder. "Excuse me, but are you ... Hudson Finch?"

I turn to see a couple of teenage girls smiling down at me. I give them my best leading man smile. "I am."

"Oh my God! Can we get a selfie?" one of them asks.

"Sure," I say, standing up and positioning myself between them, careful to keep my hands in front of me so they're in view of the camera the whole time. I make hang ten signs and grin while one of them holds her arm out (and up, always up) and snaps some pictures of us together. When she finishes, she says, "My mom is going to absolutely die when she sees this. She's your biggest fan ever."

Her friend nods. "She is. Like, she would totally leave her husband for you."

Her *mom* is my biggest fan? My heart drops to the cement, but I keep this stupid smile plastered to my face. "That's ... so nice to hear. Tell her I said hi."

They walk away and I sit down, suddenly not hungry anymore.

Gersh wipes his mouth with his napkin. "Don't worry about it. I'm sure that happens to Tom Cruise all the time."

Sighing, I say, "Yeah, probably. But I'm not Tom Cruise, am I? I just had a film shelved."

"Well… I mean, we're talking about Hollywood royalty here. Nobody else is Tom Cruise. Not even Tom Cruise."

"True, yeah."

"So…"

"So maybe I should take the job."

Gersh nods. "Yep."

"Pivot, right? Try something new?"

"Exactly."

Letting my shoulders drop, I say, "This is going to suck so hard."

And there's a ninety-nine-percent chance I'm going to fail utterly and completely.

4

Moon Dust, Homemade Gnocchi, and Overly-honest Relatives

Allie

"ALLEGRA BIANCA CAMMARERI! Don't make me call you again!" my mother hollers up the stairs.

"Jesus God, I'm not ten," I mutter, getting up from my tiny desk in my bedroom and crossing the room. I yank open the door and poke my head out into the hall, only to see her standing at the bottom of the stairs with an apron over her church dress and her messy light brown hair, that I inherited, up in a bun to keep it off her face while she cooks.

We glare at each other for a second until I finally say, "What?"

"Are you dressed? It's almost four o'clock. The family's going to be here any minute."

"Of course I'm dressed, Ma. It's almost four o'clock." The truth is, I'm in the same clothes I slept in because I was too tired to change into pajamas when I gave up on Frank at three a.m.

She narrows her eyes at me. "Don't get smart with me, young lady. I'm still your mother."

"Ma, I don't have time for this right now. I told you, I'll be down to eat dinner, but then I need to get right back to work."

If I could get out of it, I would. But missing Sunday supper is a cardinal sin in my family. My parents, along with my dad's brother and his wife, own a bakery which is closed on Sundays, which means every Sunday, we have a big meal together, and attendance is mandatory. My sister missed it once when she went into labor with their first child, Camilla, and my relatives are still talking about it because she wasn't born until Monday night at ten, which, in their eyes, means she definitely could've made it to supper.

"Pfft, work," Ma says, waving her hand. "I'll show you work. I had to make the gnocchi myself today. My hands are raw from peeling potatoes."

"Why didn't you just use premade pasta? It would've saved you hours."

Her head snaps back and she looks like I've just suggested she serve the cat for dinner. "Premade? For Sunday dinner? Okay, that's enough. You shut off that damn computer and come downstairs before you completely lose your mind."

Rubbing my temples with both hands, I say, "Mom, I'm under a crazy tight deadline. My entire career…" and Lando's demise… "depends on this. I promise I'll be around to help out in a couple of weeks, maybe even next Sunday. But today, I have to stay focused."

"You better be free next Sunday. It's Landing Day, in case you forgot."

"Obviously I know what next week is." And by that I mean technically I'm aware of the date, but only because

I'm counting down the days until the conference. As far as Landing Day goes? I totally forgot. It's a holiday my family made up to celebrate the anniversary of their arrival here in the US. It's an up-at-dawn, cook-til-you-drop event that rivals Christmas.

"You remember it's not just *any* Landing Day, right?"

"Yes, of course. It's … a big one."

"That's right, it's a big one," she answers, holding up four fingers. "It's been forty years since the Cammareris made our way across the Atlantic and set up here in sunny California. Forty."

Then why is she holding up four fingers? "Yup, got it. Forty. I'll be there with bells on, Ma. I promise."

"You'll be down here all day helping?"

"I swear on your life, all day."

She gives me a sharp look. "I don't like it when you swear on my life. It's tempting fate."

I let out a groan, then point to my room with every ounce of urgency coursing through me.

"Fine, go back to work, but as soon as that doorbell rings, I want you down these stairs."

"*Fine*," I grind out.

"And … clean yourself up a bit. You look like you smell bad."

"I look like I…? That doesn't even make sense."

She waves a hand at me and spins on her heel, walking away while I sniff my left armpit. Huh. Her theory actually holds some weight. I grab a fresh hoodie, some jeans, and some undies, then hurry to the bathroom for a quick shower. A few minutes later, I rush back to my laptop while I brush my teeth, only to see that Frank is still running the latest batch of recordings I gave him.

The doorbell chimes and I let out a heavy sigh, then go back to the sink to rinse and spit while the house fills with the sounds of hungry humans. By the time I get downstairs, I see my sister, Lucia, her husband Vinnie, and their two kids, Matteo and Camilla, peeling off their jackets. My grandparents and Zia Fernanda must have arrived at the same time because they're all squeezed into the front entry.

"There's my girl!" my nonno says, holding out his arms for a hug. Nonno is a teeny, tiny, adorable old bald man. Like, so tiny, I'm pretty sure I could pick him up and carry him around for hours. He's also the one person in my family who is completely interested in my job. He's one of the smartest people I've ever met, even though he never got a chance to go to school. If life had dealt him a different hand, he definitely could've been running NASA by the time he was forty.

I give him a quick hug, then hug my nonna (who insists on being called Grandma because she says a nonna is an old woman). The truth is, it's not the label that makes her old, it's the blue, tightly-permed hair she's been sporting since the nineties. Giving her a kiss on the cheek, I say, "Hi, Grandma. You look as young and beautiful as ever."

She wheezes out a chuckle and pats my cheek. After a second of staring at me, her face grows serious. "You look like hell. What's wrong? Are you sick?"

"You're not sick, are you?" Lucia says, adjusting her bra under her fitted sweater. "We just got over a month of head colds at our place. We don't need anything new."

"No, I'm fine," I tell her. "Totally healthy."

Lucia screws up her face. "Then why do you look so bad?"

Zia Fernanda steps closer to examine me. "She's right. You look terrible. When's the last time you had a hair mask?" (Zia has been a hairdresser for forty years, and she believes there's no problem that can't be fixed with a good hair mask.)

"Never, but I'm fine, seriously. I haven't had time to worry about my looks because I'm under a tight deadline at work," I tell them, glancing at my niece who is staring up at me dumbfounded that her auntie could look so bad. I give her a wink. "Zia's got more important things to do than worry about her makeup right now."

"What? Trying to find aliens all day and night?" Vinnie asks. "You should try finding a man instead." He barks out a laugh at his own joke, and when he's done, he clicks his teeth and shakes his head at me. "Although it's getting a little late already, isn't it?"

"Vinnie!" Lucia snaps. "It is not too late for Allie to find love."

I'm about to thank her when she adds, "It is getting a little late for babies though. Have you made an appointment at that egg freezing place I told you about? Because you better get on it."

"There's a place to freeze eggs?" Camilla asks her mom. "Why can't you just put them in Nonna's freezer?"

All the adults in the room burst out laughing (except me) while Camilla screws up her adorable face in confusion. My sister pats her on the shoulder. "Not the eggs you eat, baby. It's a different kind of egg."

She starts for the kitchen while Camilla follows. "What kind of egg?"

"I'll tell you when you're older."

"Matteo, show Zia your science project," Vinnie says, patting his son on the back of his head. He grins at me. "You gotta see this, Allie. He's been working real hard on it."

Matteo holds up his iPad with a wide smile that displays his missing front teeth. God, he's a cute kid. "Can I show it to you?"

"Absolutely. I'd love to see it," I tell him, crouching down next to him as he flips open the case.

He presses one of the icons and a picture of a massive, hairy spider fills the screen.

I immediately gag, then try to scramble away, but because I'm crouching, I wind up knocking myself off balance and fall on my ass before gagging twice more.

Vinnie bursts out laughing, and high fives Matteo. "You got her so good!"

Matteo beams down at me, then laughs like crazy. "Gotcha, Zia!"

He suddenly looks a lot less adorable to me.

I stand slowly, reminding myself that my nephew doesn't know any better, especially because his asshole dad put him up to it. "You sure did."

"What's so funny?" my sister calls from the kitchen. She pokes her head out. "You didn't play the spider trick on Zia, did you?"

Vinnie, who now has tears streaming down his face while he laughs, nods. "The gagging! Hahahaha! It never gets old."

"Doesn't it?" I glare at him, my words coming out crisp.

"Boys! That's not nice. Zia has a real phobia," Lucia calls to them. "Sorry about that, sis."

She may be sorry, but it's not like she's going to do anything to stop them in the future. I glance at my watch. *Okay, Allie, you can do this for another hour and a half. Then you can sneak back upstairs, barricade the door, and get back to work.*

The next twenty minutes are a blur of activity as we set the dining room table for the adults and the one in the kitchen for the kids. More cousins, aunts, and uncles arrive, and soon, it's a packed, noisy house. I crack open the window in the dining room to let some fresh air in as my mom puts the finishing touches on the three-course meal. First comes gnocchi in a stewed meat sauce, served with fresh baguettes, next will be the salad and roasted chicken, followed by dessert (which tonight will be raspberry and lemon polenta cake that my dad's sister, Zia Francesca, made). My stomach growls as I carry one of the serving bowls of gnocchi to the table. As irritated as I am with the stupid spider prank and tonight's topics of conversation (my lack of a man, my eggs that are in dire need of freezing, and how awful I look), I am definitely excited to dig into this dinner.

We're just sitting down when my phone rings. My dad shoots me a look while I pull it out of my pocket. "Sorry about that. I forgot to silence it."

Keenan's name is flashing across the screen. I stare at it, my heart picking up its pace a little. My boss has never called me after hours. Not one time in over ten years. Standing, I excuse myself. Ignoring my mother's protests about it being 'Sunday supper,' I hurry to my dad's den and shut the door. "Hello?"

"Allegra, I'm glad I caught you," Keenan says. "I hope it's not a bad time."

"No, it's fine."

"Good. I wanted to talk to you about a new development that's just come up. It's rather exciting, actually."

"Okay," I say, wondering what could be so important that it couldn't wait for tomorrow.

"I'm sure you're wondering what's so important that it couldn't wait for tomorrow." Keenan pauses for a second, then says, "I know you're probably quite disappointed about me choosing Chad, so I wanted to give you some exciting news. I've just got word that Galaxy Studios is making a movie about us. Well, not *us* exactly. It's about David Peck Todd."

"Like a documentary?"

"No, a major motion picture. And the exciting bit is that they've offered to donate a hundred thousand dollars to our team."

"Wow, that is exciting news," I answer, wondering what the hell this has to do with me.

"You're probably wondering what this has to do with you."

"Yeah, a little."

"They're sending an actor to come shadow one of our radio astronomers, and I thought that since you're not going to present at the conference, it would make the most sense to have him follow you around," Keenan says.

Oh, hell to the no. Not doing it. "One could also say that because Chad is prepared for the conference, he has a lot more time than I do."

"The thing is, Chad may have overstated how prepared he is. He's still got some things to wrap up to be ready in time. More importantly, this situation requires someone with a certain skill set that not everyone else on the team possesses."

He means tact. "Uh-huh," I say, just as my niece, Camilla, walks into the room, her face covered in red sauce.

I blow her a kiss, then gesture for her to leave the room, but she just stands there and whispers, "Zia, can I have your gnocchi?"

I shake my head and mouth no at her. I love my niece, but giving up my portion of homemade gnocchi? I don't think so.

Keenan's saying something about how giving and patient I am while Camilla drops to her knees and holds her hands to her chest like she's praying. "Puleeeaaaase, Zia. I'm a growing girl."

"What's that sound?" Keenan asks.

"Nothing, my niece is asking me a question," I answer, pursing my lips at her and snapping my fingers. I gesture for her to leave, only to have her pull her bottom lip out in her best attempt at looking pathetic. "Fine," I hiss, knowing she's not going to give up.

Immediately she springs to action, running out of the room, leaving the door open behind her.

I walk over and shut it just as I hear my grandma say, "Where the hell did she go, anyway? It's dinner time!"

"Sorry about that. We've got company this evening," I tell him.

"Don't apologize, I know I interrupted your weekend. I just didn't want to blindside you with this when you come in tomorrow morning. I thought it better to give you time to absorb the news."

I plunk myself on my dad's old plaid armchair, rocking back and forth a bit. "I appreciate that, Keenan."

"Well, I appreciate all your hard work, Allie. You're definitely a team player and I was hoping that being able to work with Hudson Finch would offset your disappointment about the conference."

"Sorry, who did you say?"

"Hudson Finch. He's the one who will be shadowing you."

My face immediately grows hot. My heart pounds. Hudson Freaking Finch?

"Have you heard of him?"

"Yup," I squeak, unable to get a full breath of air.

"Yes, he's got quite the star power, doesn't he?" Keenan asks. "And as I was saying, the publicity we'll get from this could draw in a lot of donations. It's a huge win for the team, so we need to put our best foot forward to maximize this opportunity."

"Right, definitely," I answer, my stomach growling again.

"I imagine trying to teach him everything you can about astronomy in a short six weeks is going to be rather intense."

Intense? I get a mental image of me standing next to him in lab coats for some reason, even though we never wear them, and him tucking a lock of my hair behind my ear. Is he going to kiss me in this ridiculous fantasy? No, he isn't. And even if he did, it would only be because he wants to use me and lose me. I'm about to tell Keenan I can't do it, but he starts talking again before I can think of a good excuse. "I really appreciate you taking this on, Allie. In fact, I'll make sure some of the studio's donation goes directly into your project."

This is a done deal, isn't it? Chad's going to get to speak in Zurich, Lando's going to beat me to the punch, and I'm going to end up babysitting a celebrity for six weeks, only to have all my dreams go up in smoke. Unless … what if he's not going to be here until *after* I get Frank working?

"Um, when does Mr. Finch arrive?"

"Tomorrow morning at eleven."

My shoulders drop. "Oh."

"Listen, Allie, I want you to know that you'll be at the top of the list for the next summit."

"Thanks, I appreciate that." No, I don't. Not even a bit.

"I'll let you get back to your company. I'm going to email the team now with the big news."

"Awesome."

"See you tomorrow, Allegra, and thanks again!"

———

GWEN

Is the family gone?

ME

Finally, yes.

GWEN

I read Keenan's email. Do you want to talk about it?

I dial her number, relief washing over me that I can talk to my bestie. She picks up on the first ring. "Can you believe this?"

"No, this is the worst thing ever."

"I was worried you'd be upset." In the background, I hear the hum of her hot tub motor. Lucky bitch. Sitting in her boyfriend's hot tub under the stars while I'm hunched over my laptop in my cramped childhood bedroom.

"I'm more than upset. I'm furious. Not only am I stuck babysitting, but did you see Keenan's latest email? The thing about moving you out of our office to make room for Hudson? I can't *not* work next to my bestie for six whole weeks. That's ridiculous."

"Agreed. I'm none-too-pleased," Gwen says. "I'm going to have to share with Edward. He mutters to himself non-stop. It's going to drive me insane."

Letting out a groan, I say, "This is the worst. I've spent the last eighteen months killing myself to get this done and just when I'm so close, I'm about to have a man-sized roadblock put in my way."

"A super-hot, famous, man-sized roadblock," she points out.

"Yeah, a super-hot, famous, dates-super-models-not-nerds distraction who's going to ruin my life and let Lando the Liar win again," I say, squinting at my screen while I wait for Frank to finish analyzing the recordings. "I can't let that happen, Gwen. I just can't. I'm in an all-out battle of good versus evil, and good has to win this time. If not, I am seriously going to lose my faith in humanity and the Universe."

"Good to know you're not putting too much pressure on yourself."

"Haha, seriously. He should be following Chad around. I mean, I get that he has no tact and he's a terrible teacher and should basically never be around other humans, but, other than that, he's not so bad."

"Yeah, when you put it that way, it's a complete mystery why Keenan chose you."

I let out a huge sigh, all my fear and frustration bubbling up inside of me. "Oh, fuck, Gwen. This sucks so hard. I'm going to waste precious hours that I don't have trying to tutor a man on a topic he couldn't care less about. He's going to pretend to listen, then go back to Hollywood, and I'll have been screwed out of my chance to prove once and for all that I'm way fucking smarter than he-who-washes-his-penis-in-the-sink."

"Maybe you can do both. Tutor him *and* finish your project. A lot of the time, you're just waiting for Frank to analyze the next batch of recordings," she says, her words almost getting lost in the sound of the hot tub bubbles. "And besides, what if Hudson turns out to be a big help?"

"Hudson Finch? The guy who once showed up to a table reading so high he couldn't actually read?"

"I don't even believe that story," she says. "Besides, you never know. Maybe he's a lot smarter than people give him credit for. Or maybe, he'll bring a fresh perspective that'll help crack this whole thing open."

"Or maybe he'll distract me for six weeks straight and

cause my only real dream to wither on the vine and die." I close my tired eyes, then say, "Sorry, I know you're trying to make me feel better, but at the moment, I'm a total mess. I'm disappointed and frustrated and exhausted. Earlier today my mother actually told me I looked like I smelled bad.'"

"What? How is that even a thing?"

"Right? Although, at the time I really did reek."

"Oh sweetie, I hate how hard you've been pushing yourself to get this done."

"It'll all be worth it if I can just get it to work, but that's not looking too likely right now."

"Listen, I know you won't want to hear this, but Virgil did offer to help you, and he's—"

"No, thank you."

"Al, I totally understand why you don't want to accept help. I get it. Really. What The Liar did was super shitty. But we've known Virgil for ten years. He's not a glory-seeker. He's not the kind of guy who will take the credit for your work. He just isn't."

I let out a long sigh. "I know this doesn't make any sense to you, Gwen. I get it. I seem like a crazy person, but I'm not. I've been scorched once and I am *never* letting that happen again."

"But what if all you need is a little tiny bit of help from a trusted coworker and all your career dreams will come true?"

"That would feel like cheating," I say, my gut tightening at the thought of bringing someone in on my research.

"It's not cheating. Everyone needs help once in a while."

"All the greats work alone—Einstein, Goddard..."

"Not true," Gwen says. "Einstein was constantly

boring his wife with all his ideas, and Goddard only worked alone because he was so far ahead of his time that the other yahoo scientists were constantly shit-talking his theories on spaceflight. But I bet if he had had another physicist who said, 'Hey Bob, I heard you're having a little trouble with that multi-stage rocket you're building, let me have a looksee,' he would have been *more* than happy to show him."

"Come *on*, nobody called him Bob."

"You don't know that."

She's right. I don't. "And *you* don't know that he would've accepted help."

"He most definitely would've because the work was far more important to him than his reputation."

"Well, I'm not Robert Goddard, okay? I'm Allie Cammareri, woman on a mission. And I refuse to let some man take credit for my work ever again. And yeah, I know kindly old Virgil isn't going to *try* to take credit for it. But you know the truth? He'll get it anyway because in my acceptance speech at the National Space Society's Space Pioneer Awards, I'd have to mention him, and the rest of the dudes out there will be all, 'Oh, we knew a man had to be behind this.'"

"Okkaaayyy..." Gwen says, her tone conveying how crazy she clearly thinks I am.

"You know what? I hear it. I do. I sound insane," I admit. "But honestly, Gwen, I'm about as sane as they come. I started this whole thing alone and I'm going to finish it alone. And I'm going to do it *ahead* of Lando and his team of hacks. And I'm going to do a much better job, too."

"In that case, I'd better let you go so you can get back to work."

"Yeah, I really need to concentrate because as of

tomorrow morning, my life is going to get a whole lot more complicated."

We say goodbye, then I end the call and sit back in my chair with a long sigh. The next six weeks of my life are going to be hell. Not just because I'm so stressed out I could cry. Not just because my niece ate all my gnocchi or because my biggest dream feels like it's about to slip through my fingers like dust on the moon. It's because I'm going to spend the next six weeks in the same room as one of the hottest men alive (and not just according to me— according to *People* Magazine), and he isn't going to so much as notice I'm there.

That's the cold, hard truth. And there is really no getting around it.

5

The Lies, the Witch, and the Wardrobe...

Hudson

"You don't think this is a bit much?" I stare at myself in the mirror while Gershwyn and my stylist, Nola, look on.

We're in the hotel condo in Palo Alto that the studio rented for me, and I'm dressed in a pair of tan slacks, a light blue button-up shirt with a navy cardigan over it, and fake glasses. I crook my left arm and stare down at it. "Leather elbow patches? You didn't happen to bring a pipe, did you?"

Gersh snort laughs while Nola shoots me a dirty look. "You can't reinvent your image in the same clothes you wore to convince the world you were a surf bum."

"But I am a surf bum."

"Nobody wants to see a sixty-year-old surf bum. That's just sad," she says, wrinkling up her nose at the idea.

"I'm thirty-nine."

"Exactly," she tells me. "Which means we need to get on this now."

I give Gershwyn a desperate look, but he just shrugs so

I focus on Nola again. "Can we at least lose the reading glasses? I feel ridiculous."

Nola shakes her head. "It doesn't matter how you feel. It's how you look. And you look hot in a very distinguished way."

"But this whole thing is a lie," I say, gesturing up and down at myself. "I have perfect vision."

"But someday, you won't."

"And when that day comes, I'll start wearing readers."

She blows out a heavy sigh and rolls her eyes. "Look, I don't need this. I'm the best. I've come all the way up to…" She looks at Gershwyn. "Where the hell are we?"

"Silicon Valley."

"Right, Silicon Valley, to help you reinvent yourself. Do you have any idea what my time—and all these clothes—are costing you?"

"I don't think I want to know," I answer.

Gersh shakes his head. "You definitely don't want to know."

I wince at him. "That bad?"

He nods, closing his eyes and mouthing, "So bad."

"Shit," I mutter, looking at myself again.

"Hudson, listen, I know this is hard for you," Nola says. "But I also know what I'm doing. I've been through this with all the greats—Leo, Brad, George, Matt, Ben, Bradley. And they've all gone on to have lucrative and long careers."

"You're telling me they all wore fake glasses and elbow patches?"

"No, for each of them, I had to come up with something unique to their circumstances. In your case, with the role you've got coming up, we've got to start convincing people you're … what's the name of your character again?"

"Dr. David Todd," Gershwyn says.

"Right. We're going to prime the audience to believe you're this Todd guy." Nola sprays some mousse in her palm, then smooshes it into her other hand and starts to work it through my hair. "We show the world a different side of you. It's a whole dark academia aesthetic thing. It's massive on TikTok and we're going to play into that. Trust me, by the time this film comes out, the world will have totally forgotten they ever heard of *Beach Cops*." She stands back and smiles at her handiwork. "And, done. Absent-minded professor achieved."

Nola goes into the en suite to wash her hands, leaving Gersh, Oscar, and I alone in the bedroom. I walk over to the bed and pick up Oscar. "I'm going to miss you, buddy. Yes, I am." I nuzzle his little head with my nose. "Yes, I am."

Glancing at Gershwyn, I say, "You'll make sure you walk him twice a day, right?"

"He'll be fine. You've left him with me before and he's survived."

"Yeah, but he always looks too skinny when I get back. I don't think he eats enough," I say, scratching Oscar's neck. "And make sure you slice up the baby carrot before you put it in his breakfast. Don't put it in whole because he could choke on it."

Rolling his eyes, Gershwyn says, "Hudson, seriously. He's a dog. I'm a responsible adult. I've got this. In fact, I'll take him for a nice walk before we drive back home."

Nola comes out of the bathroom and picks up her oversized handbag off the dresser. "All right, in the closet you'll find the outfits for the photo ops Brittany set up. She'll text you on the mornings when there's something happening that you have to be dressed for. Each outfit is carefully labeled. Do *not* try to mix and match. Don't deviate from the plan in any way or you'll ruin *everything*."

But no pressure.

Gershwyn glances at his phone. "Looks like the *Entertainment Nightly* film crew is already at the research facility. They're going to follow you around for a tour of the place, which will air tonight. Oh, and make sure you park right in front of the building so they can get a shot of you with the Range Rover. We still owe them one more photo op after this."

"Gotcha. Right in front."

"Paul said to tell you TMZ will be here twice. You'll go to the library once, and to the San Francisco opera. It's in your calendar already. The team can set up a date for you for the opera if you don't have someone in mind, and if you do, they want you to tell them who so they can vet her first. They want someone with the right image."

"The tux is in the closet," Nola adds. "It's labeled *opera night*." She pronounces the words very slowly and clearly, as if this is my first day speaking English.

"Okay, got it," I tell her.

She reaches up and adjusts my hair a little. "Listen, people are sheep. It's terrifyingly easy to convince the public of anything. If they see you doing even a couple of these highbrow, smartypants things, they'll actually believe you have your PhD."

The three of us walk to the door of the condo and I open it for her. "Thanks, Nola."

She turns to me. "I know you're nervous about this, but trust me, when I'm through with you, they'll be offering you a Nobel Prize in Science or whatever." She glances at her oversized watch, then claps her hands together. "Chop! Chop! You're not going to get any publicity standing here."

Gersh and I both jump a little, and I hold up one hand.

"Okay, I'll be down in thirty seconds. I just need to have a quick chat with Gersh before I go."

She rolls her eyes. "Your little wiener dog will be fine. Besides, if he's not, you'll make enough off this movie to buy a whole litter of them."

Screwing up my face in disgust, I pull Oscar a little closer to my chest. "What?"

"Ugh, dog people are so sensitive," she mutters. "I'm going to go down to my car. I picked up some pastries from an adorable Italian bakery this morning for you to take with you. Obviously, you need to take credit for it so we can get you on camera being thoughtful and charming," she says. "And hurry up. You're keeping people waiting which is neither thoughtful nor charming."

I let go of the door and it swings closed slowly while I say, "See you in a minute."

As soon as the door is shut, I turn to Gersh, my gut tightening at the thought of going to the research facility. "I have a really bad feeling about this. Maybe I should turn it down."

"It's only six weeks," Gersh tells me. "And you're not going to a war zone. You'll be hanging out with some nerds. You'll be fine. Oscar will be fine. It's all going to be okay, Hud. I promise."

I feel myself breaking out in a cold sweat under my triple layers of professor dress-up clothes. "It won't be okay, Gersh. I know it. This is ... not for me."

"Dude, it's exactly for you. It's an opportunity for you to stretch your wings a little. Try something new. Prove to yourself that you're smarter than you think."

"But I'm not."

"You are. Trust me. You can learn anything you set your mind to. All you have to do is set it to astronomy."

"Yeah, sure," I say sarcastically. "Maybe when I'm

done with this film, I can shadow a brain surgeon, maybe try my hand at that too."

He reaches out and gently takes Oscar from me. "You're going to be great. The people there will be very nice to you."

"How do you know?"

"Because people are always nice to you. You're rich and famous," he says. "Now, get going before Nola comes back up here. She scares the shit out of me."

"Fine," I tell him, rubbing the bridge of my nose under my fake glasses. "But this is the stupidest thing I've ever done."

———

Oh God. I'm here. The SETI Research Institute. The camera crew clearly has been informed that I'm pulling up because they're already filming. Crap, they sent Josie Pedlar to follow me around. She's the worst. She's always hitting on me.

I pull into a stall in front of the white, three-story building, get out of the truck and pick up the large white box of pastries Nola bought. Plastering my best famous actor smile on, I shut the door and nod at the crew. "Hey guys!"

"Hi, Hudson," Josie says, striding over to me. "Oh, great look! You've got that whole naughty professor thing going on. The glasses? Love it. Very hot."

Yuck. "Thanks. You look really lovely today. Did you do something different with your hair?"

Her eyes light up. "I had it colored one shade darker. I can't believe you noticed!"

The sound guy, Chuck, walks over and holds up a tiny microphone.

Smiling at him, I say, "Hey, Chuck. How's the little one?"

"Growing like a freaking weed," he tells me, lifting the back of my cardigan and clipping the battery pack to my pant waist. "And we've got another one on the way—a girl this time."

"Really? Congratulations," I answer while I stand still and let him clip the mic to my shirt collar. "When's the baby due?"

"In May. We're pretty excited."

"Okay, Chuck, you done?" Josie asks, giving him the 'get lost' look.

"Yup, we're all set."

"So, Hudson," she says, taking my arm and walking toward the building. "We'll stop in front of the doors, I'll intro the segment and ask you a couple of questions, then you open the door and welcome the viewers inside to get a look for themselves. The SETI team has a few of their best geeks waiting in the lobby to greet us. We want it all to be very natural. We'll just be a fly on the wall."

"Great." *Not great. Not great at all. I so badly don't want to do this.*

We stop in front of the sign next to the main doors and the bright light of the camera blinds me. I smile at it while Josie, who is standing next to me, says, "Josie Pedlar, here with Hudson Finch, who is looking very dapper today, I must say. Hudson, tell the audience at home where we are."

"We're here in beautiful Mountain View at the SETI Research Institute, where I'll be preparing for my most important role yet."

"Cool," she says. "What's the role?"

"I'll be playing famed astronomer Dr. David Peck Todd."

"He can't be that famous. I've never heard of him," she says with a light laugh.

I laugh along as though that was the funniest thing I've ever heard.

"Tell us a little about him, Hudson."

Shit. My mind has just gone completely blank. "Oh, I don't want to accidentally reveal any spoilers."

"Okay ... so, what made you want to play an astronomer on the hunt for aliens?"

I narrow my eyes, going for a thoughtful look. "Well, Josie, I've always been fascinated with space. Ever since I was a child, and..." I glance at the sign behind her that reads: SETI Research Institute. Are We Alone? "I've always wanted to know the answer to one of the greatest mysteries of the universe. Are we alone?"

"No, I don't think we are," she says, looking confused. "I mean, we're literally standing here with several other people, so right there you can tell we're not alone."

Okkaayy... I might not be the dumbest person here. "I think the question refers to whether humans are alone in the universe."

She laughs. "Oh, that. Right. No, obviously not. There are animals all over the place."

I open my mouth to further explain, then close it. No point.

"Speaking of animals, how's little Oscar doing?"

"He's great," I tell her. "He'll be with my brother Gersh while I'm here studying."

"He's the world's most adorable little dog," she squeals. Turning to the camera, she says, "Seriously people, if you haven't seen Hudson's dog, look him up right now. His little face." Clutching her heart, she says, "Oh, he just kills me with his cuteness." She winks at me. "Kind of like his owner."

So, so awkward. "Ha! Why don't we go inside and meet the team?"

I pull open the door with my free hand and step to the side to let Josie in. I follow her, knowing the crew will want the shot of me walking in from that angle. As soon as my eyes adjust to the indoor lighting, I see a group of people standing off to the left, near the reception desk.

"Hi there," I say, offering them a wave and a big grin. I walk over and shake the hand of the nearest person, an older woman with short gray hair who's dressed in a pantsuit that looks a bit too small for her. She grins at me awkwardly, and I can tell she's nervous. "I'm Tina. Senior engine." She shakes her head and grimaces. "Engineer. I'm a senior engineer."

I offer her a warm smile, hating how nervous this all seems to be making her. "It's wonderful to meet you, Tina."

"Thanks, you too," she says, wiping a bit of sweat off her forehead. "I've never been on television before."

Lowering my voice, I say, "Don't worry. You're doing really well."

"Really? Because I told you I was an engine just now," she says, shaking her head again.

"They'll cut that part," I say with a little wink.

She points to the older gentleman next to her. "This is Dr. Keenan Edwards. He's the head honcho around here."

I shake his hand. "Oh, my new boss," I say with a little chuckle that makes me hate myself. "It's a pleasure to meet you, sir."

"Same to you. I really enjoyed you in that film about the secret service guy." It was a bodyguard for a princess, but close enough.

"Thank you, I appreciate that."

A guy around my age sticks out his hand. "I'm Chad.

I'm the number two here, so I guess I'm sort of also your boss."

I laugh, even though I can tell he definitely thinks he's my boss. "Nice to meet you, Chad."

"You too. I enjoyed your film about the bank heist, but I do have to say there's no way the amount of dynamite you used would actually blow the door off a Trident 670," he says. "That was pretty far-fetched."

Oh great, so now I know who the giant douche canoe of the team is. "Ah, well, part of the fun of going to the movies is to suspend your disbelief."

"It certainly is," Dr. Edwards says. "Hudson, I'd like you to meet Allie."

He points to the young woman next to him, and when I look over at her, I'm dumbstruck for a second. She's gorgeous. And I mean *gorgeous*. Dark brown eyes and lovely high cheekbones. Her bottom lip is fuller than the top one, giving her a pouty look without her having to pout. She's dressed in a white button-up shirt and black wide-legged dress pants. Her brown hair is up off her neck in a messy bun and she looks like she just got out of bed, but in a good way. "Hi."

"Hi, Allie," I say, smiling at her as I watch her cheeks flush a little. I hold out my hand and when she takes it, I want to lift it to my lips instead of shake it, even though a) I never do that because it's totally cheesy, and b) it would be completely inappropriate because this is a work thing. God, her skin is soft. Like buttery soft.

"It's nice to meet you," she says, glancing down at our hands.

Shit. I'm still holding her hand, aren't I? *Let go. You need to let go.*

Not letting go. Oh, she did it for me. Well, that's just humiliating.

"Allie's a radio astronomer," Dr. Edwards puts in. "You'll be shadowing her while you're here."

I get to shadow her? Sweet! "Great! That is … great news."

Her eyes flick down to the floor and for a brief second she looks upset, but then she smiles up at me again and nods. "Yes, I hope I'll be able to help you out."

Something about the way she says it tells me she doesn't actually want to help me at all. "I'm sure you will." I glance down at the box of pastries I'm still holding, feeling super awkward all of a sudden. "I brought some treats for everyone. They're from a cute little Italian bakery near my condo."

I go to hand them to Allie, but Chad snatches them up while Dr. Edwards says, "How thoughtful of you."

"It was nothing," I tell him, hating myself for being such a phony.

"Oh, Allie, look," Dr. Edwards says. "These are from your parents' bakery!"

Allie's eyes light up. "Really? They must have been shocked when you came in."

"Um, well, you know." I shrug modestly, but even as I'm doing it, I realize she's going to figure out I was never there. But I can hardly tell the truth now, can I? Not with the cameras rolling.

"I hope you brought lots of cannolis," Chad says. "They're my favorite."

I have no freaking clue what I brought. "It's … all good stuff. Everything looks amazing."

"You'll have to fight Virgil for them," Tina tells him, and they all laugh.

Josie clears her throat. "Okay, well, how about we start the tour?"

"Great idea," I tell her.

Tina takes the box from Chad. "I'm going to take these to the lunchroom. I've already done the tour."

"Let's have just Dr. Edwards take us around, okay?" Josie says, glancing at Allie. "It gets a little unruly when there are too many people in the shot."

Allie glances at her watch. "Sounds good. Great to meet you," she says before spinning on her heel and disappearing down the hall.

Crap. She's probably going to call her parents, only to find out I'm a big, fat liar.

Way to make a good first impression, jackass…

6

When the Brain Knows Better, but the Lady Bits Aren't Getting the Message...

Allie

CRAP. I'm about to be screwed over by a man yet again, aren't I? Yes, yes, I am. I know he's a professional liar and all, but he just seems so down-to-earth and thoughtful. That smile? The eye contact? The way he can instantly make you feel like you're the only woman in the world? That hot professor look he's got going on today? I didn't know he had glasses too. Maybe he *is* a secret nerd, which would be the hottest thing ever.

And which also makes him the *worst* man to show up in my life right now.

Nope. I am not attracted to him. I'm not. I can't be, so I'm not. There, done. That was easy.

But he did buy pastries for the team, and of all the places he could've bought them, he went into my parents' bakery. If this were a romantic movie, it would be a sign that we're meant to be.

But we're not. Very clearly and obviously. He's just a thoughtful, hot celebrity that's going to sit across from me for a few weeks, then go back to his real life and forget he ever met me. Bastard.

Not to mention the seductive scent he's wearing. What is that? The smell of rubbing your body with thousand-dollar bills when you wake up? Whatever it is, it's intoxicating, which means I really don't want him in my office all day. I absolutely positively cannot smell that by the hour or I'll wind up launching myself at him, lips first.

I need a plan. *Okay, think, Allie. How do you ignore this guy while also making it seem like you're not ignoring him?* I tap my finger on my lip while I glance wildly around my office. My eyes land on the desktop fan that we have on the far counter. We normally only need it in the summertime, but today it's going to help me keep the smell away. I hurry over and take the fan off the counter, then set it up on Gwen's desk (which I suppose I'll have to start calling Hudson's desk) so that it's facing the door. I turn it on so it sucks the air toward the hall, then stand back and admire my results. Yes, that ought to do it. The intoxicating scent will no longer be a problem.

Now, all I have to do is set him up learning independently and I should be able to get some work done. I sit down and make a list:

Independent Learning Activities:
Frank Drake video
Dr. Napper tribute video
SETI Guys podcast (all 87 episodes)
Read entire Astronomy 101 textbook
Read entire Astronomy 102 textbook
Set up a day with each team member to give him a broad picture of what the team does
Have him take all the tours so he can learn how to lead them himself

That ought to take him a good two weeks, minimum. Smiling to myself, I start to feel a lot more relaxed. *This will work. I can totally do this. Now, get to Frank before he's here interrupting your flow.* I flip on my computer. While it boots up, I send a quick text to my sister.

ME

Were you at the shop when Hudson Finch came in this morning?

LUCIA

The actor?

ME

Yes. The one who's coming to shadow me at work, remember?

LUCIA

Of course I remember. He didn't come in.

ME

Then how did he show up here with the big box? Maybe you don't know which actor I mean. He was in The Honeymooner? He played that hot surfer who inherited a resort in the Caribbean?

LUCIA

I know who he is. He's on my list of celebrities I'm allowed to cheat with.

ME

First of all, seriously? You and Vinny made lists? What about the sanctity of marriage?

LUCIA

Meh, trust me, after twelve years of having the same meal every night, you start to crave some new flavors.

ME

Okkkayyy … but back to Hudson. He really wasn't there? You couldn't have gone to the back for a break or something when he came in? Maybe Ma or Pops served him?

LUCIA

I was here alone all morning. Pops had to drive Ma to the optometrist. I sold one big box, but it was to a woman with the straightest, blondest hair I've ever seen and a weird outfit. She was super pushy. What makes you think he was here?

ME

He said he was.

LUCIA

Then Hudson Finch is a big, fat liar.

ME

Yup. Apparently. You should take him off your list.

LUCIA

Nah, I'd still do him. Maybe you can introduce us.

ME

I hope you're joking right now. Besides, who do you think the blonde is? I'm guessing she's his awful girlfriend.

LUCIA

Don't ruin my fantasy. It's literally all I have left.

ME

What about your husband and two beautiful children?

Are you kidding? They're the reason I need a rich fantasy life.

Well, that's the final nail in the coffin. I now know all I need to know about Hudson Finch, phony baloney. I shall ignore him at will with a clear conscience.

As soon as I wake Frank up, I hear the TV crew coming down the hall. *Act natural, Allie. Just act natural. And try to look smart.* Wait. I am smart. *Professional—try to look professional.* I snatch a pencil out of my "Never Trust an Atom: They Make Up Everything" mug and tuck it behind my ear so I look like I've been hard at work this whole time.

"And here is our final stop—your office for the next six weeks," Keenan says.

I glance up from my screen and smile politely while Hudson and the crew invade my space.

"Whoa, that's quite the breeze," Hudson remarks.

"Oh, you won't notice it when you're at your desk," I answer. Glancing at Keenan, I see he's narrowing his eyes at me. "But if it bothers you, I can move it. I just find the air flow helps me think."

"No, that's great, yeah," Hudson says. "Good tip. See? I'm learning already and I just got here."

Oh, he's smooth. A smooth, smooth talker, who can go suck it.

Josie (who seems like a total beotch, by the way) says, "Hudson, let's get some footage of you at your desk."

"Oh sure," he says, striding over and sitting down. He adjusts the seat, sits back and puts both hands on the desk, then runs them over the faux wood surface. "This is nice."

No, it isn't. It's cheap and rickety. Oh my God, he's not just a liar, he's pathological.

"So, this is where the magic is going to happen," Hudson says into the camera. "Dr. Allie here is going to show me the ropes and turn me into a radio astrologer. Crap, astronomer. Can we cut that?"

My body goes stiff at the word astrologer and I'm pretty sure the camera caught me looking like I just smelled the inside of a sweaty hockey helmet, but I do my best to recover.

Josie grins down at him. "Of course. Try the line again."

He turns to me. "You do have a PhD, right? So I should call you doctor?"

Flatterer. I give him a quick nod that says of course I have my PhD. "I do, but you don't have to call me doctor. I mean, if you were going to, it would be Dr. Cammareri, but Allie's fine."

Look at him, smiling away at me. He's got no idea that I'm onto him. "Okay, thanks, Dr. Cammareri," he says with a wink that I'm sure makes women around the world swoon. But not me. I'm not swooning. Okay, fine, maybe I did internally swoon the tiniest bit. I'm only human.

He looks back at the camera. "So, this is where the magic is going to happen. Dr. Cammareri here is going to be my guide as I fully immerse myself in the world of radio astronomy."

"Awesome," Josie says.

Hudson smiles at me. "Allie, can you tell the people at home what you're working on?"

I pause for a second, trying to decide how much to say. "Umm, I've been working on a way to train an AI system I lovingly call Frank, after the late, great Frank Drake."

Josie and Hudson both wear matching blank expressions.

"The father of SETI?"

Still nothing.

"Anyway, Frank here is learning to analyze the data we get from outer space. He's looking for anomalies or repeated, unusual pulses of light or radio waves."

"Wow, that sounds fascinating," Hudson says, squinting at my computer screen.

"It really is," I answer, even though I'm sure he's just acting like he's fascinated. "You see, it used to be, back in the day, that we had trouble getting *signals* from space. Then it was separating the radio and laser signals from Earth with those from space. We've sorted that out and have built up our global radio telescopes to the point where now, we're getting too much data. Far more than we can analyze. But Frank is going to fix that because once he's trained, he'll be able to do the work one human would do in ten years in a matter of seconds."

"Okay," Josie says. "You can stop talking now. No way our viewers want to know any of that."

Wow, rude. She could've at least pretended.

Josie turns to the camera with a wide-toothed grin. "All right, we'll try to make it back here to check on Hudson sometime in the next few weeks, so make sure you stay tuned because you won't want to miss it. From Mountain View, California, this is Josie Pedlar signing off."

The cameraman lowers the camera to his side and Josie hands the mic to him. Then she sits on Hudson's desk and, in a low voice, says, "So, this is really where you're going to spend the next few weeks. Aren't you afraid you're going to die of boredom?"

I wait, expecting him to laugh, but he doesn't. He just

shakes his head. "Nope. I'm really excited about this. I love learning new things."

"The camera's off, Hudson. You can tell the truth now."

The sound guy walks over and starts taking Hudson's mic off. He's got his hands right on Hudson's collar. Lucky bastard. No, I mean, eww. Poor guy.

"I *am* telling the truth. I'm looking forward to this. Besides, I really appreciate Allie here taking me under her wing. I'm sure she's got a lot better things to do than help a total newbie learn about her job."

Huh, that was sort of sweet. Oh wait, he's just acting. Dammit. It is going to be *so hard* for me to remember that.

Josie glances around, wrinkles up her nose at my poster of Einstein sticking his tongue out, then shrugs. "Whatever. Do you want to go grab some lunch?"

"Thank you for the offer, but I really should get started here. If I'm going to become Dr. David Peck Todd, I need to get on it."

"Another time then?" she says, running a finger along his forearm. "When you get back to L.A.?"

"Absolutely."

Oh my God, she's not going to fall for that, is she? Does she not know about the woman with the straight blonde hair who buys his pastries for him?

That smile says that even if she did know, she wouldn't care. Pathetic. "Okay, but I'm going to hold you to it."

"I'd expect nothing less," he says, standing. "Here, why don't I walk you guys out?"

They all finally exit my office, then Hudson pokes his head back in. "Allie, which way is it to the lobby?"

I point to my left.

"Thanks."

As they start down the hall, I hear him ask the cameraman how his family's doing. Good lord, does he not have an off-switch for that charm?

7

Time to Turn Up the Charm

Hudson

IF THERE's one thing I can easily read, it's people. And Dr. Allie Cammareri does not like me. Not one little bit. I could tell by the way she was scowling as soon as the interview ended. If I had to guess, I'd say she already found out I was never at her parents' bakery. Or maybe she's just one of those smart people who looks down her nose at regular guys like me. I don't know, but whatever it is, I'm going to fix it. It's either that, or this is going to be the most awkward experience of my life.

I've offloaded the *Entertainment Nightly* crew and am now attempting to find 'my' office, without much luck. I've been wandering the halls for a good five minutes now and I honestly have no idea where I am. Poking my head into the lunchroom, I hope I'll find someone in there so I can ask for directions, but the room is empty.

The box of pastries is open on the middle of one of the tables, so I decide to bring a plate back to Allie as a peace offering. Although, since they're from her parents' bakery, she might be sick of them. Also, I'm not really sure why I need to make a peace offering at all and part of me feels annoyed to be doing this. But most of me knows that I'm going to need to really turn up the charm or this is going to go south fast.

I grab a plate from the cupboard labeled 'Plates, bowls, and mugs,' which is conveniently located next to the one marked 'NASA freeze-dried foods.' Oh, I hope they have freeze-dried ice cream. I used to love that as a kid.

Okay, doofus, forget the ice cream. You've got a job to do.

Walking over to the table, I see there's only half a cannoli left. Half. Who does that? And also, how the hell is this all that's left when I've only been here for an hour? That box was heavy with pastries.

I pick up the measly treat and place it, along with the gold lacy paper it was sitting on, onto the plate. Blerg, that looks totally lame there by itself. I hurry over to the fridge and find some strawberries in a plastic dish and set three next to the pastry. "There. Much better," I mutter.

A couple of minutes later, I manage to find the office. I put on my best smile and walk in, only to discover Allie's too engrossed in whatever she's doing on her computer to notice me. I set the snack down on her desk and using my pillow-talk voice, I say, "I thought you might be hungry for a little snack."

She glances down at the plate, and says, "Oh, thanks. That's really thoughtful of you."

This was a terrible idea. Just terrible. "I didn't eat the other half or anything. This was all that was left when I got into the lunchroom."

"Yeah, sweets move fast around here," she says, tapping at her keyboard. "Except the freeze-dried ice cream. That's been there for years."

"Oh, good to know," I tell her, glancing at the plate

again. "I found the strawberries in the fridge, but now I'm wondering if I may have just stolen someone's lunch."

She nods. "You did. Those are Keenan's."

Shiiiitttt. "Stupid. I'm used to the craft service spread on set. Everything is for everyone."

"I see," she says, her expression basically telling me I'm an idiot. "Here we feed ourselves."

"Should I … take them back?"

She pushes her glasses a little higher on her nose. "No, I'll email Keenan and tell him about the mix up. He won't mind. If you had taken something from Gwen's lunch, however…"

"Won't happen again," I say, holding up both hands and grinning at her.

She nods blandly and turns back to her computer. Wow. She's definitely annoyed because this is not how people treat me. She one-hundred-percent called her parents and found out I haven't stepped foot in their bakery. "Say, Allie, I was hoping to clear something up with you."

"Sure," she says without looking at me. "But can you give me a second? I'm right in the middle of something time-sensitive."

"Of course." I sit down at my empty desk, feeling the air get sucked away from me. If I were alone right now, I'd totally be talking into the fan. *Luke, I am your father…* Huh. I'm hungry. Checking my watch, I realize it's as fake as these stupid glasses. A fake watch? Seriously, Nola? I pull my phone out of my pocket, only to see that it's after noon already and I've missed four texts from my publicist.

BRITTANY

We need shots of you in your professor fit on day one at the job for your Instagram a.s.a.p. Send me several of the following: At your desk, with some excited-looking staff, and next to one of those huge satellite thingies, you know, like from that old movie Contact with Jodie Foster. Take your jacket off in one of them so people won't know it's the same day. I'll use some to cover us the rest of the week.

Dude, let's get on this please. I've got to get the ball rolling here.

I forgot, you get extra points if you do 20 sec videos for TikTok and Reels.

Wayne from Galaxy is already on my ass to make sure his "hundred grand was money well spent," so the sooner the better.

ME

I just finished with the EN crew. I'm on it.

I sit back in my chair and hold my phone up, trying to get the best shot for a selfie, but it looks like I'm just sitting in a chair with a blank wall behind me. I glance around and spot the picture of Einstein with his tongue out. Perfect. Getting up, I stand next to it and make the same face, then snap a few shots. The entire time, Allie's typing away, although I can feel her eyes on me. Her super smart, judgey eyes. But when I look at her, she's got them trained on her screen. I take a couple of shots of me sitting on the edge of the desk with a map of the solar system behind me, then send the pics to Brittany, hoping that'll hold her off a bit.

Allie clears her throat, which is the universal sign for 'you're being annoying,' so I sit back down in my chair. "Sorry. I don't want to distract you. It's just that the studio wants some pictures for my social media."

"Of course. Do what you've got to do."

I sit back and wait for her to finish up whatever it is that's so important. Maybe I haven't done anything to annoy her. Maybe she's just not a people person. She sure is pretty though. A pretty, slightly nasty woman who probably knows I'm a big liar and has lost all respect for me.

I can fix this. I know I can. I'll explain what happened with the pastries and ask her if I can take her out for lunch so we can get to know each other better. Only I better not say it like that because that sounds like I'm hitting on her. There's a fine line between being charming and being creepy, and that's a line I definitely don't want to cross. Although if she were up for crossing the line…

Just as she takes off her glasses (which I'm sure are real), Chad pokes his head into the room. "Say, Hudson, if you haven't had lunch yet, there's a great sandwich shop just down the street. I'm heading there and you're more than welcome to come with, if you like."

"Thanks, Chad, but I was thinking I should take Allie here out to eat. You know, get to know each other a little since we'll be working together so closely."

Allie turns to me. "You know, that's a really kind offer, but I am right in the middle of running this data so there is no way I'll be able to leave my computer for at least an hour." Glancing at Chad, she adds, "You guys go."

Chad's eyes light up. "So? Guys' lunch out?"

Oh, perfect. "Sounds great."

I stand and pocket my phone, then start toward the

door. Turning back, I say, "Why don't I bring you some-thing back?"

"No, that's okay," she says, pointing to the food I brought her. "I can nosh on that."

"That's not a proper lunch," I tell her. "I'll get you a sandwich. Is there anything you're allergic to?"

"Liars," she mutters.

Did she just say liars? She did. It was barely audible but that's what she said. I'm going to have to explain as soon as I get back from lunch. "What?"

"Lentils."

I narrow my eyes a little. "Well, I'll make sure not to get you a lentil sandwich then."

"Thanks."

My phone pings and I know it's Brittany wanting more pictures. I sigh as I follow Chad down the hall. "Say, Chad, I need a few pictures to send to my publicist of me with the team. Would you be up for a selfie?"

"Certainly," Chad answers. "Let's wait until we get outside. We can take one by the sign."

"You don't happen to have any of those satellite dishes here, do you?"

He barks out a laugh. "You mean radio telescopes."

Okay, dude, you don't have to laugh at me. "Right. That."

"No, the closest ones are up at Black Creek, which is over a five-hour drive from here."

"Really? That far?"

"Yeah, you can't set them up in highly populated areas or you get too much interference. We actually use data from telescopes around the globe. But we should arrange for you to take a trip up to Black Creek. It's a part of the job you should know about if you're going to convince anyone you know anything about SETI research."

"So I don't accidentally use the word satellite or something."

"Exactly."

All right, Hudson, new goal: get through lunch as fast as possible so I can get back here and fix things with Allie.

————

So much for my goal. When we got back from lunch, Chad walked me back to my office (which made it feel like the most awkward dude date ever), and as soon as Allie saw us, she asked Chad if I could spend the rest of the day in the server room with him under the guise of 'it being the most important thing for me to train on and him being the foremost expert on it.' Chad was thrilled. Me? Not so much.

I set her turkey, brie, and cranberry sauce sandwich on her desk and said, "I really hope we get a chance to talk later. I need to explain something."

"Of course, we'll have weeks and weeks to talk," she answered without looking away from her screen. "Just … not right now. I'm so close to a breakthrough here."

"Okay, in that case, I don't want to disturb you."

"Thanks. Talk to you later," she answered.

But it turns out *she's* the liar, or perhaps I should say she's *also* a liar, because by the time Chad was finished confusing the hell out of me, it was after five o'clock and she (as well as her laptop) were already gone. She did leave a little note on my desk:

Hudson,

I've gone home for the evening. I'll see you when you come in tomorrow morning. No rush in getting here if you want to sleep in or hit the gym or something.

Cheers,

Allie

If that's not a polite way to tell me to fuck off, I don't know what is. So now I'm back at my condo, eating supper alone, hating my life.

————

Instagram Reel: Hollywood Dish with Ferris Biltmore

The video starts up showing Ferris sitting at his desk wearing a fedora and a sweater vest with an orange shirt under it. "Hello bitches. Quit your bitching about the fact that I've left you hanging about the huge celeb who's sporting the garish rock because after the devastating news about Hudson Finch last week, I spent four days completely horizontal. But then, I got a DM from my dry cleaner who told me her neighbor's roommate's sister works for *Entertainment Nightly* and she spilled the tea that the big man himself is off to Mountain View to prepare for the role of his life. It's going to air this evening, and you can bet your biscuits I'll be watching it with my eyelids taped open so I won't miss a second.

"Apparently, his team is rebranding him as smart, like Benny Cumberbatch if he were hot. And this brings us to a new segment here on Dish called: Why Didn't You Do This Ages Ago, Morons?"

The graphic appears behind him and Ferris leans

forward, scowling at the camera. "Why didn't you do this ages ago, you morons? You no-IQs? You ... you human losers? Obviously Hudson should have been playing the smart and sexy guy all along because ... wait for it ... he is both smart. And sexy. You should've put him in these sorts of roles to start with. Although, if you had, we wouldn't have *Beach Cops* or *Beach Cops II* which would be a tragedy for all humankind, so I suppose I can forgive you for starting him out as just the hot guy. But seriously, it took you way too long to get here. And in the interim, you made him make *Beach Cops III*, and do a movie that got shelved, so, you're not forgiven for leaving him as just the hot guy until the ripe age of thirty-nine."

The graphic disappears and a picture of Hudson in his glasses and suit jacket takes its place. "And this, my little friends, is a photo taken only this morning of the big man himself, arriving at some awful science place, where apparently he's going to sequester himself for six weeks. I don't know what they do but supposedly it's something about aliens, which might actually be fun if it turns out the aliens do show up and they're well-dressed, hot, and all about the probing. But back to what I was saying: six weeks! Those lucky, lucky bitches! Spending six entire weeks with Hudson Finch. If I got to do that, I would literally die happy. Even if I knew someone was going to chop me into little pieces as soon as the six weeks was up."

He nods and mouths, "It's true."

"Now, this brings me to a special segment called: I Hate You, You Lucky Sons of Bitches!" The graphic appears and Ferris shouts, "To the people at the science place where Hudson Finch is going to be, I hate you, you lucky sons of bitches. You don't deserve him. I don't care how many PhD's you've got floating around in that dreary building. Hudson is a *god*. He should be with the other gods back here in Hollywood. But since apparently he's decided to grace you with his presence, you better treat him right. Or I'll be coming up there. Which brings us to my new segment: Don't Make Me Come Up There!"

Graphic swap and Ferris scowling. "Don't make me come up there, science people. Do not. You don't want me to come up there. And believe you me, I'm going to hear about it if there's any ill treatment of my main man. If he gets even so much as a dirty look, I'm getting in my VW Bug and setting Google Maps straight for your office. I swear to all that is holy, you will pay if you mistreat him. I'll see to it.

"But I digress, and there's no time for digressing because *EN* is going to start in a few minutes and I need to change into something formal and find my eyelid tape. See ya later, bitches! Ferris out!"

8

Noisy Furniture, Homemade Hooch, and National Television Debuts...

Allie

"It's starting!" Grandma yells, which causes a rush of people from the kitchen to the living room.

I somehow allowed myself to get roped into going to Nonno and Grandma's house to watch tonight's episode of *Entertainment Nightly* with my entire family. They've got the most seating space in their living room, so it made sense to come here. Zia Fernanda, who lives with them, is a celebrity gossip hound, so she's over-the-top excited that her niece is on the show.

Zia turns up the volume and shushes everyone.

"Welcome to *Entertainment Nightly*. I'm your host, Rock Simons. Tonight, an exclusive on-site interview with Hudson Finch as he prepares himself for his next role. But first, let's take a look at this week's make-ups and break-ups..."

Zia mutes it and jumps up from her armchair. "Quick! Let's go get the grappa!"

Oh God, not the grappa. It's a *digestivo*—or after-dinner

drink—that is supposed to aid digestion. All it does for me is up the temperature of my face by ten degrees and makes the world spin a little. It's homemade, therefore the actual alcohol content is a complete unknown, but let's just say it's somewhere between forty percent and strong enough to burn a hole clean through your esophagus.

The plastic cover on the sofa squeaks as my relatives get up and race to the kitchen. I stay put on the floor, where I strategically planted myself when we arrived. I'm sitting here so it'll be hard for my relatives to see my face while we're watching the show, on account of being terrified of allowing any sort of expression that shows one of the following two emotions: a) hurt feelings, because I know they're going to pick me apart, and b) attraction to Hudson, because if they sniff that out, it'll be a whole thing I don't want to deal with.

I look over at Nonno, who winks at me. "Are you excited, *tesora?*"

"Not really. To be honest, I don't have time for this. I need to get back to work."

He nods, then says, "Yeah, yeah, yeah," with a sigh. "You work hard, you make a lot of money, life is good when you're old."

Grandma, who is returning to the room with a tiny glass for her and Nonno, makes a *pfft* sound. "Money. She doesn't need more money. She needs to find a nice man to settle down with."

"She's a modern woman," he says, taking his drink from her. "She's making her own way in the world."

"Thank you, Nonno," I say, sitting up a little straighter.

"We can give you money, *tesora*," Grandma says. "It's time you find a good man. Money won't keep you warm when you're old like us."

On the screen, a commercial for Ozempic is playing,

which will inevitably be followed by another Ozempic commercial. The rest of the relatives pile into the room, taking spots on the sofa and kitchen chairs that have been brought into the room. Lucia flops down onto the dusty rose carpet next to me. Vinnie and the kids aren't here on account of soccer practice, so she's all-in on the grappa. She takes a big sip. "So? Other than being a liar, what's he like?"

"I don't really know. I only spent a couple of minutes with him today," I tell her.

She bumps her shoulder into mine. "Come on, what's he like?"

"Well, we've established he's a liar, so I'd say that's all we need to know about him."

Lucia shrugs. "A little white lie for the cameras. So what?"

The show starts up again and Zia jacks up the volume to 'about to blow the speakers.'

Rock Simons grins into the camera. "And now for our *EN* exclusive with Josie Pedlar…"

The video starts and my heart pounds a little harder, seeing the front of the building I'm at every day. Hudson is standing, holding the box of pastries from the shop. "There's our big box!" my father yells. The ladies in the room are all clearly more interested in Hudson. They collectively make a loud 'oooo' sound, which pretty much drowns out what that obnoxious Josie and Hudson are saying.

My dad shushes them. "Come on, we're going to miss it if you don't stop that."

Hudson's holding the door open for Josie, then the camera pans to the staff, all waiting and looking super awkward. I get a glimpse of myself and my face heats up. Oh God, I look weird. My family cheers. "There she is!!!"

"Shhhhh!!!"

"You shush. Your shushing is making it so I can't hear."

"You should've come to the shop for a hair mask."

"Stop talking already! We're missing it!"

"He's so handsome, I can't stand it!" Zia whisper-yells.

"Is he Italian?" my grandma asks.

"He must be," Zia answers. "Look at that strong jaw."

Meanwhile, on the screen, Hudson is working his way down the line, until he's talking to me. My heart is in my throat, even though I know exactly what's about to happen. I watch as we shake hands and my face turns bright pink as I say, "It's nice to meet you."

"Oooh!!!! You like him!" Zia says.

"I do not!"

Lucia snort laughs. "You do! It's written all over your red face!"

"Sssshhhhh!!!!!"

Dr. Edwards is talking now. "Allie's a radio astronomer. You'll be shadowing her while you're here."

Zia gasps. "Look how happy he is to hear that!"

"He's just being nice," I say, not wanting to let myself believe he would actually be happy about it. Although he did hold my hand for a long time, now that I think about it. And his face is lit up.

And now I'm trying to look professional as I say, "Yes, I hope I'll be able to help you out."

"I'm sure you will," he answers in that buttery voice of his.

I watch as he glances down at the box of pastries. "I brought some treats for everyone. They're from a cute little Italian bakery near my condo."

The rest of the family squeals with delight at being mentioned on national television, while I watch in disgust. He never even saw the bakery.

Chad snatches the box while Dr. Edwards says, "How thoughtful of you."

"It was nothing," Hudson says.

"What a phony," I mutter to Lucia.

"Oh, Allie, look," Dr. Edwards says. "These are from your parents' bakery!"

I see the surprise on my face. "Oh wow, they must have been shocked when you came in."

Hudson looks a little awkward as he says, "Um, well, you know."

"Damn. They didn't get a shot of the logo on the box," Pop says.

And now, Josie is telling me not to come along on the tour, so I say, "Well, that's it for me for the rest of it. I might be on for a few seconds at the end."

"Shhh! We're going to watch the whole thing," Grandma says. The tour of the building starts and Keenan is explaining what it is we do, which clearly, my family has no interest in whatsoever.

"He's so handsome!" Zia says. "Is he that handsome in real life, Allegra?"

"Pretty much."

"Because you don't look like that in real life," she adds.

"Fernanda," my dad says, sounding annoyed.

"What? It's true. She looks more sophisticated on TV."

"That's because she's dressed up to go to work. She looks very sophisticated when she's at work," he says. He's totally wrong, but I appreciate him sticking up for me.

"Does he have a girlfriend?" Lucia asks Fernanda.

"Not that I'm aware of, unless it's the mysterious blonde who came into the store, but I have to think she works for him because if he was with someone, there's no way he could keep it a secret," Fernanda says. "The paparazzi follow him everywhere, and then there's that Ferris Biltmore guy who somehow knows his every move."

"Why wouldn't a man like that be married at his age?" my mom asks.

"There's got to be something wrong with him," my dad answers. "Otherwise he'd have a wife."

"Maybe he just doesn't want to get married," Lucia says. "It's not for everyone."

Fernanda makes a smacking sound with her lips. "He's a serial dater. He picks a woman on every set and stays with her until filming wraps, then he moves on."

"Like a PR thing?" Lucia asks.

"I don't think so because sometimes the women he chooses are a bad for his career, like that redhead from the *Beach Cops* movie who likes to strip everywhere she goes," Fernanda says.

"Oooh! What if he picks Allegra to date while he's in town?" Grandma asks, sounding far more excited than she should about her granddaughter being serial dated, then dumped.

"He's not going to…" I answer, cutting myself off before I finish a sentence that sounds too insane to even be considered. "Besides, I'm not interested. We know he can't be trusted and I'm far too busy with Frank right now."

"Forget Frank. If you can get your hands on *that*, you totally should," Fernanda says, pointing to the screen.

My face heats up. "I'm not … no."

"Think of the stories you'll have to tell!" she says. "Besides, if you can date a man like that, all the other men will come running when it's over."

"Again, work colleagues only. Discussion over."

My dad speaks up. "My little girl is not going to date that man. He uses women, then dumps them, and he's not good enough for my Allegra. No. Allegra is right. The discussion is over."

"Enzo, if a big Hollywood star isn't good enough for Allegra, then who is?"

"Someone who is not him. A good Italian boy."

"Like Vinnie," Lucia says.

My dad wrinkles up his face. "Meh…"

"Enzo! We love Vinnie like a son," my mom says.

"Yeah, but…" He tilts his head as if to say, 'yeah, but Vinnie's not that great.'

Lucia rolls her eyes and *tsks* loudly. "Whatever, Pop."

"Shhh! It's Allie again!" Nonno shouts.

A quick pan of my office shows me sitting at my desk. A slight sense of pride swells in my chest. There I am doing my very important work. The video cuts to show Hudson at Gwen's desk, smoothing his hands over it. He smiles at the camera. "So, this is where the magic is going to happen. Dr. Cammareri here is going to be my guide as I fully immerse myself in the world of radio astronomy."

"Awesome," Josie says. Turning to the camera, she adds, "We'll try to make it back here to check on Hudson sometime in the next few weeks, so make sure you stay tuned because you won't want to miss it. From Mountain View, California, this is Josie Pedlar signing off."

The video ends and my family erupts in applause, while I sit, slightly disappointed that they cut everything I had to say about the actual job.

"Wonderful, Allegra! You did wonderful," my nonno says.

"Dad and I are so proud of you, sweetie," my mom adds.

"You did it," Grandma tells me.

"I can't believe you were on national TV," Zia says, shaking her head. "And with that dry hair."

"Yup. I certainly was." I was on national television, and what's more, Hudson Finch—an A-lister if ever there was one—just said my name on TV. A hot, rich, charming-as-hell, lying-his-ass-off, A-list celebrity who can have any woman he wants is going to spend the next six weeks with me. And it is going to be almost impossible not to fall for his act, even if I can see right through him. If there ever was a man to keep at arm's length, it's this man.

9

I See Crazy People. Walking Around Like Regular People...

Hudson - Three Days Later

OKAY, so when Dr. Allegra Cammareri wants to avoid someone, she does one hell of a job. She's had me whisked off every morning by a different staff member first thing when I walk in the building, each one keeping me completely busy all day, only to find her gone when I finally manage to make my way to our office. The first day, it was an engineer named Edward, who although a nice guy, is obsessed with measuring the symmetry of people's faces and got me to pose for some app. Apparently, I got a 93%, which is the highest he's seen. Whatever that means. I honestly didn't learn a thing about SETI research or engineering, but I'm a whole lot more knowledgeable about the science of attractiveness.

The next day, I was greeted by Gwen, who roped me into helping lead an early morning tour of a group of insane women who call themselves Moms and Bright Babies or something like that. They were the worst—privileged, plastic, and smug, not to mention highly competitive and obsessed with getting photos with me. I felt bad for Gwen because they didn't listen to a word she said the entire time. I don't think those babies did either. I've also got news for those women because as far as I could tell, they're just normal babies who suck on their fingers and drool. At least I got to watch a video about Frank Drake, the father of SETI research, during the tour. Fascinating guy, and someone I definitely want to study, because he's exactly the type of inspiration I need. Gwen spent the rest of the day explaining what an astrobiologist does—well, in between long pauses while she texted her boyfriend, and to be honest, I didn't pick up much of what she said because it was every bit 'over my head' as I thought it would be.

Yesterday, I was paired up with Virgil, an astrophysicist who is super jealous that his arch nemesis (some guy named Carl) has been given a position as the facilities manager at the Green Bank Telescope in Virginia. Apparently, it's not only the world's largest fully-steerable radio telescope in the world (like, taller than the Statue of Liberty), but it's also a big deal in the SETI world. Or at least for Virgil, who spent the entire day showing me videos about it and giving me all the reasons Carl has no business running a facility of that stature. And here's the kicker: Virgil didn't want the job. He didn't even apply for it. Has no intention of ever applying for it or moving to Virginia to work there. Why he's so angry is beyond me. So, what did I learn yesterday? I suppose you can say I learned that geniuses can be every bit as petty as the rest of us.

Other than that, I haven't had a chance to get Allie alone so I can fess up, I am no closer to understanding what I need to know to become Dr. David Peck Todd, and at this point, I'm not even sure if I will be by the time I go back home. So tomorrow, I'm going to try a new strategy. I'm going to come in an hour early, so I can meet her in her office before whoever she's got me set up with arrives. And I'm going to come bearing gifts.

10

The Nasty, Hairy Surprise...

Allie

WELL, this week has been one hell of a roller-coaster. Not just meeting Hudson, and having it all recorded and shown on national TV. And not just finding out Hudson's a big fat liar (which he totally is). Not just pawning him off on whoever will take him for the last few days (which is not-so-surprisingly easy due to him being famous and charming AF). But the biggest rush came just before midnight last night when Frank and I had a little breakthrough. Well, actually, it might be a *really big* freaking breakthrough, to be honest. I don't want to get my hopes up (too late—they're stratosphere-level high), but he may have detected a Black Widow Pulsar, which is a neutron star that shoots out pulses of radiation that are so regular that back in the day, they were originally thought to be actual aliens, and in fact, were nicknamed Little Green Men, or LGMs. (See? Scientists can be funny.) Anyway, this one is located approximately 6,500 light years from Earth, and if Frank really did find it, it means he's figuring out how to capture actual signals from outer space, which is really the whole damn point.

I was so excited, I could hardly sleep, so I've been back at the office since six. I gave Frank ten thousand recordings to listen to—all of which have pulsars on them. It's been over an hour and I'm still waiting for him to get through them all to see if he'll key in on the pulsars, and only the pulsars.

And as to Hudson Finch, I've managed to successfully offload him all week, which has served two very important purposes: a) allowing me to continue full-speed ahead on my project, and b) keeping me away from Prince Charming, who, let's face it, is exactly the kind of asshole I fall for. He's charming, popular, and a total liar.

I'm just about to text Tina to ask her to 'watch him for the day,' when I get a message from Keenan.

KEENAN

> Allie, I've noticed Hudson has spent the last several days with people on the team who are not radio astronomers. I thought I made it clear that he is your responsibility. Please make him your first priority going forward.

Damn. He caught me. But I can't stop now. Not when I'm so close (for real this time). I glance at the list on my desk of ways to keep him out of my hair. No problem. I'll just hand him my Astronomy 101 textbook, a pad of paper, and some pens.

I text Keenan back:

ME

I thought it prudent to start Hudson with a high-level overview of what various team members do in order to provide him with the big picture of our work, but if you want him to stay with me, I've got lots for him to study here.

My phone pings, but instead of being a response from Keenan, it's an email that makes my stomach drop instantly.

Email from Lando.Allegro@USRAO.com
To: Allegra.Cammareri@SETIResearchInsti
tute.com

Subject: How's Frank?

Al,
I saw you on Entertainment Nightly the other
night. You're going to be Hudson Finch's babysit-
ter? Does this mean you've given up on Frank?
Inquiring minds want to know.
L

Seething with rage, I hit reply.

*Nope, not even close. In fact, Frank found an LGM last
night so suck it, you rat bastard.*

I stare at it for a second, then delete it. No way am I
telling him anything about what I'm doing. He'd immediately start looking for pulsars too, and knowing my luck,

that'll be the breakthrough he needs to get his stupid AI working. Oh, and as if it's not obnoxious enough that he's also working on an AI system, he named his Drake (also after Frank Drake, you know, because he can't possibly think of anything on his own, even a name).

What should I write back? I suppose I could not reply at all. That'll feel good. Sort of. Not as good as gloating and calling him a bastard. But still, good(ish). In the name of professionalism, however, I should probably say something. Also because I want that S.O.B. running scared.

Perhaps you should consider an alternate theory. What if Hudson's shadowing me because I have loads of free time on my hands at the moment?

Okay, so this sort of makes me a liar, but not really because I'm just posing a question. Besides, lying to a lying, cheating, thieving waste of air doesn't count. I've got my mouse hovered over the send button and am trying to decide whether to hit it or not when I'm startled by the sound of Hudson's voice.

"Good morning, Allie."

Dammit. I sent it.

I glance up, only to see him looking ridiculously hot again today. He's wearing tan chinos and a light blue button-down shirt with the sleeves rolled up to show off his forearms, which are flexed, by the way, because he's carrying the largest fruit basket I've ever seen in my life. "Oh hi, I didn't think you'd be in this early."

"I really wanted to talk to you."

"Right, sorry. I forgot." I didn't forget. I'm just not interested in whatever bullshit he's about to spew about why he lied the other day.

He walks over and places the basket on my desk. "This

is for you. As a thank you for tutoring me. Well, once we actually get started."

"Wow, that's a lot of fruit." Like seriously, so much fruit. I won't need my Activia yogurt for a while. "You didn't have to do that."

Also, he didn't. He probably had that blonde lady do it.

"I wanted to, and unlike the pastries, I actually went to the store myself," he says, somehow looking concerned and flirty at the same time. How is that even humanly possible? He pulls out his phone and shows me a pic of him next to a man in a green apron. "See? That's Louis. He threw in the chocolates for free."

Of course Louis threw in the chocolates for free. This man is a shameless, shameless charmer who just goes around getting whatever he wants from whomever he wants it from. And now, he's got an innocent grocer involved. Well, not me. I refuse to be tricked into giving him … whatever it is he wants from me. I'm not falling for it. No way. No how.

Although it is sort of nice of him to go pick up a gift for me.

Sitting back in my chair, I narrow my eyes a little, not sure how to respond.

"I lied the other day when I said I'd been to your parents' bakery. My PR team wanted footage of me giving the pastries to your team so they set the whole thing up," he tells me, leaning against my desk. Oh wow, there's that scent again. I'm pretty sure they bottled him to make a new version of Old Spice body wash called Lick Me. "I couldn't admit it on TV, but I was going to fess up that afternoon, then Chad … stopped by and you pawned me off on him, then on Edward, Virgil, and Gwen, likely because you'd already talked to your parents, who told you I was never there."

"Yup. Something like that."

He rubs the back of his neck, which honestly does something to me. "How to make a good first impression, right?"

"It wasn't the best way," I answer.

"I'm sorry," he says. "The thing about life in Hollywood is that it's all just bullshit, you know? Everything you see. It's just smoke and mirrors, but if you're there long enough, you start to believe the lies yourself."

"Sounds awful."

"It can be. But it's got its perks too." He means shagging supermodels.

For some unknown reason, I stiffen slightly at the thought, then give him a quick nod. "Okay, well, thanks for telling me the truth. I mean, you were basically caught so you knew you had to, but still."

His face turns a little red and he nods, his expression filled with regret. "You're right. I was caught and I knew it. But I promise from here on out, only the total truth."

Part of me wants to tell him all is forgiven and give him a big hug—like a really tight hug where I press my everything up against his everything. It's a lonely part of me that hasn't been touched in a very long time. But the rest of me knows better. "Good, because if we're going to work together, it'll go much smoother if you're honest with me. I don't have any patience for liars. Like, none."

"I know. You're allergic to them."

Now my cheeks are the ones turning pink. I feel the heat rising and I let out a small smile. "Yes, I am."

"What about lentils? Are you allergic to them too?"

"I just don't like them."

"So, you also lied."

I let out a reluctant grin. "Yeah, but mine doesn't count."

He smiles down at me. "How exactly?"

"Because in my case, I said something snarky and I was trying to cover it up, on account of you being a VIP around here."

"Ah, okay, gotcha."

"But I promise not to lie again either. So long as you don't do it first."

Hudson presses his hand to his heart. "I swear. No more lies. In fact, while you've got me in the confessional, I don't wear glasses."

"Contacts?"

"Nope. Twenty-twenty vision. Those were fakes the other day."

"Really?" Damn, because he looked seriously sexy in them. Wait, I mean, *good,* because he looked way too sexy in them.

"Yup. Bought by my stylist, who also bought the pastries."

So, the blonde is his *stylist,* not his girlfriend. Zia Fernanda was right. "Huh."

"Smoke and mirrors, Allie, that's all it is," he says, pushing himself off my desk and standing up. I glance at his butt as he walks toward his desk. The word 'taut' pops into my mind, so I force my eyes back to my screen. The last thing I need is to get caught staring at his nice ass. Or any other totally muscular part of him.

"Oh here, I'll put the fan back on so it doesn't get too hot for you," he says, pressing the button.

A jolt of guilt comes over me. Another lie. Who am I turning into? "Thanks, that's really helpful."

"How's your AI system coming along?"

"Not bad. He seems to have detected a Black Widow Pulsar," I answer, feeling the excitement building in my chest. "Do you know what a pulsar is?"

Hudson shakes his head.

"Oh, well, it's a neutron star." I take in the blank expression on his face. "Doesn't matter. The point is, I'm proud of Frank because he managed to detect something from outer space for once."

His eyes light up. "Wow. That's impressive. I'm proud of myself when I manage to build anything from IKEA without having leftover pieces."

Laughing, I say, "As you should be. IKEA furniture is nearly impossible."

"Right? It's always those little metal brackets. I don't even know what they do."

"Nobody does."

We exchange a smile, which immediately makes me feel guilty for making him think the only reason I've been pawning him off is because I was mad at him when it's mainly because of my project. "The thing is, this system I'm building is time-sensitive. There are other teams in the world working on the same thing, and even though we should be working together, we're not. It's a race to the finish and whoever cracks it first is going to be a very big deal in the SETI world."

A look of understanding crosses his face. "So, the timing on having me show up couldn't be worse."

"Pretty much."

"Gotcha. Well, the last thing I want to do is hold you up. Why don't you stick me in a corner somewhere with some videos to watch or something? Or maybe I can just quietly observe you, you know, like Jane Goodall and the chimps," he says, quickly adding, "I don't mean to compare you to a chimpanzee. Sorry."

"I'm actually not as insulted as you'd think."

"Really?"

"No, Jane Goodall does good science," I answer.

"Look, it would be extremely helpful if I can get you set up doing some independent learning, at least for a few days. Then, when I'm past this big hump, I can bring you in and let you in on what I'm doing, and hopefully it'll help you."

"Sounds good."

A chime from my computer tells me Frank is finally finished. I glance at the screen, feeling torn between excitement to see what Frank did and disappointed that our conversation has to end just when it was getting fun.

Hudson nods. "That sounded important. Why don't I go get us each a coffee and let you get back to it?"

"That would be amazing," I tell him. "Thank you."

Standing, he says, "How do you take yours?"

"Now you're going to know all my bad habits," I answer, feeling a little embarrassed to tell a man who probably hasn't touched a grain of sugar since he was a child how I take my coffee. "There's a disgustingly sweet french vanilla creamer in the fridge that has my name on it. Just keep pouring it in until the coffee's lukewarm."

He bursts out laughing. "Okay, one disgustingly sweet coffee coming up."

"Thanks," I say as he walks out into the hall. "Oh, and you can have some too if you like."

He won't because sugar is for mortals, but I felt like I had to offer.

Okay, he's gone. Now I can concentrate for a few minutes. As soon as he gets back, I'll set him up with the *SETI Guys* podcast. But for now, I need to see what Frank was able to do.

I start reading the report he spit out, but honestly I can't even concentrate.

Okay, calm down, Allie. Just calm down and focus. You need to forget about Mr. Handsome because time is ticking. So, just ... don't think about how warm and delicious it felt when he laughed at your coffee order.

Focus.

I chew my lip for a second, then pick up my phone and text Gwen, who I still can't believe isn't sitting next to me.

ME

You in yet?

GWEN

Yup! Just caught a peek of Hudson walking to the lunchroom. He said hi to Virgil and me. He's like every Disney prince rolled together into one human man.

I put in my ear buds and dial her number. As soon as she picks up, I say, "I'm just calling to see if you can come here and slap me across the face because I really need to focus but my brain is completely scrambled at the moment."

She laughs, then says, "Good luck with that. I have a feeling everyone in the building is going to be struggling to think straight until he leaves. Is he, like, ridiculously charming or is it just me?"

"Nope, he's charming," I answer. "Oh, and guess what? He brought me the biggest basket of fruit I've ever seen to thank me for helping him."

"Seriously?" she asks, her voice going all high and squeaky.

"Yup."

"You'll be able to lay off your Activia for a while."

"I had the same thought."

"He's so sweet."

"He also fessed up about not going to my parents' bakery."

"Oh good."

"No, not good. Very bad, in fact. I need to keep thinking of him as a total dick," I say, standing up and touching the rim of the basket.

"Life's not fair sometimes. You're just going to have to put up with having a handsome, charming, thoughtful guy follow you around all day."

"Although we really don't know that he's *not* a total dick, do we? I mean, he literally possesses the ability to make thousands of women fall in love with him all at the same time, and he doesn't even have to look directly at them to do it," I say. "Someone with those skills could *easily* pretend to be a good guy. For all we know, he's really quite evil."

"Why do you sound happy about that possibility?"

"Because if he's evil, I can continue ignoring him and get my work done," I say. "Speaking of my work, I better see if I can get a few minutes in before he gets back from getting us coffees."

"He's getting you a coffee?"

"Unfortunately."

"You're nuts. Now, get to work."

"Doing it," I say, ending the call.

But instead of focusing, I stare at the basket for a second, my face heating up at the fact that an actual movie star bought that for me.

It's very sweet. And thoughtful. And it's also way too big and distracting to stay on my desk. I pick it up and carry it over to the two-drawer filing cabinet that sits against the far wall, then set it down. Hmm, what's in here? Oranges, two bunches of the freshest-looking green grapes I've ever seen, bananas, pears wrapped in gold foil (for reasons I don't understand), a box of chocolates, kiwis, strawberries, a bottle of what looks like very nice red wine, and a pineapple. Plucking a grape out of the bunch, I pop it in my mouth and take a bite, tasting a burst of juicy sweetness.

I pick up the box of chocolates and open it. "Why, yes, I think I wi—"

I freeze because, out of the corner of my eye, I spot something moving in the basket. That was probably my imagination, right? On account of all the excitement. Nope. There it goes again. My heart pounds as my brain tries to reconcile what my eyes are seeing.

It's a tarantula.

A mother fucking tarantula.

It must have been hiding in the bananas. Fucker.

I dry heave, then let out a scream, throwing the box of chocolates at it before running full speed to my desk, where I go in search of a weapon. Grabbing my stapler, I jump onto my chair so I'm kneeling, only to realize that it's on wheels. It slams into my desk, my stomach hitting the back of my chair, causing an involuntary 'oof' sound. Bracing myself, I watch, my pulse racing as I see the spider crawling out of the basket and onto the floor.

I gag, then scream, "AAAAAAAAAAAAAAHHHHHH-HHHHHHHHHHHHHHHHHHHHHHH!!! It's coming for me!!!"

Down the hall, I hear the thumping of footsteps. Thank God! "Heeeellllppp!!!" I scream, my stomach lurching again.

Hudson comes rushing in carrying two mugs, both of which have liquid dripping down the sides.

I point at the floor. "A banana tarantula!"

"What?"

"Spider! Big one! Hairy!" Dry heave. "Right there!" I point more forcefully this time as if that'll help him to actually see it.

He crouches down, glancing around at the floor. "Stay calm. I know what to do." He sets down the coffees on his desk, then picks up my wastepaper basket and flips it over, emptying its contents onto the floor. "We just trap him in this."

The spider must understand English because he scuttles toward me at a furious pace, as though I'm going to save him. "No! Scoot! Go back to the bananas!"

Oh my God, it's going to climb up my chair. Remembering I'm holding a weapon, I throw the stapler at it, only to miss completely and watch helplessly as the stapler bounces off the floor and hits Hudson, who is hunched over trying to trap the spider with the garbage bin, right on his chiseled jaw. He drops the bin.

"Oh my God, your gorgeous face! I'm so sorry!" I gasp.

The spider moves closer and I forget all about Hudson's poor beautiful face. I gag, then scream. "Get him! He knows I ate the grape! He's coming for me!" I scramble onto the top of my desk, standing with my back to the wall.

"It's okay, Allie." Hudson moves slowly, his voice quiet. "If we stay calm, he'll stay calm."

The spider scrambles toward my chair.

"He doesn't look calm," I squeal.

"That's because we're not calm," he says, lowering his voice a little more. "Now, come on, little buddy. I've got you." He takes a couple of tentative steps toward the spider, picking up the bin again.

I gag, then say, "Crush him with it!"

"I'm not going to kill him." Hudson glances at me, his eyes narrowed. "I'm just going to trap him and we'll find a safe place to release him."

Apparently, the spider doesn't like that idea because he

stands up on his back legs and rushes toward my desk, which causes me to dry heave repeatedly.

Hudson sets down the bin and says, "Why don't I get you out of here?"

"Yes, please. That'll definitely help calm things down in here," I say as if I'm not the problem.

Hudson takes a few steps toward my desk and I launch myself at him, nearly knocking him off balance. And now, he's carrying me fireman-style, as I lift my feet, head, and hands as high in the air as humanly possible. Oh, this is awkward. And humiliating. And also, I somehow feel so safe in his arms. Like there's no way that big hairy spider is going to kill me. And also, he really does smell fucking amazing. I need to find out what kind of soap he uses.

"You're okay, I've got you," Hudson says, which does all sorts of things to me that I cannot believe, given the circumstances.

"I'm not normally hysterical. I just have a thing about tarantulas," I say as he carries me to the hallway and sets me down.

"Understood. They're creepy," he tells me, placing his strong hands on both of my shoulders. "But think of it from his perspective. We're so much bigger. He's just an innocent little guy who accidentally hitched a ride from South America in some bananas. Tarantulas aren't poisonous so he couldn't even hurt anyone if he wanted to. You stay here and I'll just go get him out of your office."

He winks at me, and dammit, if that's not the sexiest thing I've ever seen. My heart is pounding, my adrenaline is rushing. I stop myself just before I breathlessly tell him he's my hero. "No, Hudson! Don't go back in there! We'll call an exterminator."

He smiles at me. "Don't worry about me. I played one on television."

I spot Chad walking toward us. "Chad! There's a tarantula in my office. You need to help Hudson get him out of here."

"Why would *I* help?"

Tilting my head, I say, "Come on, Chad. We all know you have at least one pet tarantula."

He glares at me. "I do not."

I raise an eyebrow at him, and he says, "Oh, fine, I did have one. Tarantulina Jolie. But she died."

"Exactly, so get in there and help!"

Hudson holds one hand up. "No worries, Chad. I've got this."

God, what a man. A manly, manly man. He walks back into my office, calling over his shoulder, "It's fine. Really. He's not trying to hurt any—ONE!!!!" Hudson clutches his ankle. "Fuuuuccccccckkkkkk! He bit me!"

Chad rushes in, shouting, "Hudson, noooo!!!!"

Grabbing Hudson around his waist, Chad pulls him out of the room, the pair of them reminding me very much of two soldiers on a battlefield. He shuts the door behind him while Hudson drops to the floor, writhing in pain.

"Oh God, that hurts," Hudson groans. "So, *so* much."

"That's because that isn't a tarantula," Chad says, peering through the window of my office. "It's a Brazilian wandering spider. Completely fatal if he doesn't get treated immediately. Call 911."

11

Gravy Boats and Sheet Tents

Hudson

"HUDSON, HUDSON! TALK TO ME, HUDSON!" Chad shouts. He's on my right, pressing on my upper body with both hands, doing the world's most ineffective chest compressions.

"Please ... stop ... that," I mutter through clenched teeth.

I feel like I'm in a tunnel. The sounds around me aren't quite getting to my ears. In the distance, I hear more voices, and when I look up, I see I'm surrounded by several members of the staff. Tina's on the phone with a 911 operator explaining what happened, while Keenan and Chad look on. I'm drenched in sweat, my heart is beating insanely fast, my ankle is throbbing where I got bit, but even worse, I inexplicably have a horribly painful erection. Oh my God, am I some kind of weirdo who loves pain? I double over a little more, pulling my legs up to hide it.

I glance up and see Allie kneeling beside me to my left.

Her face is filled with worry. "What can I do to help you?"

"I'm fine. It's really not that bad," I say, closing my eyes for a second as I try to get a handle on the extreme pain. Keenan starts reading out instructions from his phone. "Wash with soap and water, administer an ice pack…"

"I'm on it!" Chad says, sprinting down the hall.

Tina leans over me, and in a low voice, says, "Err, Hudson, they want to know if you have an erection."

"What?" Allie asks.

"An erection. It's a symptom of a Brazilian wandering spider bite."

Oh, thank Christ. This is normal. I nod, in too much pain to be embarrassed. "A raging one."

"Yes, he says he's got a raging erection."

Dizziness comes over me and I start to feel like I'm about to lose consciousness. I look up at Allie, wondering if hers is the last face I'm going to ever see. And if it is, I'm okay with it. Not that I want to die, but if I have to, it's so much better to be looking at her than, say, that Chad guy. "You're very beautiful."

"Thanks?" she says, looking totally confused.

Dammit, it's because of the erection, isn't it? "Allie, just in case I don't make it, please call my brother, and my parents." Oh, I'm gonna black out. "Tell them I love them, and that there was no raccoon. I'm the one who broke Nana's gravy boat."

"Okay, I'll relay the message." She nods, tears filling her eyes. "But don't think like that. The ambulance is on the way. You're going to make it."

"I don't think so. This feels like it might be it for me. I've never been in love before. God, you're pretty…"

I feel her hand on my cheek and she's saying something

but her words disappear into the ether as everything goes black.

———

Instagram Reel: Hollywood Dish with Ferris Biltmore

The video starts up, showing Ferris in purple silk pajamas sitting in bed with the covers pulled up to his chest, staring gravely into the camera. "Bitches, I have terrible, terrible news. I heard it from my acupuncturist whose niece is married to a paramedic up in Silicon Valley. Apparently, at approximately eight forty-five a.m. today, a call was placed to 911 that Hudson Finch, my sweet, sweet Hudson… Oh, I can't! I can't even say it," Ferris moans, laying his head back on the stack of fluffy white pillows propping him up. He opens his eyes. "Got bit by a terrifying, deadly spider."

He nods. "Yes, I know. I know, people. I'm scared too. I am, but rest assured, I've got all my little birds out listening for updates, and I will be right here in bed keeping vigil and waiting for word on how our Hudson is doing. There will be no segments today. I'm too upset to do segments. Except, maybe one and I don't have the strength to make a graphic. It's to the hospital staff. It's called: You Better Fucking Save His Life."

Ferris stares into the camera looking forlorn. "You better fucking save his life, bitches. I'm serious. Because there are millions of fans around the world who will never, ever get over his death. We're talking Diana-level of sorrow. We *need* him. We need *him*. And only him." Ferris's voice cracks as he goes on, "So you save him, okay? Do whatever you have to, but just save Hudson. Please?"

Shaking his head, Ferris says, "Shut it off. I can't go on."

———

Beep. Beep. Beep.

What's that sound? That's annoying. I didn't think there would be annoying beeps in Heaven.

Beep. Beep. Beep.

Am I in hell? Couldn't be. I haven't been *that* bad. I mean, I did knock the gravy boat off the counter and lied about it, but still. *Hell?*

Beep.

It's got to be hell. That is the most irritating sound ever.

"Shut that off, Satan. It's too noisy," I murmur.

"You're waking up."

No way is that voice the devil. She sounds like an angel so I must be in Heaven. Maybe it's… "Mary?"

"Um, no, it's me, Allie."

Who the hell is Allie? I open my eyes a crack. Right, the astro-whatever-the-hell-she-is. She's sitting in a recliner with her laptop, but when I open my eyes a little more, she gets up and walks over to the bed.

I smile at her. At least, I think I'm smiling. I can't really feel my face at the moment. "Hey there."

"Oh, you've got a little drool," she says, grabbing a tissue and patting the skin next to my mouth.

Awesome. "Sorry about that," I slur.

"Don't apologize. Drooling is one of the symptoms," she tells me. "I'm just glad you're finally awake."

I open my eyes fully, only to see I'm in a hospital bed and the sky has grown dark. The room is filled with balloons, flowers, and gift bags, which means word has obviously gotten out about my accident. Part of me knows I'm going to be very embarrassed about this, but at the moment I have no idea why.

It all starts rushing back to me in a very far-off, dreamy way. The spider. The bite. The pain. The ambulance. The ER team scrambling around and putting an IV in my arm. I look over to my right. It's still there with a drip bag attached to a pole next to the bed. Glancing down, I see the sheet tented up. Right, *that's* why I'm going to be embarrassed. Wait. Do I *still* have an erection? That can't be a good sign. When I look back at Allie, she nods, her expression full of understanding.

"Yeah, apparently, that might take a while to go away," she says. "Is it still quite painful? I can call for more meds."

I shake my head a little and close my eyes, because apparently, shaking my head will make me dizzy. "I can't feel anything, but shouldn't that be gone by now?"

She chews on her bottom lip. "I would've thought so. The doctors here haven't dealt with this particular spider bite before so they weren't too sure how long it would take."

"It's a bit concerning." And humiliating. So, so humiliating.

"Um, I have some hand cream in my bag. I could leave and you could ... you know."

This is by far the worst thing that's ever happened to me. Why couldn't that spider have finished me off? I force myself to look at her. "I don't think that's a good idea. Probably better to just let it run its course."

"Right. Makes sense," she says, making very deliberate eye-contact. "Oh, I called your brother and your parents. I just updated them on your ... situation—well, not *all* your symptoms, but some of them. I figured I'd leave it to you to decide who to share that with. Also, I didn't tell them about your nana's gravy boat because in the big scheme of things, I don't think they'll care about something you did when you were a kid."

"It was two years ago," I say before I can stop myself.

She covers her mouth and stifles a laugh. "I just assumed."

"Not my finest moment," I answer. "Unlike today. I'm really killing it today."

"You were a total hero today." She stares at me. Her enormous dark brown eyes are completely mesmerizing. Or is that the drugs? Nope. It's her. "Anyway, they said to say they love you, and your brother asked if you want him to come back. He said he could leave Oscar with someone named Pedro." Pointing to my phone on the nightstand, she says, "I can call him back or hand you the phone so you can call him."

Shaking my head, I say, "No, there's no point in getting him to come all the way back up here. I'm going to be fine." Wait. Am I going to be fine? "I am going to be fine, right?"

"Oh yeah, they were on it. They loaded you up with all kinds of drugs in record time."

"Good stuff," I say. "How long have I been asleep?"

"Um, about nine hours. They want to keep you here until … all your symptoms are gone," she says. "Can I get you anything? Are you thirsty or hungry?"

I lay still for a second trying to figure out if I'm feeling either of those things. "Maybe a sip of water would be nice."

"Sure, I'll go get you some," she says, standing up. "Oh, and I'll tell the nurse you're awake."

I watch as she crosses the room and disappears out the door. While I wait, my mind wanders to the moment right before I got bit—to carrying her out of the office. I had my hand just under her ass, on her upper thigh, and even though it was an intensely insane moment, I can't help but think about my reaction to holding her like that. It wasn't personal or intimate … only, it was.

She walks back in with a woman in scrubs who's carrying a glass of ice water. The woman says, "There he is. Our star patient." She sets the glass on a nearby tray, then uses the switch to slowly raise the top half of my bed. As soon as I'm propped up, she passes me the water. "Go slow. I'm in no mood to clean up vomit."

She grabs the blood pressure cuff off the wall, lifts my hand, and wraps the cuff around my upper arm. "I'm Tala. Let's check your vitals, okay, hon?" Tala glances at my sheet tent. "Oh, I see he's still up. Hmph."

I look over at Allie, who whispers, "I'll just wait outside." She rushes out before I can tell her to stay. She might as well stay at this point. Besides, there's something very comforting about her.

Tala glances at the door, then says, "Your girlfriend is very devoted to you. She hasn't left your side since you came in."

"Oh no, we're not together."

She pushes the button and the cuff starts tightening around my arm. "Why not? She's a lovely girl."

"We just met this week."

"Shhh, don't talk until this is done."

I stare at the numbers as they go up on the machine, then when it beeps, she takes the cuff off and says, "Still a little high. You two would look great together and what a story you'll have to tell your grandchildren."

"No, it's not like that. Our relationship is purely professional."

"That's what my husband and I used to say, until we finally gave in to what was obvious to everyone around us,"

Tala says, placing the oxygen meter on my index finger. "Now, are you hungry? I can go scrounge you up some supper. It's a Southwest chicken, bean, and rice bowl, which is one of the only edible things on the menu."

"I'm not hungry, but can you bring a tray for Allie?"

"We're not supposed to do that."

Smiling at her, I say, "But you could, right? If we pretend I'm going to eat it? No one needs to know."

Grinning at me, Tala says, "You're trouble, aren't you?" She shakes her head. "Fine, but this stays between us."

"I promise I won't breathe a word to anyone."

She takes the clip off my finger, then starts for the door. "I'll let your business associate know we're all done and I'll be back in a few minutes with your dinner."

"Thank you."

I lay my head back against the pillow, my mind floating aimlessly as I wait for Allie to come back. I think about what Tala said about us having a crazy story to tell our grandchildren. Then it hits me—what was going through my mind when I thought I was going to die. I'm thirty-nine years old and my most important relationship is with my brother.

Allie walks back in, looking a bit shy. She comes over and stands next to the bed. "Maybe I should take off. You know, let you have your privacy ... and rest up."

I stare at her, realizing the last thing I want right now is to be alone. "I'm sure you have better places to be, but would you mind staying?"

12

Family Phone Calls and Annoyingly Beautiful Doctors

Allie

I should leave. That would be the smart thing to do. While I have been getting a lot of work done on my laptop, I can do so much more back at the office with two screens. But Hudson did get a life-threatening, potentially permanently damaging injury while trying to save my hysterical ass. Staying would be the right thing to do. And he looks so vulnerable lying there in the hospital bed. Somehow still manly, but also vulnerable. Huh, why can't those two coexist in my mind more easily? I should probably do some digging into my own toxic masculinity when I get a chance. But first, I should go back to the office. "Sure, I'll stay."

Dammit, why'd I say that?

Oh, that's why. Look at that smile on his face. I wouldn't half mind helping him get rid of that erection myself. God, I hope he can't read my mind.

"Thanks. I don't really want to be alone right now." He lets out a sigh of relief. "Are you sure you don't need to be anywhere?"

Shaking my head, I say, "No. I'm fine to stay."

He takes a sip of water, then lays his head back against the pillow again. "Who's at home waiting for you?"

Is that a smooth way of finding out if I'm with someone? Because, fuck me, that was smooth. "My parents," I tell him, feeling suddenly embarrassed.

"Oh, you live with your parents?"

"No… Well, yeah, I do, but I used to *not* live with them, so it's not like I've never done all the adulting." Done all the adulting? I'm turning into a complete idiot in front of this man. "I lived with a roommate for years. Well, Gwen. You know her."

"Ah, right, Gwen—astrobiologist who spends a lot of time texting her billionaire boyfriend."

"That's the one," I say with a little grin. "She's the best. Anyway, my dad had a stroke a few years ago so I moved back home to help them out."

"I'm sorry to hear that," he says, and by God, he does seem sincere. "How's he doing now?"

"Great. Pretty much one-hundred-percent. In fact, he's been fully recovered for a couple of years now so I suppose I should move out again. That probably sounds pathetic to you. Living with my parents, in my old bedroom with my tiny twin bed."

Shaking his head, Hudson says, "Not at all. I think it's nice that you're close to your family. I live with my brother. Some people think it's weird."

"It's not weird," I tell him, leaning forward in my chair a little. "What's weird is how separate we all are from our families here in America. Most cultures are a lot closer to their extended family than we are. They live together and cook together and help each other raise the children."

Hudson's eyes light up. "Exactly. I love that idea. A few years ago, I was filming in the Philippines, and a lot of the local crew members lived in multigenerational households. There was a key grip that invited me for dinner a few times and I really loved hanging out there. It was kind of chaotic, but in a good way, you know?"

"That sounds like my house every Sunday."

"Big crowd?"

Nodding, I say, "*Everybody* shows up, and everyone has to help, no matter what, which means there are way too many cooks in the kitchen. It's so freaking loud."

"Sounds wonderful."

"It can be unless you need to be someplace else. Like this Sunday is a holiday my family made up called Landing Day. It's to celebrate the day they arrived in the US. It's a huge deal, and I'll be stuck cooking all day when I should be working."

"Well, surely they'll let you off the hook this time."

Shaking my head, I say, "Not a chance. It's the fortieth anniversary this year so they're pulling out all the stops. I mean, it's wonderful and I'm happy we do it, but the timing for me…"

"Gotcha."

"In the big scheme of things, I know it's a good problem to have. I'm lucky. My dad made a full recovery and I have a close-knit family which is more than a lot of people get, but I could also use a little more independence," I say. "Or a time machine so I could pause time for the rest of the world and finish this project."

"Maybe you should be working on that," he says with a grin. After a second, he glances down and says, "Hey! I'm back to normal!"

I look at his midsection and see that indeed, his sheet tent is gone. Huh, and all it took was a conversation with me. "Well, that's got to be a relief."

Hudson lets out a big sigh. "It sure is. I was really worried."

"I bet. Now the trick will be to make sure it'll go back the other way when you want it to."

Oh shit, I should not have said that. Based on the shocked look on his face, that was something he hadn't considered. He opens his mouth to say something, then closes it, so I add, "Not that it should be a problem. I'm sure everything's fine. It just might be … fatigued for a day or two."

He nods, that easy-going look returning to his face. "Yeah, I'm sure you're right."

"Definitely," I answer, clicking my teeth while I give him the 'okay' sign for some reason. "Everything is going to be right as rain before you know it."

Right as rain? Am I suddenly British now? Oh my God, stop talking.

Tala, the nurse, walks back into the room, carrying a tray of food. The smell hits my nostrils and my stomach growls immediately. She sets the tray on the overbed table. "Here you go, Mr. Finch."

"Thanks, Tala," he says. "You're the best."

God, that smells good. I am so freaking hungry right now.

Lowering her voice, Tala says, "And remember, this stays between us."

What stays between them?

"Of course," he answers, pretending to zip his lips and throw away the key. Somehow, the movement of his hand startles him, and he jumps a bit, then stares down at the floor where the imaginary key would've landed.

She glances at me and mutters, "No more drugs for him for a few hours."

As soon as she leaves, Hudson reaches up and pushes the table toward me. "Your dinner, milady."

Shaking my head, I say, "I can't eat your supper. That's for you."

"No, it's for you. There's no way I can eat right now, not with the way I'm feeling. But I figured you might be hungry."

"You did?" I ask, getting a waft of something that reminds me of Chipotle.

"Yeah, scoring you some food is the least I can do since you've blown a whole day watching me sleep. Dig in."

I stare at the tray, which holds what looks like some sort of chicken, beans, and rice bowl, a small bowl of tortilla chips with salsa, a chocolate pudding, and a glass of what I'm pretty sure is ginger ale. "What if we split it? Or we save it for you in case you get hungry later?"

"How about this? I'll take the ginger ale, you have the rest, and if I get hungry later, I promise I'll tell you."

"Deal," I tell him, standing and pushing the table toward him so he can reach the drink. I take the bowl and fork off the tray and sit back down to eat it while he has a sip of his ginger ale.

His phone buzzes and he reaches over and plucks it off the bedside table. "It's my mom. I should take this."

"Do you want me to leave?" I kind of want to leave. His parents made me uneasy when I spoke to them earlier. They're both super formal and they kept going on and on about the paperwork, wanting to make sure I filled every-thing out so Hudson wouldn't have to do it. Seriously strange. Who cares about paperwork when their son's life is hanging in the balance?

"No, definitely stay," he says before he answers her call. "Hey, Mom, how are you?" Pause. "Oh, Dad's there too and you've got me on speaker phone? Great." He gives me a 'this should be fun' face. "I've had better days, but in the big scheme of things, I'm all right." Pause. "Yeah, I know, but I thought it was a tarantula." He has another sip while he listens to her. "No, definitely don't get on a plane and come here. I'm fine. Honestly. I told Gersh not to bother coming back either. It's all good." Pause. "I'm pretty sure Allie took care of all the forms."

Again with the forms?

He gives me a questioning look and I nod. "Yup, it's all taken care of."

I eat quickly, glad that he's distracted by the call instead of staring at me while I shovel food into my mouth. Mmm, not half bad for hospital food. Although I haven't eaten since breakfast so I'm pretty sure I'd happily scarf down stale bread and cold baked beans right now.

"Don't believe everything they say on television. They're just trying to turn it into a bigger story than it is." He smiles at me for a second and rolls his eyes. "Yeah, but I *did* get to the hospital on time."

I set the empty bowl on the tray and stare at the pudding for a second. Should I eat the pudding? I really want to eat the pudding.

As if he can read my mind, Hudson gestures for me to take it and mouths, "Eat the pudding."

I mouth back, "Are you sure?"

Nodding, he says, "No, the movie is about an astronomer so I'm pretty sure I won't be in any danger. Wait, I'll put you on speaker phone so you can hear it from the real deal." Pause. "Yeah, she's still here. She stayed with me the whole day so you've got nothing to worry about. They're taking good care of me."

He presses the screen on his phone, then holds the phone closer to me. "Allie, tell them there won't be any more dangerous animals."

"I promise there won't be any more dangerous animals.

Well, unless your son buys me another fruit basket," I say, feeling super awkward.

"How's he really doing?" Hudson's mom, Dolores, asks. "Is he as okay as he says he is?"

"He's doing really well. He's actually been sitting up drinking ginger ale and chatting with me about life," I tell her, noticing how very green his eyes are. They're like a bed of moss in a sunlit forest. Oh wow, I'm losing it.

"When will they let you go home?" Douglas, his father, asks.

"Not sure," he says. "I'm guessing they're going to keep me until tomorrow."

"Well, if they do let you go home tonight, I don't want you to be alone," Dolores says. "Allie, is there somewhere he can stay the night?"

I'm just about to tell her he can stay at my house when Hudson cuts in. "Mom, they won't release me if it's not safe for me to be alone."

"But if they do…"

"They won't."

"Allie, if you think they're letting him go too early, you call me. All right?" she says.

"Or stay with him," his dad adds.

"Of course," I tell them. "I promise I won't abandon him if he's not one-hundred-percent fine."

"Thank you," his mother says. "That makes me feel much better."

"Glad I can help," I answer.

"Okay, we'll let you go so you can rest up," Douglas says.

"We're glad you're okay," Dolores says. "And thank you, Allie, for taking such good care of my son."

"It's the least I can do after he saved my life," I tell them.

"I'm also the reason your life was in danger to begin with," Hudson says. "Okay, Mom and Dad, I'll call you tomorrow."

He hangs up and smiles at me, looking adorably embarrassed. "You don't have to babysit me. Seriously. I'm a grown ass man." He rubs the back of his neck and shakes his head at himself. "A grown ass man who asked you to stay because he doesn't want to be alone."

I chuckle, then say, "Don't worry about it. I meant what I said to your parents. You were heroic today. Making sure you're okay is literally the least I can do."

The door swings open, and Tala and the doctor from the ER walk into the room. I'm not a huge fan of the ER doc, to be honest. She's way too beautiful, calm, cool, and collected for my taste. Also, I hate it when doctors tell you to call them by their first name, as if it's less pretentious to call her Dr. Blaire than by her last name. I prefer my doctors on the frumpy and formal side.

Dr. Blaire walks around to the opposite side of the bed from me and pats Hudson on the arm. "Hudson, how are we feeling?"

Blech. How are *we* feeling? Hate that.

"Pretty good," he answers.

Her eyes flick to the sheet. "I see that's gone." Looking at me, she says, "Do you mind giving us a minute?"

The way she says it is as if I should've known to leave, and my cheeks heat up a bit as I stand. Grabbing my bag, I say, "Of course," then hightail it out of there.

When the door closes behind me, I let out a sigh. What is happening right now? I dig around in my bag until I find my phone, only to see dozens of text messages, most of which are from my team, wanting to know how Hudson is doing.

I quickly write to Gwen:

ME

Hudson's awake. He's doing much better. The doc is in with him now. Can you please pass this along to the rest of the team?

A second later, my phone pings.

GWEN

I'm on it! So glad he's doing all right!

I call home and wait three rings for my parents to pick up. When I glance at my watch, I see it's a little after eight o'clock, which means they're watching *The Voice*. My dad finally picks up. "Allegra, there you are. We've been worried sick."

In the background, I hear my mom say, "Your father's been worried. I told him you're at the office."

"Nothing to worry about, Pops," I tell him. "But I'm not at the office. I'm actually at the hospital."

"*Dio santo!* She's at the hospital," he says. "I told you something was wrong."

"What happened?" my mom says, her voice getting closer. "Put her on speaker, Enzo."

The phone clicks and I can hear that I'm now on speaker phone. "I'm fine, but Hudson got bit by a spider."

"Hudson who?" my dad asks.

Oh Lord. Here we go. My mom is going to be so annoyed that he forgot.

"The one who's following her around at work. You know, we watched Allegra meet him on *Entertainment Nightly*."

"Oh right, *him*," my dad says. "Is he even a big star? I can't think of a movie of his I've seen."

"That one about the lifeguard," I tell him.

"With the blonde woman with the huge knockers?"

"Enzo, you can't say knockers anymore. It's not politically correct," Ma says.

"Can I say cans?"

Why couldn't they have just let the call go to voicemail? "Dad, it's better to find other ways to describe people than breast size."

"But it's true. And she had them made that big so clearly she wants people to notice them," he says.

I glance at the door to Hudson's room, finding myself suddenly desperate to get off the phone. "Not necessarily, but I don't have time to talk about it right now. I need to check on Hudson. I just wanted to let you know where I was and tell you I may not make it home tonight."

"Is he that bad?" my mom asks.

"It's not great, but I think he'll be fine."

"If he'll be fine, you should come home," my dad says, and I know he doesn't want me hanging around with a famous actor who isn't even a little bit Italian.

"I really can't. He doesn't have anyone else here to help him out."

"That's fine, dear," Ma says. "We have to go too. Looks like Reba's pissed at Chance the Rapper for blocking her again."

"All right. Enjoy."

I hang up, then stand, staring at the door to Hudson's room. Hudson, the sweet, thoughtful, charming, handsome man who is totally going to crush my little heart.

13

Awkward Examinations, Flirty Fun, and Guessing Games

Hudson

"Let's have a look at your penis," Dr. Blaire says. "Make sure everything's fine now that it seems to have returned to normal."

Oh God, let's not. She puts on some blue gloves, snapping them at her wrists, then lifts the sheet and pulls it down and out of her way. I stare up at the ceiling, too nervous to look down, even though I'm comfortably numb otherwise.

She lowers her face a little closer and lifts my penis, moving it from side to side. "How long will you be in town?"

God, this is awkward. "Another five weeks."

"Oh, that's nice. There's a lovely Thai restaurant not far from here. They make the best yellow coconut curry I've had, and I've actually been to Thailand."

Is she low-key asking me out? Please let go of my penis. "Well, that sounds… I'll have to check it out."

"You should." She stands and covers me back up, then

takes off her gloves and tosses them in the bin. "From what I can see, things look fine."

"Great, that's a relief," I answer. "Do you think it'll … you know … function normally after this?"

She shakes her head. "Hard to say. It's just such a rare occurrence that there isn't much in the literature about it. The closest thing I found was a guy who had an erection for thirty-six hours after one of these bites, but in that case, he hadn't received any medical attention."

"Was he okay?"

Shaking her head, she says, "He died. But don't worry about that. Your erection is already gone and your blood pressure has lowered significantly. You're getting the best care possible. I'm confident you'll make a full recovery. Just don't go trying to use it too soon. Give yourself a few days off, at least."

"Okay, yeah. Good tip."

"Seriously, don't worry," she says, placing her hand on my forearm. "You're young and you're in phenomenal shape, so you're going to bounce back really quickly, I'm sure."

"Thanks," I answer, even though she's in no way an expert on Brazilian wandering spider bites.

"Okay, well, I should go check on my other patients," she says, picking up my chart and jotting something down. "I'll see if I can swing back to look in on you before I'm off for the night."

"Excellent."

Dr. Blaire walks to the door, then swings it open to reveal Allie standing in the hall just outside. "All done."

Allie walks in and waits until the door closes before she says, "Is it me or does she not like me very much?"

"I kind of got that impression too, but for the life of me, I can't think of any reason not to like you."

Blushing, Allie looks away, her eyes landing on the balloon bouquets lined up along the wall. "I think it's got more to do with how much she likes you, which I'm guessing is the case wherever you go." Gesturing to the gift bags, she says, "Just look at all this stuff. Seriously, it started showing up when we were still in the ER. Do you know how *not* normal that is?"

"You mean most people aren't showered with gifts moments after an insect bite?"

"Technically, it was an arachnid, not an insect," she says with a little grin meant to soften the fact that she's correcting me. "But the answer to your question is yes. This isn't the reaction normal humans get."

I tilt my head to the side. "I am a normal human."

Wrinkling up her nose, she says, "I beg to differ."

"The whole fame thing … there's nothing real about it. I know it looks amazing from the outside, and there are a lot of perks, but it's also a whole lot of bullshit. People say they love me, but they don't really love *me*."

"Sure they do."

I shake my head again. "They can't. They don't know me. They love the *idea* of me. Or whatever character I played that they think is the real me, but they don't know who I am."

"Well, you seem like a lovable guy." Offering me a playful grin, she adds, "But you *are* a professional liar, so…"

I grin at her. "Well, you're getting the real me."

"I am?" she asks, walking over to one of the gift bags.

"Yup, I'm too high to pretend."

"Oh, so if I wanted to, I could get you to tell me your deepest, darkest secrets."

"Only if you'll tell me yours."

Glancing up at the ceiling as if she's deciding, she says,

"I don't know if I like those terms." She squints at the card and gasps. "Do you know who these are from?"

"No idea."

"Stephen."

"Stephen who?"

"I'm assuming Spielberg."

I shake my head. "If it doesn't also have Kate's name, it's not from him. I'd guess Colbert."

"Wow," she mutters, looking for the card on the next bouquet. "The executives at Galaxy Studios."

She goes through all of the flowers and balloon bouquets, gasping and reading the cards to me, and I can't help but find it very refreshing that she's not pretending any of this is normal. Her reactions are real. Excited. Just like I used to be when I first got my start. "Do you want me to open the presents?" she asks, clearly wanting me to say yes.

"Please do."

"Sweet!" she says, lifting a huge bag up onto the foot of my bed. "Let's see what rich people buy each other when they do something heroic."

"You mean stupid."

"Heroic," Allie answers, yanking the tissue paper out of the bag, then sliding a box out of it. "Nordstrom. This should be good." She sets the box down and screws up her adorable face. "I'm going to guess a plush blanket and some aromatherapy candles."

"Ooh, good one." Grinning, I say, "Who's it from?"

"No clues."

"Tricky. Okay, in that case, I'm going to go … bathrobe and slippers."

"Interesting. Should we bet?"

How is it possible that I'm having fun right now? "Definitely. What's up for grabs?"

"All the chocolate in this room."

"Deal," I say before my brain catches up with the conversation. "Wait. The chocolate is already mine. What are you putting up?"

"I have an *almost new* box of TicTacs in my bag," she says with wide eyes and a big smile.

"Come on, *all* my chocolate for some used TicTacs?" I ask. "You can do better than that."

"A box of pastries from my parents' shop."

Shaking my head, I say, "I'm not really a sweets guy."

"Not a sweets guy?" Pursing her lips together, she says, "That's not a thing. Everybody's a sweets guy. We're genetically engineered to crave sugar."

"Not me. I'm all salt, all the time," I answer. "Except I do love a milkshake from In-N-Out on occasion, but that's only because it's the best thing to wash down their fries."

"All right, weird, but if you say so, you're not a sweets guy." She taps her lips with her index finger, then says, "Wait. If you're not a sweets guy, why do you even care if I win all the chocolate?"

She's got me there. I have no answer for that one. "Umm, because chocolate is very important to me. It's comforting to have it around."

She bursts out laughing. "And you can have it around until I eat it all."

Now, it's my turn to laugh. "All right. Just open the box already so we can see what's in there."

Lifting the lid off the box, she then opens the tissue paper inside to reveal a robe and some slippers. "Nuts. You were right. How'd you know?"

"Lucky guess."

She puts the lid back on, then places the box back into the bag. Picking up a smaller one, she says, "Double or nothing?"

I start to laugh again. "What? Do you have two packs of used TicTacs?"

Allie lets out a loud laugh. It's a pleasing sound that makes me feel much happier than I should be right now. Somehow, making someone as smart as her laugh feels like a victory. She purses her lips at me, giving me a flirty look. "No, but I have some loose change and there's a vending machine down the hall. I bet I can scrounge up some potato chips for you."

"Okay, but only because I'm high and I could actually go for some chips."

Lifting the bag, she says, "It's a little heavy. I'm going to say ... some sort of fancy schmancy bath oils in jars made from real crystal. Oh! And the bath oils are definitely vegan, likely edible, and probably have saffron or something in them that make them cost a thousand dollars an ounce."

"That is an extremely specific guess."

She gives me a shrug. "Yeah, well, I'm pretty good at this."

"You're 'o' for one so far."

"But I'm due..." she says, causing me to laugh some more. "For all the loose change in my purse. What's your guess?"

"It's an iPad."

"Based on what?"

"The apple on the side of the bag."

She tilts her head down a little to examine the bag, then reads the gift tag. "Wishing you a full and speedy recovery, the gang at Apple." Reaching her hand in, she pulls out the box, which, indeed, indicates it's an iPad. She holds it up. "Did you go through these bags when I was in the hall?"

Placing my right hand on my chest, I say, "I swear on my dog, I did no such thing."

Giving me a skeptical look, she says, "All right. I'll believe you, but if you get this next one, all bets are off."

We spend the next half hour playing this game until all the gifts have been unwrapped. By the time we're done, I have three luxury travel shaving and toiletry kits, four sets of men's pajamas, six plush robes (all with slippers), fifteen eye masks, three baskets of food (including meat, cheese, nuts, dates, crackers, and wine), a back scratcher, enough soothing balms and moisturizing creams to start my own store, seven calming sound machines, and three more iPads.

Allie, who is now sitting on the foot of my bed, stares down at it all. "Wow. That's … a lot of stuff."

"It's crazy, right?"

"Totally. I can't believe there isn't one measly box of chocolates."

"Yeah, most people who know me know I'm not a sweets guy."

"About that—while we're here we should probably talk to a doctor. It's just not normal."

Chuckling, I say, "Don't worry. My mom had all the proper tests run when I was a kid. Turns out I can live a healthy and mostly normal life without them."

"But what's the point?" she asks, scrunching up her face as though she's confused.

We both laugh, and I find myself staring at her a moment too long. There's a shift in the energy in the room and her smile fades. After a second, she glances away, and I realize I'm going to mess this whole thing up because I like her. I mean, I really like her. And there's no way a genius is going to end up with a guy like me. I clear my throat and say, "Anyway, whatever you want, it's all yours."

"Even an iPad?"

"Definitely an iPad."

"I was just kidding. I can't take your stuff."

"Seriously, Allie, what am I going to do with seven sound machines?"

"Make every room in your house sound like ocean waves."

"I just open the windows for that."

"Oh, that make sense."

I'm suddenly embarrassed by what I just said. "Was that a flex?"

She gives me a wry smile. "A little bit, maybe."

"Shit. I didn't mean to flex. Can we chalk it up to the drugs?"

"Sure."

"That's very charitable of you," I answer. "Now, what I *meant* to say is that I'd be happy if you'd take some of this stuff, as a thank you for sticking around tonight. You are staying, aren't you?"

She glances over at the recliner in the corner. "Sure. I can use one of the plush blankets you got."

"And grab a robe while you're at it. And some pajamas. Take a toiletry kit. Whatever you like."

"How about I *borrow* some things for the night. Not to keep or anything. Well, maybe the toothbrush. You probably won't want that back."

"It's all yours. Seriously."

"Sweet," she says before rummaging around for a set of flannel pajamas, a robe, some slippers, and one of the toiletry kits. She starts toward the bathroom, then stops. "Wait. Are you sure you want me to stay? You might get a better night's sleep if you're alone."

"I really won't. As soon as you walk out that door, I'll

just lay here and worry about whether I'm actually going to make a full recovery."

She swallows hard and nods. "Well, that sounds awful."

"It would be. Whereas, with you here, I feel a lot better than I otherwise would. I'm actually having fun, which shouldn't be possible, given the circumstances."

"Well, in that case, I'll stay."

"Good, because that will make me very happy." And it will. It really, really will. I want her to stay more than I've wanted anything for a very long time. If I were sober right now, that thought would scare the shit out of me, but since I'm in a happy daze, I'm totally fine with it.

14

Hospital Bed Picnics and Pillow Talk

Allie

I STARE at myself in the mirror. I'm brushing my teeth with some sort of magical brush that feels like it's a thousand tiny hands massaging my gums. The toothpaste is a ginger mint flavor that comes from an old-timey-looking silver tube that is probably made from actual silver. I'm wearing the softest, coziest striped men's flannel p.j.'s of all time (seriously, they feel like getting a big, warm hug). The slippers are too big but the fleece lining is so incredibly soft, I want to live in them forever.

What is happening? Seriously? What? How?

I'm getting a glimpse into what it's like to be rich and famous. Well, rich, anyway. Or someone with generous rich friends. But it's not real. This isn't my life, it's his. It'll never be my life. I'm Allegra Cammareri, nerd, scientist, loving daughter, and pushover auntie. I'm not some sexy sex goddess who men like Hudson Finch fall for. They fall for voluptuous hotties from Brazil or icy blondes with perfect skin from Sweden. Not girls like me. I wasn't even interesting enough to keep Lando's attention, and he's a fellow nerd.

But it doesn't matter because that's not what this is, and I know it. But whatever it is, it's incredibly fun. And a little flirty, and totally exciting, even though it's under the world's weirdest circumstances. I'm here to hang out with a man who I don't want around (or so I thought) while he recovers from a poisonous spider bite.

And he's sweet and funny and thoughtful and sexy as hell, and … and I'm going to get so badly hurt if I don't hit the brakes on my feelings. But maybe, just for tonight, since I'm here anyway, I could just let myself enjoy being with him. As a friend.

Yes, that's what we are. Friends. New ones. Who flirt with each other while one of us is drugged. And really, I'm only flirting with him to distract him from his situation, which, when you think about it, is an act of service. So, in a way, I *have* to keep flirting with him. It's what Jesus would do. But as soon as we're back at the office however, it'll be all business. But for now … fun.

I dig around in the soft leather toiletry kit, find some mouthwash spray, and pump two shots onto my tongue. Oh my, that's nice. I feel like I'll have fresh breath for weeks.

When I walk back into the room, I see Hudson typing on his phone. He looks up and smiles at me. "Nice fit. You look ultra-cozy."

"I may have to change my mind about giving these back. I'm probably going to live in them instead," I say, setting my clothes down on a shelf in the corner. "Can I get you anything?"

"I wouldn't mind some crackers from one of those baskets."

"Crackers, coming right up." I open one of the baskets and take out two boxes of crackers, then some spreadable cheese and some grapes. A minute later, I've got a little mini picnic spread on his overbed tray.

"Come sit and eat with me," he says.

"I already brushed my teeth," I answer, then think better of it. After all, how often in my life am I going to get an offer like this? Also, that cheese looks pretty tasty. "Although, I suppose I can do it again."

I sit on the edge of his bed, my heart pounding so hard I'm scared he can tell. "I only want to eat gift basket food from now on."

Hudson chuckles, then says, "And here I was worried I put you off basket food earlier."

"Because of the spider," I answer, nodding. "I'm able to separate my fear of arachnids from delicious food."

"I'm glad." He stares at me for a second. "I um, couldn't help but notice you had a strange reaction to that spider."

My face heats up. "You mean the gagging?"

"Yeah... I've never seen someone do that before."

"I have a bit of a phobia," I say, tugging on the hem of my sleeve a little.

"I gathered as much. Anything happen to you or is it just because they're generally creepy?"

"A particularly nasty cousin of mine thought it would be hilarious to hide an egg sack in my sock drawer when I was a kid. I didn't notice until it was the middle of the night and my room was crawling with them."

"Whoa, that was crappy of him."

"Yeah, he was twelve. I was eight and probably irritated the hell out of him."

"But I'm sure you didn't deserve that."

"Definitely not. To this day, he is *not* on my Christmas card list."

"I can see why," he answers. "You should make him pay for therapy for you."

I laugh at the idea and shrug. "He was twelve. Twelve-year-olds are idiots. I mean, I'm sure you weren't, but most of them."

"No, I was pretty much an idiot." He dips a cracker into some cream cheese, and when he pulls it out, a corner breaks off. "Still am for the most part."

"No, you're not," I tell him, carefully plucking the errant piece out and popping it in my mouth.

"I'm not exactly Einstein," he says. "To be honest, I'm a little worried about my time at the SETI Research Institute."

"Why? You're fine."

Shaking his head, he says, "I don't know if I'm going to be able to grasp the finer points of astronomy. Physics isn't exactly my thing."

"The fact that you know astronomy has anything to do with physics puts you miles ahead of the game."

He purses his lips for a second, then says, "I watched a NASA video for kids."

"That's okay," I answer, plucking another cracker out of the sleeve. "They make highly informative videos."

"They really do." Hudson has another bite, and we both eat in a contented silence for a minute. It's oddly comfortable, the two of us hanging out in bed like this, even though we barely know each other, he's injured, and we're in a hospital.

He has a sip of ginger ale, then says, "So what made you want to become an astronomer?"

"Curiosity, I suppose. There's just so much out there

that has never been discovered or explored," I tell him, feeling overly excited to be sharing this side of myself with someone who seems so interested to hear it. "I mean, I get that there are a lot of places on earth that haven't been discovered yet—especially the oceans—but for me, there's just something about space. The stars, the moon, the other planets we can see. The billions we can't see. The sheer vastness of it. It's nearly impossible to wrap your head around it. And I want to know *everything*—what's out there, how it all fits together, how we can get to places in other galaxies, who we'll meet when we get there…"

He smiles at me for a second without saying anything.

"What? Do I have food on my face or something?" I ask, feeling around my mouth.

"No, you're just so lit up. It's nice."

"Really?"

Nodding, Hudson says, "Yeah. Most of the people I hang out with try really hard to seem like nothing impresses them. They're all about looking cool no matter what. It's refreshing to be around someone who's passionate about what they do."

"Well, if I'm anything, it's passionate about my work. Some would even say obsessive."

"Is that such a bad thing?"

"According to my parents, yes."

"Why?"

"Because it's not exactly getting them any closer to having more grandkids."

"Ah, I see."

"What about your parents? Do they ever bug you to settle down?"

There's a flash of hurt in his eyes, just for the briefest of seconds, but then the breezy look returns to his face.

"Not really. I think they're just happy I'm earning a good living."

I narrow my eyes at him, wondering what he means. "I'd say you do more than that."

"Yeah, I do all right," he says with a wry smile.

"But they didn't think you would?"

"Nah, it's not that. Well, sort of. I was a bit of a screw-up as a kid. I wasn't really into school," he says. "Your typical class clown. In fact, I'm pretty sure if we'd have grown up together, you would've hated me."

"I doubt that very much," I tell him, opening a bag of upscale pretzels.

"I don't. I'm pretty sure the words used most often on my report card were 'disruptive' and 'would benefit from taking his education seriously.'"

"School's not for everyone. For some people it's just a thing you have to get through until you can get on with your real life," I say, taking a tiny bite of a pretzel. "And look at what you've accomplished. You're an outlier. Rich, famous, powerful."

"Not bad for a class clown," he tells me, popping a pretzel into his mouth.

"Not bad for anyone."

Hudson shrugs. "Well, it could all be over by next year."

"What do you mean?"

"Hollywood is fickle. You can be the hottest thing going one minute and a total pariah the next."

"But I think most times when someone falls out of favor, it's because they've done something, right?"

Shaking his head, he says, "Sometimes all they do is age out."

"Pfft, what are you talking about? You're not even forty.

Besides, you're a man. Men don't age out. It's one of the biggest double standards in our society."

"That's all changing," he says.

"Seriously?"

"Yeah, it used to be just the women being judged by impossible standards, but instead of righting that wrong, it seems like things went the other way and made it harder on guys too," he tells me. "Not that I expect you to feel sorry for me or something, because I don't. I've had a good run."

I know he's holding back, but I also know that the fact that he told me this much is huge for someone like him. We finish the rest of our picnic and I clean up, then get myself ready for bed and turn down the lights. I snuggle onto the recliner under the faux fur blanket he got from his agency. My heart is still fluttering a mile a minute, so I have no idea how I'm going to fall asleep. I'm spending the night with Hudson Finch. And I know it's not like that. We're not having some wild affair that I'll spend the rest of my life dreaming about, but for someone like me, sleeping in the same room, in pajamas that belong to him, is enough. It's huge, in fact. I'll always know this night happened. I'll still be talking about it when I'm Zia Fernanda's age.

I close my eyes and listen to the sound of him breathing nearby, wishing I could give him a soft, slow kiss on his lips. Then I tell myself to go to sleep. After a couple of minutes of trying, I hear Hudson's voice cut through the darkness of the room. "You still awake?"

"Yeah."

"Me too," he says. "Can I ask you something?"

"Sure."

"Let me preface this by saying you don't have to answer and I fully acknowledge that it's none of my business. I'm just surprised you're not with anyone."

Lando's face pops into my mind and my stomach twists, like it always does. I pause long enough for him to rethink the topic.

"You know what? Don't answer that. I would normally never bring it up if I weren't drugged."

"No, it's fine." I'm so tempted to tell him everything, but I'm too embarrassed. A guy like him, who can have any woman in the world, won't understand what it feels like to be rejected. "I'm what you call book smart, but as far as relationships go, I'm a total idiot. My radar is broken when it comes to men. I tend to attract guys who want to use me for my brain, then dump me."

"If I were going to use you, it would definitely be for your body," he says.

My eyes pop open, and I'm not sure if I should be offended or flattered. Before I can answer, he says, "Wait. That came out wrong. What I meant was you're really beautiful."

My heart does a flippy thing that I don't want it to. "Well, thank you. I think."

"I'm really off my game tonight," he says. "Sorry about that."

"It's fine. We'll chalk it up to the drugs."

"That's very charitable of you."

We're both quiet for a second, then he says, "Weird that you think there's something wrong with you."

"What?"

"Your radar. You blamed the fact that you're single on yourself, instead of brushing it off as a few shitbags who used you."

"Two shitbags, and I suppose I could look at it that way, but both situations were so strikingly similar that it leads me to the question of: why do I keep attracting them? And how do I miss all the signs?"

"I think it's pretty normal to miss some signs when you're in love with someone," Hudson says.

"One of them used to come over to my place and wash his penis in the sink."

"Oh, yeah, that's a pretty big sign."

"Exactly. Best to avoid the whole thing," I say. "Anyway, it's fine. I'm happy. I have people who love me and a job I'm crazy about. It's more than a lot of people have, so I figure I should be grateful."

"Sure, but you still deserve to find a guy who will treat you right."

I turn onto my side a little more to face him, letting his words warm me as much as this blanket. "Thanks. What about you? How come you aren't with anyone?"

"Oh, I've been with plenty of women."

"But right before you passed out, you told me you've never been in love."

"Did I?"

"Yes."

"Well, I mean, that was a particularly intense moment. I thought I was about to die."

"Which usually brings out the truth, doesn't it?" I ask gently.

"Yes," he answers, sounding sheepish. "The thing is, it's hard for me to let anyone see me the way I am. Maybe it's an occupational hazard, but I sometimes feel like a chameleon, trying to be someone they think I should be instead of being myself. Someone more impressive."

My heart aches for him, and I find myself wanting to sneak into his bed and hold him tight. "For what it's worth, I think you're impressive. Not the smooth persona when the television crew was there, but how you've been today. You're honest and thoughtful and kind, which is all any woman really wants in a partner."

"Thanks, Allie. That's kind of you to say, but if you spent enough time with me, you'd be disappointed."

I lay here, shocked that he feels this way about himself and not knowing what to say. Finally, I speak up. "If you were the person I'm hanging out with right now, no one could ever be disappointed. Even though you're not a sweets guy, which is just plain weird."

He chuckles a little, then says, "Thank you. I hope the next man you're with can see what he's got because you're really lovely. Not just on the outside either."

Tears spring to my eyes and I blink quickly to stop them even though it's dark. "Thanks," I whisper. I let his words wash right through me and seep into every cell of my body. I'm lovely. Not just on the outside either.

After a minute, he says, "Can I also say I admire how hard you work."

"Sure, I'll allow it."

He turns toward me, his sheets rustling a little. "No, seriously. You're so driven. Most people would've dropped everything to work with me, but you just kept pawning me off on your coworkers so you could focus."

"Well, I sort of have an ulterior motive," I answer. "There's a huge conference coming up in a couple of months in Zurich. It only happens once every four years, and I've never had a chance to present. Keenan is going to let Chad represent our team, with what is, quite honestly, a far inferior talk—well, if I can get Frank working, that is. If he's up and running, it would be my first shot at recognition in the SETI world."

"Chad? Blech. You have got to get Frank working in time."

"Right?" I say, glad he gets it. "There are so few opportunities like this, and honestly, a disproportionately small number go to women in the field, so in a way, I'd feel like I was winning for all of us if I could make it happen." I sigh, then go on. "To be honest, Keenan already told me I can't present, but I just know everything would change if I can finish in time. It would be the biggest breakthrough in the history of SETI, so even if he couldn't swap me out for Chad, the organizers of the conference would have to make time for me. There's no way they could ignore it because everyone in the field is going to be itching to get their hands on this system."

Hudson's quiet for a minute, and I start to think he's asleep, but then he says, "That's why you were disappointed when I showed up."

"What?"

"I could tell. When I first met you—it was this tiny fraction of a second when you glanced at the floor. You were telling me you were hoping you could help me, but I knew you didn't mean it," he says. "It's because you got saddled with me instead of being able to focus all your time on Frank."

"You're extremely perceptive."

"It's my only superpower. Reading people."

"It's a good one to have," I answer, wishing I was better at it.

"Well, listen, if there is any possible way I can help you to get your project done, I'm there. Whatever you need."

Alarm bells start going off in my head, but I shut them down. There's no way I need to worry about accepting help from Hudson. It's not like he could ever take credit for my work. "Thank you. If I can think of anything, I'll let you know."

"Okay, I'm going to hold you to that."

That's not the only thing I'd like him to hold me to. Oops! Scrub that thought from my brain. No way should I be going there. "We should probably get some sleep."

"Good night, Allie."

"Good night, Hudson."

"Thank you for being here with me."

I want to tell him there's no place I'd rather be, but it would feel too cliché. Actually, that's not true. It would feel too honest. And if there's one thing I can't afford to be with this man, it's honest about how I'm feeling right now.

15

Guy Talk & Loneliness...

Hudson

Instagram Reel: Hollywood Dish with Ferris Biltmore

The video starts up, showing an ecstatic-looking Ferris sitting behind his glass desk with a bottle of champagne. "Hello, bitches, it's me, Ferris. As you can see, I've given up my in-bed vigil and I've gotten dressed, which can only mean one thing—my new segment: He's Alive, Bitches!!"

The graphic appears above his head while Ferris screams, "He's alive, bitches!!!! He pulled through. Hudson Finch is very much alive and well, which is a fucking miracle, since according to my nephew's weirdo little gamer friend, a Brazilian wandering spider bite can take down a bull with ease. A freaking *bull*, people. A BULL!!! But our Hudson survived. And of course he did, because he's superhuman. And in a way, this whole insane emergency is the perfect metaphor for his career. Because Hudson is a phoenix who will rise from the ashes and become a ...

phoenix again, making the best films to ever grace the big screen. He made it. We can go on.

"But he might not have. Which brings me to my next segment: What Were You Thinking Sending Him There?"

He shouts into the camera, "To Hudson's team and the jackals at Galaxy Studios who, if you ask me, are responsible for this whole mess: What were you thinking sending him there? To the wilds of Silicon Valley? Putting his very life at risk like this? Did you think he'd be fine? Did you believe it was totally safe outside of L.A.? Did you not care if you risked his life? What? Do you have some hulking insurance policy on him or something? Hmm? Do you?" He scowls and raises one finger into the air. "You can suck my left nut for putting him in harm's way. Suck it.

"And to those bitches out there still bitching because I haven't spilled the tea on the engagement thing, I had better things to do, like praying to the god of all the gods while my Hudson's life was hanging in the balance. The engagement is off, anyway. I heard it from my gardener's uncle's mistress, whose ex is a bartender at the Bev Hills Hotel pool. Apparently, he saw her hooking up with a certain director who she was married to back in the early 2000's. But honestly, I can't even because my world has been rocked to the core with almost losing Hudson. Which brings us to my next segment: Stay Safe, My Darling…"

Two Days Later

"Oscar, it's me!" I'm on a video call with Gershwyn, who has positioned his phone so I can say hello to my little fluff ball, who is currently curled up in his bed. "It's me, buddy. Hi!"

It's Sunday morning and I'm bored out of my mind. I got released from the hospital on Friday afternoon and have been laying around the condo ever since. I've been on a call with Gersh for the last twenty minutes. I've told him all the gory (and terrifying) details of my spider bite and my hospital stay, and we've already gotten caught up on the important things like sports. So now that we're out of topics, I've asked to see Oscar, because I'm desperate to stay on the phone. To be honest, the last thing I can face is another day alone.

Oscar opens his eyes halfway, glances around, but not at the screen, then closes them again. A second later, I'm staring at Gersh again.

"He looks skinny. Is he eating enough?"

Gersh rolls his eyes. "Dude, you can't even see his body because he's all balled up. And I promise you, he's totally fine. Eating like a champion. We've been walking every day. But back to you, because I still can't believe what happened to your dong."

"Dong? What are we? Ten?"

"Hey, it's a great word. We should totally bring it back, but stop trying to change the subject."

"I'm not. We're still talking about dongs, aren't we?"

"Yes, but you're not answering my question."

Shrugging, I say, "That's because you didn't ask a question."

"But the question was implied."

"No it wasn't. You said you can't believe what happened to my dong."

Gersh glares at me. "Which is a lead-in to a conversation. You're supposed to say 'I can't believe it either,' and then we talk about it."

"I really don't want to talk about it. Living through it once was bad enough," I tell him.

He winces and shudders. "Just the thought of it makes me feel all queasy."

"Same, which is why I'd like to change the subject."

"Okay, but I just have to know one thing. Is it ... working again?"

"Yup, it's all systems go." I give him a firm nod and a thumbs up.

"That's gotta be a huge relief."

"You have no idea," I say. "Now, what are you up to today?"

"It's better for you if I don't tell you."

"Oh shit, it's a perfect surfing day, isn't it?"

Gersh wrinkles up his nose. "Sorry, dude, but the waves are classic right now."

I slump down a little on the couch, feeling totally defeated.

"But I'm sure you'll have fun too."

Shaking my head, I say, "How? I don't know anyone here."

"What about some of those nerds from the alien place? I bet none of them are busy."

"That's not nice," I answer, feeling defensive on behalf of my new friends. "They're actually pretty cool people. Well, except this one guy, Chad. But at least he knew what kind of spider bit me, which, now that I think about it, kind of makes him my hero."

"So call him up. He'd probably love to hang out with you."

"Urg, I don't think I could handle him today. He's a lot."

"What about Allie?" he asks, waggling his eyebrows. "She had quite the sexy voice. I bet you could have a lot of fun with her."

I narrow my eyes at him, feeling unreasonably irritated

by his use of the word sexy to describe her. "Nah, she's super busy with a project she's doing. She'll be going full-out all weekend because she lost a lot of time staying with me at the hospital."

"So go help her."

"I can't help her. I don't understand anything about what she's doing."

"Well, she's gotta eat, right? Go feed her. That'll save her some time."

"She lives with her parents and they do this big meal every Sunday with all her relatives. In fact, she won't even be able to work today because she has to help out in the kitchen all day to prepare for a special dinner they're having."

"Why do you know all of this?" he asks me.

"We got pretty close when I was in the hospital."

A knowing grin crosses his face. "How close?"

"Not like that, you idiot. How was *that* supposed to happen when I was battling for my life?"

"Pfft, it was a spider bite."

"A deadly one," I tell him.

"Deadly for your dong, maybe."

"My dong is just fine, thank you."

"Ha! Made you say it."

"Oh my God, you really are ten."

"Hey, I like to have fun, so sue me," Gersh says. "Speaking of fun, the waves are calling me."

"Bastard."

"You're just jealous."

"Damn right I am. Go have fun."

"Will do. Later, dude."

"Yup."

I end the call, then look around the pristine condo. No way am I going to spend the rest of the day here. It's the loneliest place on the planet. No family, no dogs, no waves to ride. My mind wanders back to Allie, and I wonder how she's doing. She must be busy helping out in the kitchen even though she should be hunched over her laptop. I picture her in a house dress and apron (because apparently it's 1950 in my fantasy world). She's got her hair pinned up and she's wiping her forehead with the back of her arm while she stirs an enormous pot of pasta sauce. She looks gorgeous in my fantasy, by the way. Suddenly the room is cleared of everyone else and it's just the two of us. I walk up behind her, wrap my arms around her waist and plant slow kisses on her neck and slowly lift her skirt with one hand.

And *those* are the thoughts that have been torturing me since we shared a cab from the hospital on Friday. I cannot for the life of me get her out of my mind. Not that I'm trying all that hard.

I stand up and walk over to the patio doors and stare out at the gardens below for a second, feeling completely restless. Here I am with a ton of energy and nothing to do, and there she is trying to juggle more than one person can handle. If only there was something I could do to make her life easier.

Huh, maybe there is...

16

Guess Who's Coming to Make Dinner?

Allie

YOU KNOW what's worse than an angry Italian mother? A house full of angry Italians, which is what I'm trying to avoid. We're having the feast to end all feasts, which means the kitchen has been packed with cooks since dawn. It also means that I've spent the bulk of the morning chopping, dicing, kneading, and cleaning, interspersed with excusing myself so I can sneak back upstairs to check on Frank's progress and feed him new data. The crap part is that I promised my parents I'd take the day off, and they're totally onto me. There's only so many times a girl can say she's got to run to the ladies' room before her nosy relatives start to talk. The last time I went up, I came back to a whole lot of questions about a possible UTI, followed by several competing bits of advice about cranberry juice, cutting back on caffeine, and not sitting on cold pavement (as if that's something I spend a lot of time doing). At this point, I'm pretty sure if I tell them I have to pee again, I'm going to be whisked off to urgent care to get checked for diabetes.

The doorbell rings just as I'm feeding another small batch of dough through the pasta maker. The sound of pounding feet floats into the kitchen, and I know in about two seconds my nephew Matteo and my niece Camilla are going to be in a full-on fist fight over who gets to answer it. Sure enough, shouting ensues, followed by Vinnie's booming voice for them to "Knock it off and answer the GD door already!"

Here in the kitchen, Grandma makes a *tsk*ing sound and shakes her head at Lucia. "You need to tell Vinnie to stop taking the lord's name in vain like that. He's never going to get into Heaven like that."

Zia Fernanda rushes in to save Lucia with, "He didn't take the lord's name in vain. He said GD as in gosh darn."

"Still, I don't like it."

Matteo comes running into the kitchen. "Zia, there's a man here to see you!"

"What man?" Fernanda asks.

"Not you, Zia," he says, pointing to me. "*Zia*."

The kitchen goes completely silent.

A man? To see me? Oh my God, it's Hudson, isn't it? No, it can't be. He's probably lounging in bed with a model-slash-beach volleyball champion, or worse, that awful Dr. Blaire who had the hots for him. But it *could* be Hudson, like, say, if he needs help applying ointment to his ankle or something. And I look … well, not awful actually. I showered this morning and I'm wearing a clean gray tee and my yoga pants that don't have holes. Well, and this flowered apron complete with frills, but I'm hoping it's a look. Before I can ask who it is, Hudson appears in the entrance to the kitchen, carrying a case of wine. Camilla follows him into the room and announces him in her loud little girl voice. "Zia Allie, that guy from the shark movie is here for you."

Is my face bright red? Because it feels like it's on fire. He's smiling at me. Dimples. Gorgeous green eyes. Brain totally fried. *Say something, dummy.* "Hey, Hudson, what brings you by?"

Camilla answers for him. "He came to help."

My jaw drops and I glance at her, trying to process what's going on. "With what?"

She shrugs. "I don't know. Ask him."

"Right. Good idea," I answer, turning my gaze to Hudson. "With what?"

"I knew you were really busy so I thought I'd offer myself up as a tribute in the kitchen for a few hours," he says.

"Tribute?" Nonno, who is at the kitchen table playing cards with my dad asks. "What does he mean?"

"It's a *Hunger Games* reference, Nonno," Lucia tells him.

"Is he hungry? We got lots of food," Nonno says, putting both hands on the table and standing up. "Maria, get out the mortadella. I'll make him a sandwich."

"Pops, he's not hungry," Zia Fernanda says. "He's talking about a *movie* called *The Hunger Games.*"

"Well, it's also a book," I say, which really helps nothing at all. Turning back to Hudson, I say, "I'm sorry. Let's try this again."

Hudson grins, and when his dimples pop, I swear to God, you can hear the eggs dropping all around the room, even from the post-menopausal women among us. "Sure, as we say in the biz, take two. Hey, Allie, I hope you don't mind that I stopped by. I was at loose ends today and I thought maybe I could take your place in the kitchen since I know how busy you are with your project."

Oh my God, how is this happening right now? "Really? You came here to cook with my family?"

"Yeah, I know I won't be able to do all the stuff you'd normally do, so put me to work peeling potatoes and scrubbing pots." He sets the case of wine down on the floor. "Although that looks kind of fun," he adds, gesturing to the pasta maker. "Are you making homemade noodles?"

Nodding, I say, "Uh-huh. But how's your ankle and … everything? Should you even be up and around?"

Every set of eyes is on him as he walks over to me and I know they're all hearing the melody of Mendelssohn's "Wedding March" in their heads. Well, except for my dad, who's scowling.

Hudson gives me a breezy grin. "I've never been better. In fact, I'm pretty sure that spider gave me superpowers."

"Superpowers?" I ask, immediately thinking of his manly parts. Did my eyes just flick down to his crotch? Yup, they did, because I'm looking at it.

He lowers his voice. "Not like that, you pervert."

I stifle a laugh, then say, "Hey, I am *not* to blame for my mind going there."

"What's so funny?" my dad asks.

When I look over at him, my stomach drops. He's got the same expression he had on his face the time he caught Ian Miller giving me a hickey on the couch in his den. Immediately, I go right back to feeling like a sixteen-year-old girl, and it takes me a second to remember I'm thirty-five and I can do what I want. Not that I *have* been doing what I want. But I can if I want to. "Nothing, Pop. It's a long story."

"We got time," he says, running his tongue over his teeth and standing up. "I'm Enzo. Allegra's father."

If Hudson is intimidated, he doesn't show it. He walks over and reaches out his hand. "Hudson. Wonderful to meet you, sir. You must be so proud of Allegra here. She's not only a kind and thoughtful person, but a genius too."

My dad's scowl softens a little. "I know that. She's a very special one."

"That's for sure. Here she is at the forefront of the biggest breakthrough in the history of SETI research and yet she took a day off to stay with me at the hospital," Hudson says, looking around the room. "I just had to find a way to pay her back."

"Allegra, you didn't tell us about this big breakthrough," Zia Fernanda says.

Shrugging, I feel my face warming up even more. "I didn't want to say anything in case it doesn't work out."

"Oh, it'll work out," Hudson says, even though he really has no idea if I can actually do what I set out to. "She's basically the next Frank Drake."

"Really?" Nonno asks. "Our Allegra?"

"Oh yeah, you'll all be sitting at the Nobel Prize ceremony one day watching her receive her medal."

"Nobel prize, *pfft*," I say with a chuckle. "I'm not … they don't give it out for SETI research."

"Well, they will when you're done," Hudson says. "Speaking of which, you're not getting any closer to changing the world down here. Now, show me how to use that pasta grinder, then you scoot back upstairs and get your work done."

"I'll show him!"

This can be heard from every woman in the room, including Camilla, who, at the tender age of ten, is clearly as in love with him as the rest of the world.

I lower my voice. "Can I talk to you in the hall for a second?"

"Of course," he says, following me as we cross the large room.

As soon as we round the corner, I whisper, "You don't know what you're getting yourself into. They're crazy people."

"They seem fine."

Shaking my head, I say, "They're insane. And they're going to ask you all sorts of embarrassing questions and my dad's going to assume you're trying to sleep with me so he's going to be just awful to you and they're going to make you eat so much, you'll feel sick. You should just go, while you still can."

Placing both hands on my shoulders, he says, "Allie, I'm fine. In fact, I'm going to have a great time. Now, you go get to work."

"Are you sure?"

"Of course I'm sure. This whole thing was my idea," he says. "Now go."

I stare at him for a second, feeling all kinds of warm, gooey feelings. He's here to help me. He just showed up exactly when I needed him. "Okay, but only if you're sure you're sure."

"I'm totally sure I'm sure."

I start toward the stairs, but he stops me. "Wait. I should probably borrow that apron. My stylist will kill me if I get this shirt dirty."

I tuck my lips between my teeth to stop myself from laughing, and he says, "Yeah, I just heard it myself. Let's pretend I didn't say that."

I reach behind my back and try to untie the strings, only to discover they've knotted up somehow. "Just a sec," I tell him, leaning to my left as if that'll work.

"You need some help?"

"No, I'm good. I've got it," I say through gritted teeth while I attempt to twist the apron. It is not going to budge. Dammit.

"Allie, let me help," Hudson tells me, his voice a little more forceful this time.

I grunt a little, then let my shoulders drop. "Fine."

I spin on my heel and stand with my back to him, my temperature rising three degrees Fahrenheit as I feel his fingers brushing against my lower back.

"Has anyone ever told you how stubborn you are?"

"I prefer the word independent."

"I've met independent. You've crossed the line to full-on stubborn."

"Hey," I answer, attempting to turn around so I can argue with him, but he stops me with his hands on my waist.

"Stay still."

God, that felt good. It's been way, way too long.

Holding my breath, I take in every second while he fiddles with the knot, his big, strong hands only inches from the top of my bottom. My mind wanders right back to him carrying me out of my office, and it occurs to me that here he is, saving me again, when he is under no obligation to do so.

"There, got it," he says, and far before I'm ready, his hands are gone.

I turn back to him and lift the apron off my neck and place it around his, and there's that cologne again. Wow. I watch as he wraps the strings around his narrow waist and ties it in front. Grinning at the sight of him in my mom's flowery old apron, I say, "Do you want me to take some pics for your Insta account?"

He grins. "Is this a good look for me?"

"Totally." And the crazy part is, it actually is.

"Now, go get to work," he says, pointing up the stairs with his thumb.

"It's not too late. You can still sneak out."

"Never." He gives me a wink and walks back into the kitchen.

As I'm heading up the stairs, I hear my dad's voice. "So, Hudson. That blonde with the huge knockers. What's she like in real life?"

Oh, sweet Jesus. This is going to be a total disaster.

A totally wonderful, incredible, heart-fluttering disaster…

17

Confusing Food Analogies

Hudson

THIS. This is what's missing from life in Malibu. A big, noisy family cooking together and having fun. Allie's right —they are nuts, they argue about everything, but they also love each other fiercely. You can just feel it. I know I'm not a part of it, and yet somehow they're making me feel like I belong.

Well, everyone except Allie's dad, Enzo, who's acting like I'm some sort of predator, here to corrupt his youngest daughter. The truth is, I'd corrupt the hell out of her if she wanted me to. Gladly, and with fervor, over and over again. The rest of the family, however, seems to take me at my word that I'm here to help. Which I am. But also…

Allie's grandma taught me how to use the pasta maker, and together we've made enough fettuccine to feed the neighborhood. The entire dining room table is covered with noodles that will sit there for a few hours to dry before supper. Her nonno made good on his offer of a sandwich. In fact, he made them for the entire family, and wow, are they tasty—spicy mortadella, melted provolone cheese, tomato, and mayo on a sourdough roll. He starts by making piles of the meat and cheese, then fries them up to brown the meat and melt the cheese. Then he adds them to the roll, cuts them in half, then fries the whole thing. My nutritionist would be horrified because there must be a thousand calories in each one, but honestly, it's worth every second I'm going to have to spend in the gym.

We've just finished cleaning up from lunch when Enzo announces it's time for him to make the sauce. "Everybody clear out except Mr. Finch, who's going to help me."

The room goes so quiet, you could hear a noodle drop. Allie's mom's jaw drops. "You're going to show him how to make your red sauce?"

He cracks his knuckles. "He's our honored guest."

Huh, based on the look on his face, I'm not sure he actually means that. I stand, watching as aprons are hung on a hook on the wall, and the rest of the family disperses. Enzo gathers the ingredients and places them on the island, then gets out a big knife, a wooden spoon, and … is that … a razor blade? Yup, it is. I'm starting to think coming here was a bad idea after all.

"Have a seat." He gestures to a stool that's tucked under the island. I do what he said, then watch as he pulls apart a garlic bulb. "Do you know how to make a red sauce?"

"I know how to open a jar," I answer with a grin.

Okay, that joke didn't land. He's glaring again.

"No, not from scratch."

"From scratch is the only way to make it," he says. "The secret to a good red sauce is to slice the garlic so thin it melts into the olive oil and disappears."

I watch as he peels each clove, then starts to slice them with the razor blade.

"Oh hey, they did this in that movie *Goodfellas*," I remark.

Enzo looks at me like I've sprouted horns. "I didn't learn to cook from the TV."

"No, I'm sure you didn't." *All right, Hudson, dial back the jokes. Enzo's not your audience.*

The world's most uncomfortable silence follows while he painstakingly slices each clove until there's a big pile of them on the cutting board, each one paper-thin. Enzo picks up the big knife and a red onion. Chopping it in half with a loud, decisive slap, he says, "So, why are you really here, Mr. Finch?"

"I wanted to pay Allie back for helping me out the other day."

He pauses for a second and looks over his glasses at me. "The real reason."

I was lonely and bored. And I'm insanely attracted to her. "That's it. Honestly."

He stares me down while I meet his gaze, then he turns his attention back to the onion. "A good red sauce needs a lot of time to simmer on the stove. Slowly. Low heat for several hours. Time is the key ingredient because it's the only thing that allows all the flavors to come through."

In other words, don't try to sleep with my daughter for a few years. "That makes sense."

"Of course, you have to start with the right ingredients because without that, it doesn't matter how many hours on the stove you give it, it'll taste like garbage."

"I feel like I should be taking notes," I answer.

He gives me the over-the-glasses glare again. "You should, because cooking is life. What you do in the kitchen teaches you how to live. Take my wife and me—we had the right ingredients to make a good marriage. We're both from the same place, so we share the same beliefs about the world and how to raise a family. This is very important for a happy life."

In other words, Allie and I don't have the right ingredients to make a happy life. Even though marriage is the very last thing on my mind, somehow having her dad suggest I'm not good enough brings out the defiant streak in me. "Well, one could also say that having differences could keep things interesting."

"No, you don't want interesting," he says, waggling one finger at me. "Interesting means arguments you never solve. You want harmony, which only comes from growing up with the same values, and values come from one's culture."

"Sure, but we're all Americans here, right? Isn't that enough?"

He shakes his head. "No, not at all. America is big pot of too many possibilities. People throwing anything they want into the pot. This is why there are so many divorces. People like you thinking a good sauce can be made with the wrong ingredients."

People like me? Yeesh. "I've never even tried to make a sauce, so…"

"Why not? You're getting a little old to let the sauce simmer properly."

Okay, I'm getting a little confused with all this sauce and marriage talk. And also, he's calling me old? This guy is two pointy ears and some green makeup away from being Yoda. "I guess I've never found compatible ingredients or just one compatible ingredient?"

"Or maybe *you're* not the right ingredient. Maybe you're pepper, sprinkling a little here and a little there in every dish, instead of being like the tomato paste that only goes in one thing—a red sauce."

Okay, so he's got me there. I have done my fair share

of sprinkling myself a little here and a little there. But I can't exactly tell him that, now can I? "To be honest, I'm not sure what I am, but I don't think it's pepper." Glancing at the items on the counter, I say, "Maybe I'm more like ... the ground meat?"

"You don't know? A man has to know these things before he can make a sauce," he says, gesturing at me with the massive knife he's holding. "If you don't know, you could hurt someone very badly."

Seriously, does he think I'm intimidated by this?

Okay, maybe I'm a little intimidated, but it's a really big freaking knife.

"My Allegra's been hurt before by a hot pepper. Lando. She thought he was the one, but it turns out, he was the one to break her heart," Enzo says, chopping the onion so hard his forehead starts to glisten. "He had her totally fooled into thinking he was tomato paste. He was in her program at university so they had a lot in common. He was even Italian, so he managed to fool Allegra's mother and the rest of the family. Not me, mind you. A father can always tell pepper when he sees it. In this case, he was using her to get ahead at school while he was sprinkling pepper all around town, if you get my drift."

Pretty sure I can follow his train of thought, even if it does seem like it's only on the track half the time. "That's awful."

"It was awful. He broke her heart. Snapped it in half. Stole all her research and dumped her. She's never been the same. She used to have this light in her eyes and when he did that to her, it went out," he says, shaking his head. "Do you know what that does to a father? To see the light in his child's eyes go out?"

"I can imagine."

"No, you can't. It kills you," he says, tapping his fist

against his heart. "It makes you want to kill, so when another man shows up with a case of wine and a big smile, it makes you worry. Is he the kind of guy who wants to sprinkle himself all over every woman he meets? Does he turn up the heat so fast, he burns people? Am I going to have another man out there I want to kill? It's a problem for a father."

Well, this is just great. I came over to help out a little and have a nice day and now I'm being quasi-threatened. "Look, sir, I have no intention of breaking your daughter's heart. Our relationship is purely professional. Well, I'd like to think we're becoming friends, but that's it. I'm only here for a few weeks, and then I'm leaving. I'd never dream of breaking her heart."

"I hope not."

"I won't."

He glares at me. "You better not."

Oh Jesus, are we going to do this all day? "I'm not going to."

"Okay then," he says. "Because I've been waiting for years to see that light back in her eyes, and my heart won't feel right until it's there."

Allie's mom, Maria, walks into the kitchen just as I say, "Got it. And I promise not to sprinkle any pepper while I'm in town."

She makes a loud *tsk*ing sound and rolls her eyes. "Seriously, Enzo?" She turns to me. "Don't listen to a word this one says. If ever there was a man who used to sprinkle pepper all over town, it was this guy. *I* was the one who turned him into tomato paste."

"Hey! What are you doing?" Enzo says to his wife. "You can't tell him that. I'm making a point here."

"I'll tell you what you're doing. You're making this nice young man—who came over to our house to help—feel uncomfortable for no good reason. Come on, if he was pepper, he would've tried something when Allie spent the night at the hospital with him."

That's not strictly true, on account of me being incapacitated at the time, but I appreciate her faith in me. I open my mouth to agree with her, but Enzo beats me to the punch. "He might be pepper! You don't know."

She points a finger at him. "A mother knows."

"Well, so does a father!"

"No, you think *every* man is pepper when it comes to Allegra."

"That's because at the heart of every man is pepper."

He's not wrong. The last thing I'm going to do is agree with the man, but he's definitely not wrong. I sit back and watch the two of them go head-to-head about pepper and tomato paste and Allegra, and the entire time, I'm only thinking one thing. I would like to kill that Lando guy myself. Which is insane, but true. There's just something about the thought of the light in her eyes going out that gets to me.

And then it hits me—I need to protect her from me, because I'd very much like to sprinkle some pepper her way, and that's the last thing she needs right now. Because in five weeks, I'm going to disappear from her life forever.

18

When You Know, You Know. Even When You Wish You Didn't

Allie

SOMEHOW I'VE MANAGED to get some actual work done, which honestly is worthy of a Nobel Prize by itself, because the man of my dreams is in my kitchen right now cooking and being interrogated by everyone to whom I'm related. And from the sounds of things, they're having a blast. They must have cracked that case of wine he brought because the amount of laughter wafting up the stairs is unprecedented, and to be honest, it's making me a little jealous.

Also, the curiosity is killing me. Like seriously *killing me.* I want to know every word he's saying and every inane question and comment my family is throwing his way. Well, maybe not every single one because the embarrassment factor would be incalculable. When Lucia brought up a sandwich for me earlier, the only tea she was willing to spill is that he's so 'crazy charming, he could lie to her all day long and she'd forgive him' which I already knew, thank you very much.

Right after lunch, things went deadly quiet for about half an hour, which was the worst. Usually my dad clears out the kitchen when he makes his red sauce. He says it's to keep the recipe a secret, but it's really because he hates having anyone try to give him advice. The rest of the family rests for a while, some napping, some watching television, and some sitting out in the yard if the weather's nice. But where was Hudson during that time? I am so hoping he was watching TV with my mom, and not stuck in the kitchen with my dad, who I'm guessing would've done his *Goodfellas* razor blade garlic thing while he gave him a cryptic 'stay away from my daughter' lecture.

Glancing at the clock, I see that it's almost time for dinner. I tap away at my keyboard, trying to teach Frank how to ignore what we call cosmic microwave background radiation, which is basically the afterglow of the Big Bang. The trouble is, my mind keeps wandering back to that gorgeous hunk of a man every few seconds, which is *so much worse* than yesterday, when it was only wandering back to him every few minutes. The awful, horrible truth is that him showing up today has tipped me over from crushing hard to falling for him. Like honestly, the second I saw him in my kitchen holding that case of wine, I could feel my heart and soul just swell up with joy, which is just so, so bad because there's really no possible scenario in which this ends well for me.

A knock at the door interrupts my not working and I call for whoever it is to come in, except instead of my usual bark of "Who is it?!" I opt for a soothing, friendly "Come in!"

When my mom opens the door, she says, "You can drop the act. It's me."

"Is supper ready?"

"Yes," she answers. "That Hudson's a very nice boy."

I shut off my desk lamp and stand up. "Yeah, he's not what I was expecting."

"How so?"

"I don't know. He's a lot more down to earth than I thought he'd be."

"Do you think he might have some Italian in him?" she asks, which is Mom for 'you should marry him and make me some grandkids.'

"No idea," I tell her, following her out of the room. "Say, where was he when dad was making the red sauce?"

She gives me a look that tells me exactly what happened.

"Noooo, seriously?" I ask, my face already hot with embarrassment even though I don't know with one-hundred-percent certainty what happened.

Nodding, she says, "Yup."

I let out a groan. "Did he give him the pepper and tomato paste talk?"

"Oh yeah, but don't worry because I came in and put a stop to it."

God, I hope so.

———

For some unknown reason, everything tastes amazing tonight, especially the wine Hudson brought. It's a red from a region in the northwest part of Italy called Pied-mont, and I can tell by how impressed the older generation is that it's fancy schmancy. It's going down so nicely, I'm getting a little tipsy, which I know I shouldn't do since I have to go straight back to work when dinner's over. Only, I'm a bundle of hormones and nerves right now, so maybe a few more sips won't hurt.

Oops, that was more of a glug.

"Say, Hudson, do you want to see my science project after supper?" Matteo asks.

Hudson is just about to say yes when I cut him off. "No, you do not. It's a trick." Giving Matteo a hard look, I say, "A nasty one at that considering that Hudson just got out of the hospital two days ago because of ... one of those things."

Matteo snaps his little fingers together. "Nuts. You're wrecking all my fun, Zia."

Lucia sighs and gives her son a death glare. "We're not going to have fun at Hudson's expense. Especially since he saved Zia Allie's life and spent the entire day helping us."

Thank you, Lucia. For once, you've come through when I need you.

She turns to Hudson. "This wine is incredible, by the way."

"Oh, I'm glad you like it. The man at the store said it was Italy's best red."

"He was right," she answers, lifting the glass while giving him a smile that definitely means she's thinking about cashing in her one free celebrity bang card.

Vinnie glares at him. "So, Hudson? You ever do any MMA fighting?"

Oh crap, Vinnie clearly hasn't forgotten about the list.

"Uh, no, can't say I have. You?"

"Yeah, I'm big into MMA," Vinnie says, scowling at him. "I could've gone pro, but then Matteo came along. It's not the best life for a family."

Hudson narrows his eyes, looking very confused. "That is quite the accomplishment."

"It's important to be able to defend your family," Vinnie says. "Because family is the only thing that matters in this life." He points to Lucia. "This woman here? My wife? I would *kill* for her."

"Well, hopefully it never comes to that," Hudson answers.

"Let's hope not," Vinnie says pointedly.

Can this be over please?

"More lamb, Hudson?" my mom asks, lifting the platter.

"Oh, I'm stuffed, thank you though."

She smiles at him. "Where are your parents from?"

Perfect. We've now reached the part of the evening when they try to find out how Italian he is.

"Nebraska, but I grew up in New York."

"Okay, but where are *their* parents from?" Grandma asks.

"Nebraska."

"And *their* parents?" Zia Fernanda adds.

I sigh, then interject with, "They're trying to figure out if you have any Italian in you."

"Oh," he says, looking amused. "No, I'm afraid not. Irish on my mom's side and English on my dad's."

Shoulders drop around the table, but Zia's eyes light up. "But have you had one of those DNA tests done because a lot of people find out they're not from where they thought."

"Yeah, my brother and I bought those kits for my parents for Christmas one year, so I'm pretty sure we're not Italian."

The room goes silent for a minute, other than the sounds of knives and forks brushing up against the china, and I can tell Hudson's feeling a little awkward. I take another sip of wine, then say, "You don't have to be Italian. You're amazing just the way you are."

"She's right," Lucia says, running her fingers along her gold necklace. "*Just* the way you are."

A glance at Vinnie tells me he's about to lose it.

Hudson seems to pick up on it too because he clears his throat and says, "This might be the most delicious meal I've ever had."

My mom blushes. "Nah, you're flattering us. You must have eaten at some of the world's best restaurants."

"I have, and believe me, none of them have anything on this dinner. The fresh pasta? The red sauce? The lamb? You could open your own restaurant. Michelin star all the way."

Good God, that charm is lethal. I'm pretty sure at this point, there isn't an adult in this room who wouldn't go home with him—the men included.

"So, Hudson, do you have any special plans while you're in the area?" Zia asks.

He pats his mouth with his napkin. "Umm, well, other than trying to learn as much as I can about what Allie does, my publicity team has set up a few things for me. They want me to go to the museum, and to be seen at the library, and they bought me tickets for the opera."

"Why would they do that?" my mom says.

"They want to change my image. Apparently smart is the new cool," he answers with an easy smile that I can tell is hiding how he really feels. "Not sure who's going to buy me as a smart guy, but according to my team, we're going to be able to pull it off."

"I love your image," Lucia says. "You're a big star. Can't you just say no?"

He shakes his head and picks up his wine glass. "The funny thing about Hollywood is that once you reach a certain level, you pretty much have to sell your soul to stay there."

"What do you mean?" Vinnie asks. "Like gigolo stuff?"

"No, not gigolo stuff," I answer for Hudson, giving Vinnie a disgusted look. "Like, pretending he likes science

169

and posting on Instagram. Going to the opera, things like that."

"I love the opera. Which one?" Lucia asks, even though she's never been to the opera in her life.

"*Don Giovanni.*"

"Oh, *that's* Italian," Zia says.

"It's not Italian," my dad tells her. "It's a Spanish story and the music was written by Mozart who was Austrian."

"I guarantee you Mozart was a little bit Italian," Vinnie says. Turning to Matteo, he says, "Do you know how close Austria is to Italy?"

Matteo shakes his head.

"It's right frigging there," he answers. "At the very top of the boot."

My dad gives Hudson a meaningful look. "Do you know what it's about?"

"*Don Giovanni?*"

Dad nods at him to which Hudson says, "Not really, no."

"Don Juan. You ever hear someone call a man a real Don Juan?"

More wine. More sips of wine. Yes, that's making this moment so much better because I'm now comfortably detached from it.

"I haven't, Nonno," Camilla says. "What does that mean?"

My dad offers her a sweet smile. "Well, my *bambolotta*, Don Juan was the type of man who liked to sprinkle pepper on every dish he saw."

"But some food doesn't taste good with pepper!" she says. "Like ice cream."

"Exactly," he says, pointing a finger at her. "See? This little child gets it. Pepper doesn't belong on everything."

"Oh Jesus," I mutter.

My mom clears her throat, and I'm momentarily grateful that she's stepping in to save things, until she comes out with this little gem: "You should take Allegra to the opera with you. She's never gone."

Oh fuck. Seriously, Ma? I scramble to think of a graceful exit, but the only thing I come up with is sliding under the table, which is neither graceful nor helpful. "Oh no, I'm sure Hudson has someone to go with him. Like … Margot Robbie or Jennifer Lawrence."

Hudson gives me an amused look. "They're both married, and I actually don't have anyone to go with."

"You don't?" I ask, shocked that this demi-god doesn't have a date.

"Nope. You're really the only person I know in town."

I grin at him, and I'm pretty sure it's a sloppy one at that, based on how numb my face is at the moment. "Well, you know Chad."

He chuckles. "True. I do know Chad."

"You can't take Chad to the opera," Grandma says. "He's a total schmuck. You have to take our Allegra. She can wear one of my gowns."

Oh God, no. She's putting him on the spot, and I seriously cannot be rejected in front of my entire family. Vinnie will *never* stop bringing it up. I'm about to shake my head and let him off the hook, but the smile on Hudson's face as he gazes at me causes my mind to go completely blank. Damn vino.

"I'd love it if you'd go with me, Allie. That is, if you're not too busy."

"Um, well, I am, but——"

"Her answer is yes," Zia tells him. "She can definitely take the night off to go with you." She turns to me. "Grandma has the most beautiful gowns from when they still lived in the old country and you'll definitely fit into them. I'll do your hair. You'll look like a princess."

"Pfft, a princess," I slur. "I don't think so."

"I think you will," Hudson says, his face serious.

Oh my God, he does? What I wouldn't give for him to lay a huge kiss on me right this moment.

My Nonno pipes in with, "She *is* a princess, every day. Just look at that beautiful face. *Molto bella.*"

"Aww, thanks, Nonno."

"So, it's settled then," my mom says. "Allegra will go to the opera with you. You have a date."

My father looks like his head is about to pop off his neck. "But you better pay close attention to what happens to Don Giovanni because you wouldn't want to suffer the same fate."

"Enzo, he's not going to get killed by a ghost," Ma says.

"Uh-oh, spoiler alert," I mutter to Hudson, who stifles a laugh.

"Don't worry, sir," he tells my dad. "I promise to keep my hands to myself and to bring your daughter straight home when the opera ends."

"We're all aware that I'm thirty-five, not fifteen, right?" I ask.

———

"Well, that was quite the day," Hudson says. We're outside the house, both our arms loaded with containers of left-overs and bread from the bakery that my mom and Grandma insisted he take home on account of him being a man, and therefore incapable of feeding himself.

"Yeah, sorry about my family," I tell him, swaying a little as we reach his SUV. "To be fair, I did try to warn you."

"You did. You really did," he answers with a sideways grin. "Say, that whole thing your dad does with the garlic and the razor blade. Is that—"

"From *Goodfellas*? Yeah, he thinks it's intimidating."

"Oh, it is." Hudson opens the passenger door, then steps aside to let me set my things down first. "But less intimidating than him brandishing that massive knife while he talks about his daughter's heart getting broken."

I scrunch up my face. "Oh God, it's all just so embarrassing, I want to crawl under a rock."

"Why?" he asks, unloading his arms.

"Because you're obviously not interested in me, which is good because we're colleagues, sort of, in a strange way, and here he is accusing you of..." I trail off, unable to finish my sentence even though I'm half-cut right now.

"Wanting to pepper your dish?"

He is *so* gorgeous. Wow. "Yeah, that."

"Don't worry about it. He's just looking out for you, which I can appreciate."

"Is that the kind of dad you'd be? Overly protective to the point of insanity?"

He chuckles, then says, "If I had a daughter, I'm afraid I wouldn't be too far off. In fact, I'm already unreasonably mad about my hypothetical daughter getting hit on."

Lord, he's cute. I can't even take how cute he is. Am I just gazing up at him with a stupid grin on my face? I should stop that. "Listen, about that whole silliness with you taking me to the opera..." *Please take me to the opera.* "Definitely don't feel like you need to take me. I'm sure by the time it rolls around you'll have met somebody more suitable."

He scrunches up his face in confusion. "What is that supposed to mean? More suitable."

"I don't know … like someone more in your league. A supermodel, or maybe a Swedish Olympic ski champion."

"That guy really did a number on you, didn't he?" he says, his eyes hardening.

"What guy?"

"Lando. When your dad was giving me the pepper versus tomato paste lecture, he filled me in on the details," he says. "He's the guy who would wash his penis in the sink, isn't he?"

Even though I'm, well, let's face it, drunk, my stomach tightens. I roll my eyes anyway and say, "That's the one. I know my parents think he broke my heart, but he didn't mean that much to me. Honestly, I was far more upset about him taking credit for my work than I was about all the philandering and the dumping."

"Really?"

No, not really. He shattered my heart into tiny dust particles. "Seriously, I completely forgot about it."

"No, you didn't," he says, and I swear to God, his eyes are peering directly into my soul.

"How do you know?"

"Because you've completely given up on love, which is a crime." His eyes flick down to my lips. "Your nonno was right about you. You're very beautiful. And you're smart and you're fun, and any guy would be lucky to be with you."

But not him. He doesn't mean him, no matter how much I wish he did.

We stare at each other for a moment, and I feel my heart pounding a little harder than it should be for someone standing still. "Do you want to hear something crazy?" I ask.

"Yes."

"Lando is on one of the teams I'm competing against. To create the first viable AI system for SETI."

"Are you serious?" he asks.

I nod. "Yup."

"Oh my God, in that case, you need to get Frank working. Like, right now."

I chuckle a little, my heart swelling that he gets what it means to me, and we stare at each other for a deliciously long, intense moment. *Kiss me. Kiss me right here, right now.* I don't even care that my entire family is watching from the living room window. I know I should. But I don't.

But he doesn't kiss me. He clears his throat instead. "I better let you go get back to work."

"Yes, I should totally do that. Thank you so much for saving me today."

"Did you get a lot done?"

Nodding, I say, "I really did."

"Then it was all worth it because for the rest of my life, I'll know I was a part of something so much bigger than anything else I'll do with my life."

My cheeks heat up at the thought of Hudson Finch—a famous actor with the big, shiny career—thinking what I do is important.

He points to the food. "Plus, I'm going to eat like a king for at least a week."

"At least."

"I'll see you tomorrow morning," he says.

"Yes, you will," I answer, my voice all soft and silky. *Kiss me ... now.*

He glances at the house and waves. "That sure is your entire family, just standing there watching us."

I look over and give them a 'get lost' face, but let's face it, they're not going to honor my wishes. "Yes, there they are."

He holds out his hand. "Good night, Allegra. I hope you get some sleep."

I shake his hand. It's warm and big and manly and I don't want to let go but I know I have to. "Good night, Hudson. Thank you again. For everything."

"Anytime."

He lets go of my hand and walks around to the driver's side of his vehicle. Giving me a salute, he says, "Until tomorrow, Dr. Cammareri."

"Until tomorrow, Mr. Finch."

I spin on my heel and make my way up the sidewalk, knowing that standing there gawking at him while he pulls away would be nothing short of humiliating. It's what I want to do, but luckily, there's a tiny bit of my brain that's still sober and knows better. Just like she knew not to grab him by the front of his shirt and plant the mother of all kisses on him.

I kind of hate that bitch right now, but I'll be thanking her later.

Maybe.

Email from: Keenan.Edwards@SETIResearchInstitute.com
To: Allegra.Cammareri@SETIResearchInstitute.com, Hudson.Finch@ymail.com

Subject: Black Creek Trip

Allegra,

I've arranged to have you and Hudson go up to Black Creek for a day on Thursday the 23rd. This

will give Glen and his staff a day to go into
Redding to shop for supplies. I told him you'll be
there by 10 a.m., which means leaving before 5 to
get there in time. I trust that won't be a problem for
you or for Hudson.

This will be his one chance to gain an understanding of the mechanics and engineering of the
radio telescopes.

Please make sure you pack an overnight bag, as the
weather can be unpredictable this time of year in
the mountains.

Regards,
Keenan

Email from: Allegra.Cammareri@SETIResearchIn
stitute.com
To: Keenan.Edwards@SETIResearchInsti
tute.com, Hudson.Finch@ymail.com

Subject: Re: Black Creek Trip

Hi Keenan,

Sounds great. I'll arrange the transportation and
meals.

Warmest regards,
Allie

Email from: Hudson.Finch@ymail.com
To: Keenan.Edwards@SETIResearchInsti
tute.com, Allegra.Cammareri@SETIResearchInsti
tute.com

Subject: Re: Black Creek Trip

Hi Keenan and Allie,

Thank you for arranging this. I've added it to my calendar and am happy to drive. Thanks for the tip about the overnight bag.

All the best,
Hudson

19

The Problem with Happiness...

Hudson

BRITTANY

Hudson, babe, we need to talk about your date for the opera. I can get Tasha if you don't have anyone in mind.

ME

No need. I've found a perfect person to go with me.

BRITTANY

I need a name to vet her.

ME

Trust me, you won't find any skeletons in her closet.

BRITTANY

Name or I'm calling Tasha.

ME

Dr. Allegra Cammareri.

BRITTANY

Googling her now.

...

Okay, she's got potential, but she needs a
Brazilian blowout and a professional
makeup artist.

ME

There is no way I'm going to tell her that.

BRITTANY

Why not? She'll thank you for it later.

ME

Because I'm not a monster. Besides, I like
her the way she is.

BRITTANY

You're my worst client. You know that,
right?

ME

It's a badge of honor for me.

BRITTANY

Wait, are you going all George Clooney?
Hooking up with a genius?

ME

We're not getting married. She's just
coming to the opera with me as a favor.

BRITTANY

Well, see if she might want to be engaged
for a while. That would be totally above and
beyond for the movie.

ME

Yeah, that's not a thing normal people do,
so no.

BRITTANY

You're no fun. Gotta run, but you better up your post quota because you're lagging behind.

ME

Behind who?

BRITTANY

I don't know … the actors who have a future in Hollywood?

ME

Damn, that was cold.

BRITTANY

You don't pay me to be warm and fuzzy. Now, get posting.

ME

How about I disappear for a while to build the suspense? Maybe my absence will get people talking. Create a bunch of hype. And also, make it seem like I'm really busy preparing for my new role (which I am).

BRITTANY

Is this your way of trying to get out of doing a bunch of stuff you don't want to do?

ME

Maybe, but it's a little bit brilliant, no?

BRITTANY

No.

ME

Fine. Just took a shot of me at my desk. Posting … now.

I SNAP A PIC, then post it on Instagram with the caption: *Working harder than I ever have before to prepare for my upcoming role. Living, breathing, and eating SETI research. I'm going to disappear for a while so I can really focus. #SETIrocks #galaxystudios #methodactingforthewin*

———

Five seconds later:

BRITTANY
Seriously, dude?

ME
Trust me. It'll work.

———

Instagram Reel: Hollywood Dish with Ferris Biltmore

The video starts showing Ferris looking totally bored behind his desk. "Oh hey, me again. Ferris. But you might as well call me Where Is, because that's the start of my every thought. As in, where is Hudson? And yes, I know he's still at that alien hunter place up in Mountain View, but seriously, where is he? The mystery grows by the hour. Nobody, and I mean nobody, has any intel on him for me. I've checked with everyone I know, including that bitch down at the car wash who I used to date, and you know for a fact that if I'm sliding into his DM's, I'm straight-up desperate for news. And yet … nothing. TMZ caught him going into the library but other than that, Hudson's only posted twice in the last three weeks, once when he got out of the hospital and one quick, careless shot of him studying in some drab, dark office that looks like my nightmare come to life. But in that second shot, he looks happy in a way I haven't seen him, which leads me to my next segment: Did You Find Someone to Love?"

The words appear on the upper left-hand corner of the screen, and Ferris sighs wistfully. "Hudson, did you find someone to love? Did you? Because there's a sparkle in your eye that's been missing for years. It's back, so I'm guessing you're perhaps falling in love with some fabulously chic babe. Maybe some up and coming popstar or maybe a slightly older female tech billionaire who's had all the right work done so she looks both twenty-five and human? It certainly can't be because you're enjoying all that fancy book learnin'," he says, putting on a Southern accent. "No way are you lit up by learning about radio telescopes and quasars. You're far too hot for that. So I need to know, what is going on with you? Seriously. You need to call me immediately and spill the tea! Spill it! Because there's no way I can wait another three weeks for you to come back to Hollywood. I can't survive it! I cannot. It's too hard. I need you to make a public appearance. I need real footage of you moving and smiling and talking. Some sort of proof of life because what we're getting is not going to cut it."

He lets out a long sigh, then says, "That's it. I'm going back to bed. I can't do today."

————

"It's 6 o'clock. Time for a hydration break," I tell Allie, setting a cold glass of lemon water on her desk.

She thanks me and sips it without taking her eyes off her screen while I go back to my desk and slide my headphones on. Over the last three weeks, we've gotten into a routine. She works while I spend my days watching whatever videos I can find on the internet about astronomy, SETI research, and radio telescopes. There's a surprisingly sparse amount of info on David Peck Todd, but Allie found a copy of the textbook he wrote a hundred years ago in Keenan's office. So far, I haven't cracked it yet, even though I know likely nothing will get me into his head like that would. But just the sight of it makes me break out in a cold sweat because as busy as she is, there's still a chance she'd realize it's taking me forever to read each page.

So for now, I'm doing what I do best—avoiding and distracting. I'm also spending half of my days just watching Allie work, which I honestly think I could spend the rest of my life doing quite happily. I love the way she sticks the tip of her tongue out of the right corner of her mouth when she's concentrating extra hard, or the way she pushes her glasses up her nose with her index finger. I love how hard she works and how driven she is, and I don't mind taking the back seat on this, not even for a second.

When I'm not 'observing her like Jane Goodall,' I've been going along on any and all school tours with whatever unlucky person's name got drawn. My goal is to learn enough to be able to give one of the tours before I leave, because, according to Allie, if I can explain what they do here to a group of kids, I'll be ready to play David Todd.

Other than that, I help Allie in the only way I can. My contribution to her project is to use the extensive knowledge I've gained from working with trainers and nutritionists to keep her brain operating at peak levels—electrolytes, the right mix of protein, carbs, fats and micronutrients, all spaced out at the optimal times throughout the day. Since I really don't know what she was capable of before I started feeding her, I have no idea if she has more energy, but at least I know I'm saving her time she would otherwise have to spend hunting down something to eat.

Since she's supposed to be spending her time teaching me, we figured out a system with Gwen, who's in the office across from Keenan. Gwen sends a red alert text to both of us whenever he leaves his office, which prompts me to pause my video, remove my headphones, and slide my chair over to her desk, where we embark on a fake conversation. The whole thing is a little childish, very fun, and comes with an added bonus of me getting to sit right next to her, so close that our arms occasionally brush against each other, and I can smell her shampoo. It's something fruity and delicious, and it makes me want to bury my nose in her neck.

And that whole train of thought cannot leave the station because there is no way I can do anything even the tiniest bit physical with this woman. Not only did I promise her dad, but in a few weeks, I'll be leaving here to go back to my life and it won't be with someone who goes by doctor. There's also no way in hell I'm going to lead her into thinking this is going to turn into something, only to hightail it out of here. Is it tempting? Yeah. Would it be amazing? Hell yeah. Do I think about it about a thousand times a day? Yes, I do.

But it's not going to happen, which is a fact that I have to accept. She's going to meet the right guy, and when she does, they're going to have little genius babies together, and I'll try really hard to be happy for her. At least we'll have one epic date, tomorrow night at the opera. I've arranged for a limo so we can arrive in style. And no, I didn't hire a hair and makeup team. I asked her out because I like her the way she is, and I like seeing her actual face, not some makeup artist's rendition of what they think a woman's face should look like.

Allie sits back and cracks her knuckles, then turns to

me. "Well, that's about all I can do for tonight. I need to let Frank do his thing."

"What's he doing?"

"I just fed him 115,000 snippets of signal recordings, including the subset of fake alien signals. He's going to have to pick out the fakes, and if he doesn't, it's going to be off to the scrapheap for him." As soon as she says it, she puts a hand on her PC, "Just kidding, Frank. I'd never recycle you."

She gives me a sheepish look. "I know. I sound insane."

"Not at all," I answer with a wry grin. "But it may not be a bad idea for you and Frank to have a little break from each other, just in case."

Allie laughs, then purses her lips. "I can read the subtext there. You think I'm losing it."

"Anyone would lose it if they were working themselves this hard," I tell her.

She takes off her glasses and rubs her eyes. "Yeah, I could use a break. I honestly don't even know what day it is."

"Friday."

"Already?" She stretches her back a little while I do my best not to let my eyes drift down to her chest.

Whoops. There they are. Wow. And … eye contact time. "Yup. Say, speaking of breaks, do you think you'll still have time to swing by the opera with me tomorrow night?"

Her cheeks turn pink. "Yes. Oh, unless you found a real date."

I narrow my eyes at her. "You are a real date."

"Oh well, sort of, but only because I'm the only single woman you know here."

"That's not why I asked you."

"Yeah, you asked me because my family pressured you into it," she says, putting on her glasses and standing up.

I get up too and swipe my keys and phone off the desk. "Even if they hadn't suggested it, I definitely would have wanted to go with you."

She starts for the hall and I follow her, allowing my gaze to settle on her gorgeous behind. We step outside into the cool evening air, and I walk her to her car. "It's over an hour drive to the opera house, so I'll swing by around six to pick you up if that's okay."

"That sounds perfect."

"See you tomorrow," I say, my eyes flicking down to her lips.

When my gaze meets hers, she's giving me that look that says yes to all the things I'm thinking. "Good night, Hudson. Thank you for everything."

"I'm happy to be a part of it."

And I am. I'm so much happier than I've ever been in my life. Which is a giant fucking problem, isn't it?

20

Too Many Aestheticians in the Kitchen

Allie

"Ouch!" I try to move but Zia Fernanda's grip on my head is too strong.

"Stay still," she says, attacking me with the tweezers again. My right eye starts to water the second she plucks out another one of my errant eyebrow hairs.

It's late Saturday afternoon, and half my family showed up hours ago to help me get ready for my big date (which I keep telling them is not an actual date but a PR stunt). I wish it was a real date. Oh, how I wish. These last few weeks of being with Hudson all day have been pure torture. I've basically given up on the fan because his scent is burned into my brain. Even right now—when I'm being choked by a blend of cheap perfumes worn by my aunt and my sister, who is trimming my cuticles at the moment —my brain can instantly conjure up the smell of Hudson's cologne. Or his skin. I have no idea what it is, but it's got me undone. But I can't let myself believe it's a real date, because that would mean I'd start to believe we have a future together, which we definitely don't. Therefore, tempering my expectations is imperative for my heart.

Lucia stops what she's doing long enough to look at my eyebrows. "I don't think the eyebrow plucking is a good idea. She'll have big red dots all over her face when he gets here."

"First of all, she doesn't have crazy black hairs *all over her face*. Only on her eyebrows," Zia says. "And second, she will not have red marks. I've got a soothing balm I'm going to put on. I've been doing this for almost forty years, and somehow you still don't think I know what I'm doing?"

"She's got very sensitive skin, this one," my mom says, rummaging through her jewelry box for a pair of cubic zirconia studs she bought on the Home Shopping Network back in the 90s.

I wince a little even though Zia's not actually plucking anything at the moment. "Yes, my skin is very sensitive, so maybe we should just leave the rest."

She crouches over me, scouring my face for any last hairs that don't belong. "My niece is about to go on the most important date of her entire life. There is no way in hell I'm sending her out there unless she looks perfect."

My father, who just appeared in the kitchen with an empty espresso mug, shakes his head. "My daughter is perfect the way she is. She doesn't need the plucking or the makeup or anything else. And if she needs all of that stuff to impress this man, then he is not the right man. Because the right man is going to see the beauty in her no matter what's happening with her face."

I smile over at my dad, who's got that look that tells me he's terrified his little girl is about to go out with some big shot actor. And I'm not just guessing about that. I over-heard him saying it to my mom last night when I was on my way down to the kitchen for a snack. He's afraid that

Hudson is going to break my heart, just like 'the other one,' and I have to say, there's a reasonable possibility it could happen. Because no matter how hard I try to tell myself we're just colleagues, it's too late. I'm falling for him, hard. "Thanks, Pops."

"That's very sweet, Enzo," Zia says, gripping my head again. "Totally wrong, but sweet." She quickly yanks out two more hairs and then stands back to admire her handiwork. "Better. In fact, perfect."

Lucia shakes her head. "Unlike these cuticles. Honestly, Allie, I don't understand how you let your nails get so bad."

"She lets them get like this because she's busy being an astronomer all day and all night," my mother says, and to be honest, I'm not sure if she means it as a compliment or an insult.

Zia pours some type of oil onto a cotton pad, then presses it to my stinging eyebrows. It feels cool and soothing and, for the first time since everybody showed up today, I'm not completely annoyed. And I know they're here to help. Well, sort of. They also want to get another glimpse of Hudson.

"I'm going to let your face settle while I do your hair." My aunt smiles at me and pats me on the cheek a little too hard. "You're going to look like a princess."

Forty-five minutes later, my hair has been swept off my neck into a surprisingly lovely and rather complicated updo, my nails have been painted a soft pink, and my makeup is flawless for the second time in my life. The first time was when Zia got me ready for my senior prom. I'm dressed in an off-the-shoulder chiffon gown in various shades of soft pink with a raspberry-colored velvet clutch, both of which belong to my grandma. I stand, staring at myself in the full-length mirror in my parents' bedroom, with half of the family crowded into the room with me.

I glance down at my niece, Camilla. "Well? What do you think?"

"I think you can actually look like a real lady with enough help."

Children are so good for the ego, no?

My mom is busy snapping photos of me on her phone while Lucia fluffs out the long skirt of my gown. She glances at her daughter. "Camilla, can you plug your ears for second, sweetie?"

Nodding, Camilla sticks a finger in each ear. As soon she does, Lucia says, "I am so jealous right now, you lucky bitch. I'm not sure I'll ever get over this."

She gives her daughter the nod that it's okay for her to take her fingers out of her ears. Camilla scrunches up her face. "Were you talking about sex?"

Jaws drop around the room and Lucia's face turns bright red. "No! Of course not. Zia Allie is not married."

Giving her mom a skeptical look, Camilla says, "Mom, I know how it works. People don't have to be married to do sex."

Grandma makes a loud *tsk*ing sound, then says, "You never should've let them go to public school."

The doorbell rings, putting an end to the conversation and causing the entire room to erupt with squeals of excitement. Oh God, I hope he can't hear that from the front entrance.

"Okay ladies, let's keep it down," I say.

"Aren't you excited, *cara*?" my mom asks.

"No, I'm nervous. That television crew will be there again, so I'm pretty much going to be spending the entire time trying not to make a fool of myself."

"Oh God, I never even thought of that," Lucia says. "It could totally happen."

"Shush, you," mom says, waving her hand at my sister.

Turning to me, she says, "Everything is going to work out beautifully. You're a vision and he is a handsome, charming man, and tonight is the start of what will be a wonderful life together. And if you play your cards right, you're going to have the most beautiful babies."

"So they *are* going to do sex," Camilla mutters.

My face heats up and thankfully, my father saves me from the rest of this conversation by calling up the stairs. "Allegra, that Hudson guy is here to pick you up. Do you still want to go?"

I hurry out of the room and glare down at him over the railing, then whisper, "Of course I still want to go."

"I wasn't sure because you are taking so long to come down."

My relatives come pouring out into the hallway and scoot around me, rushing down the stairs to greet him while my mom hangs back a bit. "You ready?"

I nod, feeling my heart in my throat. "I just need to grab my glasses."

She shakes her head. "You can't wear glasses with this dress. That would be sacrilegious."

"Sacrilegious?"

"You know what I mean. It'll look bad. It'll ruin all of Zia's hard work."

"But what if I need to read something?"

"Get him to read it for you. Men love it when we make them feel smart." She places her hand on the middle of my back and corrals me toward the stairs. "You don't need your glasses. Let yourself be beautiful for once in your life."

"Gee, thanks."

"You know I think you're beautiful, but just not *this* beautiful most days," she answers. "No one is this beautiful most days."

I lift the long skirt with one hand and grip the railing

with the other as I navigate my way down the staircase in a pair of Lucia's heels. As soon as I turn the corner, I see Hudson standing in the front entry looking incredible. He's dressed in a tuxedo that I'm sure was tailor-made for him, and the look on his face dissolves all my nervousness in an instant, replacing it with pure joy. I don't even care that my entire family is standing here crowded into the front room, and, from the sexy smile he's wearing, I don't think he cares either. Although technically he is a professional at smiling, so...

I straighten out my shoulders and do my best to walk like a woman who knows how to wear high heels. When I reach him, I say, "Hi."

He glances down at my dress then back up at my face. "You look stunning."

"I bet you say that to all the girls."

Shaking his head, he says, "I'm not sure I've ever used that word in my whole life."

My grandma pipes in with, "Well, it's my dress."

Hudson chuckles a little and smiles down at her. "It's a beautiful dress. Thank you for lending it to Allegra."

Based on the *aww* sound coming from around the room, I'm pretty sure he just made every woman in this house fall in love with him. Looking back at me, he says, "We should probably go."

"Yes, please," I say, giving him a 'get me out of here' look.

He pushes the front door open, then holds out his arm for me. I reach up and put my hand inside the crook of his elbow as if it's the most normal thing in the world for me to be doing—to be walking out my front door all dressed up in formal wear with one of the world's most famous leading men.

I can see the entire neighborhood has been given

advanced warning of this evening's events, because somehow everyone is out working on their front yards. Actually, now that I look at them, I notice that a lot of them aren't even pretending to have a reason to be out here, and are instead holding up their phones filming us.

"Wait! Allegra," my mom calls from the front step.

Hudson and I both turn, only to see her rushing towards us. "I forgot to get a picture of you two."

"Oh God, Ma," I start to say, but Hudson wraps his arm around my waist and pulls me in, and the rest of my sentence disappears from my mind before I can even think it.

"Perfect. I can get the limo in too," she says, holding up her phone.

I smile at her, and it's a real smile, one born of hope and possibilities and the thrill of having the perfect man's arm around me on a perfect, albeit chilly, evening. A few seconds later, the rest of my family joins them on the lawn, all holding up their phones. Out of the corner of my mouth, I say, "I'm sorry about this."

"Don't worry about it. I'm used to it."

When they've all got their shots, my dad says, "Hey, Mr. Finch. My daughter's coach turns into a pumpkin at midnight, so have her home before then."

"Pop, I'm thirty-five," I hiss.

"And you're still my little girl."

"Midnight it is, sir," Hudson says, not sounding the least bit offended.

Pointing at Hudson's pants, my dad says, "And the pepper stays in the pepper mill."

My face flames with embarrassment and rage, and I give my dad the mother of all glares as Hudson carefully spins me to face the car and gestures for me to get in. I step in and slide out of his way, then watch as he settles himself next to me. I'm honestly tempted to slap my own face just to make sure this is really happening because the entire thing feels like a fairy tale. A dream that I never want to wake up from. Well, other than my ridiculously over-protective father. But the rest of it? Incredible.

How is this my life right now?

———

"I've been in a limo exactly one time—on my way to my prom," I tell Hudson as soon as the driver closes the door. I glance around at the massive light grey leather couch that wraps around three sides of the vehicle's interior. "I prob-ably shouldn't have said that. It's not exactly the type of information that makes me sound cool in any way, shape, or form."

Hudson smiles down at me. "You know what makes you cool, Allie?"

"Nothing," I answer with a little grin.

"I'm going to ignore that because it's categorically untrue," he says. "What's cool about you is you're not afraid to be yourself."

I look down at my dress. "I don't exactly feel like myself tonight."

He tilts his head. "In a good way or a bad way?"

"Somehow both at the same time. I feel a little bit glamorous for the first time ever, but also, I'd kind of love to be in that pair of pajamas Stephen sent you."

Chuckling, Hudson says, "I completely understand. To be honest, I pretty much hate these types of appearances —award shows, galas, photo ops. It's the part of the busi-ness I could do without. But tonight, being here with you is different."

"Different in a good way or a bad way?"

"One-hundred-percent good," he says, leaning over and opening the mini-fridge. "Water? Champagne?"

"Water. If I have any alcohol, I'll sleep through the last half of the opera, and I don't want to miss a second of it."

He hands me a water and takes one for himself too. "Now, tell me about your first time in a limo because I noticed you only said you took it on the way to the prom, and now I'm dying to know how you got home."

I cringe a little, then say, "My parents had to pick me up because I was so wasted the limo driver wouldn't let me back in the car. He was not wrong either because I definitely got sick."

"Oooh, been there."

"But the ride there was amazing. I can still feel the excitement of it—the anticipation of a night when anything and everything seemed possible."

"Those are the best nights," he says, his gaze so intense it's doing all sorts of things to my lady bits.

Like tonight maybe? I nod, and swallow hard. "Definitely."

"Speaking of anything being possible," Hudson says, pulling a purple velvet box out of a white gift bag. "One of the perks of my job is that people are willing to lend me things like this." He flips the lid to reveal a necklace made entirely of round diamonds set in white gold. "I thought it would suit you."

My heart pounds in my chest and my throat suddenly feels thick. "Are those real?" I whisper.

He chuckles a little. "Yes, they're real."

"It's beautiful. And so sparkly." And definitely doesn't belong on someone like me. Shaking my head, I say, "No, I can't…"

Taking it out of the box, he says, "Yes, you can. Turn around."

"But what if I wreck it or lose it?"

"You won't."

"But what if I do?"

"Then, nothing. They're going to get a lot of free advertising which is worth more than the necklace," Hudson says. "Now, turn around already so I can put this on you."

I do as he asked, my stomach flipping as he lifts his hands over my head. The necklace is both cool against my skin and much heavier than I expected, but I don't have time to think about that because his fingertips are brushing against the back of my neck, sending the most delightful surges of warmth through my entire body. After a few seconds, he says, "There."

And with that, his hands are gone long before I'm ready. I turn to him, instinctively reaching for the necklace and running my fingers over the jewels.

When I look up at him, Hudson is smiling. "It looks like it was made for you."

"Thank you," I tell him.

"Thank you for taking time off to come with me."

"I'm pretty sure I'm getting the better end of the deal."

Shaking his head, he says, "Not even close. You should see who they were going to set me up with." He pulls a face that makes me laugh.

"That bad?"

"The worst. I've never met a person so full of herself. And nasty too. Not to mention a complete airhead."

"Well in that case, you're welcome."

He grins at me, his eyes flicking down to my lips. "Yes, I'm pretty sure tonight is one of those nights where anything and everything is possible."

Oh good lord, I hope so, because I want to do anything and everything with him so badly it hurts…

21

Just When You Think It's Safe to Get Back in the Water...

Hudson

THE RIDE to the War Memorial Opera House in San Francisco is just over an hour, and believe me, I'm spending the entire time trying not to imagine all the things we could be doing in the back of this limo. Things that would mess up her hair. Things I've been trying not to imagine when I'm in her office with her every day.

Because I knew this would be a problem for me, I planned ahead and brought out a little picnic spread of grapes, cheese, and crackers. "Something to hold us over until after the show," I tell her as I set the basket on the seat between us.

"Basket food? My favorite," she says with an adorable grin.

"And the best part is, I only picked foods that won't stain our clothes if we drop them."

"Genius."

"I have my moments. Dig in," I tell her, plucking a grape out of the bunch.

"I'm actually starving," Allie says, picking up a cracker and placing a slice of white cheddar on it.

"I figured you might be. Women never seem to eat before these things," I answer. "They're always too busy getting ready."

"It really was so much more work than I thought it would be. I can see why a lot of celebrities have an entire team for these types of things."

"Yeah, that's why I generally don't show up at most of the award shows. I can't stand the idea of wasting an entire afternoon having my hair done when I could be out surfing or doing something else I love."

She has a bite of cheese and cracker, and I watch her while she chews and swallows it, knowing she has something to say. "But the guys must not need hours to get ready, right? Can't you just throw on a tux and go?"

"Oh God, you should see all the stuff we do. Skin treatments, hair masks, it's a whole thing. Mind you, it's a lot easier than what the women are doing, but still, it's ridiculous."

"Do you ever want to just quit?" Allie asks, her enormous brown eyes fixed on me.

My gut tightens at the thought of my career ending. "I don't know what else I'd do."

"You could … open a surf shop or go back to college and become something boring like an engineer or a lawyer."

"I like the surf shop idea," I answer. "Somewhere down in Mexico maybe, right on the beach. That sounds pretty good."

"It does, doesn't it?" she says. "Afternoon siestas in a hammock under some palm trees, watching the sun set over the water every night."

"Oh man, my agent is going to hate you because you're literally talking me into giving it all up."

We both laugh a little, then her face grows serious. "We can't have that. You've got dozens of wonderful movies to make."

"Well, one, anyway," I tell her. "After that, who knows? Maybe I will be waxing surf boards for a living."

"You're worried about it, aren't you?"

Nodding, I say, "This one is … really important. If I don't blow the audience away, and more importantly, the critics, I'm done for."

She scrunches up her face in confusion. "What are you talking about? You're one of the most popular actors in the world."

"Yeah, as the young, fun guy, but my last couple of movies didn't perform the way they used to, and I made one a few months ago that tested so poorly, the studio decided not to put it out," I tell her, my jaw clenching.

"Oh Hudson, I'm sorry. That sounds awful. All that hard work for nothing," she says, placing her hand over mine. It's warm and soft and comforting, and I flip my hand so I can lace my fingers through hers. We both stare at our intertwined hands, and for a brief second, I'm worried that she's going to pull away, but she doesn't. She looks up at me instead. "But I'm sure it wasn't you. It must have been a bad script or poor directing."

Shaking my head, I say, "The audience didn't like me in it. They actually said I should've been the villain."

"Ouch."

"Yeah, not ideal."

"So that's why you're here. I thought it was just a PR thing."

"That's part of it, for sure. Laying the groundwork for my new image. I have to convince the world I am Dr.

David Todd, or this whole life," I say, pointing around the limo, "is over. And even though there are parts of it I don't enjoy, I really love the job itself. It's the only thing I've ever been really good at, you know? And if I lose that, I don't know who I'll be."

"You won't lose it, Hudson. But even if you did, or you decided to walk away, there's so much more to you than just your acting ability."

I shake my head. "Before I got into this, I literally never had a day in my life when I felt remotely good about myself. I was pretty much just a screw-up."

"You were a kid."

"But most kids are good at something—music, school, sports. The only thing I could do was make people laugh, and by people, I mean the other boys. I didn't exactly have a lot of potential, you know?"

"So you were a late bloomer. Lots of highly successful people are late bloomers. Einstein didn't walk until he was two, and he had trouble learning to pronounce words. Look what he accomplished."

"I'm no Einstein, Allie," I tell her. "In fact, I'm about as far from a genius as you can get." I look up at the ceiling for a second, then add, "Except right now I'm holding the hand of a real genius, so I guess that's pretty close."

She doesn't laugh, which was what I was hoping she'd do because I really need to lighten the mood. Not just for her, but for me. This is not something I talk about with people. Ever. Instead, she stares at me for a second and chews her bottom lip. "You're underestimating yourself."

I open my mouth to object, but she lets go of my hand and puts her finger over my lips. "Facts aren't up for debate. You're definitely underestimating yourself. And I just realized I owe you an apology."

"For what?"

"I've been leaving you to your own devices this entire time when I should've been helping you learn."

"Hey, I've been learning. Those videos and the podcast? All good stuff."

Shaking her head, she says, "Not good enough. First thing tomorrow morning, we need to get to work."

"Allie, you can't—"

"I can do both. Trust me," she says in a firm voice that makes me believe her.

Smiling at her, I say, "Someone needs to make a movie about you."

She grins back. "That would be the world's most boring movie."

"Would not. You're the most fascinating woman I've ever met."

She opens her mouth, but this time I stop her with a finger to her lips. "Facts aren't up for debate."

By the time we arrive at the opera house, we've switched gears from our serious heart-to-heart to having pure unadulterated fun. We've been competing over who has the most embarrassing moments. I just told her about my first ever nude scene when the weather dropped ten degrees by the time we were ready to film, and she told me about a time when she tried to see if she could do a somersault in the ocean, only to pop out of the water with a victory leap to discover her bikini top had slid down to her ribcage.

The limo pulls to a stop, and I glance out to see the camera crew waiting. When I look back at Allie, I can see she's nervous. "You're going to be fine."

"I'm going to make an ass of myself."

"No, you won't. I'll be right there with you the whole time holding your hand."

The door opens and I get out, then turn back and hold

my hand out for her. Allie steps out of the limo, a vision of loveliness that I hope the cameras are able to capture. I smile down at her, proud to be here with her, even if it's just for tonight. As soon as she's standing next to me, I lean in and say, "You truly are stunning. Not just in this dress either."

Her cheeks flush and she offers me a soft gaze. "You're good at this."

"I'm just being honest," I answer as the flashes from the camera go off. "Come on, let's get inside."

I offer a quick nod and a smile to the crew as we hurry past them. In under a minute, the entire thing is over and we're inside the brightly lit lobby. I turn to Allie. "There. All done. We could actually leave if you want to."

Shaking her head, she grins. "No way. Let's go watch the ultimate cautionary tale for players."

It takes us nearly fifteen minutes to get to our seats. We're stopped every few feet by someone wanting to say hi or get a photo. Allie is gracious about the whole thing, even offering to take the pictures. When we're finally in the box on the second floor, I turn to her. "Thank you. You were wonderful about all that."

"It was fun."

"I love meeting fans, but it can get in the way sometimes, like tonight, when I'm trying to show a girl a good time."

She grins at me. "Don't worry. I'm having the best time."

She holds up the playbill. "My only problem is that I love reading about the cast before a play, and I let my mom talk me out of bringing my glasses."

A pit forms in my stomach because I know where this is going.

She holds it up to me. "Do you mind reading it to me?"

Desperation sweeps over me as I glance at the playbill, then back up to her face. Lifting her chin, I say, "I have something more fun in mind."

Leaning in, I leave just the tiniest bit of space between our lips. We're so close I can feel the warmth of her skin. "I know it's customary to wait until the end of the first date to do this, but I'd very much like to kiss you right now."

22

If Cinderella Had Been Set in the Time of Smart Phones...

Allie

OH MY GOD. Is this happening? Does he actually want to kiss me? Here? Now? The look on his face says the answer is yes. He wants to kiss me. In public, where any one of the hundreds of people in the audience could just look up and see us sitting in this box. Hudson Finch wants to kiss me. Every cell of my body hums with excitement. I lick my lips, then I hear myself saying, "But this isn't a real first date. It's a PR stunt."

What the hell, Allie? When Hudson Finch says he wants to kiss you, you say yes.

He glances at my lips and moves in a little closer. "We get to decide what this is," he murmurs, cupping my jaw with his hand. "And I want this to be a real first date."

Say yes, idiot. Say yes and kiss him before he changes his mind. "You do?"

Giving me that smile from his *People's* Sexiest Man cover, he nods. "But only if it's what you want, Allie."

"I don't know. I mean, it definitely sounds so much more fun than you reading the playbill to me, so…"

"Yes or no, Allie."

"Yes."

My eyelids drift shut and he closes the distance between us, kissing me softly, carefully, making sure I want this. And after a second, my grip on the playbill loosens and I feel it slip out of my fingers. I lift my hand to his jaw and feel his smooth skin against my fingertips and breathe in the scent of him that's been making me wild for three long, torturous weeks. I let out a little moan that feels suddenly desperate and slightly embarrassing, because that little sound is an admission that it's been *years* since I've been properly kissed. But his reaction tells me I have nothing to be embarrassed about. I part my lips to give him more access and he takes it, sliding his tongue into my waiting mouth, doing things to me that I never thought would happen, things I've been dreaming and thinking about when I'm supposed to be working.

Our mouths move together like they've always known each other, and yet it's also new and fresh. It's intoxicating and amazing and terrifying all at the same time. I know we shouldn't be doing this, but there's no way I want to stop. He tilts my head back a little further, his hand moving to the back of my neck, his thumb caressing my cheek tenderly while his lips and tongue wake up parts of me that have forgotten what a man can do. All this time I've been pretending I don't need or want or care about this. But I do. I want it. I want it all. And I want it from him. I've never felt more like a woman than I do in this very moment, here with Hudson.

A light cough from behind us interrupts the moment, and we pull away from each other, both of us trying not to laugh as an older couple who will be sharing the box take their seats behind us. My face flames with … well, everything … while Hudson turns to them and smiles. "Good evening."

"Hello," the man says with a knowing grin.

"Say, aren't you that actor?" the woman says.

"I'm Hudson, nice to meet you." He holds out his hand to shake each of theirs while the man says, "I'm Jack and this is Jackie, my wife. And who's this lovely lady?"

"This is Dr. Allegra Cammareri. She's an astronomer and the most impressive person I know."

Oh my God. Best introduction ever. Yes, I will marry you. I will be your wife. Not that he's asking…

Jack offers me a wry grin. "Yeah, you looked pretty impressed with her a minute ago."

Jackie smacks his arm. "Shush. You'll embarrass them." She turns to me. "We were young and in love once too. Pretend we're not here."

"They're hardly going to make out with us sitting two feet away," Jack says. "Sorry to kill the moment."

"That's fine," I tell them, even though my lady bits are yelling at me that it's absolutely not fine at all. "It's probably better that we stopped there."

The lights dim and the audience starts to applaud. Hudson and I turn to face the stage, my mind swirling and my heart pounding as the opera starts. He slips his hand onto my lap and interlaces his fingers with mine, spreading warmth from the top of my head to my toes. This is a proper date. A proper *first* date, he called it, which means he wants more of them. We're all dressed up and I look beautiful for once in my life and he's holding my hand and I have no idea what's happening on the stage because my thoughts are booming and sparkling like fireworks and my heart is exploding with joy and all I can think about is how very badly I want to climb onto his lap and crush his mouth with mine and run my hands all over him and frantically take off this dress and his tux and go so much farther than would be considered even remotely smart with a man like him.

The entire first half of the opera my mind races like this, thoughts of all the lusty, wonderful things I want to do with him swirling around in my head. What if we do them all as soon as this is over? What if we get in the limo and pick this up where we left off? Would I actually have sex with him? In the back of a limo? Yes. I would. I'd happily go for that ride. And it may sound cheap or sleazy, but it wouldn't be. Not with him. Not with the way he takes care of me at every turn. He's everything I've always wanted, and the truth is, I'm in love with him. Totally and completely in love with him. As much as I've been trying to convince my heart to stay dammed up, he's managed to break it open and now all the emotions are just pouring through me. There is literally nothing I can do to stop it. Not that I'd want to. So I'm going to sit here holding his hand, and after the standing ovation, when we get back in that limo, I'm going to have a glass or two of champagne to bolster my courage, then make it very clear that I want him. All of him. And I want him tonight.

The lights come up for the intermission and Hudson turns to me. "How about a glass of champagne?"

"I'd love one."

We stand, then slowly follow the crowd in the direction of the lobby. I can feel his hand on my lower back and it's all I can do not to press myself against his fingertips. When I look back, I see he's got his phone out and his face is screwed up as he stares at the screen. "Shit," he mutters.

"What's wrong?"

"I'm really sorry, but we need to get out of here," he says. "I'll explain it when we're in the car."

My heart beats a little quicker as I take in the worried expression on his normally relaxed face. He types something into his phone before we walk down the wide staircase to the main floor. "Come on. We need to go out the back."

He takes my hand and leads me to the back entrance, then stares out the window. As soon as the limo pulls up, he says, "Let's go. We need to hurry."

The driver steps out and opens the door for us while Hudson and I rush to the car. I get in first, then slide out of his way and wait, my stomach twisting as I wonder what the hell is going on.

Once the door is closed, he lets out a sigh and stares at me for a second. "Someone was filming us when we were in the balcony."

"What do you mean? It's already on the internet?"

He nods. "Unfortunately, yes."

I stare at him for a second, watching as his jaw clenches and he glances out the window, wondering if my coach has already turned into a pumpkin far before the clock struck twelve. "Well, that's not such a big deal, is it? We were just kissing," I say as the limo crawls through the alley.

"In theory it's not a big deal, but now that it's on video for public consumption, it's going to create a whole new level of interest in you," he says.

I open my clutch and pull out my phone, one part excited and one part terrified. I let a little grin escape at the idea of Lando the Liar seeing me snogging a Hollywood superstar. Suck on that, Lando. I'm moving up in the world. "Let's see what they have to say."

I search Hudson Finch opera date and immediately a bunch of videos pop up. "Whoa. That was fast. The opera's not even over yet."

"Yeah, that's why I wanted to get you out of there. By

the time it is done, the paparazzi will be swarming." The limo pulls out of the alley and when I look out, I see camera crews setting up in front of the opera house. A guy with an enormous lens on his camera spots the limo and comes running toward it, but the driver pulls out and takes off before he can reach us.

"This is not how I was expecting this evening to turn out," I mutter.

"It's a lot to take in, I know."

I offer him a small smile and a shrug. "Well, the whole idea was to get some good publicity, so I suppose we could say mission accomplished."

He smiles back, trying to look reassuring, but I can see in his eyes, he's concerned. I look back down at my phone, my curiosity taking over. I scroll through the videos until I get to a famous celebrity gossip blogger. "Ooh, Ferris Biltmore has already posted about us."

"I don't think you should watch that."

"Why not? He's hilarious."

"But he's not exactly kind. Let's just ... forget about all that nonsense and try to enjoy the rest of the evening."

I glance at him for a second, then press play, my stomach in knots.

Ferris stares at the camera for a second, then says, "Okay, bitches, breaking news out of San Fran tonight. My Hudson is out on a date and it looks like they're heating up the opera house. Check it out." The feed cuts and a video of us starts up. We're sitting in the balcony and just as I'm holding up the playbill, the camera zooms in on us. I watch as Hudson tells me he would very much like to kiss me. You can't tell what he's saying on the video, but his words are burned into my soul. We talk for another few seconds, and now he's kissing me.

Oh God, is that what I look like when I'm kissing? Why is my chin doing that? And why are there two of them? I don't have two chins. Do I?

The video stops and Ferris bites his knuckle. "Okay, so here's the scoop on the woman in question. I already got the dirt from my cousin's best friend's pet psychic who knows a guy who went to school with her. Her name is Allegra Cammareri and she may look pretty here, but trust me, she ain't in Hudson's league."

"Okay, let's shut this off." Hudson tries to take the phone from me, but I pull it away.

Ferris rolls his eyes. "This brings me to my first segment of the night, 'Hudson, What Are You Thinking?!'"

The words appear next to his head and Ferris shouts in the camera, "Hudson, what are you thinking?! Making out with this … less-than-average person?!"

A terrible photo of me that Lucia tagged me in on Instagram pops up to replace the graphic. It was taken on my thirtieth birthday, and I was sweaty after being out on the dance floor at the bar. I also had just taken a shot of Sour Puss and my face is all screwed up like the cat on the bottle.

"You're fucking with this?! This?!!!" Ferris says, his pitch going so high I can hardly hear him.

My body goes numb as Hudson slides the phone out of my hand and shuts it off. "Shit. Sorry."

I sit, stunned, humiliated, and hurt, tears stinging my eyes as Ferris's words blare through my brain.

"I know it's hard, but try not to take it personally. He wouldn't be happy no matter who I was with."

I nod a little, trying to pretend I'm fine with the whole thing. "It's all good. I know he's got a thing for you. And that picture of me is probably the worst one anyone has ever taken. I'm going to kill my sister for posting that."

"You're fine. You just look like you're having a really fun time," he says. "Unlike now."

I chew on my bottom lip, my mind racing to figure out what this is all going to mean. "Okay, so the team is obviously going to find out, and oh, crap, my family too."

Hudson winces. "Your dad."

Nodding, I say, "Yeah, and you thought it was awkward when he just *suspected* you of wanting to…" I trail off, not finishing the sentence because I honestly don't know what Hudson wants from me. "Maybe don't come over tomorrow for Sunday dinner."

"Yeah, that would be the smart play," he says, rubbing the back of his neck. He lets out a long sigh. "I shouldn't have kissed you like that. I knew better and I'm sorry."

My entire body feels hot, but not in a good way—hot with shame. I stare down at my hands and fold them on my lap, not knowing what to say.

"That didn't come out the way I intended. I'm not sorry I kissed you, I'm sorry I kissed you in such a public place because now your life is about to get a whole lot more complicated."

"I'll be fine."

"Just … don't go looking online. It won't do you any good to read the shitty things people have to say."

"Some of them may be nice."

"You won't remember the nice comments. Only the nasty ones. Trust me. I know."

We're quiet for a long time, then Hudson says, "Hey, would you like to get something to eat? I hate that the night is ending so early."

I shake my head, my stomach too tied up in knots to want to eat. "No, thanks. I think it would just draw more attention."

"What if we go through a drive thru? In-N-Out Burger?"

"I don't want anything, but we can stop if you're hungry."

"That's okay. Why don't I just get you home?"

"Yes, that would be good," I answer. "I can't wait to get into some cozy pajamas and crawl into bed." Alone. Without the man of my dreams.

I stare out the window for a few minutes, then feel Hudson's arm wrap around my shoulder. He gives me a kiss on top of my head and pulls me close. "I'm sorry."

I let myself lean into him, basking in the warmth that is his body. "Don't be, it's not your fault."

"No, it is."

He holds me like this for the rest of the ride home, neither of us saying or doing anything more than just snuggling together as my mind tries to wrap itself around reality. This is what it would be to be with him. It wouldn't be a fairy tale. It would be the relentless pursuit of privacy. It would be me never measuring up to what society believes Hudson should have. It would be me getting hurt over and over again. I close my eyes and let my thoughts drift, feeling hollow and alone, even though he's right here.

When we pull up in front of my parents' house, the lights are still on, which means my parents are still awake. I reach up and unclasp the necklace, letting it drop into my hand. My skin feels cold and empty where the jewels were, and I hand them to him with a sad smile. "Thank you for the lovely evening."

"It wasn't lovely. I screwed it up," he says, sliding the necklace in his jacket pocket.

"You tried. That's what matters," I answer. "Besides, even half a date with someone like you is a once-in-a-life-time thing for a girl like me."

The driver opens the door and Hudson gets out, then holds his hand out to me, and I take it, allowing him to help me. He grips my hand and turns toward the front door, but I stay put. "I think it's better if we say goodbye here."

Hudson opens his mouth to protest, then closes it and nods. "All right. The last thing I want is to make things harder for you."

"I'm fine. I'll see you Monday, work buddy," I tell him with a little punch on his arm.

"See you Monday."

I start toward the house, but he stops me with his voice. "Allie, wait. Let's not end things like this."

Turning to him, I say, "It's the only possible ending. I've already gone through all the possible scenarios in my mind and they all end exactly like this, only much, much worse."

He was right when he said I wouldn't remember the nice comments, not that there are many of them. I will remember the nasty ones forever, because they feel like they've been branded into my soul. It's two a.m. and I'm lying in bed still scrolling, even though I should've been asleep hours ago. Even though I should be working. Even though it's going to do me absolutely no good to read about how I should never wear anything without sleeves until I spend at least a year hitting the gym to tone these sausage arms. It's definitely not good for my self-esteem to read about what a mismatch Hudson and I are or how I should be the poster girl for 'skinny fat,' or how he's really scraping the bottom of the barrel as far as dates go. Oh, and here's another one: CuteGirl24 has posted to Hudson that she's right here in L.A. waiting for him to come back and that she literally has no gag reflex, so that's lovely.

I finally force myself to shut off my phone and put it on the charger. I close my burning eyes, wishing I had never agreed to go out with Hudson. Wishing I'd never met him. And certainly wishing I'd taken his advice about not reading what the trolls have to say. It's hard to believe that only a few hours ago, the world was full of possibilities. I was filled the excitement of the start of something new and wonderful. Only it wasn't. And it can never be. And believing that it could be anything more than something professional makes me the stupidest person to ever walk the Earth.

23

The Fallout

Hudson

"So, you and Allie, hey?" Gersh asks.

"I don't want to talk about it."

"Then you shouldn't be making out with her in front of hundreds of people with smart phones," he says.

It's Sunday morning and I am just realizing I should not have picked up the phone when I saw his name. "Yeah, already figured that out, but thanks."

"Seriously, dude, you might as well have just taken her up on stage and went for it right there."

Plunking myself on the couch, I say, "Yup. Got it. Big mistake. Filled with regret. Don't need you to make it worse."

"You literally pay me to give you advice, which is what I'm doing."

"Oh, so you're talking to me as Gershwyn my manager right now?"

"Of course."

"Because it sounded like you're talking to me as Gersh,

my big brother who wants to break my balls over an already-shit situation," I tell him.

"Maybe it's a bit of both. It's hard to separate one from the other."

"Okay, well, how about you switch to being a supportive big brother who tries to make his sibling feel better about hurting an innocent woman?" My gut tightens even more than it already was. "Seriously, she was totally blindsided. And have you looked at what people are saying about her?"

"Yeah, I saw the whole 'send her to space and leave her there' hashtag," he answers. "Pretty shitty. Maybe she won't see it."

"She'll see it. She's the most curious person I've met. No way she just went to bed and forgot all about it last night," I answer.

"You like this girl."

"Of course I like her. She's … there's nothing not to like," I answer, not wanting to start listing the thousand things I like about Allie to my brother who will definitely use it against me later—specifically to embarrass me if he ever meets her.

"So, if you like her and she likes you, who cares? Just go about your business starting a relationship with her and see where it goes."

"It's not that simple."

"Why not?"

"Because she's a doctor, Gersh. A literal rocket scientist. I think. Maybe being an astrophysicist isn't the same thing, and the fact that I *don't* know the answer to that means she and I aren't going to wind up together," I tell him, knowing it's true. "She could spend the next year slowly explaining what she does to me like I'm a five-year-old and I still won't fully understand it."

"So what? Lots of perfectly happy couples don't have an intimate knowledge of what their partner does for a living."

"Name one."

"Umm... Bill and Melinda Gates."

"Okay, worst couple you could've brought up."

"Why? They seem happy and there's no way anyone understands what Bill Gates did for a living."

"First of all, they're divorced. Second, do you even know how they met?"

"No," he says, sounding slightly sheepish.

"She worked in product development at Microsoft, so I have a feeling she understood exactly what Bill did for a living."

"And see how unimportant that was? They're divorced. If anything, *not* knowing what your wife does is a plus."

"Nobody's getting married here. It was one kiss. And when we left, we both realized it wasn't going to go any farther."

"Seriously? Nothing? You didn't give her the old hot beef injection when you got in the limo?"

"Oh my God, how is it that I let you manage my money?"

"Don't change the subject," he says. "You clearly like this girl and so far you've provided no good reason not to give it a go."

"She's already married to her job, and since my career is teetering on the edge, I can't exactly move up to San Jose, now can I? And don't bother suggesting we have a fling because she's not that type of girl."

"Why not? She's an adult—a highly intelligent one at that. She can make up her own mind about that, can't she?"

I chew on my lip for a second before I answer him. "She's not built that way. For meaningless flings."

"How do you know? Did she tell you that?"

"She didn't have to. I just know." Standing up, I walk across the living room and stare out the patio doors. "She's not exactly sophisticated when it comes to relationships. She's been hurt before, and I can't be just another guy to…"

"Hit it and quit it?"

"Exactly," I say, running my hand through my hair out of pure frustration. "Which is why I never should've kissed her in the first place. In public or not."

"So why did you?"

I think back to the desperation I was feeling when she asked me to read to her. Not wanting to admit that, I say, "I guess I was overcome by the moment."

"And clearly she was too, which, if I'm not mistaken, could be the sign that you have some serious chemistry. You can at least give it a try," he says. "And before you say it, don't give me the 'I'm too stupid to date someone like her' bullshit because in case you don't know, you bring a lot to the table yourself."

"Yeah, like trolls and raving maniac fans who will make her life a living hell."

"So she'll have to delete her social media apps or learn to ignore it. Every relationship has trade-offs."

"She won't have to because there is no relationship. I'm only here for another couple of weeks, then I'm leaving and she's staying here to do her important work and probably marry a fellow genius so they can eventually populate Mars."

"Wanker."

"Asshat."

"I'm hanging up now."

"Fine, but do you know what the saddest two words in the English language are?"

"You're fired?"

"Haha, very funny," he says. "What if?"

"As in, what if I get so sick of your shit, I fire you? Huh, not that sad, actually."

"As in, what if she's the love of your life and you just let her slip away and end up growing old alone?"

"I'm sure you'll still be squatting in my house when I'm ninety."

"Sad."

"Yeah, it is. Goodbye."

"Bye bro. Think about it. It's not too late."

"It's not going to happen." I hang up on him before he can say anything else. A second later, my phone buzzes and I see a text from him.

GERSHWYN

What if?

He follows that with a gif of a toddler who looks like he's about to cry.

GERSHWYN

That's the son you'll never have because you're being a stubborn idiot.

ME

You just made my point for me, so thank you.

I stare at our exchange for a second, then shake my head. I don't have to ask 'what if' because I already know. She and I are not meant to be, but only because she can do much, much better.

———

Instagram Reel: Hollywood Dish with Ferris Biltmore

The video starts with Ferris sitting outside at a coffee shop sipping a large drink in a to-go cup. When he lowers the cup, his upper lip has a frothy mustache. "Hello, beotches, I've been up all night to get you intel on what happened with our sexy sex god, Hudson, and his date who I'm dubbing Miss Match, as in she's a total mismatch for a man that fine. Hence the Americano with a double espresso shot topped with an espresso foam. I've been sucking these babies back all day and I have no intention to stop now, so if you want to buy me a coffee for all the sacrifices I make on your behalf, hit the button below. Pulease and thank you."

He has another sip, then says, "It took me until nearly six this morning, but I finally heard back from my landlord's nephew's girlfriend whose brother is a limo driver. No, not the limo from the now-infamous video of Hudson and Miss Match fleeing the opera at half-time. But someone who knows someone at that company and who managed to get a peek at the records for the night. Apparently, Hudson the Hottie dropped her off at home, and left immediately. And get this, it turns out Miss Match still lives with her parents!" Ferris bursts out laughing. "Even though, all signs point to the fact that she's 35-years-old. OLD, people! Far too old for Hudson, who should be just about ready to settle down with some 24-year-old temptress who can make lots of perfect babies without worrying about her aging eggs. I'm too tired and wired to do a bunch of segments but because you bitches are so desperate, I'm going to do one, but it'll be a good one."

The words: *Run, Hudson, Run!* appear on the screen.

"Run, Hudson, run like hell! You have *got* to get away from this walking disaster. This, this queen of the geeks. This!" The words disappear only to be replaced by the photo of Allie after her Sour Puss shot. "Look, I don't know what came over you last night. I don't know if she went all Cosby on your ass and you didn't know what you were doing, or maybe you were swept up in a whole *Pretty Woman* at the opera thing, or if this was some sort of Make-a-Wish thing, only for terminally pathetic women, but Hudson, honey, this has to stop. Now. Before she kills your reputation completely and you never get to pork another supermodel again in your life. Think it through, Hudson, and run. Seriously. Run like hell."

The Next Day

Well, this blows. Allie has completely gone into professional astrophysicist-mode. She can barely look at me, and when she does, the pain in her eyes is a clear indicator that she spent way too many hours reading all the shitty things people said about her on the internet. She's given Frank a quarter of a million recording snippets to analyze and the two of us have been sitting next to each other for the last hour as she goes over the highlights in her Astronomy 101 textbook for me. It's awkward and uncomfortable and hard as hell to be so close to her without getting to touch her.

I've been doing my best to focus on what she's saying because I know it's important and I owe it to her, but I just can't concentrate. Not with this whole shitstorm happening.

The rest of the people on her team aren't exactly helping either. There's been a lot of winking and giggling and 'Hey, you two certainly seemed to be having a good time on Saturday,' and honestly, each comment makes me feel a little smaller. Not because I don't want people to know I'm attracted to her, but because this whole thing blew up in her face before we could even figure out what was going on between us. And I wound up doing the last thing I meant to do—hurting her.

"Are you sure you don't want to write some of this down?" she asks.

"No, keep going and I'll read through it on my own later, and take notes then," I answer. "I don't want to waste your time."

"Okay, well, I get the feeling you're having trouble concentrating. Do you need a break?" She finally looks at me, her beautiful brown eyes killing me.

"I think we need to talk about what happened," I say. "I have a terrible feeling you went down the rabbit hole after I dropped you off."

Shrugging, she looks back down at the book. "I couldn't care less what a bunch of idiots hiding behind their keyboards have to say about me. What I do care about is my project and getting you ready for your movie. And I'm going to lose an entire day going up to Black Creek on Thursday, so let's stay focused on the matter at hand, okay?"

Ugh. Being in a vehicle alone together for a total of ten hours is going to suck hard if I can't fix this. "Allie—"

Holding up one hand, she says, "Nope. None of that

matters and dwelling on it won't fix anything. It'll just rob us of time we don't have."

"Can I at least ask if your family has been giving you a hard time?"

"They've been surprisingly supportive. Except my idiot brother-in-law who thinks the whole thing is hilarious. And my dad, who threw out the pepper mill."

"Seriously?"

"Yeah, supper was on the bland side last night, but it doesn't matter. We need to get this done."

"Allie, I'm really sorry—"

"Don't be. It wasn't your fault that some thimble-headed douche decided to record what should have been a private moment and posted it for the world to see."

"But it *is* my fault. I know people are watching me. I just … momentarily forgot."

"Who would think someone at the opera would do something so low?" she asks, looking completely disgusted. "The *opera*?"

"There are assholes literally everywhere."

"Yeah, well they can suck it," she says. "And so can all those trolls and half your fans who very clearly have an unhealthy obsession with you."

"Yes, they can. They can all suck it," I answer, glad to see her looking angry instead of hurt.

"And I take back what I said about Ferris Biltmore being hilarious, because he's actually really awful. And I feel bad that I ever watched his videos to begin with because I now realize that every time he's doing that, a real human being is getting hurt."

"I wish he would stop. Or at least move on to someone else. And I'm sorry that you got caught up in this whole thing because the last thing I intended was for you to get hurt. I wanted to take you out and give you the kind of night you deserve."

She tilts her head, then says, "It really started out that way. Things just kind of … spun out of control in a very big way."

"They really did."

We stare at each other for a second too long, then she clears her throat and looks away. "Okay, good. Now that we got that out of the way, let's get back to stellar evolution because there's no way I can let you leave here without knowing that."

"For what it's worth, I'm not sorry I kissed you. I'm just sorry that it all blew up."

Her cheeks turn pink and she looks back down at the book. "So, stars are formed from clouds of dust and gas as they collapse."

"It's kind of disappointing, isn't it?"

"That things blew up?" she asks, scrunching up her nose a little. "Yes, I mean, obviously it's not how I thought the night would end."

"I was talking about the stars," I answer. "But out of curiosity, how *did* you think the night would end?"

Her entire face turns red and she glances at the ceiling. "I refuse to answer that question on the grounds of trying to salvage a professional relationship."

Grinning, I say, "Come on, you can't just leave me hanging like that."

Clearing her throat, she says, "I most certainly can. Now, what exactly is so disappointing about stars?"

"You're not going to tell me, are you?" I ask, two parts turned on and one part horribly disappointed that whatever she had in that beautiful mind of hers is never going to happen.

"Definitely not." She taps her textbook with her index

finger. "Back to stellar evolution. You were talking about how disappointing the billions of stars are, which, quite frankly is unimaginable to me."

"It's just that all those bright, twinkly stars are just big balls of dust and gas."

She gives me a hint of a wry smile. "Yeah, kind of like the ones from Hollywood."

"You *are* mad."

"I'm not mad. Well, not at you."

"But you just compared me to a ball of gas."

"Don't forget the dust."

"That too."

"I kind of had to. You set me up so perfectly," she says with a tiny grin.

I smile back as relief washes over me. Maybe the next couple of weeks won't be as awful as I imagined. It's not going to go back to what it was before, with the incredible sexual tension and the lusty thoughts. Well, the thoughts will be there, but the potential for acting on them is totally gone. I've already pushed things way farther than I should have. It's time to get smart and do the right thing. Even if it kills me.

24

Seat Warmers and Sweet, Hot Coffee...

Allie - Thursday

IT's four a.m. and I'm already dressed and ready to go for the day. I'm a bundle of emotions, partly from lack of sleep, but mainly from being in love and being extremely confused about being in love. On a scale of one to ten, I'm a thousand confused. He seems to have feelings for me. That kiss certainly felt real. And the hand holding. But then he backed off so easily, it's made me realize I have to accept the fact that nothing is going to happen between us. Whatever that was on Saturday night, it's over. Dead. Turned to dust and blown into the wind. Not coming back. We've taken three steps back to acting like very professional work colleagues, which is better, even though I hate every minute of it. It's nearly impossible to pretend I'm indifferent to him, not with all these thoughts of all the things I want to do with him floating in and out of my mind without my permission.

I just have to survive the next two weeks with him, then I can move on with my normal life. He'll go back to L.A., the trolls will move onto someone else, and I can start the process of forgetting all about him. But first, I have to get through a very long day alone with him without confessing my undying love. Should be no problem, right? Even though this desperate part of me wants to blurt it out every few seconds whenever I'm around him.

Hudson and I are on our way up to Black Creek so I can show him the radio telescopes. It's over five hours each way and when we get there, I'll be relieving the small team that works there, so they can all have a day off at the same time. They'll come back around dinner time, and Hudson and I will start the long trek back.

I'm standing at the door with a small overnight bag packed and two travel mugs filled with coffee. He pulls up in his truck and I sneak out the front door, hoping not to wake my parents. There's a cold wind that whips my hair around and chills me to the bone by the time I reach his truck.

Hudson's already standing at the passenger door, holding it open. Damn him for being such a gentleman. He takes the coffees from me and sets them in the console cup holders, then slips my bag off my shoulder. "Good morning."

"I'm still calling this night," I tell him as I climb into his Range Rover.

Opening the back passenger door, he puts my bag on the seat, then hurries around to get in out of the cold. I immediately notice that my seat is toasty against my back and thighs. "You pre-warmed my seat for me, thank you."

"And you brought coffees. Thank you," he says. "Which one is not going to give me diabetes?"

I chuckle a little and point to his. "Black like the soul of a man who breaks his Nan's gravy boat, then blames an imaginary raccoon."

He laughs, then pulls away from the curb. "How are you feeling this morning?"

"I haven't decided yet. I'm still forty percent asleep."

"That's oddly specific."

"I'm a scientist. We're a specific bunch," I answer. "How are you feeling?"

"Good. I'm used to long days from being on set."

Of course he is. Mr. Perfect. Oh dammit, I can't be sarcastic about him. He actually *is* perfect. He has a sip of the coffee, then replaces it to the console. "I really appreciate you taking an entire day away from work to go with me," he says. "Not that you had much of a choice in the matter."

"I might as well go. Frank and I need a bit of a break from each other," I answer, yawning. "We're not exactly getting along right now. Besides, I'm happy to go. I like it up there. It's very peaceful."

"Have you spent a lot of time there?"

Nodding, I say, "Just after grad school. Keenan sends everyone up there for a few months so they can learn how to monitor and troubleshoot any equipment problems. It's important that each team member knows this stuff so we can keep the telescopes working."

"Makes sense. He's a great boss."

I let out another yawn, covering it with my hand. "The best."

"That's one of the weird things about being an actor. No real boss, no team that you stay with. I mean, there's always the director, but that changes every job. Unless you're doing a series, that is, which I haven't done since I got my start."

"Do you miss it?"

"Yes, and no. I like trying new things. I love the freedom of what I do, but I miss working with the same people every day. When you're doing films, you get really close to the cast and crew, then a few weeks later, it's over. It reminds me of graduating from high school over and over. You're excited that it's over but you're also sad because you have to leave everyone behind."

I nod, thinking about what Zia Fernanda said about him picking a woman on each set, then ending the relationship. Another good reason for me to not get involved. "Sounds difficult."

"It can be, for sure. You get to see each other again on the press junket to promote the movie, but it's not the same as sticking with a team year after year."

"Although working with the same people has its drawbacks too. I mean... Chad?" I ask with a wry smile.

Hudson laughs, then says, "Aww, he's not so bad. A little goofy but he means well."

"Try being a woman who works under him."

His phone pings and he grunts a little. "That's a reminder from Brittany, my publicist. Would you mind doing me a giant favor and taking a picture of me driving, then posting it on Instagram? She wants one as early in the morning as possible to prove how dedicated I am to science."

"Sure."

I take his phone and hold it up to his face to open it, then take a few shots of him looking absolutely delicious in a dark green fleece jacket and a white T-shirt. How? How can anyone look this good at this hour?

Opening his IG app, I select the best one, which is hard to do since they're all pretty much perfect. "Okay, what do you want to say?"

"Out the door at 4:30 this morning to drive to the Black Creek Telescope Array. Can't wait to get there and learn all about them. Hashtag SETI, hashtag galaxy studios, hashtag radio silence the movie."

I quickly type what he said, then hit the post button and put his phone back on the console. "There, done."

"Thank you. That ought to make her happy for a few hours. I'll have to get some video and pics when we get there."

Ooh, it's so cozy in this seat. And so dark outside. My eyelids drift down but I snap them back open again and have a few sips of coffee.

"Feel free to have a nap, if you want."

"No, I couldn't possibly."

"Can't sleep in a car?"

"Oh, I can sleep, but then you'd see me with my mouth hanging open and drool on my chin."

"You spent an entire day looking at me like that," he says, smiling over at me. "When you think about it, it's really only fair if you have a nap in front of me."

"Okay, but only for your sake," I tell him, snuggling into my seat. "And not because I need it."

When I wake, it's fully light out. And bright. I blink my eyes a few times, then realize it's snowing. Like, really snowing. "Wow," I say. "The forecast called for a little snow but nothing like this. This is serious."

"Yeah, hopefully it lets up soon."

"Good thing we're in your big SUV and not my little car."

Glancing at the navigation map on the dashboard, I see that we're only a few minutes from Black Creek. "Oh my God, I slept for over four hours."

"You must have needed it."

"You must have been so bored," I say, then realize how that sounds. "You know, because it's such a thrill ride to be around me and all."

"I know you're joking, but you're actually a very interesting person."

Interesting. Blech. I don't love that description. It's very bland.

When I don't say anything, he adds, "In the best way possible."

I look over at him, my heart swelling at the very sight of him. "Do me a favor, okay?"

"Sure."

"Don't be too nice to me today."

He narrows his eyes and glances at me for a second. "Why not?"

"I just… I don't think I can explain it, but it'll just be easier for me."

He nods and lets out a sigh. "I think I understand."

"See? That. Right there. You should say something like 'that makes no sense at all,'" I tell him.

He chuckles a little. "Sorry. I'll try harder to be an obtuse jerk."

"Thank you. That means a lot to me."

25

How Can It Be So Cold and So Hot at the Same Time?

Hudson

BY THE TIME we pull up, it's snowing so hard, it's a whiteout. I crawl up the long, winding driveway, hoping I'm not about to go off into the ditch. I pull to a stop next to a long one-story building and look down into a field with rows of enormous radio telescopes all lined up. "You don't happen to have winter boots, do you?" I ask her, thinking ahead to how cold our ankles and feet are going to be if we actually trek out into that field.

"No, but they have several sets inside. Goose down coats too. Glen, the senior engineer, will get us all set up."

We hurry inside the lobby, and when I look around, I see that to our left is a large office with three desks set up and a whole lot of computers and other equipment. To our right, there's a lunchroom. A note is taped to the door leading to the office, and Allie reads it aloud.

Allie and Hudson,

Welcome. We beamed out early and will be in Redding for the day. Should be back by five and are excited to meet Hudson. The diaphragm pump on 3E needs replacing and I thought it would be a good way to show Hudson how the telescopes work. All the parts are in the shed. Help yourselves to whatever's in the fridge and cupboards. We'll be back as soon as possible with fresh haircuts and lots of food. Hopefully you can stay to have supper with the team so we can catch up with you and answer any questions Hudson may have.

All the best,

Glen

"Beamed out. Is that a radio astronomer joke?" I ask her.

"It is."

"I had no idea how funny your people are."

"You didn't laugh."

"Exactly."

She grins at me. "Why don't I take you on a tour of the facility first. Hopefully the snow'll let up by the time we're done."

We spend two hours on the tour. The facility is all under one roof, including the living areas and the offices. The kitchen leads to a living room with a fireplace and a big television, then four small bedrooms and two bathrooms. It's pretty basic, but it's cozy and has everything a person would need to live comfortably. Most of our time is spent in the observatory room, looking at computer screens. Allie's full of enthusiasm as she explains how they capture the data and we sit, side-by-side, watching as the information is displayed in real time. "See that line there? It's a quasar. You can tell by the very broad emission lines on the chart."

"How long did it take you to learn to tell everything apart?"

"A few weeks. But once you start to see the patterns, it gets easy. For someone like Glen, who's been doing this for decades, each of these charts is like reading a story. He knows exactly what's going on up there."

God, I want to kiss her right now. So, so badly. "Fascinating."

"No, it's not."

"Agree to disagree on how fascinating you are."

"You're supposed to stop being so nice, remember?"

"Totally forgot. My apologies."

"An obtuse jerk wouldn't apologize."

"Damn, I screwed this up again, didn't I?"

"It's okay. I'll let it go this time." She stands and stretches her back while I shamelessly stare at her. Pointing to the window, she says, "I think my plan of waiting out the snow isn't going to work."

I look out to see that, if anything, it's snowing harder.

She looks at me. "Come on. Let's go get kitted out. This is going to be the coldest pump change in history."

"Awesome. Let's do this."

Thirty minutes later, we're bundled up in borrowed winter gear and we're out in the shed where Allie has gathered all the tools and parts we need to replace the pump. I smile down at her. "If you need me to use the tools for you, just let me know. You know, since you're a woman and all."

She grins up at me, immediately catching on. "Nice."

"I thought being sexist would be the fastest path to pissing you off."

"You thought right, but it's not going to work since you're only doing it because I asked you to."

"This is a no-win situation, isn't it?" I ask, glancing down at her lips.

"I'm afraid so."

"In that case, maybe I should just go back to being myself."

She slings the tool bag over her shoulder, then I reach up and slide it off. "Here, little lady. Allow me."

Allie bursts out laughing. "What are you going for now?"

"Old timey western gentleman?"

"Nailed it. All right? Should we brave the cold?"

"Do we have a choice?"

"Not really."

"Then, yes," I tell her. "Oh, and I need to get some pics of me out there next to a telescope to send to Brittany. According to her, if it's not documented, it might as well not have happened."

"In that case, let's go feed the beast."

As soon as she opens the door, we get a blast of frigid air. I follow her out and soon, we're trudging through knee-deep snow as white flakes swirl down and stick to us. "Is it far?"

"Yup. Unfortunately, it's one of the ones at the very end."

"But once we get out there, it'll go fast, right?"

"I wish."

———

"Dammit, this just isn't going to tighten," she says, twisting the screwdriver to the right.

"Want me to give it a try?"

"Yes," she answers, sounding slightly defeated. "Apparently this is a lot harder when it's minus a thousand out."

She sets the screwdriver down, climbs down from the ladder and blows hot air on her red hands. Without thinking about it, I take off my gloves and take her left hand in mine, rubbing it and blowing on it. Then I put my mitt on it and do the same to her other hand.

"Worst. Jerk. Ever," she says.

"Hey, a guy can't be good at everything."

"What if you had to play a bad guy in a movie?"

"I could totally do it."

"I'm beginning to doubt that."

Picking up the screwdriver, I say, "All right, enough playing around. It's time for a man to take over."

Allie bursts out laughing. "Much better."

———

"I can't believe I broke it," I tell her. "Who knew there was such a thing as too much torque?"

When she doesn't answer, I say, "Everyone. Everyone knows it's possible to use too much torque, right?"

"Not everyone," she says. "Just … most people."

We both laugh, and when we're done, I let out a groan of regret. We're finally back inside the building and are both stripping off our coats and stepping out of our boots.

If I were here with anyone else, there is no way I'd find this even remotely sexy, but with her, it's different. All she did was take off her parka, and my mind just kept on going, imagining her pulling her shirt over her head and tossing it on the floor. Her curly brown hair is wilder than ever when she takes off her beanie and her mascara has transferred from her eyelashes to her skin, but she still looks beautiful to me.

She glances up at me. "It's not really broken. It's just ... temporarily out of service. But the good thing is we learned something valuable."

"Not to let me touch the tools?"

"That too. But more importantly, that we shouldn't do maintenance in these weather conditions."

Her cell phone pings and she digs it out of the pocket of her parka. "Crap."

"What's wrong?"

"That's a message from Glen. The state troopers closed the road, which means they're stuck in Redding and we're stuck ... here."

Try not to smile. Do not smile, jackass. "Oh, that's ... inconvenient."

She bites her lip. "Yup."

She types something back and gets an immediate response. "They won't have it cleared until tomorrow morning at the earliest."

"So, we're stranded for the night?" I ask, my body humming with possibilities.

We lock eyes and the tension between us builds. "Yeah. Good thing we packed overnight bags."

"That was smart thinking," I say, my gaze flicking down to her full lips. "Since we'll be here overnight."

She clears her throat, then says, "Yes, it'll give us a lot

of extra time in the observatory room. We'll be able to make so much progress."

She gives me the most bland smile possible, clearly trying to douse the flames between us, but honestly, it's not working because all I can do is imagine pressing her up against the lockers behind her and picking up exactly where we left off in that opera house.

———

Instagram Reel: Hollywood Dish with Ferris Biltmore

The video opens to show Ferris sitting on a lounge chair in his backyard, dressed in a parka and beanie. He sighs wistfully. "Hey, bitches! Finally, some news from my love, my heart, my world, Hudson Finch. And no, he hasn't decided to switch teams and declare his undying love for me. But he did something almost as good. He posted a hot, hot, HOT vid of himself doing some manly work on a massive satellite thingy they use to hunt for aliens. Check it out here."

Footage of Hudson standing on a ladder, holding a screwdriver, starts up. "Hello from Black Creek, California, where an early spring storm has hit. I'm here to learn all about the mechanical side of radio telescopes. I'm trying my hand at changing out something called a diaphragm pump. It's basically a part used to keep the telescope from overheating, although we're in no danger of that today." The camera zooms in on the pump, then back to Hudson's smiling face. "Anyway, back to it for this guy so we can get out of the cold. I'll catch you later!"

Ferris's face fills the screen again. "Be still, my beating heart. No one can pull off goose down like Hudson. Not even geese. He's … just everything a man should be, no? I watched that video four times before I realized one very important fact. Someone else is there with him. The person making the video, which brings us to my first segment of the day: Who's Taking the Video, Hmmm?"

The words appear next to Ferris, and he shouts, "Hey, Hudson, dreamboat! Who's taking the video, hmmm? Who is it? Is it that Allegra Camma-boring person? I hope not, for your sake. Because, BORING! And if it is her, you better not be kissing her because no. And that leads us to our next segment: No, Just No."

The graphic appears and Ferris shouts, "No! Just, no, Hudson! Don't you dare fall in love with her! She is not for you. She belongs with some graphic-tee-wearing geek with ingrown toenails and halitosis. Not you. No! Your perfect match is someone like … Emma Stone, who can act and sing and dance and make us fall for her, or … Sophia Loren in her prime."

The words disappear, and Ferris's face fills the screen. "Okay, so one last segment, then I have to get out of this coat before I die of heatstroke. And that segment is called: Look at You, Being Brilliant.

"Hudson! Hudson? Hudson. Look at you, being brilliant. You've got a screwdriver and you're using words like diaphragm pump! I told you you were smart! And the rest of Hollywood better sit up and take notice, because Hudson Finch is not only fire, he's also a fucking genius. Mic drop. And I'm out. Time to go jump in the pool."

———

Text to Gershwyn:

ME

Just in case you try to reach me, I'm up in
Black Creek, in the mountains, visiting an
array of telescopes. Also, we're snowed in
for the night, but not to worry because
there's lots of food and I'm in a building
with heat and running water.

GERSHWYN

Who's we???

ME

Allie and me.

GERSHWYN

Really??? Just the two of you? Alone? In a
cabin in the woods?

ME

Yes, but it's a research facility in the
mountains.

GERSHWYN

Hmmm ... what will you do to pass the
time?

ME

She wants to spend a few hours going over
the computer equipment with me.

GERSHWYN

That's boring.

ME

No, it's really nice of her. She's definitely
helping me out.

GERSHWYN

Okay, but if the opportunity presents itself, I
say go for it.

ME

Not having this conversation again.

GERSHWYN

Why? Is she reading over your shoulder or something?

ME

No, she's in the shower, and I'm going to make some supper.

GERSHWYN

Sounds very domestic.

ME

Good night, Gersh. Give Oscar some behind the ear scratches from me.

GERSHWYN

You're no fun at all.

ME

I'm here to do a job, not amuse you, you weirdo.

I stare at our exchange while I wait for the oven to heat up. Texting Gershwyn is smart. He knows right from wrong. He has no intention of sweeping the computer off a desk in the observatory room, setting Allie down on it, and having his way with her. And I'm going to have to turn this evening over to that guy. The one who knows right from wrong, because, honestly, the only thing I can think about is getting her naked.

26

Blame it on the Lemon Fiesta Coolers

Allie

So ... a little bird told me you and Hudson are stranded for the night up at Black Creek? (You can't see me, but I'm waggling my eyebrows as I type.)

YES!!! Is there any way Daddy Warbucks can send a helicopter to save me? Because I have a very bad feeling I'm about to make a fatal error.

1) Daddy Warbucks? Newp. Don't like that nickname. 2) Trust me, you do NOT want to travel via chopper. They're just giant fish bowls of death that have no business flying around like that. 3) What if NOT sleeping with him is the fatal error, and you wind up missing out on your one chance at true love?

ME

I know your frame of reference can't help but be skewed by the fact that a hot billionaire fell madly in love with you, but trust me, in my case, it is not going to happen. So, yeah, sleeping with him will be fatal for my poor heart.

GWEN

You're forgetting I saw the kissing video. Plus, I've seen the way he looks at you in real life. It's like you're the only woman in the entire Universe. Go for it and report back later. I want all the details.

ME

Not going for it, which means any details will be about things like having supper and spending the evening teaching him all about the Big Bang Theory.

GWEN

Yeah, you should definitely focus on some big banging. Maybe big bang him a few times, since you've got him trapped in the mountains all night.

ME

You're not helping.

GWEN

I am, but just not in the way you want me to. Your goal is to stay as far away from that hot man candy as possible, and my goal is to encourage you to take advantage of a once-in-a-lifetime opportunity to shag a celebrity.

ME

He's so much more than just a celebrity. He's a human being. A thoughtful, kind, generous person.

GWEN

Agreed. He's a thoughtful, kind, generous, hotter-than-molten-lava hot man who is totally into you.

ME

I'm ending this conversation now. I need to have a shower, then spend the rest of my evening NOT sleeping with anyone.

GWEN

Fine, but let me just say this: You should totally have sex with him.

ME

Good night. Have fun with your billionaire.

———

Text to Lucia:

ME

Hey, I need you to relay a message to Ma and Pops from me.

LUCIA

Why can't you call them? Camilla's got dance class in half an hour and we haven't left the house yet.

ME

Because it'll be a whole thing if I call them. You don't have to do it now. Wait until you're at the dance studio. Tell them I'm snowed in up at Black Creek, but that everything's fine, and they should have the highway plowed by tomorrow morning.

LUCIA

Please don't tell me you're stranded alone with Hudson Finch.

ME

Okay, I won't tell you that.

LUCIA

OMG! You ARE!

ME

And our parents know he's with me, which is why I can't call them.

LUCIA

You lucky, lucky bitch.

ME

So, you'll pass the message on?

LUCIA

Fine, but what do I tell them about the fact that you're not calling them yourself?

ME

Just ... tell them there's no cell reception to place calls. Only to text.

LUCIA

That's not a thing.

ME

It could be. I'm not a telecommunications engineer.

LUCIA

Who are you? My sister hates liars, and one date with this man and you're ready to sell your soul to the devil.

ME

Am not. I just can't handle the pepper vs. tomato paste talk right now. Hey, I thought you were in a big rush?

LUCIA

I'm still waiting for Camilla to get off the toilet. I think she's constipated.

ME

Okay, not sure she would want her auntie to know that.

LUCIA

Oh, she's out. Gotta go. I'll call Ma in a bit, but you owe me.

ME

Thanks.

———

"You can't sleep with him. You can't. No," I say to the woman in the mirror. She just had a shower, and it should've been a cold one because the thoughts going through her head belong in a letter to Playboy. "Just no."

Oh, but I really, really, *really* want to. Like really, really, more than anything I've ever wanted to do. In fact, I'd honestly hand Frank over to Lando right now if it meant one night with Hudson. Guilt hits me immediately. I could never do that to Frank. But the fact that I even thought that shows how very badly I need to stay away from Hudson. Only I don't want to. Not even a bit. There's a devil inside me that's urging me to walk out of this bathroom, drop my towel and say, "How about it?"

But that's not who I am. At the end of the day, I'm boring. So boring, I can't hold a man's attention. And Hudson isn't just any man. He's a man who can have whoever he wants whenever he wants. He may seem interested in me, and maybe he is, but only in a curious sort of, 'what would it be like to sleep with a total nerd' type of way. But even if we did somehow fall into some sort of weird, mismatched relationship, he'd get bored. Fast.

And even if it did last a few glorious weeks or months,

there's all that online hate I'd have to deal with. And I know me. I won't be able to ignore it. I could try, sure. But eventually, my need to know will get the better of me, and I'll break, and spend hours scrolling through shitty comments people are saying about me, which will hurt more than it should and bring out every last one of my insecurities. It'll eat away at us. I know it will. So that's that. Time to woman up and go spend a very chaste evening with my dream man. That's what I'm going to do. Keep it professional and go to bed early if I feel like I'm going to crack.

I pull on my leggings, a long-sleeved tee, and some wool socks, and give myself another quick lecture in the mirror. "You can do this. You've managed to go years without sex. You can last one more night."

I pull open the bathroom door and follow my nose to the kitchen, only to see Hudson setting the table, his arms flexing with the effort. Damn him for wearing a fitted t-shirt and jeans and having all those muscles. How's a girl supposed to resist that? "Something smells delicious."

It's him. He's the thing that smells delicious. And not just because he showered already.

He smiles at me. "You must be really hungry then because it's just frozen pizza."

I pick up the box. "Oh, but it's extreme meat lover's which sounds very decadent."

"It's the word extreme. It really classes up any food."

I laugh at his joke. It's a giggly girlish sound that should not be happening. *Please stop being so fun and amazing.* I busy myself getting out a couple of glasses, then open the fridge. "We've got beer, lemon fiesta coolers, and Coke."

"I say we go with lemon fiesta. You know, make it a party."

I grin at him, knowing I should probably go for a Coke.

But somehow, I find myself pulling two coolers out. I hand one bottle to Hudson, brushing his fingers with mine accidentally on purpose. We unscrew the caps and he holds his up to mine.

"What are we cheersing?" I ask.

"Cheersing?"

"It's a new word. I just made it up now. Go with it," I say.

"In that case, we're cheersing to forgetting about the world for a while."

I stare at him, realizing how hard it must be to be in the public eye all the time. Everywhere you go, being recognized and approached. Then I think about how nice it is to be away from my own work today, and to just ... be. There's no Chad irritating me, no family in my business, no race against time. Just us. "To forgetting the world."

We sit down to eat a few minutes later, both of us starving from being out in the cold for so long. The pizza is piping hot, and loaded with pepperoni, Italian sausage, bacon, ham, and cheese. "They weren't kidding about the extreme amount of meat."

I have a few sips of my drink to wash it down, and I already start to feel a bit of a buzz, which should be sending off warning signals for me to leave it at one drink. Inhibitions are an absolute necessity, especially tonight.

After we eat, we work side-by-side to clean up the kitchen, him washing and me drying and putting everything away while he tells me about the worst person he's ever worked with—a total male diva who constantly had the crew waiting for 'the moment to be right,' and I tell him about my biggest brush with fame before I met him. The time I took a flight from Vancouver to Denver and Dennis Quaid was on board. "I spotted him in business class as I was walking to my seat at the very back of the plane, obviously. He was on the phone and we made eye contact, and he definitely could tell I recognized him. I smiled, and he … pulled his hat down and turned away. Super rude, right?"

He clicks his teeth. "Well, it's a bit of a tricky situation because if he strikes up a conversation with you, it'll delay boarding."

"Good point. So maybe he wasn't so much rude as responsible," I say, taking the last plate from his hand so I can dry it. "Now, my question is this: Was he on a real phone call or a fake one?"

He glances up at the ceiling for a second. "I'm going to say fake, which is a good strategy because people are far less likely to talk to someone who's on the phone."

"That's what I thought. Although, the truth is, if he hadn't been talking, I wouldn't even have noticed him sitting there."

"Oh yeah, good point, so he was actually drawing attention to himself."

"Exactly. So, what do you do to avoid fans in that situation?"

"I wear a hat and pretend I'm already asleep. Works like a charm."

"You should tell him that if you ever meet him."

He laughs, then says, "I'll definitely do that."

"Good." We stare at each other for a second, then he pulls the plug on the sink and lets the water drain. I hand him the dish towel so he can dry his hands. The whole thing feels so natural and comfortable, as if we've been doing this our entire lives. When we're finished, we're left with the dreaded question of what we should do next. My lady bits have a few ideas, all of them very, very bad.

I lean against the counter with my hands behind my back to keep myself from running them all over his everything. He's standing a couple of feet in front of me, staring down at me. His eyes flick down to my mouth and back up.

My heart pounds and I'm filled with butterflies that need to calm the hell down already. "So, I was thinking, since we're stuck here, maybe we should spend some more time in the observatory room. We'll go over those charts again, only this time I was thinking you could take some actual notes."

He moves closer, his body nearly pressing up against mine. "That's probably a good idea. To read through those charts again…"

"Yeah, it would be the smart thing to do." Did I just slowly lick my lips? I should not have done that because it's clearly sending a message I shouldn't be sending.

"But I thought we were going to forget about the world," he says, moving a little closer.

"Is that what we said?" I ask, my voice coming out all breathless.

He puts his hands on either side of me and grips the counter. "We did. We even cheersed to it, remember?"

"Oh right," I say, my entire body coming alive as he leans down. "But surely we didn't mean we should forget about work, did we?"

"Pretty sure we did." His lips are almost on my neck and I can feel the heat from his body as he whispers in my ear, "What if we give ourselves this one night to do all the things I know you've been thinking about?"

"What have I been thinking about?" I ask.

His lips brush against my neck. "This."

I let out a moan, tilting my head to expose my neck a little more while he works his way up. Oh God, that's good. So, so good. His teeth skim my earlobe, completely silencing that voice in my head that was sounding that pesky alarm. I grab his shirt and pull him to me so he's now got me pressed up against the counter. He reaches up with both hands and places them on my cheeks, then kisses me hard on the mouth, melting the rest of my resolve. I run my hands up and down his back, feeling his muscles flex while he does the most amazing things with his tongue. After a few deliciously delirious moments, he pulls back and gazes down at me. "Is that what you had in mind?"

I nod, not wanting him to stop. "How did you know?"

"Because it's all I can think about too," he answers, nipping my bottom lip with his teeth. "I want you, Allie. I've wanted you since the moment I first laid eyes on you."

"No, that can't be right," I say. "That's just something you think you have to say."

His eyes harden. "It's not. It's the truth. I'll never forget seeing you there in the lobby. I was awestruck by your beautiful full lips, your perfect skin. You're gorgeous, Allie. Stunning."

He kisses me again, and I feel myself melting like butter in his arms. "You're the most beautiful woman I've ever met, both inside and out."

"But you've been with—"

He kisses me hard on the mouth to stop whatever comparison I was about to make. "Facts aren't up for debate." His words come out as a low growl, and I let out a little involuntary squeak.

"Okay, I won't argue with you then," I say.

"Good."

He crushes my mouth with his while I tell that awful voice in my head—the one who can't let me believe he means any of this—to shut the hell up. Because if I don't, I'm going to talk my way out of the most incredible night of my life.

I lift myself onto my tippy toes and kiss him again,

wrapping one hand behind his neck and pulling him closer.

I'm pinned between his hard body and the counter, and it's all I can do not to start yanking off both our clothes. Instead, I give in to the moment, letting myself feel what he's doing to me with his hands and his mouth. I breathe in the scent of him. The masculine, fresh, irresistible smell of his skin. We stay like this, making out until we're both worked up into a frenzy. He pulls back, causing me to let out a little whimper—it's a sound I've never made before in my life. It's desperate and whiny and it makes him smirk as he pulls off his t-shirt, tossing it on the floor behind him.

My eyes drink in the perfection that is his body, and I only now realize how very thirsty I've been for basically my entire adult life. "Wow," I mutter, running my hands over the ridges of his abs and up to his muscly chest. "Yeah, wow."

I don't even care that I'm fawning over him when I should be playing it cool. There's no way *not* to fawn over the absolute perfection that is Hudson Finch. Every woman who's ever seen him on screen wants to do exactly what I'm doing right now, which makes me the luckiest human on the planet. Reaching down, he pulls my shirt over my head, forcing me to lift my arms—and lose contact with his glorious body for a second. He smiles as he stares at me without my shirt on. Just when I start to feel a hint of self-consciousness, he says, "God, look at you. You're so fucking beautiful."

His hands are on my waist, and he pulls me to him, kissing me some more. I feel the heat of his skin against mine, and I'm suddenly desperate to have all our clothes off so I can feel more of him against me and all of him inside me. He works his way down my neck with torturously slow kisses that trail across my collar bone, then pulls my lacy bra down to give him full access to my breasts. His mouth captures my right breast and he teases my nipple until it's puckered and hard, sending a ripple of pleasure through me. I moan again, shameless in my desire for him.

He lifts his head and says, "Is this what you were thinking about?"

"God, yes, all of it," I answer, my words breathy.

He works his way back down and gives my left breast the same perfect attention, his tongue swirling around my nipple and doing all sorts of amazing things to me. I barely notice him unclasping my bra, or it falling to the floor, but somehow it happens. He drops to his knees in front of me, pulling my leggings, panties, and socks off, leaving me completely exposed. The cool air of the kitchen causes goose bumps across my skin, but his hands warm me as he moves them up the sides of my legs and onto my hips. I should feel self-conscious, here in the brightly lit room in front of this Adonis of a man, but the look in his eyes tells me I have nothing to feel bad about.

"I'm going to do everything you need," he says, gripping my ass with both hands and planting kisses across my tummy. "All the things you've always wanted."

"Yes, please," I answer, unable to think straight enough to say anything coherent. I stare down at him, my breath ragged, as I take in the expression on his face. It's adoration and animalistic and everything I've always wanted in a moment like this. I feel sexy. I feel beautiful. I feel seen. And it's utterly addictive. I want to be looked at like this forever.

I grip his shoulders and pull up. "Come here," I whisper.

"Not yet," he says, gently parting my legs. "We've got all night and I intend to make this last."

He kisses and licks me, his tongue doing things that are so intense and amazing, I can hardly hold myself up. I grip the counter behind me to stop myself from collapsing onto the floor. His fingers grip my ass as he pleasures me in ways I didn't know were possible. Closing my eyes, I let my head drift back until it's resting against the cupboard, feeling him lift my right leg a little higher so he can bring his tongue in deeper inside me.

A distant part of me feels like she's observing this from across the room, shocked and delirious and thrilled at what's happening. She can see us together like this, with Hudson showing me how a man should love a woman. Just like this. He's not quick or selfish. He's not here to just get whatever he can from me. He's paying attention to every little moan and sigh and movement of mine, and adjusting to bring me closer to the edge. I press myself a little harder against his smooth face, writhing over him as I tighten my muscles and let one hand drift from the counter to his hair. I grip his head and pull him in even more, his tongue rubbing inside me, setting off a wave of intense pleasure that rips through every cell of my body. Spasms of satisfaction take over as I call out, "Yes, yes, yes!" in a raspy voice.

He stays right where I need him as I ride every wave. When it's over, he holds onto my waist with both hands while he plants lingering, adoring kisses from hip to hip, the heat from his mouth warming every part of me. When he finally stands, I kiss him hard on the mouth, tasting the pleasure he just gave me. It was incredible, powerful, and all-consuming, but somehow, it's left me desperate for more. For him, and only him.

I fumble with the button on his jeans, somehow managing to undo them, then I let my hand slide inside, feeling his hard length through the fabric of his boxer briefs. God, that's big. And hard. And I want all of it inside me right now.

Hudson tugs off the rest of his clothes, then stands in front of me, nude and hard and perfect. "Should we go find a bed?" he asks.

I shake my head, frantic to feel him inside me before he can change his mind. "No, let's stay here."

"Are you sure? I was hoping to romance you," he says, lifting one hand to cup my jaw.

"Fuck romance. We can do romance later," I murmur. "I need to do this now."

27

You CAN Touch This...

Hudson

"You can't say things like that," I tell her, nipping her bottom lip with my teeth. "That's the type of thing that can make a guy move too fast when he's trying to take it slow."

"I don't want slow. I want now," she answers, her eyes blazing with lust. She grabs me by the back of my neck and pulls me down, kissing me hard on the mouth, showing me with her tongue what she wants me to do.

I'm more turned on than I've ever been in my entire life. I want this every bit as much as she does. Likely more, in fact. But I can't get caught up in some frenzy, only to have this end all too soon. With some other woman, I'd gladly do it. I'd give in and go for it, but not with her. With Allie, I need to show her how incredible she is, how lovely, how sexy. She needs that from me. She needs to see herself the way I see her—as perfection itself. I need to give that to her more than I need to feel myself buried inside her.

More than I need the release that's been building in me since I first laid eyes on her.

But what she's doing with her hands—running them over my abs and down to my cock—is making me forget everything I told myself when we got started. Her warm fingers against my skin, the scent of her as I nuzzle her neck, the moans and sighs and the way she's breathing, are all too much for me to take. I let my hands slide down to her gorgeous ass, then grip her and pick her up. She immediately spreads her legs and wraps them around my waist. "Yes, Hudson, right now."

Setting her on the counter, I press myself against her, the silk of her skin against my body bringing me closer to the edge. I line myself up against her wet heat, a throbbing need building as she presses herself against me. Her kisses grow more frenzied, her breathing more jagged and filled with need. I watch her beautiful, flushed face as she closes her eyes and licks her lips.

I let out a groan, then manage to say the only thing that's on my mind. "You're so fucking sexy."

"So are you," she answers, gazing at me while she wiggles her hips in desperation. "You're the hottest man to ever live."

Her words come out sounding pouty, almost like a complaint, and I find myself smiling through our kisses.

"Are you laughing at me?" she asks.

"Never. I'm just fully enjoying your enthusiasm."

She glances down at my cock, then gives me a wry smile. "I can see that." Kissing me again, she says, "Now I want to feel it too."

Unable to hold back for another second, I slide inside her with one long thrust, feeling how hot and wet she is. Kissing her hard, I let my tongue mirror what I'm doing inside her with my cock, slowing down so I can feel every movement and take in her every response. She lets out a moan that almost causes me to lose control, but I force myself to hold back, needing to make sure she's ready. Her muscles tense around me as she grips my back with her hands and she pulls me in closer with her legs that are wrapped around my waist.

I open my eyes and watch her while I thrust into her again and again, each one causing her breasts to bounce a little more, making me wild with lust and longing. A deep need builds inside me—a need for her to know that this is so much more to me than just one night of passion. A need to tell her I think I'm falling for her. I want her, not just for tonight, but forever. But I can't very well say that. Not with how complicated this is. Not when I'm hiding so much from her. But right now, in this moment, it almost feels like I can tell her the truth about me, and that she would understand. Maybe even accept me anyway. "I…" Love you. "You're perfect, Allie."

She starts to say something, but I crush her mouth with mine, not wanting to give her a chance to argue. I lift her off the counter so I'm holding her up, the weight of her body bringing me in deeper as I lift and lower her onto my now-throbbing cock. She wraps her arms around my neck and kisses me, fully letting herself go, writhing and wriggling with the euphoria that has been building.

"Yes, Hudson, yes!" she murmurs, her words raspy, her chest heaving. "Just like that. Don't stop."

The sound and the sight and the scent of her pushes me over the edge, as I thrust into her again and again, each time with more force, as we build to the climax that got started so many weeks ago. Her muscles tighten around me as she lets go, moaning and panting as she comes. I give in to my own release—something more powerful and intimate and amazing than anything I've known.

"Oh yes, Hudson, I can feel you coming!" she pants. "Right there, right there, yes, yes, yes!"

I let out a loud groan, as the most powerful orgasm of my life rips through me. She bites my lip, then kisses me hard while I finish. We stay like this for a long time, kissing and panting and pulsing with satisfaction. Resting my forehead against hers, I try to find the perfect thing to say. Something that will let her know how much she means to me, without making promises I can't keep. "I have another indisputable fact for you," I say, panting a little. "You're an absolute goddess."

She gives me a sloppy, happy grin. "Oh, you're good at the sexy talk."

"You're good at the sexy everything," I answer, kissing her again.

"I'm pretty sure you did almost all the work."

"Trust me. You're amazing."

I set her down on the counter, but she doesn't unwrap her legs, and I don't even want her to. I want to stay buried inside her forever, just like this. The two of us alone where the outside world can't touch us. No media, no trolls, no publicists insisting I feed the machine, no deadlines. Just us, here together. We kiss and caress each other, and feel our bodies tangled up together, as close as two people can be for a long time.

Just when I'm starting to think I might be ready to get things going again, the power goes out, and we're left in complete darkness.

"Well, that's not good," she says.

Nuzzling her neck, I murmur, "We don't need lights for what I have in mind."

"As much as I love where you're going with this, without power, we don't have any heat," she says, kissing me again. "We'll need to get a fire going in the fireplace so the pipes won't freeze, but after that…"

———

An hour later, we're snuggled up in front of the fireplace on a pull-out sofa, where we're going to spend the night. The flames flicker and the sound of wood popping and hissing fills the otherwise silent space. We're laying on our sides facing each other, and even though we just finished round two, the sight of her like this, laying here in my arms, has me ready to start all over again. I pull the blankets up over Allie's shoulder to keep her warm and give her a lingering kiss.

"God, I love the snow," I tell her. What I mean is, God, I love you, but I can't exactly say that.

"Me too. I can't believe I've gone thirty-five years without knowing how wonderful it could be," she answers, running her fingertips over my forearm. "But it's so, so wonderful. Dreamy, even."

Grinning down at her, I say, "Totally dreamy. I hope it never stops snowing."

She gives me a skeptical look. "You'd get bored if you were trapped alone with me for very long."

"I wouldn't. I already know I wouldn't," I tell her. "Eventually, we'd both get hungry, but otherwise, I'd be completely happy."

"You're supposed to be acting like a jerk, remember?"

"But then I would've missed out on all this," I say, kissing her forehead. "And that would never do."

"I'd say of the two of us, I got the better end of the deal," she says, snuggling into me a little more.

"How so?"

"Because you're … you and I'm just … me."

Lifting my head off the pillow, I give her a hard look. "You've got to stop that."

"Stop what?"

"Stop discounting yourself. You're an incredible person, Allie. Seriously. You're smart and funny and sexy as hell, so stop thinking I could do better, because it's the other way around," I say, hoping my words find their way to her heart. "You can do so much better than me."

"Nobody can do better than you."

Shaking my head, I say. "Not true. Everything about me is ... manufactured. I'm just a guy who's good at pretending to be something he's not. I wasn't born with this body. I built it at the gym."

"But you built it. You did that work. No one else did."

"But I never would have, not if I was, say, a plumber or something," I answer. "It's all just for show. The whole damn thing."

She reaches up and touches my cheek. "Now, you're the one who needs to stop because if you don't get how amazing you are, there is something seriously wrong with this world." Rubbing her thumb over my skin, she goes on. "You're the most kind and charming person I've ever met, not to mention thoughtful. I mean, showing up at my house to cook so I could keep working? And keeping me fed and hydrated when you could've just sat around studying?" Shaking her head, she says, "And the way you make me feel ... it's like you think I'm special, and if I hung around with you long enough, I might even start to believe it too."

"I said those things because I meant they're true, and helping someone out is just being a decent person."

"But do you know how *rare* that is? Having someone to support you like you've supported me? You're amazing, Hudson. And not because you can act, or because you have a lot of money. It's because you're the way you are in spite of those things." She sighs, and it feels like she's seeing into my soul—all my hopes and dreams and insecurities. And it terrifies me.

Needing to push away the thoughts I'm burning to say, I prop myself up on one elbow and kiss her hard, rolling her onto her back. She lets out a moan that tells me she wants to go with me where I want to take her, and soon we're tangled up in each other again, our bodies moving together like we've always done this and always will. I banish all thoughts of tomorrow morning, when all of this is going to come to an end, and, instead, focus on showing her exactly what she means to me. I'm saying how I feel about her without uttering a word, without risking anything. I'm in love with her. I feel powerful and loved when I'm with her. I feel like I could take on the world and win.

But I'm also too much of a coward to tell her the truth that she deserves to hear. And that is possibly what's most disappointing about this entire thing because I know myself. I'm never going to tell her the whole truth. I'm never going to let her see the real me. And not just because I'm not even sure who he is anymore. It's because deep down, I know she deserves more than what I have to offer.

28

Baby Ducks and Snuggles

Allie

I'M IN LOVE. Like fully, completely in love, which is a huge problem. Enormous. And even worse, I'm relatively certain it's unsolvable. When we woke up the next morning, the power was on so we were able to make a big breakfast together while we waited for the snowplow. Eggs, bacon, and pancakes. Followed by some plowing of our own until the road was cleared—wink, wink. We held hands almost the entire way home. That's *five hours* of hand-holding. By the time we got back, it was too late to bother going into the office, so Hudson dropped me off at my place, where I quickly showered and packed an overnight bag, grabbed a loaf of peasant bread to-go, then explained to my parents that I'm thirty-five, a responsible not-so-young woman, and that I was going to spend the night at Gwen's because Ty is out of town. So not only am I in love with a man who's definitely going to break my heart, I'm also turning into something I hate—a liar. But honestly? Totally worth it because the D is fire.

Anyway, it's now Saturday morning, and I'm laying here in Hudson's bed, watching him sleep. I know it's creepy, but honestly, I can't stop. I want to drink in every last drop of whatever time we have together. And there's a tiny part of me that believes this might, just maybe, be forever. I'm trying my level best to convince her that this isn't a permanent situation—because it's not. It's just a fling. But she's not buying it.

Every cell of my body, every bit of grey matter in my brain, all of it, belongs to him. This is so different than with Lando. First of all, what I thought was good sex was actually garbage. Lando had absolutely no game. I just didn't have a frame of reference. I guess I should've realized it though, based on his lack of interest in my satisfaction. With Lando, I had to race to make sure I got there before him, because he was definitely going to fall asleep ten seconds after he was done without a thought to whether or not I had a good time. Also different is the complete lack of red flags with Hudson. Well, other than the crazy fans and the trolls, but those aren't his fault. Plus, I can totally learn to ignore them. I'd happily light a torch to my iPhone and get myself a flip phone so I can live in ignorant bliss for the rest of my life if it means I get to be with him.

Although if I did that, it would be so much harder to text my bestie, which would totally suck. I pick up my phone, only to see a message from her.

GWEN

How's our sleepover going? Are we having fun?

ME

SO. MUCH. FUN. I'm exhausted but also have never had more energy in my entire life, if that makes sense.

GWEN

Totally does. Let me guess, you're lying there watching him sleep?

ME

How'd you know?

GWEN

Been there. In fact, doing that right now, to be honest.

ME

Ha! Same brain.

GWEN

Aren't you glad you took my advice and slept with him?

ME

Not sure yet. Immediate Gratification Allie is thrilled, but Future Allie might be furious with me for listening to you. He's leaving in a matter of days. What if I never see him again? Do you know how far it is to Malibu from here? 5 h 53 min by car, 2 days by bike, and 6 days of walking! That's a long fucking walk, Gwen.

GWEN

First of all, that's what airplanes are for. Second, you wouldn't walk to visit him if he lived five blocks from your house, so why are you looking up the amount of time it'll take to do something you're never going to do?

ME

Because I might be panicking a little here.

GWEN

You might be? Girl, you are full-on panicking. But seriously, I've seen how he looks at you. It's the real thing. Now let yourself enjoy this moment. It's the start of something amazing for you.

ME

How can you be sure? He's never been in love before, which seems odd since he's nearly forty and can pretty much snap his fingers and any number of women would come running, all of whom would be ready to have his children. So the question is, what's been holding him back? And is it remotely possible that whatever it is won't be an issue with me? Which leads me to the next question—what makes me so freaking special? Because honestly, I don't get it.

GWEN

I'm not even dignifying that last garbage question with an answer. Don't overthink this. Ty was over forty when I met him and he'd never been in love before either. Maybe H has been waiting for you this whole time.

ME

Aww. That's so sweet. Highly unlikely, but sweet. Also, even if he is in love with me, he could easily change his mind about me and realize that we're just too different. I mean, we really are. We're complete opposites.

GWEN

Ty just woke up and told me to tell you you're overthinking this whole thing. He also suggests you stop laying there watching H sleep because it's creepy and he hates it when I do it.

ME

Okay. Tell Ty thanks for the tip. The last thing I want is for H to know how creepy I am. ;)

GWEN

Gotta go. We've got some stuff to do. Just let yourself enjoy this moment, Al. You deserve to be treated like he treats you. Because you are totally a queen.

I put my phone down and stare at Hudson for another few seconds. Just look at him, sleeping there like a hot, muscle-bound angel. So content and peaceful. And hot. He's the world's best distraction from my failing career. My gut twists when Frank pops back into my mind. The time away from him hasn't helped spark any creative solutions for how to get him to separate out the fake alien signals from the real noise. I keep waiting for some inspiration, but it's not happening and time is running out fast. Gah! I should go back to the office and get to work because spending the day relaxing and having sex with this gorgeous, gorgeous man isn't exactly going to get me anywhere. But ... *sex*...

His eyes flutter and before I can look away, he's staring at me. "Were you watching me sleep?"

"Yes, but not in a stalker way. More like ... just imprinting you on my memory."

"Like a baby duck?"

"Exactly," I tell him. "It was either stare and commit you to memory or take unauthorized photos and I thought you probably wouldn't like the second one."

"Yeah, that would feel creepy." His phone chimes and he reaches over and picks it up off the night table. "That's my brother."

"Oh, do you want me to hide?" I ask, pulling the sheet up to my nose.

He laughs at me. "No! Of course not." Swiping the screen, he says, "Hey, buddy."

A man that sounds a lot like him says, "I've only got ten minutes before I have to be out the door, so we need to make this quick."

"I'm fine, thanks for asking," Hudson says. After a second, his voice goes up two octaves. "How's my boy? How's Oscar?"

I narrow my eyes in confusion for a second, then lean in so I can see the screen. An adorable brown mini-wiener dog is filling up the screen. He's not looking at the screen and he doesn't seem to be reacting to Hudson's voice.

"Hey, Oscar! Do you want to meet Allie?" he asks, turning the phone so I'm now in view of the camera.

"Hi, Oscar. You're so cute." Turning to Hudson, I say, "Man, he's cute."

Suddenly the video goes blurry and I'm staring at Hudson's brother. "Oh, so this is Allie!"

My face goes immediately hot with embarrassment. This is not the time to meet new people. What if I look like I smell bad? "Hi," I say, giving him a small wave. Thank God, I'm wearing a pair of silk pajamas from the hospital haul. "Nice to meet you, Gershwyn."

"You too," he says. "My brother won't shut up about you."

Now my skin is hot with the best compliment ever. Grinning at him, I say, "Really? What's he been saying?"

"Oh, just that you're—."

"She doesn't want to hear that," Hudson says in an urgent tone.

I smile wider now. "Oh yes, she does. Every last word."

"He said you're super-hot and that he loves watching

you work because you always tuck a pencil behind your ear even though you never use it, except the one time when you were writing down your lunch order, and that—"

"Yeah, okay, that's enough," Hudson tells him. "She already knows the great things about Allie because she's been living with her for years."

"Some would say my entire life," I add. "But it's always nice to hear nice things about yourself, so please do go on, Gershwyn."

"He can't because he's in a big rush," Hudson says.

Gershwyn nods, then says, "Actually I do have to run, but there's a bit of a work thing I need to talk to you about first."

I take that as my cue. "I'll leave you boys to talk business. Nice to meet you Gershwyn."

"You too, Allie. I hope we'll meet in person sometime."

I slide out of bed and into a pair of slippers before rushing out of the room and closing the door behind me. As soon as I'm in the kitchen, my stomach growls, and I realize I've expended way more calories than I normally do on a Friday night, watching TV with my parents.

I dig around in his fridge and pantry, finding some eggs, a jar of red peppers, and some cloves of garlic. Grabbing the peasant bread, I cut four thick slices, then set out the rest of the ingredients to make eggs-in-the-hole when Hudson finishes his phone call. Next, I brew a pot of coffee, so happy, I'm practically singing to myself *a la* Snow White. He's been talking to his brother about me, and the particular detail he told him isn't something you'd share about someone you consider a fling. I wonder what else Hudson's been saying.

I pour myself a mug of coffee with cream and sugar, then wander into the living room, spotting the script for his movie on the side table next to the sofa. Settling myself on the sofa, I pick up the script and turn to page one. "Let's have a peek."

I stare at it for a second before I realize the font is one I've seen before. It's used by people who have dyslexia. My heart stops for a second, as it hits me. Hudson has dyslexia.

The door to the bedroom swings open, and I quickly shut the script and get up. His bare feet slap against the hardwood floor as he wanders in wearing only a pair of low-slung pajama bottoms, looking all sexy-disheveled, with his thick brown hair standing straight up in the back. My heart surges when he looks at me and smiles. "There you are. I thought maybe you decided to leave me and went back to Frank."

"Don't worry," I say, walking over and giving him a kiss. "I'm not the type to get it and forget it."

"Lucky me," he answers, pulling me into his arms and leaving a trail of soft kisses down my neck.

My stomach growls in response, and he lets go of me. Grinning, he says, "But first, food."

"I'm going to make you a family favorite," I answer, letting go of him even though I don't want to and walking over to the stove. "Eggs-in-the-hole with red peppers."

"Sounds amazing," he says. "Can I help?"

Shaking my head, I smile at him. "Just keep me company while I cook."

He pours himself a coffee and leans back against the counter next to me while I sauté the peppers and garlic. "A woman of many talents."

"Yes, I can fry things at will," I answer. "Say, I had a peek at your script."

"Oh yeah?" he asks. "Did you find any glaring technical mistakes?"

"I only looked at the first page, but I couldn't help but notice the font."

He freezes for a fraction of a second, but it's long enough for me to know the truth. Giving me an easy smile, he says, "Oh really? Are you a big font aficionado?"

"No, but I've seen that one before when I was working on a joint project with a team at NASA. It's for people with dyslexia." I look up from the pan to try to gauge his reaction.

He's suddenly very interested in his coffee. "Is that so?"

"Yeah," I tell him.

He pushes away from the counter and walks over to the island. Plunking down onto a stool, he says, "That's weird. Why would they use that font?"

"Because fifty percent of the people at NASA are dyslexic."

His face turns a little pink, but he manages to keep a nonchalant expression. "Seriously? How'd that happen?"

"It happened when the people who run NASA figured out that dyslexia often comes with an ability to map out problems in one's brain, which leads to creative problem solving that other people can't do."

"Huh, well, you learn something new every day," he says, having a sip of coffee.

I turn back to the stove and slide the peppers and garlic onto a plate. Adding more butter to the pan, I then place the slices of bread in and start cracking eggs into each hole. The entire time, I'm waiting for him to admit it. To tell me himself. But he doesn't say anything. My heart picks up its pace a little. He's definitely trying to avoid the topic, and I'm not sure how he'll react if I push it. But, after all the things we've said and done, surely he can admit something so minor to me. When I turn back to face him, he's staring at the island while he chews his bottom lip.

"You okay?" I ask him.

He smiles up at me, the mask of the happy go-lucky A-lister returning. "I'm great. Why wouldn't I be?"

"No reason," I say. "It's not something to be ashamed of. I mean, if a person has dyslexia."

He tightens his jaw. "Yeah, well, that's easy for you to say. You don't have it."

29

So This is What Intimacy Looks Like...

Hudson

WHY DID I leave that damn script lying round? And who the hell recognizes a font? Seriously, dating non-geniuses is so much easier. My gut churns. This is it. The moment she'll start to look at me differently. I don't see it yet, but that's because I haven't come right out and admitted it. But as soon as I do, everything will change. She'll have all sorts of questions about what it's like for me to try to read and how it's affected my life and suddenly I'll go from being someone who's not quite as smart as her to someone she pities. And there's no way I can handle that.

We're both silent while she plates up our food and brings it over to the island. Setting it down, she says, "Sorry, I didn't mean to pry. I was just ... totally prying."

Crap. Now I made her feel bad. "It's fine. Let's forget about it, okay?"

She sits next to me. "Sure. Whatever you want. It's your thing."

"Thanks. I appreciate that," I say, picking up my fork

and knife and slicing into the bread and egg. "This looks amazing."

"It's an old family recipe."

Taking a bite, I let out an appreciative moan. "So good."

"Thanks," she says, taking a bite of red pepper. Her tone is flat and I know she's not happy with the abrupt change of subject. But she's just going to have to get over it because like she said, it's my thing. Not hers. And I don't want to talk about it.

We eat in silence, and other than the food being fucking delicious, there's an awkward tension between us now that I wish I could erase. "So, what do you want to do today? I was thinking we could maybe go for a walk. There's a little coffee shop a few blocks from here that I've been meaning to try."

"Umm, yeah, maybe. I should probably go back home soon. Do some laundry, get back to work."

"Right, big deadline and all," I answer in a light tone.

"Exactly," she says before popping her last bite in her mouth.

"Well maybe you could come back tonight or … tomorrow?"

"Maybe." Allie gets up and takes her plate and cutlery to the sink.

Fuck. This is going south fast, isn't it? Clicking my tongue a few times, I say, "Look, it's not something I tell people, okay? Nobody knows, other than my parents and Gershwyn. Not even my agent."

"Is that why you're upset? Because you think I'm going to blab it all over town?" she asks, leaning against the counter and folding her arms.

"No, obviously not. I trust you," I answer, irritated that she'd even think I'd think that of her.

"So what's the problem?"

"I already told you, it's not something I talk about."

She stares at me intensely, then says, "I thought we were being honest with each other."

"We are."

"But not about *this*."

I let out a big sigh. "Look, someone like you will never understand what it's like to be someone … who's got what I've got going on in my brain."

She wrinkles up her nose. "Is that what you've decided? That I'm going to judge you or think less of you? Because if so, that's pretty insulting."

"Come on, put yourself in my shoes. I'm barely keeping up with you as it is. If we throw that other thing into the mix, it's just too much."

"Why don't you let me decide what's too much for me?" Pushing off the counter she starts for the bedroom. "You know what? I should go."

I get up and follow her. "Yeah, of course you're going. That's exactly what I knew you'd do if you found out."

She spins on her heel and glares at me. "Is that why you think I'm leaving? Because I think less of you?"

"Oh, come on. Are you trying to stand there and tell me you think *more* of me now that you know I sometimes struggle to read even a menu?"

"My nonno can't read and he's one of the smartest people I know," she says, jutting out her chin.

"Yeah, in English maybe, but in Italian, I bet he's a total whiz."

She shakes her head. "Nope. He had to work on their farm when he was a little boy. His mom taught him just enough to be able to go shopping and take a train. And I have nothing but respect for him. He's also the only person in my family that understands what I do for a living. Sometimes we talk about my job for hours, and he *gets it*." She picks up her overnight bag and sets it on the bed. "And the people on that joint project at NASA? Brilliant. The ones with dyslexia could totally see things I couldn't. I was completely jealous of the way their minds work."

"Yeah, well, maybe that's how I feel about you," I blurt out.

Her head snaps back and she stares at me.

Shaking my head, I say, "I just ... see you working on things I'll never understand and I wish I could do that too. I'd kill to have things come so easily to me."

"None of it came easily to me. I had to work my ass off for years to learn what I know," she says, yanking a pair of jeans out of her bag. She pulls off her pajama bottoms, giving me the best view of her toned legs before she quickly covers them up with her Levi's.

"It's not the same thing, Allie. And I'm not some NASA genius who can map things out in my head. I'm just ... ordinary."

She scoffs. "Says one of the most successful, famous actors in the world. You're anything but ordinary." She pauses and gives me a piercing look. "You know, you've talked a lot about how I should learn to overcome my insecurities, but it seems to me like you should be taking your own advice."

"It's different."

"It's really not," she answers. "We're exactly alike—using our insecurities as an excuse not to let someone in."

"I have let you in."

"But only so far, right?" She gives me a sharp glare. "Maybe I'm completely naive, but after everything we've told each other and all the things we've done, I thought we were a lot closer than this."

Oh fuck. I'm about to lose her. "We *are* closer. I'm

closer to you than I've ever been to any woman in my life." I walk over to her and take both her hands in mine. "I promise. I've never let someone in like this before."

"I don't think this is how relationships work," she says softly. "You have to let the person in *all* the way."

I let go of her hands, my palms sweaty and my gut twisting. I walk over to the bed and sit down, rubbing the back of my neck. "I know what you're asking doesn't sound like much, but it feels enormous to me. My whole life, I've just been so ashamed."

She drops to her knees in front of me and places her hands on my thighs. "But why? So many successful people have dyslexia—Tom Cruise, Keanu Reeves. Nobody thinks less of them."

Everything in me is shouting for me to shut this conversation down. It's too much. I can't do it. I won't. But when I stare into her deep brown eyes, I can see what I'm pretty sure is love staring back at me.

She gives me a hopeful smile and whispers, "It's okay."

I get a lump in my throat, knowing in my heart that she means it. She's going to accept me for me. I take a deep breath and I start to talk. For the first time in my life, I talk about it with someone who isn't my brother. "My parents moved us to New York when I was three and Gersh was five. My dad had gotten a job as the principal of a fancy boarding school—kindergarten through senior year. The kind of place only the most elite of the elite can afford to send their kids to. At the time, they didn't know about my affliction. Coming from a hick town in Nebraska already put my dad as an outsider from the start. He needed everything to be perfect in order to prove he could measure up to what they wanted— including my brother and me. Only I didn't measure up. I wasn't learning. Wasn't hitting all the milestones, whereas

Gersh was always ahead. Reading at a fifth-grade level in second grade." I pause and shake my head. "He'd go on and on about his oldest son. He's going to be a lawyer or a doctor someday. But with me? He'd say nothing. In first grade, my mom was tasked with 'fixing me.' We'd practice sight words all evening, every evening. All summer too. When all the other kids were out playing, I'd be at the kitchen table trying to memorize every word we'd learn the following year, so I wouldn't embarrass the family."

"Oh, Hudson," she says. "I'm so sorry. That sounds awful."

"It wasn't great." I glance at the floor, emotions swelling in my chest that I'd rather not feel. "By the time I was in seventh grade, I couldn't take it anymore. I started to rebel and became the class clown. I spent half of my time in my dad's office, which drove a wedge into our relationship. But the truth is, he would have been embarrassed by me either way, because by the time I was a sophomore, I was so far behind, there was no catching up."

"But none of this makes you stupid, Hudson."

I clench my jaw, then say, "It doesn't exactly make me smart."

"Of course, you're smart, you jackass," she says, squeezing my legs a little. "Look at how you learned to adapt. And how long you've kept this secret from the world, especially given your career-choice. There must be countless times you have to read out loud."

"Gershwyn's the genius, not me. He handles everything so I don't have to," I tell her, thinking maybe she'd be better off dating him. The thought makes my blood boil, and I brush it away. "He quickly picks up anything that requires reading, while I distract and redirect people. Sometimes, when they push it, I act like I have better things to do or that I can't be bothered at the moment, but I'll get to it."

"You charm them."

"Exactly," I answer. "Once, I even stooped as low as to pretend to be high at a table reading."

"Wow," she says, and the look on her face terrifies me. I'm one-hundred-percent sure she's about to tell me how disappointed she is in me, but she doesn't. Instead, she says, "And that story has followed you for years."

"Yeah, pretty stupid. If I had kept that up, I would've been out of a career real fast." I lean down and press my forehead against hers, not wanting her to see the shame I'm feeling.

We stay like this for a minute, then she lifts her hands and places them on my cheeks. "I'm sorry you went through all of that," she says.

I shake my head. "Half of it was self-inflicted."

"No, I'd say your parents inflicted it on you." She gives me a soft kiss on the lips, followed by another one, this time, more urgent. "There's nothing wrong with you, Hudson. They're the ones who should be ashamed of themselves."

I kiss her back, not wanting to talk anymore. Not wanting to feel ashamed or embarrassed or less than. Pulling her up onto my lap, I kiss her harder, feeling loved and accepted. I run my hands along her waist and up her sides, feeling her breasts through the silk pajama shirt. She grinds against me, through the fabric of our clothes, and I'm suddenly desperate to have her again, to feel her skin against mine, to taste her, touch her everywhere. And I know damn well it's what she wants too. In a frenzy of movements, we help each other get naked, and soon, I'm on top of her, with her legs wrapped around my back, as close as two people can be.

It's everything. This moment. The two of us together like this. It's love. I know it is. She's showing me how she feels, that she accepts me the way I am. A distant part of my brain is telling me not to trust this. That she doesn't know how pathetic it is when I have to read something for the first time, but I silence that thought and focus on her—on how she feels under me, how powerful I am when I'm with her like this, moving over her, bringing her as much pleasure as I'm giving myself.

When it's over, we collapse into a heap, tangled up together, panting and satisfied. "You've got some serious gifts," she tells me with a smile.

I chuckle, then kiss her again. "You do too."

She runs her hands lazily up and down my arm while I plant kisses along her neck. After a few minutes, she says, "You know how I'm relentlessly curious?"

"It's one of the things I love most about you."

Grinning, she says, "I want to hear about how you learn your lines."

"Oh, that," I answer, surprised that I'm actually happy to talk about this. "Gersh scans my scripts and changes them to the Dyslexie font, then records himself reading them out loud. I listen to it over and over while I follow along until I've got the entire thing memorized."

She stares into my eyes, and I can feel the love radiating from her. "So, you're secretly an extremely hardworker masquerading as an easy-going surfer dude."

"It's been the greatest role of my career."

"Wow," she says. "I'm not sure if anyone's told you this lately, but you're amazing."

"You're only saying that because you want me to shag you again."

She lifts one hand and caresses my cheek with her fingertips. "I'm serious. You're amazing, Hudson. What you've accomplished is incredible. Only someone who's a really fast thinker could do what you've done."

Shrugging, I say, "Meh, I may be fast, but I have my limits."

She gives me a serious look. "Listen, because I'm about to say something you need to hear. Everything you've learned, every skill you've developed—it took determination and intelligence to do that. I've never met anyone as good at reading people as you, and that's one of the most important skills a person can have."

"I don't know about that. I could never do what you do."

"So what? You've built an incredible life for yourself, and it took guts and talent."

"All right, I'll shag you again," I say, doing my best to sound reluctant about it.

She laughs, then says, "Oh good. But first, can I ask you one more thing?"

"Seriously? I'm offering you a mind-blowing orgasm and you want to ask more questions?"

"You knew what I was like when you got involved with me," she answers. "Besides, I'm pretty sure the offer will still be on the table in a few minutes."

"Oh really? Someone thinks highly of herself," I say with a big smile.

"If I do, it's only because you're as hard as a rock right now," Allie tells me.

I burst out laughing, then say, "Okay, you got me there. Now, out with it. What's your question?"

"I know for a lot of people with dyslexia, the words seem to jump around on them. And I'm wondering if that's what it was like for you when you were trying to learn to read."

"You do know this is the worst pillow talk of all time."

She winces, then says, "Scientists, right?"

I snort laugh. "You're a strange bunch. Okay, fine. You know how there are twenty-six letters in the English language?"

"I'm familiar with the alphabet, thank you."

"Well, those twenty-six letters make a whopping—and if you ask me, an unnecessarily confusing—forty-four sounds. So before you can learn to really read, you have to be able to figure out which combinations of letters make which sounds," I say. "That's hard for anyone, but imagine if you're doing that while the letters are switching themselves around on the page, and your super-impatient father is staring over your shoulder shouting at you to 'try harder.'"

"That sounds awful," she says, looking like she might start to cry.

"Can we change the subject now? Because I'm definitely losing my erection."

"Of course," Allie answers. "I'm sorry I brought it up."

She kisses me hard on the mouth, and within a few seconds, I've completely forgotten about what I was just saying, and apparently she has too, and she's super turned on, because she just gasped and shouted, "Oh my God!"

"Wow, already?"

"No, not that," she says, sitting up suddenly. "I definitely loved what you were just doing, but the letters and the sounds and the decoding…"

"*That's* what turned you on?" I ask. "I'm not judging. I'm just asking for future reference."

"Frank. I just realized why he hasn't figured it out yet!"

"Seriously?"

She nods, her eyes wide with excitement. "It's what you said about decoding the sounds. Frank's struggling because I haven't broken down the signals enough for him. I've been feeding each one as a whole unit." She laughs a little, covering her mouth with one hand. "Sorry. I'm totally killing the mood."

I grin at her, thrilled to see her so happy. "Don't be sorry. You gotta go."

"Really?"

I detangle myself from her. "Of course. We can pick this up later. Right now, you've got a world to change, and you've got a total shitbag to vanquish. Come on, let's get dressed."

She gets up and kisses me hard on the mouth. "Best. Boyfriend. Ever." As soon as the words are out of her mouth, her mouth drops. "Oh, not boyfriend. *Pfft.* You're leaving in a few days. I meant 'guy I'm sleeping with.' No, that doesn't sound right. Friend with benefits? Best friend with benefits ever. Oh wait, that's too much pressure, I didn't mean you're my best friend. Gwen is, but not with the benef—"

I kiss her to shut her up. "If we were going to label it, I would be in favor of the word boyfriend."

"You would?" she whispers.

"Yeah, it's got a nice ring to it. Now, you have to get going. There's no time to lose."

30

The Vanquishing of the Shitbag...

Allie

"WE DID IT!" I say, patting my monitor, you know, like a crazy person. Tears fill my eyes and I let out a single, happy sob. Late last night, Frank sorted the fake alien signals from all the other noise from space. Every single one of them. So I quickly whipped up a new batch of fakes, and he found those too, with no errors. Just perfect detection of unusual anomalies. "We fucking did it, Frank!"

"You did it?" Gwen asks, poking her head in my office.

"We did!" I jump up and rush over to her. "He's going to detect extraterrestrials for us! If they're within range, he'll find them."

"I'm so proud of you!" Gwen says, holding out her arms.

We give each other a big hug, squealing about what is the most thrilling moment of my life. Well, career. The whole Hudson boyfriend thing is pretty fucking thrilling.

After a quick second, Gwen recoils. "Oh wow, I take it you've been at this for a while?"

Pulling back, I give my left armpit a sniff. "Whoa, bad. I got here Saturday morning and have been at it non-stop. What are you doing here?"

She blinks once. "It's Monday morning and I work here."

"Oh God, seriously? I should go home and shower before Hudson sees me like this," I say.

"You mean your new boyfriend?" she asks with a waggle of her eyebrows.

I make a 'keep it down' gesture with my hands. "I don't want him to think I'm blabbing to the whole world about that."

Pursing her lips, she says, "I'm not the whole world."

"Good point. Okay, I should go," I say, rushing over to my desk, searching through the empty freeze-dried ice cream wrappers for my cell and my keys.

"Oh my God, you ate the ice cream."

"I was desperate." I find my cell and hold it up. "Ah-hah! There you are. God, I've missed forty-two messages, and I'm guessing at least thirty are from my relatives about missing supper last night." I find my keys, then realize I can't leave yet. "Oh wait. I need to send a quick email to Virgil, Chad, and Keenan to see if they'll do the verification for me. Then, I should go home and eat some real food and get some sleep."

Gwen grins at me. "I can't believe you did it, Al. You really freaking did it! You're going to be famous."

"Well, SETI-famous," I say with a little shrug. Then, unable to contain my excitement any longer, I let out a squeal. "Which is really the only kind I care about."

I force myself to sit down, and quickly write an email, then attach the report and send it to my makeshift verification team. Just as I hit send, Hudson walks into my office. As soon as I see his face, I realize I have nothing to feel self-conscious about.

His eyes are shining and I know he's as invested in this as I am. "Well?"

I nod. "We did it."

He lets out a loud whoop, then hurries over to me. "I knew you could do it!"

When he's close enough, I tell him, "You may not want to hug me. I've been at my desk since I left your place."

"Are you kidding? This is the biggest moment of your life. Of course I'm going to hug you!" He pulls me out of my chair and wraps his arms around me.

It's a truncated hug, and when we pull back, I can see he's trying not to look like his sense of smell has been severely assaulted. "Well done, Allie! I'm so proud of you." Turning to Gwen, he says, "She's amazing. Isn't she amazing??"

"She's *completely* amazing," Gwen answers. "One thing about this woman is that when she sets her mind to something, she's going to do it. Even if she has to exist on freeze-dried ice cream all weekend."

His face falls. "Oh, dammit, I knew I should've come in to feed you."

Shaking my head, I say, "No. Honestly, this happened the way it had to. I needed to be completely alone and focused the entire time. You would've been a distraction."

"I'll take that as a compliment."

"That's how I meant it," I say, pulling off my glasses and rubbing my weary eyes. "Oh God, I have never been this tired in my life. I think I could sleep for a week."

"I'll give you a lift home," he says.

"No, that's okay. I have my car here."

He raises one eyebrow. "And yet, I'm still going to drive

you. There's no way you should be behind a wheel right now."

"Good point." Turning to Gwen, I say, "Do you mind telling Keenan I'm taking the day off to sleep?"

"Will do."

"Oh, and what about you?" I say to Hudson. "What will you do all day?"

"Tomorrow's my big tour so I'm going to practice for that."

"You sure you don't need help?" I ask.

"He's got it, Allie," Gwen says. "He's been on enough tours now to know the routine. Now go get some rest."

I give her a wide-mouthed grin again and try to give her another hug, but she shakes her head. "Tomorrow."

"Right," I say, snapping my fingers. "I stink."

I start for the exit, with Hudson right behind me, his hand resting gently on my lower back. Oh wow, that's definitely something a real boyfriend would do, isn't it? I turn back to Gwen to see if she sees it too, and clearly she does because she's giving me a huge smile and double thumbs up.

Hudson notices the exchange and narrows his eyes a little. "What?"

"What what?" I ask.

"What are you two doing there with the grinning and the thumbs up?"

Gwen, whose brain is clearly functioning better than mine, says, "Oh, we're just excited about karaoke night this Wednesday. Did Allie tell you about it?"

"No, she didn't, but that sounds fun."

"It's the best. You have to come," Gwen says. "Allie here does the world's worst version of '9 to 5' by Dolly Parton."

My head snaps back. "Hey, it's not as bad as you singing 'You're So Vain.'"

"I gave that song up, thank you very much," she quips.

Turning to Hudson, I say, "Yeah, now she and Ty do a cringe-worthy performance of 'The Power of Love' by Celine Dion."

Hudson chuckles. "Well, in that case, I'll be there."

"He's in!" Gwen says, then she turns back to Hudson. "Do you sing?"

He gives her a cocky look. "Do I sing? Come on. That's like asking Allie's father if he uses confusing food-related analogies."

Gwen and I both laugh, then I say, "What're you going to sing?"

"I don't know. If Allie likes to sing Dolly, I might drag her up on stage for a little 'Islands in the Stream.'"

"You'd be my Kenny Rogers?"

"I'd be happy to be your Kenny," he says.

My entire body warms at the thought, my heart flutters, and I'm suddenly giddy. Is this really going to happen? Like all of it? The dating and the falling in love and the whole having a life with someone? Someone pinch me please, because this is all too good to be true.

———

The entire ride back to my place is a blur for me. My mind is pretty much incapable of thought and I'm not even processing what's happening. When we pull up in front of my house, Hudson smiles at me. "You really did it."

I smile back, so happy I could cry. "Thank you. If you hadn't said what you did about decoding language, I never would've figured it out."

"You would have. I know it," he says.

"Thank you anyway."

"I'm not taking any credit for this," he answers. "Not even an atom's worth."

I click my tongue, then say, "Did you just make a physics metaphor for me?"

He chuckles. "Maybe. Why? Did you like it?"

"Super-hot. If I wasn't exhausted and disgusting, I'd be all over you right now."

"You're still beautiful."

"We said no lying."

"It's a fact. And facts aren't up for debate." He leans over and gives me a kiss on the lips. "Go get some rest, and call me when you wake up."

"I will." I open the door and float up the sidewalk, feeling like I'm in the best dream ever. At thirty-five, my life is falling into place. I've just made a major discovery that's going to help the world, and I've found love. Real love with a good man who loves me back and supports me.

I eat a huge breakfast—eggs, toast, orange slices, and yogurt—glad my parents are at work so I don't have to try to talk. I write them a quick note to say I did it and that I'm sleeping, so when they get home from the bakery, they won't wake me up. Then I take a long hot shower and drop into bed, listening to a chorus of birds outside my window. I lay there for a minute, thinking about how incredibly lucky I am. I not only got Frank to work, I'm madly in love with the most perfect man ever, and after our big talk yesterday, and how he opened up to me, I know he loves me too. Even though we haven't said it yet, it's there. He knows I accept and love him just the way he is, which is true love. The kind that lasts forever. Just like he accepts and wants me, even when I'm a total mess. We've done the hard part. The rest is just logistics. And all signs point to this relationship being a go. I fall into a deep sleep, feeling content in a way that I can honestly say I've never felt before, thrilled that soon, I'll be back in his big, strong arms.

————

"Wake up. Allegra, wake up," my mom says. "It's almost supper time."

I grunt and turn away.

"Come on." She yanks my covers off and pats me on the back. "If you keep sleeping, you'll be awake in the middle of the night and tomorrow will be another write-off."

Why does she have to be right? "But I'm so sleepy," I murmur, feeling too hot and too cold at the same time. Without opening my eyes, I reach down, searching for my blankets with my hand, even though I know they're too far away.

"Let's go. I made baked ziti to celebrate your work project."

"I'm not hungry."

"But you gotta eat so you can show your body what time it is," she says. "Come on. Up with you."

Yanking open my curtains, she lets the early evening light into my room. Walking over to my door, she says, "If you're not downstairs in five minutes, I'm coming back with the bucket."

The bucket is something she used to wake us up as teenagers when we'd try to sleep till noon. It's metal. She brings a stainless-steel spaghetti spoon and makes a god-awful racket with them. "The bucket? You do know I'm a grown woman and a highly accomplished scientist, right?"

"Five minutes. It's for your own good."

I groan and drag myself out of bed, then stumble to

the bathroom to pee and brush my teeth, still completely disoriented. In some distant part of my mind, an alarm is going off, and I have no idea why. I grab my phone and text Gwen, then Hudson, to tell them both I'm awake and that I'm going to eat supper and force myself to stay awake for a couple of hours before bed. Immediately, I get a text from them both.

GWEN

Rest up, my friend! You've earned it. See you tomorrow.

HUDSON

Do you want me to pick you up and bring you back here? I can help you stay awake...

ME

As tempting as that is, I'm completely wiped.

HUDSON

Totally understandable. I'll swing by and drive you to work tomorrow morning.

ME

Thank you. See you around eight?

HUDSON

I'll be counting the minutes.

If ever there was a man who was boyfriend material, it's this man. So, why is there a niggling feeling at the back of my mind? Something's wrong, but I don't know what.

"Allegra! Do I need to come up there?" Ma yells up the stairs.

"No, I'm coming down."

Supper is a blur. The food is hot and delicious, and I have to admit my mom knew exactly what I needed. I coast through helping with the dishes without saying much more than two words. Then we sit down in the living room to watch *Law & Order* and *20/20 True Crime*, both of which scare the shit out of my father, who repeatedly tells me that 'this is why you should never move out. Because of whack jobs like that guy.'

"Sure, Pops," I tell him, too tired to argue. By the time my dad shuts the television off, I realize that strange, yucky feeling has grown exponentially. Something is definitely off, and I know it's got something to do with Hudson, but I can't put my finger on why.

Finally back in bed, I convince myself I'm just not used to being this happy. That's got to be it. Being *this* happy is making me uncomfortable. It's like I'm waiting for the other shoe to drop. But this time it won't, because this time, I've fallen for a man I can trust.

As I drift off, a voice in my head tells me there is something I'm missing. Something big and important. I have to find the pattern. The pattern is the key.

But the key to what?

31

And the Truth Shall Set Your Life on Fire...

Hudson

I WAKE to a text from Allie that gives me an uneasy feeling.

ALLIE

Don't worry about driving me to work today. I've got a ride. See you when you get there. The class won't arrive until 10 so feel free to take your time.

That is not the text of a woman who wants to see someone. It's reminiscent of the note she left on my desk my first day here, telling me to feel free to hit the gym and relax before I came in. I quickly write her back.

ME

Everything okay?

ALLIE

Yup. Just tons of stuff to do. I'll be super busy preparing the instructions for how to use Frank for the verification team. I'll be done in time for the tour though.

I stare at our exchange, deciding to take her at her word and assume she's just really busy. She's also probably worried that the other astronomers won't be able to verify her results, which will mean she won't be able to present at the conference. It's a whole lot of pressure.

Yes, that's probably it. I'm sure everything between us is fine. How could it have changed overnight? That would be bananas.

I arrive at 9:45 bearing coffees and find Allie at her desk typing away furiously. I set her coffee down and give her a quick kiss on the top of her head. "Don't let me distract you."

"I won't," she says without looking up.

Taking a seat at the desk, I have a sip of coffee, then open one of her textbooks and flip through it so I'm not just sitting here watching her. After a few minutes, she stops typing, then gets up and closes the door to the office. Turning back to me, she says, "I need to ask you something."

I offer her an easy smile, even though I can tell something is wrong. "Sure. Anything."

She settles herself on the corner of her desk and crosses her arms. "One of the most important skills an astronomer can have is the ability to detect patterns, even if they're not obvious."

"Okay…" I say, having no clue where she's going with this.

She bites her bottom lip, staring at the floor for a second, and I can tell she's fighting back tears. Needing to be near her, I get up and walk over, putting my hands on her upper arms and rubbing them. "It's okay. Whatever you're worried about, we can sort it out."

She gives me a dead look. "I'm not sure we can."

I let go of her and wait while she takes a deep breath.

"I've noticed a pattern in our … whatever this is … and I thought it best to come right out and ask you about it, because I could be wrong." She blinks a few times, then says, "I hope I'm wrong. I've been going over the more pivotal moments we've shared—the kiss at the opera house, the first time we had sex—both prompted by a request that would have risked me finding out about your dyslexia. And then when we talked about it, you said something that's been bugging me ever since. Like way at the back of my brain, but I was too focused on Frank to let it come to the forefront. This morning when I woke up, however, it was all there, plain as day. You said you distract and redirect people to keep from being found out. And I said, 'you charm them,' to which you said, 'yes.'"

Fuuuuccckk. "Allie—"

"Please let me finish because this is hard enough to get through without being interrupted."

I close my mouth, my heart sinking as I stare at her beautiful face.

She lifts her chin. "So, if you have a habit of charming people to hide your dyslexia, then that means both of those … events … would not have happened when they did. Or possibly at all."

"They definitely would have happened. Maybe not at those exact moments, but trust me, I very much wanted them to happen," I say, desperation coming over me. "I didn't kiss you because I was trying to avoid the truth, and that's certainly not why I slept with you. I did those things because I wanted to. Because I wanted *you*."

She gives me a hard look. "I need the truth. Not what you think I want to hear, not some smoothed out version of what happened to placate me. The whole truth, because I'm trying to figure out what we are, and the timing of those things isn't a coincidence, is it? You were doing that thing you've always done to hide."

I open my mouth to protest, but then realize I can't do that with her. It wouldn't be fair. Running a hand through my hair, I say, "You're right. I did do that thing I've always done."

She gets up and walks to the window, clearly needing to be as far away from me as possible.

"But I also really *wanted* to kiss you at the opera. In fact, I've been wanting to kiss you since I first saw you," I tell her, wanting to close the distance between us, but knowing I need to give her space.

She nods, doing her best to hide how hurt she is. "Okay, that's really all I need to know."

My palms go sweaty, my heart pounds, and my gut churns. I'm going to lose the only woman I've ever loved, and all because I was too much of a coward to let her see the real me from the start. "Allie, wait, it's not that simple. If I hadn't wanted to do all those things, believe me, I would have found some *other* way to distract you. Like, at the opera, let's say I went with Chad instead of you, and he wanted me to read the playbill, I would've … pointed out some beautiful women in the audience and suggested we go meet them at the intermission. Then I would've gotten him to figure out their seat numbers so we could send a note down to them."

Okay, based on the disgusted look on her face, I can tell this isn't helping. "I'm making this worse, aren't I?"

"Yup."

I take a couple of steps in her direction, then stop myself. "I meant everything I said to you. Every word of it. I feel things for you I've never felt for anyone."

"Please stop," she says, her eyes filling with tears.

My heart moves up to my throat, but I force out the words that need to be spoken. "Allie, I'm in love with you."

"No, don't say that." Her words wobble and her chin quivers, and I know I've hurt her beyond repair. "Not when the whole thing was based on a lie."

"It really wasn't. I promise you. Okay, at the opera it may have started out that way, but as soon as I kissed you, I knew. And you can't tell me you didn't feel it too, because I know you did."

"I don't know what I felt anymore, but I know that right now, what I feel is betrayed. You lied to me. Maybe not with your words, but with your actions. You tricked me. I have never felt so stupid in my entire life," she says. "And I had a boyfriend who would wash his penis in the sink, Hudson. *In the sink.* Yet somehow you've made me feel worse than he ever did."

I rub a hand over my mouth, not knowing what to say, hating like hell that I've hurt her like this. Hating myself. "I never meant to—"

"Oh yes, you did. I'm just another sucker. Somebody you managed to fool so you could keep your secret," she says, shaking her head. "That's not love. It's a cheap magic trick."

"Allie please—"

She shakes her head. "No more. Whatever this was, it's over. Let's just get through today and then you can leave like you were always planning to do."

A knock on the door interrupts us, and Allie quickly wipes under her eyes. I turn in time to see Chad poke his head in. "Hey, Hudson, you coming to karaoke tonight? I do a pretty mean 'Livin' on a Prayer.' Plus it's dollar-off highballs."

"Uh, I'm not sure," I tell him, glancing at Allie, only to see her staring at the floor.

"I'm not supposed to tell you this, but the team's been working on a song for you, to celebrate your time with us."

Rubbing the back of my neck, I say, "In that case, I'll be there."

"Sweet. It's going to be epic," he says with a grin. Looking at Allie, he says, "Oh, your tour arrived already. They're in the lobby so you guys better get down there."

She nods and strides past me. "Okay, thanks, Chad."

"I'm going to get back to playing with Frank," he tells her. "So far, he's smarter than I thought he'd be."

"Awesome."

As soon as she walks out of the room, he squints. "Is it me, or is she in a bad mood?"

"I should go."

"She's probably got her period or something."

I shake my head at him. "You're better than this Chad. Seriously. Do better."

Hurrying down the hall, I realize I should be taking my own advice.

32

I Should Have Listened to My Father...

Allie

I'M A PROFESSIONAL. I can do this. I can get through a two-hour tour with the man who tricked me into falling in love with him. I'll do it for the kids. I'll keep it fun, light, and educational, even though my heart shattered the moment he admitted he was just hitting on me to avoid having to admit he struggles with reading. Today, *I'll* be the one giving the Oscar-winning performance because I'm going to smile and laugh and pretend everything's fine when what I really want to do is go outside and key the word LIAR into the hood of his fancy schmancy SUV.

I feel a lump in my throat as I hurry down the hall to the lobby. *No. Do not cry. Do not. You can do that when you get home. Or when you get into the car to go home, but not until you've left the parking lot. Just get through this with your dignity intact.*

As soon as I get to the lobby, it's clear that the students are already restless—shuffling around and elbowing each other. Two of them are playing keep away with one poor kid's beanie. Normally, I'd be concerned because I'd have to find a way to rein them in, but today, it's not my problem. In fact, I'll have the pleasure of watching Mr. Smooth-Talking-Lies-Out-of-His-Ass try to wrangle them and fail miserably because no one can effectively deal with nine-year-olds.

I hurry over to their teacher, Mrs. Brutain, a no-nonsense woman in her forties who I've met numerous times before. "Welcome back."

She lowers her voice. "Is it true that Hudson Finch is here?"

I suddenly realize she's not dressed in her usual teacher style of khaki pants, a button-down shirt, and a long cardigan. Today she's in a sleek black skirt and a slightly-sheer button-up shirt that has one too many buttons open. *Et tu, Mrs. Brutain? Et tu?* Is no one immune to his charms? I give her a tight smile. "Yes, in fact he's going to be giving the tour today."

Her face turns bright red and she reaches up and touches her hair. "Really? He is?"

"Yup," I say. Turning to the class, I say, "Hi, kids! I'm Allie. I'm so glad you're here. Who's excited to learn about the world of SETI?"

A few of the children smile at me, and one little girl nods enthusiastically. She's my people. She totally reminds me of me when I was that age. Well, other than her straight teeth, the well-behaved blonde hair, and the obvious sense of style and self-confidence.

Hudson comes to stand beside me. "Hi, everyone, I'm Hudson. I'll be helping Dr. Cammareri here give you a tour."

The kids gasp, their eyes growing wide as they all start to whisper. One of them shouts, "Hey! You're the beach cop!"

Hudson gives them his stupid leading-man smile. "I sure am. Who's seen *Beach Cops?*"

All their hands shoot straight up in the air. "I've seen it eight times," one boy says.

"Wow, that's a lot of times," Hudson answers. "I think you've spent more time on that movie than I have."

"It shows," I mutter.

Hudson turns to me. "Excuse me?"

Setting my jaw, I say, "We should show them around." I turn to the class. "Hudson is going to be your tour guide today and I'm tagging along to see if he's learned anything in the six weeks he's been here. He's been studying how to be a radio astronomer, which is what *I* do for work. Does anyone know what an astronomer is?"

When the kids shake their heads, I say, "Well, let's let Hudson explain it."

He smiles at me, but I can see in his eyes, he's hurt. Well, good. That makes two of us.

He turns to the class. "I'd be happy to. An astronomer studies outer space—things like planets, stars, and other galaxies. There are lots of different types of astronomers, but in the case of the people here at the SETI Research Institute, their specific area of interest is in seeking out and communicating with extraterrestrial intelligent life forms. Does anyone know what that means?"

Hands shoot up, and little me says, "Like E.T.?"

"That's right," he answers, all warm and smooth and despicable. "Someday they're going to make contact with aliens like E.T."

Clearing my throat, I say, "Well, they won't *look* like E.T. of course. That was just a *pretend* version, designed by someone who clearly doesn't understand evolution because honestly, there's no way his species would have survived with those stubby little legs. They never would've been able to outrun predators, therefore their civilization wouldn't have survived long enough to achieve spaceflight."

The kids all stare at me like I've suddenly sprouted a goatee, but Hudson just nods. "Man, she's smart, hey kids? Dr. Cammareri knows everything there is to know about space and evolution. Now, should we get started on the tour?"

"Yes!" the class shouts, which is just so irritating. Not once, in my eleven years of giving tours, has a class cheered. Not one damn time.

He gestures for them to follow him, and they do exactly that. I wait and bring up the rear, frustrated beyond all imagination that this is going to be so easy for him. He's got them all fooled, just like the rest of the world. But I've seen behind the curtain, and the Great and Powerful Hudson isn't who they think he is. He's not the super-handsome, charming, easy-going, charismatic person he's masquerading as. He's a wizard of deception. A master of manipulation. Another man pretending I meant something to him.

My mind wanders back to when I first opened my eyes this morning. My chest was tight and my stomach felt heavy. And I knew what the pattern was. My brain must have been working on it all night while I slept—figuring out every moment he charmed me out of thinking clearly. His whole 'I have something more fun in mind,' bullshit, followed by the 'I know it's customary to wait until the end of the first date to do this, but I'd very much like to kiss you right now.'

Urgh! How could I have been so stupid to fall for that? I knew he couldn't be interested in me. I definitely knew it. And yet, I let the wool be pulled over my eyes so easily. I fell for all of it—the gifts, him constantly feeding me, the listening to every word I said, the showing up at my house to charm the pants off every living relative of mine. Except my dad. He knew better the whole time. That's it. From now on, I'm letting my father make all my decisions for me. Well, personal ones, anyway. Obviously, I'm killing it professionally. I just made what is likely going to be the greatest advancement in SETI research history. Me, Allie Cammareri. So, suck on that, Hudson and Lando. And screw love. Screw it. Not worth it.

Yes, forget men forever. From now on, I'm going to focus all my energy and attention on my job. My job has never let me down. Really, this is for the best. It's not like someone with my potential should split her attention between her job and a man. Being in love is just a huge waste of time. Just think of what I can accomplish if I stay single.

We crowd into the server room, and I'm on alert, in case one of the kids tries putting their sticky little fingers on one of the computers. They always do that. Every single time. Except, apparently not today. Today, they're all fascinated while Hudson the Hoodwinker explains how the computers in this room are receiving signals from radio telescopes from all over the planet. He smiles at me and says, "Have I missed anything yet, Dr. Cammareri?"

"Nope, you seem to have covered it all." Dammit. He has too, when a very petty part of me wants him to fail.

"Excellent," he says. "Remember kids, if you have questions about anything, she's the expert. I'm just going to play one in a movie."

Oh, stop sucking up. There is literally no possible way I'm falling for your act again.

"Wicked!" one of the boys says. "Is it going to be like *Guardians of the Galaxy*?"

"No," he says. "It's set on Earth and it's about a scientist like Dr. Cammareri here."

The boy's shoulders drop. "Oh. Sounds boring."

Mrs. Brutain makes a *tsk*ing sound. "Braxton, that's not nice." She turns to Hudson, batting her eyelashes at him. "I'm sure it's going to be a thrilling movie."

Blech. I'm *glad* we're done. Who would want to put up with women hitting on your man all the time? Not this lady. No siree. No thank you.

Hudson leads the kids back out into the hallway, calling, "Who wants some freeze-dried ice cream?"

They all cheer while I stomp along behind them trying not to scowl or shout at them not to let the smooth-talking, womanizing, very bad man fool them. Because oh my God, does it ever hurt.

33

Breaking Up is Hard to Do...

Hudson

THIS IS NOT how this evening was supposed to go. I was planning on taking Allie out for a dinner at a cozy little Japanese restaurant before karaoke, where we'd talk about the future, plan a duet to sing, and celebrate her victory. It was supposed to be the start of a new phase in our relationship—the totally-worth-it, long-distance phase, which would involve lots of weekend flights and late-night phone calls until we could figure out phase two—the being-together-all-the-time part.

Instead, I ate supper alone in my condo while I waited for her to answer my *can we talk?* text, and I'm now just pulling into the parking lot of the Off-key Emporium, even though I know going in there is quite likely a horrible idea. But it's not like I have much choice, especially when the team has some fun send-off planned for me. I can only hope she'll give me a chance to explain, although I guess technically I already did and it's not exactly helping my cause. I fucked up. Big time. And I'm not sure if she'll ever be able to trust me again. And the thing is, I don't blame her.

Her car is already here, and my stomach tightens, knowing she's inside. She managed to avoid being alone with me for the entire day, and ducked out early when I was distracted with Edward, who downloaded a new 'facial symmetry' app that he was dying to try out.

I hurry through the parking lot, a cool wind against my face that fits my mood. I screwed up. I get that. There's nothing I can do to change what happened. All I can do now is convince her that I love her, and that I'm never going to make that type of mistake again.

The entire team is already here, sitting at one long table near the front. Gwen and a guy I assume is her boyfriend are up on stage, singing an ear-splitting version of a Celine Dion song. The only positive of them being up there is that there's an empty seat next to Allie at the moment. She's dressed in a red V-neck top and her hair is piled on top of her head in a bun. The sight of her nearly does me in because she's so incredibly gorgeous and there's a distinct possibility that as of a couple of days from now, I'll never see her again.

As soon as I sit down, I can feel her mood change from relaxed and happy to cold as ice, even though her eyes haven't left the stage. I wave a quick hello to the rest of the team, then lean in to Allie's ear. "Hi. I really need to talk to you."

"You really don't."

On stage, Gwen is belting out, "SOMETIMES I AM FRIGHTENED BUT I'M READY TO LEARN…!!!!!!"

I wince, but Allie stares up at her friend as if she's Celine Dion herself. "Allie, I need to fix this."

"Not possible."

"ABOUT THE POWER OF LOVE…."

"Definitely possible and absolutely necessary. I need a chance to explain."

She scoffs, then turns to me. "Explain what? How you tricked me into sleeping with you?"

The crowd erupts into applause, which I'm pretty sure is because they're finally done torturing us all.

"I didn't trick you," I say, feeling my desperation morph to irritation. "I wanted you just as much as you wanted me."

Shaking her head, Allie says, "Don't bother. Seriously. There's nothing you can say that will change anything." She gives me a hard look. "I don't even know why you're here."

"I'm here because I'm in love with you and I need to find a way to get back to what we had."

"What we had was a giant lie," she says. "Now, you're sitting in Gwen's seat, so if you don't mind…"

"No, of course," I answer, getting up. I turn and see Gwen standing in front of me.

She smiles, seemingly unaware of what's going on. "Hudson! I want you to meet Ty." She turns to him. "Ty, this is Hudson. Allie's new fella."

Urgh. Not anymore. I hold out my hand and we shake hands. "You do a mean Celine."

He rolls his eyes in a self-deprecating way. "If you had told me a year ago that I'd be on stage singing, I'd have said you had the wrong guy," he says, throwing a smile at Gwen. "The right woman'll change you in ways you never expected."

While we're talking, Gwen pulls an empty chair from the table behind ours and pulls it up to the table. "Here, now you and Allie can sit together."

Allie stiffens, and out of desperation, I say, "You know what? I think I'm going to get up and sing. You know, get it over with early before I overthink it."

Gwen claps her hands and grins at Allie. "He's going to sing for you!"

I walk over to the DJ, whose face immediately lights up when he recognizes me. "Whoa! You're Hudson Finch."

"Hi, nice to meet you," I tell him. "I'd like to go with The Righteous Brothers, 'You've Lost that Lovin' Feelin'.'"

He gives me a nod. "Solid choice. Watch the beginning because you have to start singing before the music kicks in, so you really have to follow the prompter."

"Good tip. Thanks," I say, giving him a thumbs up.

A second later, I'm standing with the microphone in my hand, feeling stupid. I take a deep breath and say, "This one is for the beautiful, talented, incredibly smart Dr. Allegra Cammareri, who's just made the most important discovery in SETI research since the late, great Frank Drake." The team starts to cheer, but Allie just purses her lips and gives me a quick eyebrow raise that says she's not impressed.

I give the DJ a nod and he starts up the song. "You never close your eyes anymore…"

My heart pounds and I feel a cold sweat break out on the back of my neck, but on the outside, I'm giving Tom Cruise in *Top Gun* vibes. I'm really going for it, occasionally pointing at Allie, smiling at other people from the team, holding the mic out on the chorus to get everyone to join in. Pretty soon, everyone in the place is clapping along and belting out the lyrics with me. To anyone here, I look like the most confident guy in the world, but inside, I'm dying. This isn't working and I don't know why I thought it would. I just want to throw her over my shoulder, take her back to my place, and beg her to give me another chance.

But since obviously that would be illegal, I just keep performing. When the song ends, the group gives me a standing ovation, and I high five people as I make my way back to my chair.

As soon as I sit down, Allie gets up. "My turn to sing."

"Oh! Some Dolly?" Gwen asks.

"Nope. I'm going with something different for a change."

Gwen grins at me while Allie walks away. "I bet it's for you!"

That's what I'm afraid of.

Allie takes the mic and says, "This one's an oldie but feels particularly relevant today."

It takes me a few seconds to recognize the tune, but when I do, my heart sinks. She's singing Nancy Sinatra's 'These Boots are Made for Walkin'.' I sit, watching her, embarrassed at the thought that her coworkers might pick up on the fact that this is for me.

"Huh, this seems like a weird choice," Gwen says, having a sip of some sort of fruity-looking cocktail. "I didn't even think she likes this song."

Trying to look nonchalant, I say, "Oh really? That is odd, then."

I stare at Allie as she dances a little to the beat while she keeps on singing, her glare growing stronger by the second. She's really selling it as a woman who's about to leave a bad man in her dust, and the crowd is loving it. They're all cheering while I sit here, knowing I'm the bad man who deserves to be left behind.

Gwen leans over to me. "Hey, is she pissed at you about something? She looks pissed."

Rather than give a direct answer, I say, "You know her better than me. Do you think she's pissed?"

She squints, then nods. "Yeah. She's pissed."

As the song starts to wind down, Allie puts the mic back in the stand, then makes her way over to the table, keeping her steps in tune with the beat. She grabs her handbag and her coat, then struts her way through the tables and right out the door.

Ty narrows his eyes. "Huh. She's really committing to this."

Tina, who's sitting on the other side of the table, says, "Is she ... actually leaving?"

Yes, yes, she is.

I grab my jacket off the back of my chair and follow her out.

Chad shouts, "Hey, Hudson, we haven't done our song for you yet!"

"I'll be back."

I hurry out into the dark parking lot, jogging over to her car just as Allie's hunting around in her bag for her keys. She glances up at me, then shakes her head. "Dammit, why can't I ever find my keys in this thing?"

"It's because of all the partially-finished packs of TicTacs," I tell her, hoping a private joke will help soften her up.

It totally backfires of course. She stops digging through her purse long enough to glare at me. "Nope. No callbacks. You do not get to make me laugh. Or smile, or do anything else fun or otherwise pleasant ever again."

I rub the back of my neck. "Ever again?"

She stares at me, the pain in her eyes nearly killing me, then turns her attention back to her bag. "You heard me."

"I know I screwed up. I promise, I get it, and I would never, ever think about doing anything remotely that dishonest again."

"When we first met, I made it one-hundred-percent clear to you how I feel about liars," she says, starting to pull things out of her bag and place them on top of her car. "And you told me you would never lie to me again. I shut off all the alarm bells going off in my head—the ones telling me you were just too smooth and too perfect to be real, the ones telling me a guy like you was never going to fall for a girl like me, the one telling me I had already seen how easily lying comes to you." She tosses a couple of lipstick tubes and some balled up napkins on the roof so hard they bounce. "But did I listen? No! I ignored all my instincts because I wanted to believe for once in my stupid life that I was worth something. That maybe *I* could be the girl who gets the guy for once. That maybe fairy tales do come true. I mean, Gwen got her fairy tale ending, so it didn't seem so far-fetched somehow, but it was all bullshit."

"It was all real. It still is."

"It was all bullshit." She digs around some more, and I pull my phone out of my pocket and turn the flashlight on, then hold it so she can look inside her purse. She *tsks* loudly, then says, "Oh my God, can you stop please?"

"Stop what?"

"Being so fucking helpful?" she asks, lifting her keys out of her purse and giving me a hard look. "It's impossible to hate you when you do shit like that."

"I don't want you to hate me. That's the last thing I'd ever want."

"Well, then you shouldn't have pretended you wanted me when all you wanted was to distract me. It was a shitty thing to do."

"Yes, it was."

"And it ruined everything," she says, furiously tossing everything back into her bag.

"Yes, it did. And I'm asking you for another chance. One I know I don't deserve."

"One you're not getting," she tells me, her voice shaking. "It's over. This is over. I have to get out of here. You should go back inside and let the rest of the team serenade you. They've worked really hard on it and they'll be super disappointed if you take off on them."

I glance at the building, not wanting to let her leave and not wanting to go back inside, but knowing I really don't have much of a choice about either thing. "Allie, I would do anything to fix this. Anything."

"You can't. I know you're not used to people saying no to me, but believe me, this is a very real, very hard no with absolutely zero chance of me changing my mind," she says. "Please do me a favor and don't come back to the institute. Just … say goodbye to everyone tonight. Tell them you got called back to Hollywood for some … movie emergency or something. And don't be there tomorrow when I get there. That's really the only thing left that you can do for me."

I stare down at her, wanting with everything in me to wrap my arms around her and kiss her until she remembers how perfect we are for each other. But obviously, that's not an option. "Okay, that's what I'll do then."

"Good."

"If you ever change your mind—"

"I won't." She yanks open the car door and tosses her bag on the passenger seat, the contents spilling everywhere. "Shit," she mutters, before turning back to me. "Goodbye, Hudson. Good luck with your movie. You're ready."

"If I am, it's because of you."

She wrinkles up her nose as if I just let out a huge belch. "You seriously can't stop yourself, can you?"

"Not really. I think it's some sort of disorder," I tell her.

"Fuck," she mutters, getting into the car. "Ridiculous."

Shutting the door, she starts up the engine, then pulls out, leaving me standing alone in the cold night air, wishing there was something, anything I could do to convince her to give me a second chance. But there isn't, and I know it. That was goodbye forever. And I know, without a doubt, I will never finish getting over her.

34

The Truth, the Whole Truth, and Nothing but the Truth

Hudson - Malibu - Two Days Later

INSTAGRAM REEL: Hollywood Dish with Ferris Biltmore

The video starts with Ferris at his desk with a red light therapy mask on. He lifts the mask and rests it on top of his head. "Hey, bitches! I'm getting my glow on because someone very special is back! Yes, you guessed it. Hudson Sex God Finch the First has finally returned from that cold, awful, yucky Mountain View place, all smartypantsed up and ready to wow the world with his new-found knowledge of all things space. I heard from my housekeeper's uncle's best friend, who owns a landscaping company in Malibu, that the man himself pulled into town yesterday afternoon, alone. Which brings me to my first segment: Thank You, Jesus!"

"Thank you, Jesus, for bringing him back safe and sound. Thank you for making sure he came back here ALONE, without that dull-as-dishwater scientist who was seriously in danger of bringing his hot level down from raging inferno to Carolina reaper-hot. Thank you."

He nods and lets out a happy sigh. "Oh, and I've got some exclusive footage sent to me by one of my little birds who happens to have been at the same awful karaoke bar that Hudson was at a few nights ago, in which you can see the end of their happily never after. And you know what that means kids?! It's time for another segment of I Got the Scoop, Bitches!"

A glittery graphic appears on the screen, then a video starts, showing Allie and Hudson standing next to her car in the parking lot while she digs around in her purse. "Oh God, just look at that perfect man. Then look at her. Yick. Now, there's no sound so I've been putting my team to work doing some lip reading, so I'll play the parts of both Hudson and that boring science woman." Putting on a high-pitched voice, Ferris says, "I'm furious with you for no good reason other than that I'm a miserable, awful person who can't stand to be around perfect men like you. Now leave me alone so I can go home to my parents and my twenty cats." He lowers his voice and smooths it out. "You're amazing and even though I know I'm too good for you, I somehow find you attractive."

Imitating Allie, he says, "Shut up. I need to concentrate while I look through my handbag from Target for my cold sore medication. Here, I'm going to put all these dirty tissues on my car, along with things I've had in this bag for twenty years. You stand there and watch me. Now I'm going to throw things at my car because I'm so mad about nothing."

"Don't be mad, baby. Let me help you find your medication." Hudson turns on his flashlight and holds it up for Allie.

"Oh my God, can you stop please?! I hate thoughtful men who do nice things for me."

The video stops and Ferris fills the screen again. "Anyway, it's just more of that for another couple of minutes until she gets in her car and tries to run over his foot. So, at least that's over. She can go live in a cave until she dies. The point is, Hudson is back. He's rid of her, and he's moving on to bigger and better things in life."

Ferris lets out a happy sigh, then slides the mask down onto his face again. "And ... back to making myself look perfect just in case the world's most perfect man comes calling..."

———

"So she just kept on walking?" Gershwyn asks. "Right out of the bar while the song played out?"

"Yup."

"Did she have boots on at the time?"

"No. Ballet flats."

"Huh," he says. "Pretty baller move, when you think about it."

"Right? You can see why I'm gutted," I say.

We're sitting on the beach, having just spent a good chunk of the morning surfing. Yesterday, when I got home, I wasn't ready to talk about Allie. I told Gersh I was too wiped to even think, so we spent the entire evening watching basketball while Oscar snuggled up next to me on the sofa. Gersh only asked once if I was okay, to which I replied, "I will be. Someday." He nodded and said, "I'm here when you want to talk about her."

When I woke this morning, I immediately got into my wetsuit and made the most of the waves, hoping that doing my favorite thing in the world (well, favorite thing I can do without her) would take my mind off how horribly I fucked up. It didn't. Instead, I felt totally dead inside even though the waves were perfect.

"Why didn't you just deny it?"

"Because lying isn't exactly conducive to a healthy relationship," I answer.

"Yeah, but it's not really lying. It's not like you were grossed out by her or something. You *wanted* to kiss her, right?"

I watch as a wave rolls into shore. "Of course I did. I also wanted to have sex with her up at Black Creek, but in both cases, I was also desperate to hide my dyslexia from her, so I did exactly what she accused me of doing—making a move to avoid the truth." Shaking my head, I say, "Honestly, it was the worst thing I could do to someone like her. I made her feel used and ... unworthy, and she's had a history of guys who have already done that to her."

"But you didn't use her, and you're not the one who hurt her in the first place, so don't start taking responsibility for shit you didn't do," Gersh tells me.

"But I *am* responsible," I say, picking up a rock and tossing it toward the water. It doesn't make it far enough and bounces on the sand. "She told me when I first met her what the line was, and I crossed it over and over. Hell, I danced over it like a total idiot, thinking she'd never figure it out."

"Like ninety-nine percent of women would never have put that together."

"Hmm, I think you're underestimating the fairer sex there, but yeah, most of the women I've dated certainly wouldn't have." I chew on my lip for a second. "That's the problem with falling for a genius."

"I could see it having its drawbacks."

"Yeah, if you're a total fuck up."

"You're not a fuck up." Gersh gets up and grabs his board, and I know it's time for us to get ready for a meeting with Paul and Brittany. "As usual, you're being way too hard on yourself. You made a mistake."

Standing up, I grab my board. "I made the same mistake multiple times and totally blew her trust, and the thing is, Gersh, she was the one for me. We had so much fun together, and I could talk to her, you know? Like, really talk to her. And I wanted to know everything about her. And when I was with her, I could just be myself. Well, mostly. Obviously I was holding back, but when she figured out I have dyslexia, she managed to make me feel *good* about it. Can you even imagine that? Me feeling good about something I've been ashamed of my entire life?"

"No, I can't."

"Well, somehow she did it. She talked about it being a superpower instead of a problem."

"Shit, man," he says, as we walk across the beach. "If only our parents could've made you feel like that. It would have saved you so much heartache."

"Yeah, well, they didn't," I answer. "But it was my job to get over it. I'm almost forty, for God's sake. I shouldn't be acting like a child, hiding all the time."

"Cut yourself some slack. You had nearly forty years of them programming you to be ashamed of yourself. That would be hard for anyone to get past."

"Please don't make excuses for me," I tell him. "I know you're just trying to make me feel better, but honestly, I need to own this. It's the only way I'm going to be able to change."

"Okay," he answers, as we get to the stairs leading up to the house. "So, what are you going to do about it?"

"Stop fucking hiding."

———

Paul and Brittany sit at my dining room table with their mouths agape. I just told them everything, and now I'm waiting for them to respond. This conversation has been one of the hardest fucking things I've done. I broke out in a cold sweat as soon as they showed up at the house. When I started talking, I could barely get the words out, but I forced myself to do it, knowing that this is the first step in becoming the man I should've been for Allie. And I know it's over, but there's a tiny part of me that is hoping that if I can show her I've changed, that she'll give me another chance.

Brittany closes her mouth first, then says, "You've always had it?"

Oh God, this sucks. Nodding, I say, "It's something you're born with."

"How did we not know?" she asks. Then, turning to Paul, she says, "How did *you* not know? You're his agent. You must have gone over dozens of contracts and scripts with him."

He shakes his head at her, and says, "I had no idea." He gasps and looks at me. "Oh my God, you never once read any part of a contract in front of me. Or a script. How did I not realize that?"

"Gersh and I have a pretty good dog and pony show going," I answer, picking up Oscar, who was standing on his hind legs and pawing at my knee. I hold him against my chest and he licks my chin a couple of times as a thank you. "He immediately picks up any contracts or scripts while I distract you or change the subject."

"We've been working together for almost twenty years. How have I never noticed this?" he asks, scratching his forehead. "Am I *that* clueless?"

"Don't start thinking there's something wrong with you," Gersh tells him. "We've had our entire lives to get this down to an art. No one knew about it. Not even our grandparents or Hudson's teachers."

"Wow," Brittany whispers. "And here I always thought you were a marginal actor, but it turns out you're like fucking Pacino."

Narrowing my eyes, I say, "Thanks. I think. Anyway, the reason I'm telling you all this is because I need to start being honest. With you, with people in the industry, with the public. I want to share my struggles in case it helps some kid out there who's dealing with a learning disability."

Paul opens his mouth, and I'm certain he's about to lavish all sorts of undeserved praise my way, about being brave and a true role model. Instead, he says, "Terrible idea."

Gershwyn wrinkles up his nose. "Seriously, Paul?"

"Yeah, I mean, eventually, sure, but not right now," he tells Gersh. "Not when we've been working overtime to convince the world he's a total brainiac."

"You can still be a brainiac and have dyslexia," Gersh tells him.

"Yeah, in fact, half of the people at NASA have it," I add. "Half. Can you believe it?"

Paul squints a little. "Is that a TikTok fact? Because it feels like a TikTok fact."

"No, it's real. You can Google it if you like," I say. "I looked it up after Allie told me that. It turns out there are some pretty cool gifts that can come with dyslexia when it comes to problem solving and creative thinking. Well, for some people anyway."

Gershwyn nods. "It's probably why he's so good at

hitting his marks after only seeing them once, and why he's so good at connecting with people."

"The point is I don't think it'll hurt my new image. If anything, finally being open about how my brain works will let people connect with me."

"And we can share the stuff about NASA, which will really solidify things for Hudson as far as the role goes," Gersh adds. "In fact, we can talk about the problem-solving stuff and Hudson can talk about how he helped solve an issue the team was having with this new AI system."

Scratching Oscar behind his ears, I say, "No way can I take credit for Allie's work."

Gersh sits forward a little in his chair. "I'm not saying you take credit for her work, but you told me yourself that it was something you said that sparked the big fix she needed to make to get it working."

"Wait. Allie the opera date?" Brittany asks.

I give her a deadpan expression, not wanting to talk about her. "Yup. That's the one. Anyway, all I did was explain how difficult it was for me as a kid to decode the English language. We weren't even talking about her system at the time so it's not like I even knew I was helping her."

Brittany tilts her head. "Tell me about this language thing. I'm curious."

A sense of relief comes over me, knowing that another person knows the truth and isn't judging me. "Well, there are twenty-six letters in the English language and they make a total of forty-four sounds, depending on the combination of letters. For someone like me, when I see a new word, it's nearly impossible to figure out which sound the 'c' is making, for example. I needed it all broken down into the smallest chunks so I could memorize the combinations."

"And him explaining that to Allie helped her realize she needed to break down the information she was feeding her AI system," Gersh says. "So, you can see how, if Hudson hadn't been there, it may not have ever gotten solved."

I shoot him a dirty look. "She would have figured it out eventually. Probably the next day even."

Gersh gives them a knowing look. "He's a pretty big fan of hers."

"Anyway, I'd like to get back to the matter at hand. I really want to go public with this. I think I can help a lot of people." *Myself.* I can help myself get Allie back when she finds out I'm finally being honest. Obviously, I do want to help other people feel better about themselves too, especially children. But I also really, really want Allie back.

Paul taps his stylus on his iPad. "Why don't you let Brittany and I have a think on this, and I'll talk to the studio about it so we can figure out the best way—and the best time—to go public with it."

"So long as we're going to actually do it, Paul," I tell him. "I'm serious about this. It's important to me and I don't want to wait a second longer than necessary."

"Don't worry about a thing. We've got your back."

Brittany offers me a big smile. "We're here for you, Hudson. Don't forget that."

I smile back even though in my mind I'm saying, *why don't I believe you?*

35

A Kick When You're Already Down...

Allie

WHY DID I DO IT? I have so much going for me right now. Like SO much that I should have completely forgotten about Hudson by now. The team was able to verify Frank's results yesterday, which means he's ready to present to the world. I ran half a million snippets of data through overnight, and when I woke up, Frank had found three anomalies that can't be explained by anything we know. *Three!* That means he might have already found proof of intelligent life. It's too early to say, but even if they turn out to be something else, at least we'll have found three more things that we can catalog and teach him to ignore.

Keenan's so excited, he's gone back to the conference coordinators with a copy of my report, and a request to find a way to squeeze me in. Because the conference is only a week away, it would definitely be a hard no if it weren't for how huge this is. I have a very good feeling that they're going to come back with a yes, which is why I should be working on my speech instead of doing the stupid thing I'm currently doing—Googling Hudson.

Why did I do it? Seriously, why?? I knew it would be a horrible idea. Even if it were just some pics of him surfing (which there were), it would hurt. But what I found is *so* much worse.

Some dirt-eating, mouth-breathing, son of a spider videoed us in the parking lot, and it's been making the rounds on the Internet. There are dozens of edits of it, some with people reacting (and hating me with a passion), and even a couple with filters that make me resemble the devil, a cow, and one filter I looked up that's called 'disgust,' that gives me a full-on scowl the whole time. And let's face it, I look like a crazy person in that conversation while he looks all rational and kind and thoughtful. But no one knows what he did to me. Not even Gwen. Because I'm not telling her the whole truth. Telling her the whole truth would mean sharing his secret, and I won't do that, no matter how hurt I am. I've given her a very vague explanation of what happened, in which I told her that it turns out his feelings for me were 'less than sincere,' and that I was going to have to leave it at that, even though I know normally we'd spend weeks dissecting every word spoken between Hudson and me until we beat the topic to death with a couple of spoons. Being the awesome best friend she is, she left it alone, thank God, because if she had pried, even just a tiny bit, I would have spilled the tea so fast, we would've both been scalded.

She walks into my office with two cans of Coke for us. "Oh no, you're not watching more videos, are you?"

"I know I shouldn't, but can you blame me?" I ask her, taking the Coke. "It's just so hard knowing thousands of people hate you this much."

"They don't hate you. They're just using the video to get attention for themselves."

I point to my phone, on which an Instagram reel has the words 'MOST HATEABLE WOMAN EVER' across my face.

She tilts her head. "Okay, maybe they hate you, but the truth is, they don't even know you, so it's not really *you* they hate. Now, shut it off!"

I scroll all the way to the top, planning to close the app, when I see a new video has just been posted by that awful Ferris Biltmore. The title is: Hudson the Genius Makes Huge Science Breakthrough.

"What the fuck?" I mutter. "Gwen, come watch this."

"Allie—" she starts, but stops when she reads the title. "What the actual fuck?"

"Ferris here, bitches! And I've got some big news straight from one of my sources at Galaxy Studios. I can't even tell you how I know this source because she's so high-level, even one tiny clue would give it away. Anywhoo, back to the huge news: turns out our Hudson is not only the most perfect specimen of man candy to walk the planet, he also is an actual genius who solved a problem those science nerds were struggling with for years before he got there. Now, I don't understand all the details because quite frankly, they're too fucking boring for me to listen to, but suffice it to say, those people at that alien hunting place never would have figured it out without him. Never ever. He just waltzed in there, immersed himself in their weird little world, and dominated. Within a few weeks, he managed to develop some sort of AI system for detecting little green men, which brings me to my first segment…"

Gwen shuts the video off while I sit, stunned, confused, and ready to lose it. I look up at her, and whisper, "He's taking credit for Frank."

"Well, you don't know that yet. I mean, it definitely sounds like it, but maybe there's some sort of mix up?"

My stomach rolls and my body feels numb. "There's no other explanation, Gwen. He needs the world to think he's smart. That's the reason he came here in the first place. And now, he's found a way to convince people. He's taking credit for the most important thing I'll ever do."

"Come on, Allie, there must be some other explanation for this. Hudson's not like that. He's a good guy."

I shake my head. "No, he's not. He only plays one on TV."

"What the hell happened between you too?"

Letting out a sigh, I say, "It doesn't matter. What matters is that history is repeating itself, and I'm about to get fucked over again."

Gwen shakes her head. "No, that is not going to happen. Maybe people who don't know anything about astronomy will believe he had something to do with it, but the people who matter—the people in our field—are *never* going to buy that. I mean, come on, an actor created an AI system in six weeks? That's crazy talk."

"Yes, it is crazy talk," I say, chewing my bottom lip. "You're right. No one in SETI will believe that. It totally makes him a bigger shitbag than I thought he was, but at the end of the day, it changes nothing. I was never going to see him again anyway."

My phone buzzes and I see an email from Keenan asking me to come up to his office for a minute. "Okay, that's Keenan. He must have heard back about my speech."

Gwen gives me a confident smile. "Perfect. That is just the thing you need to distract you from all of this nonsense."

I get up and nod at her. "Yeah, exactly. The speech is what matters. Not this garbage."

———

"Allie, have a seat." Keenan stands and lifts a pile of papers off his desk and sets it on the floor to make a window for us to see each other through. "I've had a rather strange phone call this morning and, quite honestly, I don't even know what to say about it."

My heart pounds and my palms get clammy because I have a horrible feeling about what he's about to say.

———

"Wait. I don't understand. *Hudson's* doing the speech?" Gwen asks, her head snapping back. "Hudson Finch, the actor?"

We're in the ladies' room on the third floor, where I immediately went when I left Keenan's office. I'm sobbing into some one-ply toilet paper she grabbed off the roll for me. I blow my nose, then nod. "Yup. Keenan said I'll be given time in a breakout room to talk about Frank and answer questions, but just not on the main stage. He said the attention will be good for all of SETI so we have to let him do it." I sniffle, the injustice of it all pouring out of my eyes. "He'll bring international attention and millions in donations."

"Fuck the donations," Gwen says. "Like seriously, fuck it. We don't need it. No. You go back there and tell Keenan we're going to fight this because there is no way we're letting some smooth-talking, fake-ass man steal your thunder. Not on my watch!"

"We do need the donations, Gwen. Keenan made that

very clear, and before you offer to ask Ty for more money, I would never want you to do that," I tell her, wiping my cheeks with the palm of my hand. "It would be bad for your relationship."

"No, it'll be fine. He's a billionaire, for God's sake."

"But you can't treat him like an ATM or it'll ruin everything."

She stares at me for a second before she answers, and I know she knows I'm right. Letting out a big sigh, she says, "Allie, I'm not letting some asshole step in and take credit for your hard work, and you can't just sit back and let it happen either. You're the genius, not him. This is *your* discovery, and you're the one who's going to change the world. He's nothing. And if he dares to show his face in Zurich, I'm going to tell him as much. In fact, I'll tell every single person there that this is all a big bullshit lie."

Shaking my head, I say, "Keenan said he understands how hard this is going to be for me, and he's going to make sure the truth comes out, but only at the right time."

"When? Like now? Because now feels like the right time to me!"

"Like *after* the donations stop coming in."

"But that could be months from now."

I blink, trying to hold back a fresh round of tears. "Could be, but I have to just trust that no one who matters will believe the story."

"But ... some of them will. In fact, a lot of them will. They'll all be men, of course, and they're going to be totally obnoxious about it."

I nod, my gut aching. "Like Chad."

"Oh my God, I didn't even think about Chad. He's going to be awful about it. Smug. Smarmy. Slimy. I'm going to punch him in his weasely mouth if he dares to say one word to you."

I chuckle a little, then start to cry again. Gwen pulls me in for a big hug. "Listen, we are not going to take this lying down. No ma'am. We're going to find a way for the entire world to know the truth, including all those shitty trolls. We'll expose Hudson for the fraud that he is. And it's going to be glorious."

"God, I hope so."

"I know so. We're fighters, Al. You're a fighter. And there's no way we're going to let this happen." She pulls back and puts her hand on my shoulders. "So get yourself cleaned up and get your game face on because we're going to war."

———

Email from Lando.Allegro@USRAO.com
To: Allegra.Cammareri@SETIResearchInstitute.com

Subject: Congratulations

Heard you got some help with your AI system. What a shame since I know you like to pretend to do everything yourself. See you in Zurich!
L

Email from Allegra.Cammareri@SETIResearchInstitute.com
To: Lando.Allegro@USRAO.com

Subject: Congratulations

Fuck off.

————

HUDSON

Allie, I've been trying to reach you. I'm assuming you don't want to pick up, which I totally understand. I swear I never told anyone I made Frank. Please call me back.

I know this looks bad, but I promise I can explain. Please call me.

If I don't hear from you by tomorrow, I'm coming up there to see you. I need you to know the truth.

ME

Don't bother. You wouldn't know the truth if it was growing on your ass.

36

Guess Who's Back?

Hudson

IF THIS IS what it means to love someone, I'm glad I never fell in love until now, because what a huge, giant pain in the ass it is. Feeling this lost, this hopeless, this powerless? It sucks rotten fish balls. But if I can somehow turn this around and wind up with her? Nothing but fresh fish balls from now on. Blech, that was the worst analogy I've ever come up with. Oh God, I'm going to have to do so much better than that when I see her.

I'm currently in the back of an Uber on the way to Allie's house from the airport. I strategically timed it so I'd arrive on Sunday afternoon, when I know she'll be home.

Unfortunately, this means her entire family—all of whom I'm sure hate my guts by now—will also be there. But so be it, a man's got to do what a man's got to do. I'm going to march up that sidewalk, knock on that door, and tell her little niece and nephew that I refuse to leave until I see their Zia Allegra. And if they say no, I'm going to bribe them with two crisp hundred-dollar bills.

My phone pings and I pull it out of my pocket, hoping beyond all hope that it's Allie.

But of course it's not.

GERSHWYN

You there yet?

ME

I'm about five blocks from her house.

GERSHWYN

You sure you want to do this? It's a house full of angry Italians.

ME

I'm positive, so if you don't have any words of encouragement for me, I suggest we end this conversation now.

GERSHWYN

All right. Good luck, you poor bastard.

ME

Thanks. I'm going to need it.

The car pulls up in front of the house and I take a deep breath before I get out, then make the long, lonely walk up to the front door. I picture going inside and seeing her in the kitchen in an apron, and saying, "Okay, if this is where it has to happen, this is where it has to happen," just like the scene in *Jerry Maguire* when he gets Renee Zellweger back. But this isn't a movie. It's my life, and I'm not here to put on a show or pretend to be someone I'm not. Allie deserves the real me, and that's exactly who she's getting.

My heart pounds so hard, I can hear it in my ears, and there's a voice in my head that's yelling at me to turn and run, but I won't. I force my hand to push the doorbell, then wait, my stomach twisting while I listen to the sound of pounding feet rushing toward me. The door swings open, and I see Camilla and Matteo jostling to stand in front of each other. When they look up, their mouths drop in unison.

Camilla raises her eyebrows. "Oh, snap!"

"Hi, Camilla, is your Zia Allegra here?"

"Nope," she answers. "And even if she was, I would *not* recommend trying to talk to her."

"I know she's upset with me. And she has a very good reason," I answer. "Now, can I see her please? She's going to be so much happier after we talk."

Matteo shakes his head. "She's *furious* with you. Like, worse than my mom was when my dad bought a boat."

"That bad, hey?" I ask, swallowing hard.

"Way worse," Camilla says. "Like, I'd run from here if I were you."

"Not running, Camilla," I tell her. "She means too much to me to run away."

I hear Allie's dad in the background. "Who are you kids talking to?"

They both turn and say, "Hudson Finch."

"Oh, no," he answers, his voice getting louder as he says, "He better not be here."

He comes to stand in front of the door wearing a death glare.

I give him a small wave. "I am here."

Shaking his head, he *tsk*s about twenty times, then points a finger at me. "You screwed up."

Another voice comes from behind the door. "Who screwed up?"

"Hudson Finch," he tells them.

Zia Fernanda squeezes her way around the kids. "Oh yeah, you screwed up more than any man in the history of love. And I know a thing or two about this because I work at a salon, so I've been hearing about stupid things men do for over forty years."

"I know. I really did screw up," I tell her. "And I'm here to fix it."

"Some things can't be fixed," Enzo says.

"I came all this way. I have to try," I say. "Your daughter is the best person I know. I'm in love with her and I want to spend the rest of my life with her."

"Then you shouldn't have done all the things you did," he answers.

"Agreed. I messed up royally, but I have a way to fix it. I just need to explain everything to her."

He gives me a stern look, then says, "She's not here."

"Come on, Enzo, of course she's here. It's Sunday."

He shakes his head. "She knew you were coming so she left."

Fernanda nods. "It's true. She didn't want to see you. Not that I blame her."

"But it's Sunday."

Her mom appears next to her aunt. "We gave her a pass today." She shakes her head at me and sighs. "Oh boy, you really messed the bed, didn't you?"

Letting my head hang down a little, I say, "Yes. Yes, I messed the bed."

The kids both burst out laughing, covering their mouths with their hands. Behind them, I hear their idiot dad's voice. "What's so funny?"

"Hudson Finch messed his bed!" Camilla yells.

Awesome. A little louder so the whole neighborhood can hear it.

A second later, I'm faced with Allie's sister and brother-in-law, her nonno, and her grandma, three of whom are *tsk*ing and shaking their heads at me, while Vinnie shrugs. "Meh, you dodged a bullet. Trust me."

"Oh nice, Vinnie," Lucia snaps. "Real nice."

"What? She's weird."

I glare at him. "She's perfect."

Lucia pulls a face like she just saw a tiny kitten. "Aww, that's so sweet. You must be in love to think that my sister is perfect." She turns to her mother. "Ma, he came all this way. Tell him where she went."

Maria shrugs. "I don't know. She wouldn't tell me. She was afraid I'd crack under the pressure." She nods a little, then says, "Which I would have. Look at that sad face. Do you want to come in and eat something?"

I glance at Enzo, who looks like he wants to slice me up with his garlic razor. "Do you think she'll show up?"

"Not a chance. She packed an overnight bag and said she'd go straight to work from wherever she's staying tonight."

Fuck. She's like the master of avoiding people she wants to avoid. I rub my hand over my mouth, trying to decide what to do. "All right, will you please do me a favor and tell her I was here, and that I really need to talk to her before she leaves for Zurich. It's important."

"I'll pass the message along," her mom says.

"Thanks," I tell her. "See you, everyone. Take care."

I turn and walk down the steps, then stand for a second, feeling completely lost. I pull out my phone and open the Uber app. I'm just about to request a ride, when I hear the front door shut. I turn, my heart in my throat, thinking maybe Allie is there after all, but it's her dad. He points to his car, which is parked on the driveway. "Come on. I'll give you a ride to the airport."

Newp. Bad idea. Very bad idea. "That's okay, sir. I don't want to put you out like that."

"Get in the car. I need to talk to you."

––––––

We drive for a full five minutes before Enzo says anything. Five terrifying minutes, because he might be the worst driver I've ever seen. He nearly sideswiped a truck getting onto the freeway, and now he's going ten under the speed limit in the fast lane. I grip my knees, hoping that we'll make it to the airport alive while yet another car passes us on the right, honking at us.

"I don't know what to think," he says finally. "I was so sure you were pepper, but then you showed up here, which is not something a man who just wants to sprinkle pepper would do."

"That's because I'm not pepper."

"Maybe not. I don't know what you are then, which is troubling because, as a father, I should know. But you … you've got me all confused."

"How about if I'm just a man who's in love with your daughter and who screwed up and wants nothing more than to fix it?"

He over-steers and we almost hit a guard rail. I close my eyes, not wanting this to be my last car ride. When I open them again, he's looking straight ahead, shaking his head. "I don't know what's going on. Allegra's not saying much. Only that you're taking credit for her discovery, which, if that's true, is a pretty evil thing to do, Mr. Finch."

"I'm not taking credit for anything, I swear."

"Are you going to give a speech at the conference?"

"Yes, but not the one she thinks I'm giving," I answer. "If I could just explain everything, she'll understand why I'm doing this, but she won't give me a chance."

"Explain it to me. If I think you deserve a second chance, I'll talk to her."

I start to talk, telling him everything from the beginning. I tell him about my dyslexia and how hard I've worked to hide it my whole life, and how I've spent my entire life playing a role until I met her. I tell him about how I kissed her at the opera, but I skip what happened at Black Creek, for obvious reasons. I talk about how intimidated I was to work with her, but how close I felt to her that night at the hospital. I explain how I feel like I have to show up at the conference because I know I can get them international attention and the funding they need. I also tell him what I'm planning to say when I get there, and that I need her to be ready to present Frank, because I'm going to make that happen.

By the time we pull up at the airport, I've spilled it all to a man who, worst case scenario, can't stand me and never will. He listens quietly without saying much. Then we park and he lets out a big sigh. "Okay, I'll talk to her for you."

"You will?" I ask, relief washing over me in a perfect wave.

He nods. "Yup. You're tomato paste."

"Really?"

"Yes, and I know why I was having a hard time figuring out what you are," he says, giving me a hard look. "It's because you didn't know yourself. You tried to be pepper, but only because you were scared, which is the only reason any man pretends to be pepper. It's a scary thing to love a woman. I know, because that's how I felt when I met Maria. I'm still scared, but now it's because we're getting old and I know I won't be able to live without her." His eyes look glassy for a second, then he clears his throat, and when he talks again, his voice is deeper than it was before.

"Anyway, that's something you'll have to face in the future. For now, you need to find a way to get Allegra to take you back. I'll pave the way for you, but I can only do so much. She's like her mother. She's got a mind of her own."

"Which is a good thing, if you ask me," I say.

"I didn't ask you," he answers. "Besides, what you think is good now turns out to be a real pain in the buttocks when you're married."

I chuckle a little and Enzo offers me a tiny grin. "All right. I better go home. I might just make it in time to eat. I'll talk to my daughter for you, but no guarantees."

"Got it. Thank you, Mr. Cammareri. I appreciate that you're willing to try."

He clicks his tongue. "Someday you may not appreciate it that much."

"No, I'll appreciate this every day for the rest of my life. I know I will because loving your daughter is the most important thing I'll ever do."

His eyes fill with tears and he mutters, "Yeah, yeah, yeah. You're tomato paste. Poor bastard."

37

Angry Packing and Unwanted Advice

Allie

"Why don't you bring a bathing suit? I'm sure the hotel has a hot tub and it'll be good for your bones after that long flight," my mom says.

"Meh, I really don't feel like being in a swimsuit around people I work with." The truth is, I don't feel like going. Not even one bit. I'm bitter and angry and furious and ... what's another word for angry? Filled with rage. Well, that's a phrase, but it fits. I'm also late. I should have left for the airport already, only I couldn't bring myself to pack on account of all the rage.

"Why not? If I still had a body like yours, I'd be walking around in a bikini all year," she tells me.

I open my underwear drawer and count out six pairs, then toss them in the general location of my open suitcase. "It's not about how I look. It's about me trying to get some respect, which is apparently the world's biggest uphill battle for some stupid reason. On a hill made entirely of ice and I'm wearing Teflon shoes."

My mom picks up my pajama pants and folds them neatly, then places them in properly. "I wish I knew what to say to make you feel better, *tesora*. What's happening is not fair, but I still believe it's going to work out."

"Why on earth would you think that?" I ask, zipping up my overstuffed suitcase.

"Because it's true. You've worked so hard for so long, and it doesn't matter if some actor is going to get credit for your invention as far as the public goes. What we all think means nothing. None of us even know what the hell you do. Everybody who knows *will know*."

Sighing, I say, "I guess."

I pick up my passport and stuff it in my handbag while my mom calls down the stairs. "Enzo! Allegra's ready to go. Come get her suitcase."

"Ma, I can carry my own luggage."

"Not down the stairs."

"Of course down the stairs," I say, giving her my handbag. I sling my laptop bag over my shoulder, then pick up my insanely heavy suitcase and fight my way to the front door just as my dad comes out of his den. "You ready?"

"All set. You two have a wonderful week. I'll see you when I get home."

He shakes his head at me. "What are you talking about? I'm taking you to the airport."

Oh God, I do not have time to go dad-speed right now. "No, that's okay. It's too much trouble. You'd have to drive there, then turn around and drive all the way back here. I'll drive myself." Holding out my arms, I say, "Okay. Let's hug it out, then I really have to run."

He waves off my hug and picks up my suitcase. "I'm taking you."

Ma nods. "Your father is taking you. End of discussion."

I open my mouth, but he says, "I need to talk to you."

Crap. He's been trying to convince me to give Hudson a second chance since he showed up last Sunday, but I'm not having it. To be honest, I feel pretty damn betrayed that my own father would take his side. "I don't want to talk about it."

"It's not about that. It's something else. Something important."

I narrow my eyes at him, and he says, "For real. Let's go."

Two minutes and four hugs from my mother later, we're finally on the road. I grip the armrest on the passenger door while my dad drives toward the freeway.

"What did you need to talk to me about? Are you okay?"

"Healthy as an ox," he answers. "It's not about me."

"Is it Ma?"

"She's good too. Strong woman, that one."

"Okay, well you're just going to have to tell me because I'm not in the mood to name every member of the family right now."

He slowly makes his way onto the freeway, crossing all four lanes until he's in the left one. "It's about you."

I close my eyes for a second, knowing exactly where this is going. "I told you, I don't want to talk about it."

"You're not going to talk. I'm going to talk," he says, pointing a finger at his chest. "You're going to listen."

"Sweet Jesus," I mutter.

"He's tomato paste, Allegra. I know it. As a father, I know it."

"I don't think you do. You told me he was pepper."

"I'm willing to admit I was wrong. He's tomato paste."

"He's a big fat liar," I tell him.

"No. He's a man who was ashamed of something he

had no business being ashamed of. He didn't come right out and say it, but I'm pretty sure it's because he has terrible parents."

My heart picks up its pace, and not just because he almost hit the guardrail. "He told you about his dyslexia?"

Nodding, he says, "He told me everything."

Oh God, I certainly hope not. "Yeah, well, he only did that because he's trying to offload all the guilt he should be feeling about what he did."

"He showed up because he loves you. Because he's sorry he hurt you. Because he's finally figured out who he is."

"He's been a grown up for a long time. He should have figured his shit out by now."

"He couldn't do it before, but he's doing it now."

"Oh really? And just how do you know he's actually doing it now? He's a *professional* liar, Pop. He's made millions pretending to be people he's not, and that makes him dangerous and unreliable, neither of which make him a good candidate to be with your daughter. So why you're on his side is beyond me," I say, staring out the passenger window just long enough to make eye contact with an elderly woman who passes us on the right with her middle finger aimed at my father. "You should be on my side."

"I am on your side. I've always been and will always be on your side," he tells me. "But it's my job as a father to tell you when you're about to ruin your entire life."

"Oh God, I can't deal with this right now. I'm late for my flight, I'm stressed out about this stupid trip, and the last thing I need is a big lecture from you."

"I'm telling you the truth, *cara*. Hudson is a good man. He's a hard worker. Life dealt him a crap hand but instead of giving up, he made something of himself, and that is to be respected. He's also a brave man. He came all the way up to our house, on a Sunday, knowing your entire family would be there, just so he could talk to you. That's not something pepper does."

"He only showed up because he doesn't want me to make a big fuss at the conference. I could really embarrass him."

"No, he showed up because he loves you and he wants to make it up to you."

"Oh yeah? If that's the case, why the hell is he going all the way to Switzerland to steal my thunder?"

"That's not what's going to happen."

"Of course it is. They already printed the agenda and he's the keynote speaker, and the topic is "The Future of AI in SETI Research!" That's my topic. Mine. And if he cared even the tiniest bit about me, he would've turned them down," I say, my voice raising. "But he didn't because he doesn't care about me at all. He used me. That's all he did. He used me and made me believe something was possible that isn't possible. He's cruel and selfish and I hate him. And nothing is ever going to change that."

I expect my dad to argue, but all he does is shrug. "We'll see."

"Yeah, we will see," I answer in a clipped tone.

We're both silent the rest of the drive. I fume while my dad turns on the radio to a country music station. He hums along as though he doesn't have a care in the world, which quite frankly makes me even more furious. When we finally pull up, I let out a big sigh. "I don't know why you felt the need to tell me all this stuff I don't want to hear. It's not going to change anything."

He looks at me, his face filled with love. "Because I know my opinion matters to you, and I didn't want you to turn down your one chance at happiness because you think

I don't like him. I like him. He's a good man." Shrugging, he says, "He's not Italian, but nobody's perfect."

"My one chance at happiness," I scoff. "That's ridiculous. There are plenty of good men out there."

"Not like this one, *cara*. This one makes your eyes light up."

"He does not," I snap. "Maybe he did for a minute, but that's over."

"Is it possible that you're fighting so hard to believe he's pepper because deep down, you don't think you're good enough to finally have tomato paste?"

I stare at him for a long moment, not wanting to think about what he just said. "I have to go."

He pats me on the hand. "You deserve tomato paste. You always have. You just have to believe it."

38

And It All Comes Down to This...

Allie

ZURICH IS one of those places that would be perfectly romantic if you're in love. It's like something out of a movie—a beautiful, historic city on the banks of Lake Zurich. There are endless options for dining, shopping, and chocolate. A blanket of fresh snow gives the city a serene feel, and if I were happy, I'd love everything about it. But I'm not happy. I'm miserable. And this stupid gorgeous city isn't helping. The snow only reminds me of being stranded at Black Creek with today's stupid keynote speaker. The chocolate only reminds me of him telling me he's 'not a sweets guy.' Talk about a red flag. How did I not pick up on that? Not a sweets guy is code for 'I'm pure evil.'

But at least I've come to a very important conclusion—I'm not to blame. I'm not to blame for being tricked by a man who has spent his entire life lying. I'm not to blame for Lando using me, then stealing my work and dumping me, and fifteen-year-old me certainly isn't to blame for stupid Ian Miller either.

I spent most of the flight thinking about what my dad said, and he was right about one thing—I do deserve tomato paste. There's nothing wrong with me. In fact, I'm pretty damn great and I have got to stop being so fucking hard on myself. *They're* the problem, not me. I won't be dipping my toes in the dating pool anytime soon, but when I do, I'm not going to rush into it. I'll take it nice and slow. Maybe get to know the guy as a friend for a year or two before even attempting a date. I'll run background checks and ask all sorts of questions and analyze the answers for red flags. Have you ever washed your junk in the sink? Yes? Move it along. Are you dating a cheerleader at the moment? Get the fuck out of my house. Not a sweets guy? No thank you. But that's all stuff for Future Allie to consider.

Right Now Allie has shit to do. My most important job is to wow everyone with Frank at that breakout panel, which is happening tomorrow. Today's focus is to avoid Hudson like he's the plague and the world just ran out of antibiotics. So far, so good on that front. Our team arrived at the hotel and conference center last night, and I haven't seen Hudson even once yet, even though I know he was already here when I arrived. I could tell by the excitement in the air and the horny women everywhere. Also because of the all-chocolate gift basket he had delivered to my room with his room number and a note:

Allie,

I really need to talk to you before I give my speech tomorrow. There are things you need to know.

Love,
H

I read it over again while I nosh on a magical hazelnut, dried fruit, and creamy dark chocolate bar. "No, thank you. I already know enough."

And I'm going to be late for the opening of the conference if I don't get my butt down to the auditorium. I drop the note in the waste bin and hurry out of my room. My plan was to arrive right on time, and not a minute early in case it means we cross paths. All I have to do is get through his stupid keynote speech without looking at him, heckling him, or rushing the stage and pulling a Will Smith, and I'll be fine. It's going to be really fucking hard—it'll require every ounce of self-control I have and then some, but I cannot let him get the better of me. Not in front of Lando and Chad and all the other assholes that will be in the room (and there are plenty).

Yes, I shall keep my dignity intact throughout the day. I am Allegra Cammareri, serious astrophysicist, and future global leader in SETI research. One day, I'll be the new Frank Drake, except they'll call me the mother of SETI for obvious reasons. But first, I have to get through today without any sign of weakness.

I get off the elevator on the main floor and walk down the wide carpeted corridor to the auditorium. A sign next to the door says, "SETI Conference in Progress."

Pulling the door open, I step inside and stand at the back of the room, scanning the audience for Gwen, who has saved me an aisle seat. She turns and waves to me, and I hurry over to her and sit down.

"You okay?"

"Yes, I have a plan. I'm just not going to look at him the entire time."

"How will that help?"

"Because then I won't have to see him," I say, as if it's the most obvious thing in the world. "I'll be fine if I never have to look at or smell him again."

She nods, but I can see she's skeptical. "Well, that's a plan all right."

"It's really all I've got, so…"

A man's voice comes over the loudspeaker. "Please welcome our very special guest and keynote speaker, Hudson Finch, to the stage."

The place erupts with applause and a couple of cameramen sneak up to the front to take photos of him. I look to the left of the stage, only to notice a few film crews set up. I quickly lower my gaze to the back of the chair in front of me so as not to accidentally see him.

Even though I mostly hate Hudson now, my heart is in my throat because it hasn't gotten the message that we don't love him anymore, and therefore we certainly don't have to worry about him screwing this up and embarrassing himself. "What's he doing?" I whisper to Gwen, keeping my eyes on my lap.

"He's striding purposefully over to the podium. Now he's adjusting the microphone to the right height," she whispers. "Oh, he just found you in the crowd and he's staring at you."

I battle the urge to look up. Instead, I say, "What expression does he have on his face?"

"Sad."

"Welcome, everyone, I'm Hudson and I have absolutely no business being your keynote speaker. I'm not an astrophysicist, or a space engineer, and I certainly don't have fifteen minutes-worth of important things to say. In fact, two months ago, I didn't even know what SETI stood for." Murmuring can be heard around the auditorium until he says, "No, it's true. I had no idea. Six weeks ago, I showed up at the SETI Research Institute in Mountain View to prepare for an upcoming movie role, totally green. I had the incredibly good fortune to work with Dr. Allegra Cammareri, who taught me what she could, even though she was busy working on a project that is far more important than anything I'll ever do. Anyway, she was gracious enough to help me out, and I learned more from her in those few weeks than I did the entire time I was in school."

He pauses for a second, and I know without looking that he's staring at me. Not falling for it, Mr. Liar Liar Kisses on Fire Pants.

Okay, that sucked, but I'm barely hanging on here.

"She taught me that science is the relentless search for truth, even if you have to forgo meals or showers or sleep, which she did on a regular basis while I was there observing her."

He pauses and I whisper to Gwen, "Is he reading this or just free-styling it?"

"Free-styling it," she answers.

"She also taught me that facts are not debatable. That's what makes them facts. Like the fact that I'm standing up here and she's sitting down there, when the fact is she should be up here delivering this speech, not me."

Unable to help myself, I look up at him, only to see him staring back down at me. Damn him for looking so hot and for doing that stupid thing where he makes me feel like the only woman in the world.

He swallows hard, then keeps talking. "The fact is that Dr. Cammareri—and only Dr. Cammareri—is responsible for her AI system. I had nothing to do with it, and the fact that I've been given any credit at all is an insult, not only to her, but to all of you who work so hard in this field.

"I was asked to speak because I can bring attention to your program, which will bring in money. And that's the only reason I'm here. It's because those cameras are rolling and people who don't know and don't care about what you do are hearing about it today, many of them for the first time. So I'm going to help out in my own small way, to give a lift to an endeavor I've come to believe is very important for humanity. The search for extra-terrestrial intelligence is something more people should know about, because it's the ultimate marriage of true science and hope. It could one day present humans with partnerships that could solve the major problems we face around the globe. It could bring us new technologies, new foods, new energy sources, and new medical procedures. And in my humble opinion, as an outsider—and again, as someone who really has no business even sharing his opinion—I believe this is something worth pursuing. I'd even go so far as to say it's not up for debate. SETI research is something worth pursuing."

He pauses and the auditorium fills with applause again while he stares at me. My heart swells in my chest, even though I tell it not to. I'm failing so, so badly right now.

"In a minute, I'm going to ask Dr. Cammareri to come up here and use the rest of the time that was wrongly given to me, because she deserves to be up here sharing her discovery with you. And you deserve to hear about it. But before I do that, I want to explain how the rumor got started that *I'm* the person who managed to get her system to work, which is pure fiction, I assure you. After my time at the institute, when I got back to L.A., I was so proud of Dr. Cammareri, that I told my team about what she had done. Inspired by her commitment to truth, I told them the truth about myself for the first time.

"I've had a secret I've been keeping my entire life. Something I was ashamed of, when there was no need to be. I have dyslexia, and in my case, it's presented me with significant challenges with reading my entire life, in spite of my parents' best efforts to fix me. The studio wanted me to keep that under wraps until my movie had come out so they're going to be pissed that I'm going public with this right now, but the thing is, nothing is more important than honesty and being authentic. Dr. Cammareri taught me that too. And when you believe in something, you have to start living it now. Not just when it's convenient or when it doesn't scare the shit out of you. You have to live it every day. Which is what I'm going to do, starting today. No more hiding. No more pretending. Just pure honesty."

Am I crying? Yes, I'm crying. Dammit. I do not want to cry in front of these people. This is so much worse than wearing a bathing suit.

"Anyway, while I was telling my team about my dyslexia, I accidentally made it seem like something *I* said caused Dr. Cammareri to find the final missing piece to the puzzle, when in actuality, I didn't even know that what I was saying was in *any* way related to what she was doing. In my team's effort to make the world believe I'm some type of genius—which I'm not—they didn't just bend the truth. They broke it. And I'm sorry that happened, Allie. I'm sorry I didn't stop them the second it happened. And I'm sorry that while I was so busy hiding who I really was, I didn't think of how I was hurting you. And I know I hurt you, and that's the last thing you deserved. What you deserve is to be respected for the remarkable scientist—and human—that you are. You are strong and honest and brave, and you have more integrity than anyone I know. Your dedication to your work is truly inspirational, and I want the world to know your name because *you* are the one who should have the cameras on you. Not me. So please come up here and introduce the world to Frank, because it's high time they get to meet him."

He stands back from the mic and starts to clap while I sit, stunned and yet somehow more alive than I've ever been. Everyone else joins in with his applause, and I know it's not because they suddenly respect me. It's because they're following his lead. But it still feels fucking amazing.

"Go on, get up there," Gwen says.

"But I'm not—"

"You are. Now go show these bastards who's boss."

I walk up to the stage, my legs feeling wobbly as I make my way up the stairs. Hudson holds his hand out to help me up. Of course he does because he's a mother fucking gentleman and I'm totally done for because there's no way I can not love him now. He whispers in my ear. "I love you, now go give 'em hell."

I hurry over to the podium, a new-found strength growing in me with each step. When I'm finally standing there, I face the crowd—a moment I've fantasized about for years. I spot Lando and my lips curve up in a smirk I don't even want to hide. *Yes, fuck you, Lando. I won.* And also, what was I thinking with him? He's actually kind of gross.

I take a deep breath and start to talk, trusting that I already know exactly what to say. I talk and talk for what feels like hours and somehow only a few seconds at the same time. I don't have my computer with me, so I can't demonstrate, but I tell them all about what Frank can do. Before long, I have people in the audience asking questions, and I can see they're all growing more excited by the minute about the possibilities.

When I'm done speaking, I stay perfectly still while I get a standing ovation. Tears fill my eyes and even though I promised myself I wouldn't show any emotion, I don't even care. Because I did it. I really did it. I worked my ass off and I believed in myself and now I'm standing here while everyone in the SETI world claps for me. This moment is huge—it's everything I've always wanted. I'm finally being recognized for my work, and I'm not ashamed that I'm so happy I'm letting a few tears slide down my cheeks.

I don't even remember how I wound up backstage, but now I'm here, standing in front of Hudson between the curtains. He's smiling down at me with that look that says *all* the things. I close the distance between us, wrap my arms around his neck, and kiss him hard on the mouth, those feelings rushing back to me. The way he smells, the way he holds me, the way our bodies feel so perfect pressed against each other. We pull back and I say, "I can't believe you just told the world *everything* you just told the world. How do you feel?"

"Incredible. And a little scared." He tilts his head, then says, "Actually, really fucking scared."

"Are you worried the studio will drop you?"

"No, I'm worried you won't take me back."

"But I already kissed you," I say, narrowing my eyes a little.

"But that could've been just a reaction to the moment."

"It was a reaction to being near you. I can't help myself. I'm in deep here, even though I was trying so hard not to be."

"I promise I will *never* give you another reason not to be

in love with me again." He gives me a slow, gentle kiss, then rests his forehead on mine.

"My dad was right about you," I tell him. "You are tomato paste."

He chuckles and kisses me again, pulling me in tighter. "Great speech, by the way. Even though you weren't prepared, you really knocked it out of Earth's orbit."

I grin at him. "Aww, an astronomy metaphor?"

"Yes, and it took me an embarrassingly long to come up with it," he says. He lets go of me and takes his phone out of his suit jacket pocket and turns on the camera.

"You're not going to post a picture right now, are you?" I ask.

Shaking his head, he says, "Nope. This one is just for me. Well, I'd really appreciate if you'd send it to your dad for me. I want him to see that the light's back in your eyes."

39

Redemption, Love, and All the Good Things...

Hudson

"THERE'S MY LITTLE GUY," I say into the phone. "Hi, Oscar! I'll be home in twenty hours."

I called home to give Gersh a heads up on my speech, in case he hadn't heard yet. But it turns out, he already knew. Paul and Brittany are in 'damage control' mode, which is basically just pumping out all the stuff I told them to say originally. According to Gersh, the public's response has been overwhelmingly positive.

"Oscar, buddy, where's your chewie ball? Where is it?"

Oscar yawns and curls up with his back facing the camera.

Gershwyn's face fills the screen. "You know he doesn't understand video calls, right?"

"He does, but he's upset that I left again."

"I'm not so sure that's it," he says. "I think it has a lot more to do with the fact that he's a dog with a tiny brain who lacks any understanding of technology whatsoever."

Shaking my head, I say, "He's mad."

"So? Have you talked to Mom and Dad since you came out to the world?"

"Not yet. You?"

"Yeah, Mom called me about an hour ago. I guess Aunt Lydia called her as soon as the story broke. Then Lydia called every one of our relatives to tell them. Shit's hitting the fan because Mom kept such a big secret from her sisters all these years. Dad's been getting calls from former staff too. Apparently he's hearing the word 'disappointed' a lot." He smiles at me, then says, "There's a certain poetic justice to it, isn't there?"

I grin back. "I'm not going to lie. That feels pretty good."

"Let yourself enjoy the moment. You deserve it," he says. "Speaking of enjoying the moment ... you and Allie?"

My heart expands three sizes at the thought of her. "Oh yeah, me and Allie. In fact, she should be here soon. We went for dinner in the hotel's Japanese restaurant and she got mobbed by fans when we were leaving. She's holding an impromptu Q&A in the lobby right now."

"That's awesome."

"It really is. I couldn't be happier for her. She's finally getting her due. She's so talented and hard-working, and I'm just so damn proud of her," I say, meaning every word. "Anyway, I should let you go so I can call our parents. I'm sure they have a few things to say to me."

"If one of those things isn't sorry, hang the fuck up."

"Will do, bro. Catch you soon."

"See yah."

I hang up, then take a deep breath and dial their number. My dad picks up. "Hudson, I was wondering if you'd call."

"Hey, Dad, you know you can always call me, right?"

357

"We weren't sure if you'd want to talk to us."

In the background, I hear my mom's voice. "Is that Hudson?"

"Yes. I'll put him on speaker. Hang on."

I walk over to the minibar and grab a bottle of water while he switches over. My mom says, "Hello, Hudson."

"How are you doing?" I ask, even though part of me doesn't want to hear the answer.

"A little worn out," she says, her voice cracking. "This has been a very big day for Dad and me."

"For me too," I tell her.

"Of course, of course it is. Silly of me. I just … wish we would've known you were doing this so we could have prepared for it."

Walking over to the window, I stare out at the evening skyline. "I was worried you'd manage to talk me out of it, and it was something I had to do."

"Why?" my father asks. "Why now?"

Not wanting to talk about Allie, I say, "I think a better question would be why not thirty-three years ago when you found out."

"It was a different time back then," Mom says. "And with your father's job, we were worried it would reflect poorly on him."

"Believe me, I know. I know it by heart."

"We never meant to make you feel ashamed," Dad tells me, his voice a little wobbly too. "But I know that's exactly what we wound up doing, isn't it?"

I sigh, not wanting to hurt them, but also knowing that I need to say this. "You did. You really did. My whole life, I have never fully let anyone know me because I was scared that if they found out, they'd think less of me."

"But we thought you were over it. You're such a huge

star. You've got everything," my mom says. "How could you possibly feel bad about yourself?"

"Because I grew up believing I was seriously flawed. Beyond repair. That I was unacceptable to my own parents. That's not just something that goes away because you make a lot of money."

She sniffs, then says, "No, I suppose it's not."

"Hudson, I'm ... your mom and I are so sorry we did that to you," my dad says, his voice barely above a whisper, which is sort of shocking for me to hear.

"It's true," Mom adds. "If we could go back, we'd do so many things differently. *So* many things. We just thought we were doing the best thing for you and for the family. We were worried that if people knew, they wouldn't give you the same opportunities. We didn't want this to hold you back, so we thought if we worked with you enough, we could..."

"Fix me?"

"Yes," she says. "We know now that it wasn't the right way to think about it. To think about you."

"No, it wasn't, but I appreciate you admitting it now."

"We mean it," Dad answers. "If we could take it back..."

"Sometimes parents screw up so badly, but they can't see it when they're doing it," Mom tells me. "That's the hardest part of being a parent. The last thing you want is to hurt your child, but you inevitably wind up doing it anyway."

"We really bunged things up with you," Dad says. "You turned out to be this amazingly successful person, and I now see that you did that in spite of us, not because of us."

"You did a lot of things right, too," I answer. "And I appreciate what you were trying to do."

"Are you okay?" Mom asks. "Now that the story is out?"

"Yeah, I'm great," I answer. "In fact, I've never felt this good in my entire life. I feel like my life is finally starting."

"Really?" she asks.

"Really. And I'm sorry that you're going to take some heat from people. I hope it won't be too bad, but I think the main thing is that I can help a lot of people feel better about themselves. And I can stop hiding, which is an amazing feeling."

There's a knock at the door and I hurry over, knowing it's Allie. "Listen, I have to go, but I'll call you when I'm back home."

"Okay, we love you," my mom says.

"And we're really sorry," my dad adds.

"I know. I love you too."

I hang up and open the door, only to see Allie grinning at me. "Hi."

"Hi."

"Are you doing anything this evening?"

Taking her hand, I pull her into the room and let the door shut, then press her up against the wall. "I thought I'd spend the entire night showing you how I feel about you." I nuzzle her neck, then plant a slow, soft kiss on her collar bone.

She lets out a little moan. "That sounds nice, but I have to be up early because I've got a big presentation to give."

"That's going to be a problem because I have a lot of feelings." Kissing my way up her neck, I murmur, "Big ones."

"Is that so?" she asks, capturing my mouth with a kiss.

"Yeah, it is. But if you're worried about being tired, we can always wait for a more opportune time."

She grins at me and bites her bottom lip. "That's why coffee was invented."

"Really?"

"It's a fact," she says, unbuttoning my shirt. "The first person to ever grind up and brew coffee beans had just been on a sex-bender."

"Is that so? I had no idea."

"I'm a bit of a history buff, so…"

I burst out laughing, then say, "Now who's the liar?"

"Me, I'm the liar, but we should only allow it for comedic purposes."

"Deal. Otherwise, complete honesty." I pick her up under her knees and kiss her hard before carrying her over to the bed. I set her down on it and she lies back, looking absolutely perfect. I lie on top of her and rub her jaw with my thumb. "To be completely honest, I've never in my life loved someone the way I love you, Allie. I have never been as happy as I am right now, knowing you're giving me a second chance. These past days without you have been awful. I've never felt so alone, so hopeless—because I knew without a doubt that you're the one for me and I couldn't have you. I couldn't talk to you or listen to you or know what you were doing. I couldn't watch you work or share in your excitement or tell you how proud I am of you."

Her eyes glisten and she lifts her head up to kiss me. "I'm so proud of you too. What you did today was incredible."

Shaking my head, I say, "It's something I should've done a long time ago."

"But you did it, and that's the important thing."

"I only did it because of you. You made me feel worthy," I tell her, rubbing her cheek with my thumb. "You made me feel whole for the first time in my life." Tears fill her eyes and I kiss her. "Thank you for that, Allie."

"Thank you for what you did today."

"It was nothing."

"It was everything," she says, reaching up and taking my face in both hands. She pulls me toward her and we kiss again. We're both more urgent this time, and I know in about thirty seconds, we're going to be fully undressed and I really will spend the entire night showing her how I feel. How much I love her and how desperately I want to be with her always. How I only know who I am when I'm with her. Because it's true. I'm the best version of myself when we're together, and I'm going to be that man for her every damn day for the rest of my life.

Epilogue

The video starts with Ferris laying back on a lounge chair sipping a fruity drink. "Hello, bitches, I'm popping in for a quick vid from here in beautiful Belize. I don't have a lot of time because I have a very full schedule of relaxing today. But I had to share some a-MAH-zing news with you. I heard from my insurance broker's brother's best friend, who works at Galaxy Studios, that *Radio Silence* wrapped today and even though they're not even in post-production yet, Hollywood is already abuzz with Oscar talk. Hudson knocked this one out of the park, people, like I knew he would. Which brings us to our first segment: I Knew He'd Kill it, Bitches!

"No graphics today because I refuse to make graphics when I'm on vacay. Anyway, here we go. I knew he'd kill it, bitches! You … you naysayers, you non-believers, you … haters of all things good and pure in the world. You know what you can do. That's right, you can suck my left nut because Hudson freaking killed it. He killed it!! Everybody's talking about it. They're saying Peter Ma is the new Scorsese and Hudson is the new Leo. The new Leo, people!" He lowers his voice to a whisper and says, "Leo."

"I also got a text from my dog walker, whose boyfriend's sister works for someone who's sleeping with some nerd at that drab SETI place up in Mountain View, you know, where Hudson prepared for *Radio Silence* and fell in love with his permanent leading lady, the beautiful, smart, and talented Allegra Cammareri, who I know totally forgives me for all the terrible shit I said about her when she and Hudson first went public, because in the last six months since Hudson made his now-infamous speech, telling the world he has dyslexia and defending his lady, I've done nothing but be on her side. Where was I going with his? I think I've had too many daiquiris. Or too much sun. Or both…"

He clicks his tongue a few times, then says, "Oh right, the text. Anyway, apparently the second the movie wrapped, he picked up Oscar and flew directly to Silicon Valley, where Allie is hard at work on her next huge science discovery. Her family is having some big meal for him to celebrate, then he, Allie, and Oscar are going to sneak off to the mountains for a few days of making up for lost time. Which brings me to my next segment: Give Them Their Privacy, People.

"Seriously. Give them their privacy. They're madly in love and they deserve it. So if you happen to be staying at a cabin nearby or see them out for a walk, just put your damn phones away and let them enjoy this special time together. Okay?! Just let them have this. Unless you're planning to send me the footage, that is. Then all bets are off."

Allie

There is one thing I hate in this world: spiders. But I'm working on it because it really isn't their fault I'm scared of them. I'm also over my blinding hatred of liars, because the truth is, we all lie from time to time. And the truth can be complicated. It's not always cut and dried. For example, earlier this evening, Hudson made me a very romantic dinner of overcooked steak, undercooked baby potatoes and carrots with way too much dill. And when he asked how everything was, I said, "Perfect," which wasn't exactly true, on account of the food tasting pretty bad, but was absolutely true because the two of us are spending four days at a secluded cabin in the mountains. (Well, the three of us, because little Oscar Mayer, who I love fully and completely, is here too.)

We've been official for six months now, and even though he's had to be away a lot of it filming, and I've been crazy busy with work, this has, by far, been the best six months of my entire life. When we're not together, we talk on the phone every day, usually until way too late in the night. Sometimes, he's in Mountain View at a condo, and sometimes he flies me to Malibu for the weekend, where he's teaching me to surf. Now that his movie has wrapped, we're going to start house-hunting in San Jose, near my parents, but not too near. That'll be our home base, but we'll also spend as much time in Malibu as we can too, because … Malibu.

Gershwyn has met someone too. Well, he's always known her, but I guess they finally realized they were perfect for each other. Nola, Hudson's stylist. So it's happily ever afters for both of the Finch brothers.

Speaking of happy endings, I just heard the shower shut off, which means Hudson is going to be walking out of that en suite all steamed up. I quickly try to arrange myself on the bed so I look alluring. I'm wearing a silk nightie he gave me for my birthday, and I have to say, I'm feeling pretty sexy this evening, and it's not just because of the lemon fiesta coolers we had with supper.

The door swings open and he comes out, dressed in only a towel. My heart surges with joy, as it does every time I see him like this, because I know he's all mine, in a way he never has been or ever will be with anyone else. Our love is so strong that there aren't enough trolls on the Internet to break us up. Our love is forever.

He gives me that panty-melting grin. "Wow. You look incredible."

"I was just thinking the same thing," I tell him, patting the bed beside me.

"That you look incredible?" he asks.

"No, that you do," I say. "Although, I wouldn't mind if you lost that towel."

He puts his hand on the part tucked around his waist. "You mean like this?" He whips it off and drops it on the floor, leaving him totally nude.

"That's exactly what I meant." I gaze over his entire body, fully appreciating the view as he strides over to the bed. "God, you're perfect. You know that, right?"

"Nobody's perfect." He lowers himself over me and kisses me on the neck, in the little spot that drives me wild.

Before I completely lose my focus, I say, "Normally, I would agree with you, but in your case, perfection."

He lifts his face up and opens his mouth, but I hold a finger up to his lips. "Facts aren't up for debate."

"In that case, let's have sex instead."

"Deal."

And now he's kissing my neck again and working his way down my body and I know I'm in for one of the best nights of my life. Because the way he loves me is exactly what I need. He's thoughtful and caring and generous. He puts me first every chance he gets. And he shows me how much he wants me every time we're alone together. And there are days when I still pinch myself that I get to be with him, but each day, I trust this a little more. Because I trust him. And I'm the person he can trust too. We're each other's soft place to fall. We cheer each other on and pick each other up when things get rough. We're exactly what true partners should be for each other. And I'm grateful every day that he walked into my office all those months ago because this love is a love that was worth the wait.

THE END

Now Available: The Honeymooner

He's tall, dark, and built. The kind of man whose abs have abs. And I only want one thing from him —to forget the last twenty-four hours. Forever.

It was supposed to be the best day of my life. The sun was shining. The church was packed. I was dressed in white and ready to marry my steady-as-a-rock fiancé.

There was just one big, fat problem—he didn't show up.So I did the only thing a girl can do under the circumstances —escape to the Caribbean for our honeymoon.

Alone.

Enter Harrison Banks.

Somehow he brings out a side of me I didn't know existed —a carefree adrenaline junkie. After a few days together, Harrison's got me wondering if the life I always wanted was meant for some other girl.

369

I should go back to my safe, comfortable life, right?

That would be the sensible thing to do.

I can't risk everything to live out some tropical fantasy with a guy I've just met, even if he is the only man who's ever made me feel truly alive…

The Honeymooner is a laugh-out-loud, opposites attract romance about a heroine who's used to staying inside her comfort zone and a hero who knows exactly how hard to push. It'll have you laughing, swooning, and sipping fruity blender drinks.

About the Author

Melanie Summers is a multi-award-winning, Amazon best-selling author of romantic comedies and women's fiction. She's written over thirty books for people who have 'had it up to here' with the real world and need to laugh, feel good, and sigh happily. When she's not writing or reading, she's usually out for a walk with her two adorable dogs, hanging out on the beach with her husband and their three teenagers, or curled up on the couch for family movie night. Melanie resides on Vancouver Island, Canada where her life goal is to become one of those fabulous people who take daily ice baths in the ocean. So far, she can get in up to her ankles, which is not awful, thank you very much.

If you'd like to find out about her upcoming releases, sign up for her newsletter on www.melaniesummersbook s.com.

Made in the USA
Middletown, DE
28 June 2024